The Rat Eater

A Note on the Authors

Anand Ranganathan is the author of *The Land of the Wilted Rose* and *For Love and Honour*. A graduate of St Stephen's College, Delhi, and Pembroke College, Cambridge, he is a scientist based in Delhi.

Chitra Subramaniam is the founder of CSD-consulting, Switzerland, working at the crossroads of public health, media and development. An award-winning journalist and author, she is one of India's best-known media personalities.

'Seldom has deep philosophy mixed so effortlessly with the language of the street. *The Rat Eater* is penned from the gut, with the ink of blood and bile. It is, at once, angry and kind, real and imagined, heavy and light. *The Rat Eater* just might be the undefinable defining novel India has been searching for.'

—R. Jagannathan, writer and editorial director, *Swarajya*

'Part mystery, part rebuke, *The Rat Eater* is an experimental, pacy, honest, modern novel by two immensely admirable writers.'

—Manu Joseph, author and columnist

'*The Rat Eater* breaks new ground through its Dalit protagonist, in that he breaks the shackles and the glass ceiling and rises to shine in an unwelcoming India rather than play victim to his circumstances. It brought back memories of my own childhood when hunting field rats was a sport for us. The book simmers with real tension and realism, capturing the rawness of the human struggle against bigotry and barbarism.'

—Chandra Bhan Prasad, Dalit writer and activist

'*The Rat Eater* shakes the reader up. Its philosophies draw you in. A dark murder mystery, this is an important novel.'

—Amish, author and columnist

'*The Rat Eater* is a brilliantly written, fast-paced, satirical, sometimes philosophical, but ultimately a brutally straightforward book. Heaven and hell, they are all here, with passages that seem to be sculpted in time. It weaves a tapestry of society, politics and the unforgettable history of our country, with flashbacks that are told in a pinch-and-zoom manner to reveal in detail the nooks and crevices of a creaking system. This book is a must-read, and it is to be read again and again.'

—Keshav, artist and illustrator

'*The Rat Eater* is at once a thrilling and chilling read that goes from the paan-stained expletives of corrupt cops, living in loopholes framed by the local thana, to the exulted juxtaposition of Greek philosophy with schools of Indic thought. This book is full of shit, entire hierarchies full of it, from caste to class in rank and file, and a reminder that you are standing right in it. We are looped into endless cycles of birth and death such that salvation, when it comes, must hang on the incarnation of the breaking out. The line between the fiction and the non-fiction of our lives blurs in this book. And should you choose to be silent, it seems to say, then you contribute every day to manipulations that lower the highest truths into sullied trenches. A must-read'.

—Gayatri Jayaraman, author and editor

The Rat Eater

Anand Ranganathan
Chitra Subramaniam

BLOOMSBURY
NEW DELHI • LONDON • OXFORD • NEW YORK • SYDNEY

BLOOMSBURY INDIA
Bloomsbury Publishing India Pvt. Ltd
Second Floor, LSC Building No. 4, DDA Complex, Pocket C – 6 & 7,
Vasant Kunj New Delhi 110070

BLOOMSBURY, BLOOMSBURY INDIA and the Diana logo are trademarks of
Bloomsbury Publishing Plc

First published in India 2019
This edition published in 2019

ISBN: TPB: 978-93-89000-16-0; eBook: 978-93-89000-18-4

2 4 6 8 10 9 7 5 3 1

Typeset in Manipal Digital
Printed and bound in India by Thomson Press India Ltd.

It is, now, the hope of death that keeps me alive.
—Mirza Ghalib

Let me walk you through the light and the darkness, through the joy and the sorrow, through the pain and the pleasure, through the beginning and the end; let me walk you through the real and the imagined. And then I will ask you which is which.

Contents

1

2004—Darkness at Noon

The policeman spat before he entered; you don't shit where you eat.

Right foot in and he stumbled on a mooda. He kicked it in anger, staring blankly at the few hula-hoops the mooda completed before it settled on its base, a scooter tyre. His pupils dilated in reaction to the near darkness of the room. Shapes appeared. Tucked away in one corner was the interrogation table over which dangled a battered tin cone. A woman sat under it. The policeman noticed her as his eyes swept the room—the sharp features, the fair skin, the missing sindoor.

He swaggered toward the table and the woman, and dragged a chair out. The woman recorded the arrival with a shudder, bile clambering up her throat.

The policeman flicked free two buttons of his khaki shirt, unshackling his belly, which seemed at once grateful in the way it poured forth and thrust complainingly at the remaining buttons. The woman lifted her eyes only to hurriedly look down again. Unmindful, the policeman withdrew a burlap pouch from the pocket of his vest and pulled at the strings. He stole a pinch of tobacco, placed it carefully in the centre of his left palm and began rubbing it in small concentric motions with his thumb, all the while staring at the woman who kept her eyes firmly on her shiny slippers and her orange-nail-polished toes.

Grinding over, the policeman patted the tobacco with a flurry of quick slaps, making the chaff mushroom and glitter as brown tinsel under the cone. The woman coughed.

The policeman gathered the tobacco with his thumb and the first two fingers of his other hand, tucking it between his teeth and his overhanging lower lip. As the sting worked its way through his lacerated gums, he opened his eyes, lids laden, and dusted the leftover tobacco with a clap. Quite deliberately, he began making cattle-herding noises, at times hissing like a snake, in an effort to pull together the goo that had started to seep from the corners of his mouth.

It was time, decided the policeman. But he noticed that he was sweating profusely, his shirt bearing salt-encrusted patches round his armpits and just above the belt where the ever-increasing dampness was beginning to resemble a contour plot. Sweat beads were jostling for space on his forehead. He jerked his handkerchief free from the pocket of his pants with a flourish and mopped his forehead. One bead of sweat escaped and snaked its way down to the tip of his nose. He noticed this first as a mild and drifting wet sensation and then by focusing his eyes on the hanging drop. In time, the drop ripened—other, smaller droplets now supplementing it—and then began to wobble, threatening to detach. He flicked at it with sluggish pleasure. The pearl exploded into tiny droplets, some peppering the woman's face, forcing her finally to look up. The policeman was waiting with lust and intent.

'What is your relationship with Dev?' began Deputy Superintendent of Police Mohan Kumar Sharma.

'What?'

'What is your relationship with Dev, that ban-cho lying in the corner there.'

'Sorry?'

'You deaf?'

'…'

'Teri ban…What-are-you-to-*him*?'

'To whom?'

'To Dev.'

'Friend.'

'What?'

'Friend.'

'Louder!'

'Friend.'

'Friend?'

'Friend.'

'Just *friend*? We don't believe you.'

'Please, sir, it is true.'

'What is?'

'That he is just my friend.'

'Not a lover?'

'No, sir, please.'

'No?'

DSP Sharma clenched and unclenched his fist, curling his fingers in slowly. 'Where does he stay?'

'Who?'

'*Dev*, you—'

'I don't know, s-sir.'

'Really? Tell me, what were you doing behind those bushes?'

'Please, sir, I beg you. It wasn't like that.'

'Like what?'

'Like that.'

'Then tell me.'

DSP Sharma paused, heard his breathing for a second or two, then slapped his open palm on the table. '*Tell me*!'

'W-we got off early from college, so we thought we'd spend some time together and compare notes.'

'You were comparing notes?'

For the first time, the woman showed resolve. She brought her trembling hands together and placed them up on the table, fingertip touching fingertip. Realising her bravado, she withdrew them hurriedly to the comfort of her agitating thighs.

'Stop that. You were at it, weren't you? Weren't you? Haan?'

'No, sir, please, I am from a respectable vegetarian family.'

'Respectable? My foot respectable!'

'Sir, I beg you, please.'

'You couldn't smell it?'

'Believe me, sir, I promise. We didn't even look behind the bench.'

'You have never been near a dead body?'

'No, sir, I haven't.'

'The smell of a dead body. I mean, will it smell like dhoop? Couldn't you have guessed?'

'Really, sir, there was no smell coming from the plast...'

'But just now you said you didn't even...'

There was panic in the woman's eyes, delirium in the policeman's. 'Haan?'

Gasping, the woman dug her toenail into the tender underside of her other foot. 'S-sorry, sir, I am getting a little confused n-now. I-I'll tell you exactly what we saw.'

'Listen, you bitch. I'll hang both of you from a lamp post right outside your house—saali, messing with me.'

'Sir, please, honest-to-'

'*Start.*'

'Y-yes, sir. The park was deserted. We had just sat down on the bench when we noticed a black bag behind us. We decided to ignore it and just sat there co-com-comparing notes of the p-practical…'

DSP Sharma lifted his buttock so his palm could slip into his back pocket. Like a surgeon who removes a tricky piece of shrapnel and then stares at it in awe, DSP Sharma pulled out a discoloured and heavily chewed toothpick. Flagging it, he gestured for the woman to continue.

'We didn't notice any smell, sir, God promise. Some fifteen minutes later, we thought we should leave. Right at that moment, three men appeared from nowhere, sir, and they jumped over us, knocking us down flat. Before we knew what was happening, we found ourselves here, locked up—no food, no water, no phone, nothing, sir. Wa-wa-one, one of the three was him, sir—behind you—but he wasn't wearing his uniform then.'

Toothpick firmly in the company of his teeth, only moving side to side, DSP Sharma swivelled his upper half and looked beyond the limit of the cone of light. He couldn't see much more than a gloomy outline but addressed it nonetheless. 'Oye, Jatinder, you were there? Ban-cho, you didn't mention it.'

The shadow emerged in the form of Sub-Inspector Jatinder, who adjusted his sweat-drenched potbelly and stood to attention, just. 'Yes, sir, I was in the team. I was told to wear plain clothes and hide near the body and wait in case the murderer returned.'

DSP Sharma cupped his nose in disbelief. 'Why would he come back, bewakoof!'

'Point, sir, very sorry. But I couldn't reach you at that time and inspector saab was adamant that I stay put.'

'Who, that Gokhale?'

'Yes sir, Inspector Gokhale.'

'For how long were you hiding in the bushes?'

'Full three hours, sir—no food, no water, no phone...'

'Yes yes, now what about these two?'

'We found them snuggling up on the bench, sir—real tight.'

Sub-Inspector Jatinder demonstrated by giving himself a hug that would have made a boa constrictor proud.

'Snuggling up? She says they were comparing notes.'

'Jhooth, sir, they were holding hands. It looked to me he was trying to pass on a mobile phone.'

'Wait a minute; you saw a phone?'

'No, sir, I think it was a phone, the way it caught the sun. I am sure they threw it away the moment we jumped on them.'

DSP Sharma plucked the toothpick from his mouth in a flash. 'But you did retrieve a phone from the spot afterwards?'

'No, sir, we couldn't. We'll resume the search shortly.'

DSP Sharma punched the cone brutally, the mystery of its many dents now solved. 'So let me get this straight. You brought these two here just because they were holding hands on a bench? No knife, no mobile, no blood on them…'

The swinging cone made the sub-inspector appear and disappear in the hyper-agitating arc of light; now his belly, now his face.

'You brought them because they were holding hands. Bastard, Jatinder, are you mad! *Gadhe ki aulad.*'

'But, sir, I am convinced...'

'Shut up.'

The sub-inspector kept his head down, his mind now idling, waiting for the storm to pass.

'Ban-cho, SP saab will be here any minute; is this all I have for him? Do you even *know* who was in that plastic bag? Jatinder, what are we going to do?'

The sub-inspector raised his head—'Sir, I have an idea.'

'Chup.'

—only to pull it back quickly within the folds of his crumpled and greased collar.

'Anyway, what is it?'

The childlike vivacity returned. 'Sir, we can request SP saab to apply for a seven-day judicial for these two. Meanwhile, let me run upstairs and get that mobile phone we recovered from Lakhan Kitla's body yesterday. Place it in Dev's pants for SP saab to get an underworld angle.'

The toothpick, which had once again found its way to DSP Sharma's mouth, slumped off his lower lip. He caught it in mid-air and replaced it in his mouth. 'Saala.'

'Thank you, sir.'

'One minute, what about the SIM card? Why, you ass? What if it comes out in front of magistrate saab that Dev here has no underworld connection?'

'Er, sir, we can make sure the hearing goes to cell number two. Our Tilak has some fitting with Srivastav saab—the magistrate.'

'Oye Jatinder, you seem to have thought of everything, hain.'

'Victory in this investigation is only because of your efforts, sir.'

'Haan, haan. Now come close and pay attention.'

Realising his folly, DSP Sharma gestured quickly with his free hand for the sub-inspector to retreat a few steps.

'Ban-cho, Jatinder, do you ever take a bath? *Scent toh laga liya kar, gandu.*'

'Sir?'

'Uff. Take this Dev fellow to the water cooler and give him a nice cold wash. Scrub all those belt and buckle marks, you understand? Get Tilak in the next room, give him a few tight ones on the face, two on the ear, you know the sort. Struggle has to be established.'

'Tilak, sir?'

'Why, are you volunteering?'

'No no, sir, I...'

'Then shut up and do as I tell you. We need to...'

The sub-inspector's ears stood up. 'Sir, ahem, careful now, here he comes, I can hear him coming.'

'What, who?'

'SP Kharbanda is behind you.'

'Who? Ban-cho, am I deaf to...'

'SP saab is behi… Hello, good evening, sir.'

The chirping, churning sounds of creamed and polished shoes ceased abruptly as the bulk they were carrying came to a standstill. 'Good evening, good evening. And you are?'

'Sub-Inspector Jatinder, sir.'

'Yes yes…' SP Kharbanda dismissed the reply from his attention even before it was uttered. Such must power be—real, visible and shoe-chirping. His attention was fixed rather at his direct subordinate and not some lowly sub-inspector. He got hold of the backrest of the chair DSP Sharma was perched on and shook it branch and root. 'Arey DSP saab, so angry with me that you won't even turn and look at me, hain?'

'Who, what… oh, *hello* sir *hello*, we were just talking…welcome, sir, take this chair—oye Jatinder, some chai-shai, quick.'

Vanity restored, SP Kharbanda became almost gentle. 'No need for that, please keep sitting...arey keep sitting, Sharma saab.'

Adamant, DSP Sharma jumped up and then realised he'd done so too fast. He wobbled, looking for support, which he found in the drenched half-sleeve of the sub-inspector's shirt. He tugged at it a couple of times and restored his balance. 'We have made good progress in this case, sir.'

'I knew I could rely on you. Well done. Now tell me.'

DSP Sharma tilted his head inquisitively. 'What, sir?'

'What what sir. Who is this girl? And that young man over there—was there a struggle? He looks a little...'

'Well, yes, sir. We hit the jackpot, alright. Jatinder here has done a commendable job. You see, I had instructed him to keep an eye on the dead body. Since morning, he has…'

SP Kharbanda sat himself down, donating his baint and his headgear to the welcoming hands of the sub-inspector. 'If you please,

Sharma saab, just the results, no details—file them in the report later. I don't have time for this. A team is on its way from Delhi as we speak. The case will be out of our hands by tomorrow. DIG saab, Special Branch, someone called Ajay Banerjee, has been put in charge of this investigation.'

'Not Banerjee, Biswas sir, Biswas. He's in charge, sir? He is well known, sir. I mean in police circles.'

'Yes yes, one and the same, Sharma, one and the same.'

'Er, yes sir.'

SP Kharbanda had had enough of the chit-chat. He cleared his throat loudly. 'Haan, now tell me.'

'Y-yes, sir. In short, Jatinder caught these two at the crime scene, a full forty-eight hours after Saane's death. Rathod of the forensic branch estimated the time of death. Mr Saane is currently—sorry sir—his body is currently undergoing autopsy. We knew Rathod would give us something in the meantime. He is very good sir, our Rathod. Also, the eyes of Mr Saane...'

'Sharma saab, please, what did I tell you? Just give me some maas-machhee on these two.'

'Er, yes sir. In short, Jatinder caught these two at the scene. This man, sir—Dev—he was trying to pass a mobile phone to this girl. We confiscated the phone and found that Dev here is a sleeper of the Mitoo gang.'

'Hm... is this Mitoo fellow the same as that Andheri? The three ban-chos who were killed in yesterday's encounter—they belonged to the Mitoo gang, didn't they?'

'Yes, sir. Lakhan Kitla was one of them. Dev here was passing on Kitla's mobile phone to his girlfriend just before they were jumped on by our Jatinder. You see, sir, Lakhan Kitla and Babloo were...'

SP Kharbanda scratched his day-old stubble with care. 'Who is Babloo?'

'One of the three who were killed yesterday. The third was Jhingaa, sir. This Mitoo gang has the support of the ruling MLA, Madhav Godbole. Inside information. Looks like a simple job—poor Mr Saane.'

'Leave the politics-volitics, Sharma. I am in enough shit as it is.'

'No doubt, sir.'

'But tell me, how did Kitla's phone land up with this Dev? And who is this...what's your name, miss?'

'Payal, sir.'

'What?'

'Payal.'

'Louder, madam, please.'

'Payal.'

'Oh, Payal...good, beti, good. Now go and sit next to your friend Dev.'

'Yes, sir.'

The woman edged her feet into her chappals and laboured off to be with her friend.

SP Kharbanda pondered over the pitiful sight. 'Haan, so Sharma, how are these two involved in all this? They don't look very underworld to me.'

'I am coming to that, sir. The man who killed Saane, and most likely it is Kitla, dropped his mobile at the spot—this we know. Sensing that the area would be heavily guarded in the aftermath, he simply asked this sleeper Dev to go over and retrieve the phone. We knew something like this would happen, so I stationed Jatinder there in plain clothes. Sure enough, Dev arrived to carry out the job and was caught.'

Something rattled. It made SP Kharbanda drum his knuckles on the table. 'One minute, let me get this straight. You mean to say that Kitla killed Saane on the orders of Godbole a full two or more days ago, given that Kitla himself was killed yesterday?'

'Well, sir, exactly.'

'What exactly? It doesn't add up, Sharma. You mean for two days, Saane saab's body was rotting in that bag and no one noticed it, or the smell? And what about Kitla? He must have realised very soon that his mobile was missing and given that the bastard was killed yesterday, he must have asked Dev to retrieve it *before* he was killed. No?'

DSP Sharma wheezed for air. 'Y-yes, sir.'

'What yes sir? And this means Dev had two days to go and get the phone but decided to go there only *this morning?* Why? No, Sharma saab, this is too hi-fi for me.'

There was silence in the room, except for the distant moans of the male suspect. SP Kharbanda waited. He drummed his fingers on the table twice and inspected his giant topaz ring. 'Well, Sharma saab?'

The last recourse for a subordinate: throw in the towel, lunge at the feet of your superior, clasp the ankles if only to be dragged along—all of which DSP Sharma had now commenced in sequence. 'S-sir, I am sorry. Jatinder here convinced me...'

SP Kharbanda snatched his baint from the sub-inspector's light grip. 'Sharma, *you*...one minute, you mean to say you made this all up?'

'Er, s-sir...'

'Ban-cho. This sort of thing is good at sub-inspector, inspector level. You are a DSP!'

SP Kharbanda pushed back his chair and got up. 'We are screwed, ban-cho, that's all there is. Saali Dilli team arrives tomorrow and what's more, I was so sure of our success that I told the higher-ups we have had a victory in the case. What will I do now? The team will kill us, Sharma. We'll be the laughing stock of the whole department. This will not do. You hear me? This just will not do!'

DSP Sharma stood rooted to his spot, head lowered.

'Well, don't just stand there like an ass! Say something!'

Don't say anything. Don't say anything, DSP Sharma counselled himself repeatedly.

SP Kharbanda roared. 'And you, what was your name? Satinder? *Watinder*? You think you are some RAW agent who can cook something up in a minute? You get out of my sight, right *now*.'

There was an immediate shuffling of feet.

'Oye not you, Sharma. Where do you think you are off to?'

'Sorry, sir, I...'

'Listen, there's no denying that you and this bastard, whatever his name is, are two of the most senseless ban-chos I have seen in a while...'

'So sorry, sir.'

'You better be. But now we can't leave everything like this, only for the team to hang *us* out to dry. We have got to recover the situation.'

SP Kharbanda kicked the chair, bringing it into position for him to sit on. 'Now listen—and no mistake this time, you understand?'

DSP Sharma couldn't believe his luck. 'Anything, sir, please.'

'But first you tell me exactly where we are right now on this case. And *if* I catch you making up stories again, *I* will make sure a formal procedure is constituted and *I* will personally ban-cho strip you of all your seva medals, rank, shirt, pant, right down to your soiled VIP, you got that?'

'Believe me, sir, I will myself strip in front of you if I am found lying…that bastard Jatinder put me to this scheme of his. I am so sorry, sir.'

'I said, *go on.*'

This was easy for DSP Sharma. All he had to do was add a dash of fact to a bubbling and steaming cauldron of fiction, something that he was adept at, having supervised the drafting of post-mortem case reports early on in his career.

'Believe me, sir, this is all we know: We found the body this morning after a jogger phoned the PCR control room. Almost immediately I was on the scene and realised at once that it was Mr Saane, still wearing his Gandhi cap. His body had been stuffed inside a black plastic bag. I ordered Jatinder to stick around and asked for the body to be sent to forensics. Just after lunch, when I was having my tea and rusk, Jatinder brought in these two. This girl, Payal, has since been under the supervision of a female constable as per the rules, and this fellow here, Dev, was taken to the next room by Jatinder, for, er, some further interrogation. Sorry, sir, but we haven't been able to get anything more on this case. Bastard Jatinder coaxed me into involving Dev in an underworld connection story, sir, otherwise I would never have...'

SP Kharbanda grunted loudly. 'Enough! What is done is done. Now, you listen very carefully. All is not lost. We can still give the Delhi team some results.'

'Definitely, sir.'

'Here's exactly what you have to do. And I mean *exactly*. Don't bother to think on your own—just do what you are told.'

'Sure, sir.'

SP Kharbanda lowered his voice conspiratorially. 'Take Dev to the water cooler and give him a nice cold wash. Scrub all those belt and buckle marks. Get one of your langoors in the next room and give him a few tight ones on the face, two on the ear—you know the sort.'

'That'll be Jatinder, sir, who else.'

'Yes yes, anyone, it doesn't matter. Blood must be seen on the officer. If a tooth comes out, that's a bonus.'

DSP Sharma looked cheerfully thought of the sub-inspector. 'Sure, sir.'

'Then call up magistrate saab. You have a connection?'

'Sure, sir, all our landlines are in full working order...'

'Oye ban-cho Birbal ki aulaad, by connection I didn't mean a phone connection, you...'

'Oh. Sorry sir, yes sir, Jatinder has, he mentioned Tilak having...'

'Yes yes, fix it. Make Jatinder record his statement in front of magistrate saab. No, don't let that idiot write down anything. You do it for him. Got that?'

'Yes, sir.'

'Your underworld connection story will do for the time being. But some loose ends must be tied first. This mobile phone that you confiscated—I mean, what exactly did you have in mind?'

'Sir, we would have used Kitla's phone, only removed the SIM card.'

'No need for that. Put back the SIM card. Make Dev call up Kitla using Dev's phone, you got that? I am assuming Dev has a phone. Otherwise get one for him for this purpose. Ask Dev to speak hello shello, anything—you make it up. It should be clear to the magistrate that Dev has a connection with Kitla.'

'Sure, sir. But who will speak to Dev? From the other end, I mean.'

SP Kharbanda punched the cone, only to quickly inspect his topaz ring. Relieved that the bone-crushing sound was probably because of something else, he stalled the belly-dancing light cone with his paw. 'My great-grandfather, that's who. Ban-cho, obviously magistrate saab has never heard the real Kitla speak, and thankfully now never will. Get someone to speak as Kitla. You got that?'

'Sure, sir. Er...'

'Yes? You want to say something?'

'No no, sir, all is fine…er, it's just that if Dev, I mean, you know what I mean when I say Dev...'

'Out with it, ban-cho.'

'S-sorry, sir, but won't magistrate saab get to know the date and time of the call that Dev makes to Kitla? Er, but if you...'

SP Kharbanda thwacked the table with his baint. 'Yes, good point.'

'Th-thank you, sir.'

'One, don't mention the date and time of the calls in your report—and also when you are saying all this to magistrate saab, try and hurry him up, you understand? Two, as backup, get someone from the technical wing to sort this out. Ban-cho we can send that Chawla chhori into space, but we can't change a simple date and time on a SIM card?'

'Yes, sir, got you. One last thing, sir, this girl Payal…'

'Yes yes, I was coming to that. Tell her that if she doesn't cooperate, we'll bring in her mother, father, brother—well, you know the rest. Tell her we will portray her as a call girl involved with a Mitoo gang sleeper. These things usually stick and give some credibility to our story.'

DSP Sharma was beginning to see it through to the end. 'They do, sir.'

'Tell her she is a nice girl and we wouldn't dream of doing any of this, if only she says in front of the magistrate that Dev was moving about the spot under, under… what's that nice official phrase that I forget, ban-cho–'

'Suspicious circumstances?'

'Yes, suspicious circumstances. Tell her to say all this to the magistrate saab. Haan, and also that the bastard followed her while she was doing, I don't know, yoga-shoga in the park, and then forced her to keep a mobile phone for the time being.'

'Perfect, sir.'

'Remember, only Payal and Jatinder must give statements in person to magistrate saab. Dev must not. So do something to Dev saab so he cannot speak in front of the magistrate. Or do I have to do that, too?'

'No no, sir, got it.'

'Get magistrate saab to sanction a fourteen-day police custody. And ring up Inspector Bhujangi, that *Sansani* fellow. This case needs all the sensationalising it can get. Now, if we are finished, I have too much to do before the team arrives. You got all that?'

'Sir, you are a genius, sir, a one hundred percent genius.'

SP Kharbanda raised himself up clinging on, as usual, either the hairy arm or the sweaty shirt of a fellow officer or sometimes, even a dangling amulet. He was nonchalant but in need of a little more flattery. 'Yes yes, alright.'

DSP Sharma was only too pleased to oblige. 'That's why, sir, I am just a DSP and you are an SP.'

'Yes, now don't butter my hairy ass.'

DSP Sharma hunched over and touched SP Kharbanda's kneecaps, one by one. 'What a relief, sir. Thank you—really, sir, thank *you*.'

'You are welcome. Jai Hind.'

'Jai Hind, sir.'

Have you ever been to an Indian thana, say in Pipli or Nidadavolu? Don't know where that is? Correct, it's next to Salem, Connecticut.

Thana. Go on. Step inside. Be brave. You will be raped in twenty-seven languages and a million dialects. You will be spat on. You will drink urine. And if you are lucky, you will die. But if you are reading this, there's a good chance you are not among the lucky ones.

Policemen in India are a scared lot. They will shit on you because that's what they know—they have been shat on all their lives and this here is their chance. Those people huddled in corners and shaking at the edges. This is the opportunity for policemen to strike back. And there are so many ways to give back—why not, why not, indeed. All is fear in life and death.

We are so subservient it has altered our morphology. In photos of Indians next to other Indians—or for that matter anyone—we stand in what is now called covering the crotch position. Hands juxtaposed strangely in front, for ladies and gents. In football it is necessary before a free kick. This is the Indian version.

The police is afraid of the police who is afraid to police. Shoulders lunging forward, arms covering pot bellies, breath-holding selfie moment. Awkward? What awkward. Their dictionary starts and ends with 'Do you know who I am?', which is also the favourite line of famous people. When they get an opportunity to know themselves, they hit us. Who is to blame—us, them or kismet? Zindagi? It is not easy being a cop in India—in fact, it is especially bad to be one.

Oh look who just swung in through the saloon doors. *'Saaley, kuttay, masoom pe haath uthate ho? Maa kasam…'* and six policemen lie dead on the floor. A few minutes ago, he had just rolled over a few bones on the curb. No, footpath. Amchi Mumbai or Namma Bengaluru—how does it matter? Same skeletons, another place. Another bitia, tibia, skull, socket joint, humerus, fragments from a crushed foot. That's all that remained anyway, one fateful night in Mumbai. Stupid skeleton, wanted to sleep on a pavement and that too in the middle of the night. But one or two bones squeaked. How dare they! An FIR should be lodged against squeaking bones for noise pollution. Ban bones. Oh, sounds so chic. These beggars—who do they think they are? And for years now, a certain thana in Mumbai is quivering with fear, wondering what being human means to a monkey. Do monkeys have biceps?

What do policemen in India do after the criminal has been caught in the movie and after we have all clapped and whistled? The khaki uniform is so disrespected even the starch revolts, especially when policemen wear half and full pants so stiff the canvas crackles as if you were sharpening a knife with the crease. They call it the unicorn. Can't run, can't sit, can't lie down, can't stand. All they can do is sweat. People fear sweat-drenched khaki more than they do khaki. Sweat denotes anger as much as fear.

Indian police stations are places where everything except a leaking tap can be fixed. This is where false is true and true is false, where body parts are made to appear and disappear, sometimes swiftly, sometimes with studied deliberation, as the dead come alive and the alive jump out of their skin. Don't have evidence? Manufacture it. Have evidence? Destroy it. Defile the file. Too many files? Destroy the building. Easy. Set fire to it. Damp matchbox? Then go on leave, or better still, say there's nothing to hide. Destroy, defile, deny. Here, behind that wall, across the hallway, are stacks of files. No one knows, few care and even fewer come to find out.

Welcome to my cell where a six-foot-tall man can be found hanging from a six-foot-high ceiling. Or where a man dies because he bit a live wire. Yes, that's how justice is delivered in India while holders of positions and carriers of justice speak about it as a miscarriage.

One gets a strange sense of an India, which is forever pregnant with Justice—she's either delivering it, aborting it or suffering a miscarriage. Feminine gender.

What is the ratio in India of people to police? Some say three lakh to every cop, some put the figure upwards of half a million. But who knows and who cares. Probably as many as the rats that run around our ration shops.

The police officers in India know when to produce evidence and when to do a Houdini. They watch before they act. But before they watch, we do. Crime has to be given a name these days. It is no longer just a murder, a rape or a lynching. The context makes all the difference; otherwise, it is just another dead rat. A girl lies strewn, bleeding to death. We don't stop our cars because we are in a rush to buy candles and placards with which to manufacture outrage over her coming death. We are such cowards that we even deprive a woman of her name. But crime has a name. Own it. Face it. Embrace it. It is yours.

Naming is distancing, naming is owning, naming is disowning, naming is belonging, naming is abandoning, naming is deriding, naming is defeating. And naming is defining. We are sanitised, we are globalised, we are immunised and we have given ourselves a number to dial in case of an emergency...

100. There's a government notification which requires that the three digits should be displayed prominently in all public places across India. These include skeletons and police stations where the sun goes down and there is darkness.

Don't fool yourself into thinking that you can carry on with skeletons as witnesses. In the grand scheme of things, you are only as alive as long as you feel for others, share their grief, lend a hand, spare a thought and remember that loved ones will refer to your body as 'it' even before rigor mortis sets in. The rat eater has only just started talking. It is about you, everything you hold dear and everything about which you know nothing. Ready to jump without nets? Brahmandam. Growing into deep silence to reinvent yourself as a revolutionary, a karma yogi?

In the meantime, before you laugh at India's police, stand straight. Order yourself a Manhattan—darkness at noon. Huh?

We are all rat eaters—make no mistake. Even the one that got away, is, in the final analysis, a rat eater. The cuckoo that flew over the nest also had a defined trajectory.

2

1966—A Brave New World

Amma thumped the tarpaulin-sheathed wickerwork basket on Bela's head with such force, the poor girl nearly collapsed on her knees.

'Hold it. Steady,' she said, clamping Bela's upper arms. 'Yes, good.'

The commotion upset Amma's husband and father to her nine girls. 'Arey Laxmi,' he said, mopping the hollow of his armpits with his gamchha. 'What are you shouting about this early, hain?'

'*This* early, Mala-ke-Baba?' said Amma, shoring up her enormous belly with meshed fingers. 'Look at me, all bloated up and still off to work.'

Amma did not wait for her husband's retort and hurried out of the shack, driving away damp strands of hair from her face with exaggerated breaths. One by one, five of her girls tumbled out with baskets on their heads. They formed a line and waited, giggling, murmuring, nudging and bumping each other with their elbows and shoulders. The banter would have carried on unabated were it not for the spray of mynahs that exploded from the kikar under whose sparse canopy the girls had lined up. The basket-laden heads moved hither and thither in delight, with the youngest and the shortest craning their necks to steal a better view of the melting and forming patterns.

'*Enough.*'

Amma turned around slowly, moving her feet in tiny shuffles like a danseuse, and looked at the girls with deliberately enlarged eyes. A hush descended. The girls were stared into getting on with the detail of the drill. Soon, the jingle-jangle of cattle collars filled the air. The alarm had sounded.

But Amma went down on her haunches instead, a smooth capsize. Arms extended, elbows resting on her knees, hands wilted at the wrists, she waited.

An uneven chant of huffing and puffing broke the dusty stillness and made Amma turn her head. A thin man, ribs showing through shifting skin, a plough bearing down on his shoulder, bounced past, swinging his free arm as help. Amma's eyes followed him. Slowly, the blur of dust dissipated, some of it resettled and the man was gone, but Amma was searching for him, her gaze wistful.

She raised herself up, pushing hard at her knees with her palms, and walked past the line, adjusting a basket here, rectifying a posture there. The sun, pitiless already, was turning the sky from blue to silver. '*So soon,*' thought Amma, looking up and then at the mile-long dirt road that would take them to the village. *So long, the road*, she said to herself, twitching her elbows to better position the load.

Work. Cruel and merciless.

Amma snatched a basket that lay upturned on the thatched roof. Crowning herself with it, she asked the girls gently, 'Chalain?'

Meanwhile, at the other end of the mile-long road, another household was waking up. Multicoloured morning sun poured through the stained-glass ventilators lighting up all the fifteen rooms of the Thakur Haveli, gently nudging the sleeping residents to wakefulness. Badey Thakur craned his neck to investigate, then threw his head back on the pillow like a deadweight. He turned this way and that and proceeded to get up from the only available side of his single bed.

Badey Thakur slept alone. An otherwise violent and terrifying man, the one cardinal virtue of Gandhiji he had chosen to imbibe was to see the sexual act as a means of procreation. Nothing more, nothing less. In his entire life of fifty years, Badey Thakur had performed the said act seven times, resulting in four sons, one daughter and two miscarriages. Abstinence conferred on him a saint-like status. The villagers anointed him as their own mahatma, and his every word, his every decree soon became sacrosanct, a paththar ki lakeer.

Badey Thakur's wife, like Bapu's before her, accepted her husband's decision with grace. She too slept on a single bed and in a separate room so as to avoid any kind of temptation, worried that Kamdev, the unrepentant God of carnal jugglery, was forever lurking behind curtains and bedposts.

Man, though, is largely an animal, and much as Badey Thakur and Badi Thakurayin pressed the virtues of sexual restraint, their exhortations were largely ignored by the villagers who proceeded to do what they did best behind closed doors. Fame spread, not the message, and so the axe fell on the nearest and dearest. Inwardly reluctant men and women of the Thakur household outwardly volunteered to sleep in single beds once their quota of five children had been exhausted. The haveli turned rife with unrequited sexual energy, which found its release in the terrifying repression and atrocities towards the lower castes of the village. They were trampled beneath the angry Thakur feet, their backs bore the bloody gashes of the angry Thakur whips and they drowned in the angry sea of unused Thakur semen.

Badey Thakur now got up from the bed and slapped his morning erection to a cowering withdrawal. He staggered out of his room holding one end of his dhoti and shouted: 'Arey, Thakurayin?'

'In a moment,' said Badi Thakurayin. A muffled shout from afar made her instinctively quicken her pace. The ghoonghat slipped down her head, the haveli keys jangled by her waist, the saucer and cup trembled in her hand, as she rushed to keep appointment with her lord. The couple almost collided in the corridor that opened on to the front veranda. Badey Thakur lost no time.

'Where is my chai? *And* my newspaper *and* my mug of water.'

'I-I am sorry. I was held up in the kitchen,' said Badi Thakurayin, slipping her ghoonghat back on as she passed her husband his tea.

'Held up in the kitchen. What were you doing there? Scheming to ruin my day? Now get lost.'

'Ji.'

'And wait.'

'Ji?'

'Have the latrines been cleaned?'

'I think so.'

'You *think* so?'

'But they are, I am sure. That musahurin comes early to do them—Laxmi is her name.'

'I don't care what her name is. Heaven help you if I find any smell in there. Now go and check whether the latrine has been cleaned.'

'J-ji.'

The morning sweet nothings over, Badi Thakurayin strode quickly down the long corridor, moving in and out of the jagged planks of sunshine seeping through the archways that ran all along its length. She entered the central veranda and stopped under the neem tree, which was draped with an assortment of sacred threads that criss-crossed round its girth.

'*Now what.*'

While contemplating her next action, Badi Thakurayin tore a branch and ran her enclosed palm all along the stem. Having chewed one end adequately, she spat out the froth and looked in the direction of the many rooms along the quadrangular balcony.

'Arey, Sushma? Subhadra? Mandakini?' she cried. 'Where are all of you? Don't know why I put up with this. One of these days, I'll pick my jewellery up and disappear, clean latrine or no clean latrine.'

A door opened, revealing a cheerful woman as yet unaffected by the cruelties of the day.

'Arey, bhabhiji? Good morning.'

Badi Thakurayin was not in the mood for a friendly chat.

'Bhabhiji ki chachi. Yes, that's right—you just stand there yawning and stretching while your bhabhi runs around like a slave.'

'Kyaa bhabhi ji, drop it na. Achha tell me—what is to be done? You just have to say.'

'Then go and find out if that musahurin Laxmi has cleaned the latrine.'

The incredulous look on Choti Thakurayin's face betrayed annoyance. '*What*?'

'You heard me.'

'But bhabhi, I have just got up and…and Chotey Thakur might ask for a cup of tea, and...'

Badi Thakurayin was seasoned at such talk. 'See? Didn't I tell you? No respect—none.'

'*Uff bhabhi*. Achha na, you win. *Only for you,* my sweetest, dearest bhabhi.'

'Spoken like a true princess. Now go.'

Resigned, Choti Thakurayin gently closed the door behind her, lobbed the key bunch tied to her pallu over her shoulder and commenced her trek round the haveli, climbing up a hundred stairs, pushing open and pulling shut heavy doors, all the while mumbling protests that only she could hear or understand. She came finally to the end of the tour at the last door, the one that opened on to the back alley. She pushed it open and peered out.

'Arey is anyone here. *Laxmi*? Laxm...there you are. What are you doing standing near Kusum chachi's house, mui?'

Laxmi—Mai to her children—was busy with her morning duties along with her staff of five. The shouting made her turn around. She let go of her hand shovel and straightened.

'Arey, Choti Thakurayin? Coming in a minute, please wait.'

'What did you say?'

'I said, Choti Thakurayin, I am just...'

'Hurry up, mui. I can't wait for you all day.'

'Ji. Come now, Mala, Sarla, Bimla. Pick your baskets up. Only Badey Thakur's house to go. Careful, Mala. Cover your mouth with the dupatta—like this. Where is…What took you so long, Bela, you stupid girl?'

Bela, all of seven, burst into tears. 'Mai, that Kania—he threw a rock at me and I lost my footing-and-and, everything from the basket fell on the road. Mai, the smell…it was terrible.'

'Bas bas, don't make trouble for your mother, you hear? I have enough as it is—nine months heavy and then having to take care of you lot and in this heat. Now come along. The last thing I want is Choti Thakurayin mouthing me off—that'll really make my…Oh! Ai-ma. Mala, here, just take my basket. It's coming, I am sure of it—today itself, I am telling you.'

'What...what's happening, Mai, *what*?'

'Your brother, or ooh-maa…s-sister, is coming today, that's what's happening...Now don't trouble me. Give me back my basket.'

The caravan of manual scavengers wound its way and came to rest by the unwelcoming sight of Choti Thakurayin. The line formed, and this time, Mai was in it.

'What took you so long, mui?'

'Forgive me, Choti Thakurayin. That third house from the end—there, you see? We had to wait a while as Thakurji hadn't finished his visit. Some food poisoning from chicken, it seems.'

'Did I ask you? *Did I*? Listen, *you*. I am not interested in your stories of waiting in line for Thakurji's prasad.'

Mai was swaying under the weight of her basket.

'I promise it won't happen again, Choti Thakurayin. I should have brought along Ganga too. But she had to go to a Harijan basti to get the day's water. Very sor…Ooh. Ma!…Aiyaah.'

'Shut up, mui; you and your lies. And why are you screaming your head off?'

'Nothing-g, Choti Th-thak-urayin-n...Ooh. It's just that I think… I'm going…into labour…my water's just…ai-maah!'

'Keep your voice down, you'll wake everyone up! So you are in labour. Is that my problem? Another rat on the way. Is this your fifth? Sixth? Must be eighth?'

'T-tenth, Ch-choti Thakurayin.'

'*Tenth*! Hey Bhagwaan. What is it with you people. One doesn't come out fully and the next starts to grow in the same womb. Now stop wailing—you are not the first woman to be giving birth. Hold it, hold the rat till you have done our latrine.'

'Y-yes, of-coa-course, Choti Thakurayin…Maala, Sarla…G-go-on…empty the can-canisters…B-e-l-a…h-here…take this phenyl and wash the trench up, munni.'

The girls set to work under Mai's eagle eye, moving expertly around her like little soldiers, emptying the canisters, splashing fistfuls of raakh inside the cans to wipe them clean, then pouring phenyl in the trenches. Choti Thakurayin ordered them to be more generous with the noxious liquid. The painful, smelly minutes ticked by. At long last, but not before two of the girls had to climb down into the trenches with handle-less brooms and fill their little baskets to the brim, the army lined up one more time, looking up at their mother with a hint of pride.

Amma parted her trembling lips with great difficulty. 'T-h-e-r-e, Choti Thakurayin…d-done.'

'Sure? As it should be? Let me not come over and find any stench.'

'No, n-no, n-o sm-ell. Come, see f-for yourself.'

'Hm, no need. Good. How much do we pay you for this?'

Amma compressed her lips a few times before she could muster enough strength to answer.

'T-ten paise, Th-thakurayin.'

'That much? And even then you rats come late. Here…take this five—that'll teach you to come on time. Now go.'

'J-ji, Choti Thaku-rayin. Come Maala, Bimla, everyone.'

And the convoy set sail again: tired, defeated and humiliated. It was the Indian file of scavengers, owners of skills passed down from generation to generation, with a guaranteed job they had no worry of losing. What was lower?

The sun beat down on their heads while the tar took care of their soles. Slowly, silently, they walked on. After a while Mala, the lead, turned her head. 'Mai? Can we stop for a minute? Choti Thakurayin threw the coin in my basket. Let me fish it out.'

'L-leave it, Mala. That bitch. Leave her paanch paise in that Thakur shit. Don't touch it; we don't want it. Ai-mah…ooh...a-animals! Listen, I can't walk any l-longer. W-water…Where's your father…'

'Baba should be in the fields by now, Mai…'

'Call him. Run. I t-think it's coming. I have to sit now. M-Maala... ai-maa. Mala, hurry, call your father. Get him-m.'

'Yes, Mai.'

'It's coming. Oh G-God, no. No-u-u...S-Sar-l-a, listen munni, we don't have a choice…dispensary is too far...*Da-dai, dai* will take too long to come. You sisters will have to do it.'

'Oh no, Mai.'

'Yes-s...till Mala gets back, one of you g-get some water. Go!'

'But, Mai, we don't have a can, and there's only the Thakur well nearby. What are we going to do, Mai? I am so scared.'

'Listen, S-Sarla. Bimla. You don't be scared, you f-fools. It's n-nothing. Haven't you seen gou-mata giving birth to her calf? Haan? It's n-nothing...now go, get me some water.'

'But Mai, there are only some puddles…near there, can you see?'

'Then go…fi-fill your mouths with water…from those p-puddles…c-come back and spill it on me…water…I need some water…ai-ma!'

'Yes, Mai. Come on, Bimla, hurry.'

'Ai-maah! Diee...let me diee.'

Meanwhile, a fair distance away, Mala's little legs hopped and skipped through the steep incline of wild grass that demarcated each plot of land, the abrasive edges of the grass stalks slashing her limbs, unnoticed. She spotted her father without much difficulty. There he was, surfing the barren earth, his legs perched on the plough mouldboard and his hands holding the reins tight for dear life.

'Baba...Baba!'

Baba let go of the reins and jumped off the contraption; the yoked beasts continued their run.

'Arey, Mala? What happened. Is everything alright?'

'Stop working at once Baba! Mai is in trouble...she's delivering the baby on the road near that tree. Baba, please hurry, Mai may die. Oh God! Mai will die Baba...come Baba. There's no water a-a-and we are too far from the house...we cannot call the dai. Baba...m-m-my Mai...my Mai is surely going to die Baba. Oh no! Baba please hurry right now. She's lying in the middle of the road there Baba...there's no water there...Baba help!'

'Oh my God. Slow down, slow down, Mala. Where?'

Mala started to cry. 'Near that bargad. Hurry.'

'Yes yes, let's go.'

Baba doubled up his lungi and gazed into the distance. The bullocks had come to rest dutifully by the boundary of his field and were foraging the sliver of green turf next to the water channel. He caught hold of Mala's wrist and hurried down the slope, dragging his daughter who could barely keep up with his giant strides. Soon, the two stood next to the wailing mother, staring at her, not knowing what else they could do.

'Laxmi? Arey, Mala-ki-Amma? What is happening? Are you...'

'B-baby is happ-eningg, you f-fool. Maa...A-ae!'

'Oh my God! Oh my God!'

'Shut up. Shut up! It is *you*. *You* have done this. *You* have killed me. *You* are responsible, Mala-ke-Baba.'

'Don't say that, Mala-ki-Amma, please don't. Calm down. You need to calm down.'

'Don't say one word. *One* word. Who called him? Mala, who called him!?'

'You did, Mai...Mai, please calm down.'

'Mala-ke-Baba? Arey, Mala-ke-Babaa...are you there...?'

'Yes.'

'Then do something...say something!'

'What?'

'Say pushh!'

'Push.'

'Say push-sh-shh...ae-maaa!'

'Pushh! Push...Pushh.'

'Diee...just let me diee.'

'It's coming. I can see the head—it's very black, the head.'

'Say pushh.'

'It's coming...pushhhh...push!'

'S-Sarla, hold the head...beti, hold the head...and pull...diee, let me die...'

'Push, Mai, push! Push, Mai...with all your strength.'

'Haiiiiii! Raaaaaammmmmmm!'

'Yes, that's good. More, more.'

'Raaaaaammmmmmmmmmm!'

'It's coming. Just a few more, Mai...'

'Raaaaaaaammmmmm!'

'Push, Mai, push. Nearly there. Sarla. Bela. Empty your mouthfuls here. *Quick*.'

'Aaaathhhoooooo!'

'Bimla. Go get some more mouthfuls! It's nearly there, Mai. It's sliding, it's sliding out,' said Sarla.

Baba offered to help. 'Keep calm, Mala-ki-Amma, keep calm.'

'Shut up! *You* try it...next time *you* try it. There'll be no next time-mm…I promise.'

'Don't say that, Mala-ki-Amma. What if it's a girl?'

'Never in a thousand y-years.'

Baba insisted. 'But what if it comes out a girl?'

'Never again-n.'

'But...'

Mala had heard just about enough of this. 'Baba, shut up! Can't you see mai is in so much pain?'

'Kill me. Enough. Enough! Hain-Hain-uunnhhh, Haan-uunhh. Maa! Ay-eema.'

Mala was in command. 'Bimla. Spit out. *Now*.'

'*Aaathhooooo*!'

'There…Mai! It's come out...it's a boy. A boy. A brother! Did you see? A brother.'

'Hain-Hain-uunnhhh, Haan-uunhh! Hain-Hain-uunnhhh.'

'Mai! A baby boy.'

'Hain-Hain-uunnhhh, Haan-uunhh.'

'Baba! Can you see? A brother...for us!'

'Yes. *Yes*. A boy! *A boy*. A son.'

'Hain-Hain-uunnhhh, Haan-uunhh.'

'Arey, Mala-ki-Amma, can you hear it? Can you not hear his beautiful, sweet cries; can you not see it?'

'Hain-Hain-uunnhhh, Haan-uunhh.'

'It's a boy. My son.'

'Hain-Hain-uunnhhh, Haan-uunhh.'

'Tenth time lucky. Tenth time lucky. Thank you, God. *Thank you*.'

'Hain-uunnhhh.'

'He is my son.'

'Hain-Hain-uunnhhh, Haan-uunhh.'

'My only son.'

'Hain-Hain-uunnhhh, Haan-uunhh.'

'He will be strong.'

'Hain-Hain-uunnhhh.'

'He will rise.'

'Hain-Hain-uunnhhh, Haan-uunhh.'

'He will lead us.'

'Hain-Hain-uunnhhh, Haan-uunhh.'

'He will feed us.'

'Hain-Hain-uunnhhh, Haan-uunhh.'

'Protect us.'

'Hain-Hain-uunnhhh.'

'He is our saviour.'

'Hain-Hain-uunnhhh, Haan-uunhh.'

'Our avatar.'

'Hain-Hain-uunnhhh, Haan-uunhh.'

'Dashavatar.'

'Hain-Hain-uunnhhh.'

'Did you hear, Mala-ki-Amma?'

'Hain-Hain-uunnhhh, Haan-uunhh.'

'Dashavatar.'

'Hain-Hain-uunnhhh, Haan-uunhh.'

'The tenth reincarnation.'

'Hain-Hain-uunnhhh.'

'I will—we will—call him Kalki.'

'Hain-Hain-uunnhhh, Haan-uunhh.'

'Kalki!'

'Hain-Hain-uunnhhh.'

'Kalki has come. *Kalki has come.* Kalki has entered this rotten godforsaken world. But he has come. Yes, my son has come now.'

'Hain-Hain-uunnhhh, Haan-uunhh!'

'Did you hear?'

'Hain-Hain-uunnhhh.'

'Are you listening, Kalki-ki-Amma?'

Can you smell the shit? You are standing on it. After she ensured your safe passage. Aisle, corridor, sky, veins, arteries, windows, mainframe, firewall. Fire. Agni. It is all around you, it is you—from head to toe—and all you can see is a son. Son. *Fils*. Son. *Figlio*. Yes, yes. Finally, a son, the heir, the inheritor, the independent procreator, the powerful, the pitiful, the pitiless, the conqueror, has come knocking on your door. Lottery.

The womb, the garbh, is but a taxi. *Uber alles*.

Can you smell the hurt? It is odourless. It is colourless. As colourless as that foetus found in a fridge. Headline, breaking news, star-studded panels, outrage that would make the sound barrier shy. Lament. Lament between G&T and single malt and, unknown to you, cheap wine. Perfect for the display of handloom saris at the next innovation summit. Even better with a prêt-à-porter and chipped shoes and craggy elbows at a women's conference—where else, where else can the foetus go? Think up some possibilities for the Travelling Foetus. *Over men and horses, hoops and garters; lastly through a hogshead of real fire. In this way the travelling foetus will challenge the world.*

Can you smell the thought? It comes sealed in a tank. Think tank. Can't speak about misery in miserable conditions. Chi. Thoo. Who will go to Patherdih. Can't think when hungry and far away. Research and more research must be done about women in India. It's a generational ATM—perpetual seminarists.

Indian women are struggling.

That canapé is tasty.

Indian women are trapped.

I have a new iPhone.

Millions for researching the obvious. Lawyers, journalists, experts, interns—everyone but those who die a little every day. Of course. Can't trust poor people with money. They will buy sunglasses and chips when what they really need are micronutrients. Grunts, grants, grunts, grants and frequent flyer miles. Even the World Bank has said poverty is feminine. And virginity? Is it also feminine? Now that's a good headline for a speech. But we have to be careful, you see. Actually a multicoloured PowerPoint presentation might fit the bill better. What is the colour of the hurt that is running in the gut? Next slide, please.

Why on earth would anyone stuff a foetus into a fridge? New desperation, new deprivation, new place but same shit. Normally we bury them in sand—girl foetuses and newborn babies—just deep enough for vultures and other birds of prey to take them away, upwards and ever more, higher and higher, to an abode called heaven. On earth, in India, it is called a girl child, a dead child, a curse, a cost, a shame, a burden, a disease, a disaster, a prostitute. The lettered call her a responsibility to be passed from hand to hand.

Passing the parcel.

In books, in cultural tradition, in scholarship, she is Goddess—forgiving: she is Ma Kali; she is Mary; she is Durga; she is Mahishasuramardhini. But when Mahishasuramardhini wears trousers and drives a Vespa instead of coming astride a buffalo, she is leered at, spat on. In Bollywood, for decades she used to be a swing. *Nari jeevan jhoole ki tarah, iss paar kabhi, uss paar kabhi; hothon pe madhur muskan kabhi, aankhon mein asuwan dhar kabhi.* That has changed. She now advertises for razors for men and performs acrobatics to make tea. She has been liberated, by men. Liberian Girl. *You came and you changed my world.* In this plastic return to modernity, she is neither jeev nor jantu, neither dark nor fair, neither inside the house nor outside it. Evolving, revolving—that is what is expected of her. Smiling, serving, servant. Smiling, servile, survive. Oh, alliterations after alliterations.

Spot the foetus, start saving. Shame if you can't see the shame.

What exactly is shame? Who defines it? Is there an upper limit? More girls, babies and otherwise, disappear in India than anywhere else in the world. Those who start saving for the curse are also women. Those who pour kerosene over brides are also women. Those who cover up household rapes are also women. Those who ignore their victimised colleague's cry for help at a workplace are also women.

It is not enough to look like a woman to be a woman. It is important to be one in all the manifestations that are known and continue to be. Tell the stories first, then whisper whatever little remains of the day.

Stories, what stories? Of plastic bottles inserted into the vaginas of toddlers? Of women being burnt alive because they dared to step out of their homes without a male escort? Of khap panchayats ordering the lynching of a girl who married in the same gotra? Sagotri is okay if you have an obliging priest. You can do a gotra-swap for a bit. God is kind, very understanding, and above all, very accommodating if you have money. Accounts in heavens are of a different nature.

And what if God was one of us? A woman and black and not amused at all?

Stereotype, separate; stereotype, segregate. A girl who wears a skirt is fast. A girl who wears a sari—is she slow? What does God wear if she wants to go jogging? Pinga—got you! The pant and the Pinga have to go out and earn a living; in some cases, they are the sole breadwinners. She drinks, she must have no morals; she doesn't drink, so she has several. She can take care of herself in a city. But wait, she's not a foetus anymore. What happened? Money came calling and so Lakshmi came blessing.

How do they manage to get into buses that never stop, trains that spit them out, crowds that grope them, husbands who harass them? We are civilised. We use words like naukrani and bartanwali and jhadoowali. Celebrate—their principal tool is now an election symbol.

The inconsistencies are jarring. Naming is shaming, naming is respecting. Widows of Mathura—we make films about them as if they are animals in a zoo to be photographed and pitied. We celebrate festivals that pointedly exclude widows. Sumangali prarthinai excludes young widows of tragedy from family prayers. What kind of an animal does this? Such atrocities in the name of gods and goddesses no one has seen. If god is Brahmandam, where then, is the exclusion? It is in the dirt of the uninformed, the vacuous and the vile mind that segregates to survive.

There is no point in getting angry, for this type of anger, the helpless one, is the anger of a loser. It is the first step to cynicism, to betrayal, to complicity. There is no point in citing the wisdom of texts and knowledge in the whispers of cultural practices and traditions. Try this. Tell people the *Bhagavad Gita* can also be seen as a violent text and see them bristle. Tell them that it throws you over the cliff without nets—that dharmakshetre, kurukshetre is not obvious.

The *Gita* is alive. It is scary. It seeks you as you seek it, and if you have the courage, it throws you right back on the roller coaster. What has the *Gita* got to do with women? Nice try.

To the self-styled oracles, the middlemen speaking for gods, any gods, everything is in the religious texts when it suits them. Everything from going to Mars to blasting the atom to developing a stem cell to driving a Ferrari to overtaking a Tesla—we know it all. Overlook parts that teach us to live like human beings. Compassion, empathy—*atmavat eva paraan api pashyata.* Okay. Sure, with some ice please.

Privately, we cheat. Publicly, we chat. Privately, we want a Madonna. Publicly, a Virgin Mary. So many women in India get acquainted with their feminine or masculine—yes, you read that right—aspects the first time they are assaulted. If reading this is difficult, think about the living dead.

She is all around you. Fear what we are doing to her. Fear yourself. Fear the Brave New World.

3

2004—A Guest of Honour

Out of nowhere, the north-bound Swami Gangeshwar Janta Mail approached platform two of Mumbai Central like an angry bolt of lightning, leaving the waiting mass of humanity scampering for cover. The speed was as unrelenting as the sound was thunderous, and the coaches continued to boom and go, boom and go, allowing the crowd only hazy glimpses of platform three and the trains waiting on the adjacent tracks through the gaps in-between or when the opposite doors of a coach were both left open.

Dust from the tracks invaded the platform in no time and the wind gave birth to a tornado of plastic bottles, paper cups, biscuit wrappers, crumpled newspapers, pattals, bidi ends, zarda sachets and cigarette butts. Only the driver of the train and its passengers saw the joke. They looked at the fog of screaming and cursing people and laughed their hearts out. An uneasy hush descended as the last coach sped by—as though the train had sucked the soul and the sounds of the platform and dragged them in its wake.

Slowly, people began to recover their postures. The coolies were the worst-hit as they had formed an Indian file close to the platform edge, expecting to hop on to the normally slow-moving train in order to save time. They waved their fists and swirled their turbans like lassoes at the now-vanished train, heaping curses on the obviously punch-drunk driver and his immediate family.

As the dust settled, the thriving ecosystem of the tracks became visible. Gigantic rats emerged from their holes by the sniffing the upturned filth with their twitching noses. Pigeons fluttered in and, once they had perched on the iron girders that supported the corrugated cement roof of the platform, they trotted, but guardedly. A pack of stray dogs arrived from across the tracks—shrivelled udders long dead, wounded tails incapable of wagging, mottled looks driven by fear; they hopped on to the platform ledge and vanished amid the human sea.

Bisleris lay strewn like dead soldiers in a battlefield. Urchin managers scrambled all around the confused crowd to collect as many as they could, punching and shoving their fellow gatherers, arguing heatedly over territories. Meanwhile, the announcer resumed her disjointed babble, the coolies revamped their Indian file and finally, when the mothers risked their toddlers to the platform edge for *soo-soo*, normalcy was restored.

Having missed all the fun, SP Kharbanda emerged from the Left Luggage Room exercising his knee joints and zipping up his trousers. Well aware that *Men* must be avoided at all costs, he had slipped past the Left Luggage Room attendant unnoticed and selected a corner.

'Arey bhai, where's my tea?' he said, having spotted DSP Sharma. 'This ban-cho Agast Kranti is always late. Platform number two, na.'

'Yes, sir, two,' replied DSP Sharma, discarding his chana cone in a flash. 'Not to worry, it should be arriving any moment. Arey Jatinder, get a steaming cup for sir.'

'Haven't slept a wink. I say too much pressure in the force these days, no Sharma?'

'Indeed, sir. And then they want quick results.'

SP Kharbanda dropped his shoulders and massaged his potbelly. 'What to do, Sharma saab, what to do.'

'True, sir. There are days when I don't get to see my Tanisha and Shiv at all. Sometimes I even forget whether Tanisha is in class nine or ten. And the wife is always nagging: Why are you late again, kids are growing up so fast, why aren't you investing in mutual funds,where's that Honda City you promised...'

'Bas bas, same at my end, Sharma, just the same. Arey what happened to my tea?'

DSP Sharma craned his neck and tried to locate the sub-inspector. 'Arey Jatinder? Oh, he's getting it, sir.'

Sub-Inspector Jatinder hurried his steps and hunched forward in respect as the kullarh switched hands. 'Here, sir. *Garma-garam.*'

SP Kharbanda would have acknowledged the effort with a thank you, but that would have meant breaking the habit of a lifetime. He nodded dismissively and blew hard into the chai.

'Hmm…aahh. Good tea. Come, Sharma, let's stand under a TV. You select.'

'Sure, sir. Arey, Jatinder, just get the mooda near that TV.'

'No need, Sharma.'

'No problem, sir…come, please sit.'

'Sharma, any biscuit?'

'In a minute, sir. Arey, Jatinder?'

Even as the sub-inspector scurried round the platform searching for Hide & Seek—SP saab's favourite—the object of his affection had collapsed on the wobbly mooda and was complaining to a passer-by about the TV not being loud enough. It was left to DSP Sharma to hunt down the stationmaster and get the remote. Both the DSP and the sub-inspector hurried back with their respective pickings and took their positions on either side of the mooda. SP Kharbanda winked—he was happy. He dunked his first of many Hide & Seeks into the kullarh and spat out something, not entirely sure what.

'Now, what is this Star News harami saying? Sharma? Volume…'

DSP Sharma dutifully commenced fiddling with the Sellotaped remote, muttering 'volume…volume…volume' under his breath, trying to decipher which of the rubbed-out buttons signified volume control. The channels changed, so did the colour; next was contrast, after which came the aspect ratio. The TV switched to AV until, finally, he managed to make the volume bars run helter-skelter on the screen. He cursed the stationmaster once more and restored the screen to the news channel SP saab was interested in.

The reporter sounded confused, much to SP Kharbanda's irritation. *'Rohit, can you hear me?...Rohit?...Please inform us of the latest update on the Saane murder.' 'Ji, yes, Pritam, as I was saying before the break, this case has shaken Mumbai to her core. People on the streets seem to be saying: if this can happen to a minister…er, we have with us Inspector Gokhale, in-charge of the investigation. Inspector Gokhale, please, this way…'*

SP Kharbanda was flabbergasted. '*Oye, saala*. Arey Sharma, where did this Gokhale come from?'

'I don't know, sir. I strictly told him...'

'Did you explain to him the underworld connection to this case? Please tell me that you did.'

'Of course. But I also told him to redirect all media queries to us, just us. Let me go back, sir, I'll...'

SP Kharbanda breathed a sigh of relief, followed by one of goodwill. 'Arey leave it, Sharma. Let him get some sunlight, bhai.'

Inspector Gokhale, meanwhile, was trying to convince the reporter, and through him the general public, of his extraordinary efforts at fighting crime: *'So, I have been on top of this case since yesterday, with the honoured support of my seniors, DSP Sharma and SP Kharbanda saab.'*

'Saala. Did you hear that, sir? Bastard's saving his ass. I'll slice him in two, just you wait and see.'

'Leave it na, Sharma. Listen…'

'So Gokhale saab, what you are saying is that the body was found behind a bench and in a plast...' 'Look, all I am saying is that we apprehended a Mitoo gang sleeper, who we believe was trying to help the real murderer, none other than a Mitoo gang member called Kitla, who we know was killed in a police encounter day before yesterday, which was the very day he murdered Mr Saane. You see, it...'

'Thank you, inspector, please stay with us, we have many more questions; back to the studio.'

SP Kharbanda threw away the kullarh in disgust. 'Well, I'll be... Sharma? This bastard Gokhale is spilling the beans completely. Who gave him permission to do all this?'

'Well, sir I..., er…sir, the train announcement.'

Not quite Aakashvaani, the sonorous voice from the clouds, but more of a loud and sharp grunt, filled the already heavy air. *'Passengers, meeters, and, greeters are, notified, this, that, two, nine, five, four, down,*

Mumbai, August, Kranti, coming, from, New, Delhi, to, Mumbai, Central, via, Hazrat Nizamuddin, Mathura, Sawai Madhopur, Kota.'

SP Kharbanda was not used to being made to wait. He addressed the loudspeaker.

'C'mon, c'mon, bitch, what's taking you so long?'

DSP Sharma thought it fit to fill in the blanks. 'Sir, believe it or not, this is a recorded message. The words are spoken by a lady, then put inside a computer that then assembles them in the correct order for transmission. That's why, sir, if you notice, the ending tone of every word doesn't fit with the starting tone of the next word. It's quite clever actua...'

'Shut up.'

'Sorry, sir.'

'...*Nagda, Ratlam, Vadodara, Bharuch, Vapi, and, Borivali, scheduled, to, arrive, at, eleven, hundred, hours, on, platform, number, two, is, now, arriving, at, eleven, hundred, and, thirty, hours, on, platform, number, twelve. Any inconvenience is greatly regretted, thank you.'*

SP Kharbanda flung the empty Hide & Seek packet and gave the mooda an almighty kick, making the sub-inspector instinctively chase it.

'What the.... Arey Sharma, did you hear that. Saali train's now coming at number twelve. I'll hang that bastard stationmaster. And this bitch.'

'Yes, sir, really sorry for this inconvenience. These railwaywallahs, taking this country for granted. Now we'd have to go up the stairway, to the overbridge, all the way to twelve and then all the way down the...C-2, sir, C-2 is the coach number.'

'I don't ban-cho care, Sharma, why are you telling me? What a life.'

The men raced the stairways and the connecting bridges, brushing aside coolies, hawkers, beggars and one or two unfortunate sufferers of elephantiasis obstructing the passageway, descending finally on the new platform, hands on knees. In celebration, the old lady crossed the T and put in the dot. '...*to, Mumbai, Central, has, now, arrived, at, platform, number, twelve. Any inconvenience is greatly regretted, thank you.'*

The officers watched helplessly as coach after coach slid past with no intention of stopping. *'Rukti nahi saali.'* The three sighed in unison.

Meanwhile, near the entrance of the vaataanukulit C-2, an anxious couple was scanning the crowded platform.

'Can you see him, Api? He should be here if he got my email. Draw the curtain a bit more. Can you see him?'

Aparajita swung her head round excitedly. 'Yes, I see him. I see him. That's Akhil alright. There he is. We have gone past him now. Looks just the same, Ajay, just the same. And what's this? It appears someone has sent a paltan in our honour.'

Ajay, too, had noticed the three officers trying desperately to keep pace with the train that refused to slow down. 'Oh, good. My message reached them in time. Damn, will this train ever come to a stop?'

When, finally, Lord Jagannath came to rest—half of it beyond the platform—there was an immediate commotion, not in the least caused by the throng of coolies who insisted on getting in first. Sweat, bone, flesh, D-cups, talcum powder, hairy arms, colour, backpacks, coconut oil, suitcases…

'You go from the left, Ajay. Careful, with that...'

'Haan haan…Arey, Api.'

'Haan bhai…uff, beta, just let me pass. Thanks… Sir, could you, yes, just move, move please, just a bit? Thanks. Ajay? *Ajay*?'

'Ya ya, I am coming. Why does everyone have to get down all at once. Goddam...'

Ajay broke through and in the same instant managed to spot a familiar face on the platform. 'There, I can see him. Akhil? Oye, Akhil!'

Akhil, who had had to run the entire length of the platform, overlooked the discomfort at the sight of his friend, now dangling from the entrance railing.

'Ajay? *Abey, saaley!* How are you? C'mon get down, man. Where's Api? Did she come? I got your email yesterday night. Fifteen years, and all you write is one sentence, you bastard.'

'I wasn't sure of your email id, man. Got it from the IIT website—took a chance.'

'Where's Api?'

Ajay got down and rushed to greet his friend.

'Hi, saaley. Just wait a sec till this crowd thins out. She's at the other exit. Do you see her?'

'Ajay, you dog. Now let me see. Api?'

Aparajita, struggling to get down from the train, heard her name being called by a familiar voice. Magically, she appeared at the door and jumped, her suitcases following behind.

'Hi, Akhil. How *are you*? Good heavens, you haven't changed one bit.'

'What—in fifteen years? Here, let me take that bag. Come, give me your hand. Great you could come, too.'

'Had to. Ajay told me of his trip—said it could take him a while, a month. So, like the loving wife that I am...'

'I believe you.'

'No, actually the Uni's closed for the summer. Here he comes.'

Ajay hurried over, a part of him worried they now had one suitcase less. 'Hi, Akhil.'

'Hi, AB. Great to see you two after all these years.'

'You look just the same, Aks my man, you bastard.'

'But you *have* changed, you bugger. Grey hair, double chin, glasses, wrinkles, paunch.'

'Enough. I can get you arrested for this.'

'On what charges?'

'Outraging the modesty of a police officer.'

'Guilty as charged.'

'Oh man, so good to see you, Aks.'

'Listen, some chaps behind you, with a garland.'

'What? Oh, hello there.'

There they were, indeed—Mumbai Police's finest—drenched by their own and other peoples' sweat, belt buckles adrift, caps no longer on their heads, shoes almost opening at their mouths, standing to attention but not at ease. Sub-Inspector Jatinder was the first one to react, hiding the mooda behind his legs. DSP Sharma inspected the garlands and dusted the out-of-place petals. But it was SP Kharbanda, the senior-most among them, who was the first to open his mouth.

'Hello, sir. Welcome to Mumbai. I hope the journey was safe and sound.'

Ajay smiled. 'Yes, very. Thank you.'

'Great to see you, sir—finally. Have heard so much about you.'

'What have you been hearing?'

'Just this and that, sir. Climbing the ladder of success so fast and all.'

'You are SP Mohinder Kharbanda, no?'

SP Kharbanda beamed. 'Yes, yes, you know of me? That's an honour, sir, indeed. This is Superintendent of Police Mohinder Pratap Kharbanda reporting, *sir*.'

'Arey, what's this, Kharbanda saab, please. No reporting-shiporting, bhai. And these two are…'

'DSP Mohan Kumar Sharma and Sub-Inspector Jatinder.'

'Well, thank you for coming over to receive me.'

SP Kharbanda spoke for all three. 'No problem, sir, it is our holy duty.'

'Oh. Kharbanda saab, this is my wife, Api—Aparajita. She's a lecturer of English at Delhi University.'

SP Kharbanda was all grace and charm. 'Very pleased to meet you, madam. Welcome to Mumbai.'

'Thank you, Mr Kharbanda.'

'And this here, SP saab, is my best friend—Akhil Sukumar. BA, MA, PhD, Cantab.'

Akhil rolled his eyes even as Ajay continued: 'Assistant professor of chemistry at IIT Mumbai. I have known him from the time he'd take Kachuachaap in one hand and a Nestle Everyday in the other and sprint off before you could say: shit man Akhil, that flush ain't working.'

Api admonished Ajay with a slap on his wrist. 'Ajay! Take no notice of him, SP saab. Actually, both Ajay and I know Akhil from our Delhi college days—Stephen's. And we haven't seen him for fifteen years, can you believe it?'

'Is that so? Oh, how nice. My pleasure to meet you, Professor Akhil. And, er, sir, you mentioned something like kitab…'

'No, Cantab. Cambridge. That's where the idiot wasted most of his adulthood.'

'Well, an honour to meet you, Sukumar saab.'

Akhil shook SP Kharbanda's hand warmly. 'Likewise, SP saab. Anytime you'd like to visit IIT, please let me know.'

'Sure, Professor saab, thank you.'

Ajay looked at his watch. 'Right then, Kharbanda saab, I think we should make a move. There are a few things—first of all, were you alerted by DSP Vijay Kumar and his three colleagues who are also arriving today?'

The pecking order was suitably uninformed and clueless. 'Er, no, sir. Sharma, did you know of this?'

'No, sir, I didn't. Jatinder?'

'No, sir, definitely not.'

Ajay stroked his chin. 'That's strange. They called me up and confirmed that a message had been sent to Mumbai headquarters. Well anyway, they are arriving today. If I remember correctly, by Golden Temple Express.'

SP Kharbanda displayed his attention to detail. 'But, sir, Golden Temple was supposed to arrive at five-forty in the morning.'

'Really? Then either they have arrived, looked around, not found any party and left for the headquarters, or…can you find…has the bloody train arrived today at all?'

'I'll get it checked at once, sir. Arey, Sharma, just find out.'

'Ji, sir. Arey, Jatinder? Yes, Golden Temple.'

'Ji, sir. Arey, coolie? Did the Golden Temple come in this morning?'

'No saab, it is late by eight hours.'

SP Kharbanda felt duty bound to convey the results of the police investigation to his higher-up but was cut short by Ajay.

'Shit. Ya, I heard that. Well, Kharbanda, we can't leave them in the lurch—poor fellows didn't have any reservations. Buggers must have sat huddled up next to the toilet, and in this heat.'

'That's terrible, sir.'

'Listen, Kharbanda, can you ask someone to receive them while we get going? I'd appreciate that.'

'Sure, sir, no problem. Er, Sharma? Can you and Jatinder stay back and receive the team? It's only one or two more hours.'

Sharma looked up, trying to decipher the colour of the sky.

SP Kharbanda broke the silence. 'Sharma saab?'

'Er, no problem, s-sir, no problem at all.'

Ajay patted Kharbanda's shoulder. 'Thanks, Kharbanda. That'll cheer them up. Even more so when they see the garlands.'

SP Kharbanda collected the garlands from Ajay and passed them on to the waiting hands of DSP Sharma. 'Er, yes sir, of course.'

'So, this is the plan. Api? You go with Akhil to the guest house while Kharbanda and I go down to the HQ and get a grip on things. I'll see you guys in the evening. Okay, Akhil? Kharbanda saab?'

Api protested. 'But, Ajay, what's the big hurry—we have just landed, *yaar*. Can't this wait till tomorrow? Besides, Akhil may have things to do.'

'No, that's alright guys, I took the day off. Hey, what's this about a guesthouse? No way.'

Ajay tried to soften Akhil's disappointment. 'Arey Aks, this time you'll have to excuse us, man. The case has to be cracked pronto, you know. I thought it best not to trouble you. Besides, we'll make sure we get together almost every other day.'

'Hey man, it's no trouble. The house is vacant when I am in the lab. And you can't have Api all locked up in a guesthouse—didn't you say it could be a month?'

'No formality-vormality, yaar. Listen, why don't we start off with the guesthouse and then maybe after a week, shift to your pad? It's just that this place is quite near the headquarters—convenient. Your place is way off. Promise—in a week's time.'

'Alright, but I don't like it one bit. I better see you in the evening. Where's this guesthouse?'

'Just off Pedder Road—listen, thanks man.'

'Shut up and piss off.'

'Talking of pissing off, the bloody toilet in there was straight out of *Trainspotting*. Seen *Trainspotting*, Kharbanda saab?'

'What, train...potting...sir?'

'Arey never mind. The toilets?'

'Sir, if you could kindly, er, hold in for just thirty more minutes, we'll be at the HQ. The toilets at this station are a photocopy of the ones in the trains, believe me, sir. Once I discovered the urinal had its connecting pipe missing. Bastards. And that day I was wearing my new shoes.'

'As you say, Kharbanda.'

'Promise, sir.'

'Api, Aks, if you could take the luggage as well. Let's plan on going out tonight.'

Akhil wagged a finger. 'You better.'

'I give you a policeman's word, my sweet boy. What more do you want. Now. Shall we, Kharbanda? I take it you have arranged for a car.'

'Sure, sir. Please follow me. This way.'

SP Kharbanda thought it fit to counsel his juniors even as he cleared the way for his senior.

'Arey Sharma, just handle the situation here. Get the team to the headquarters, okay?'

DSP Sharma thought he'd convey his disappointment through some peace and quiet but SP saab was never one to let go of a tail.

'Sharma?'

Silence.

'Sharma!'

'Er, yes, sir, sure. No problem. You go ahead, sir, I'll manage.'

Satisfied, SP Kharbanda resumed his official duty, which was to guide DIG Ajay Biswas through the limited mess and into the unlimited variety that lay in store for them just outside of the station.

Akhil, too, decided to make a move. 'Let's go, Api. Give me that suitcase. You'd like a Coke or something? One sec, let me just light up.'

'So you haven't quit.'

'Many times.'

'And you found?'

'That I am not a quitter.'

'No seriously yaar, you should quit. One fine day. Decide. Then just quit.'

'What about you. When did *you* quit? Or have you?'

Api threw her head back and laughed. 'Not really, no. Just once in a while though, in the bathroom, with the exhaust on. Actually, wouldn't mind a little drag right now. What is it? Thanks.'

'Gold Flake. So. Has Ajay changed? His gait certainly suggests he is in serious need of some uthhak-baithhak.'

'Seriously yaa. Have told him hajaar times to go out, jog, run, at least walk to the office.'

'Look at him pulling up his trousers to hide that paunch of his—just look at him.'

'Arey, that's intentional. He has started wearing his belt one hole to the left so he can do that pulling up thing and tell his friends he has lost weight.'

'What a bastard. No, I mean changed—from how he was back in college.'

'I don't know. Perhaps he has. You knew him best, you should know.'

'But I am not married to him. Thankfully. Haan, how much boss? Do thanda and one badi Gold Flake.'

'Twenty rupees, saab.'

'Here…Shall we, Api?'

'Ya, let's go.'

DSP Sharma and Sub-Inspector Jatinder watched Akhil and Api depart. Much to his relief, DSP Sharma realised he was the senior-most now.

'Just us two now, Jatinder. There they go, the memsaab and her professor.'

'Yes, sir.'

'Arey Jatinder. Bastard, was there any message at the headquarters? About Golden Temple?'

'Er, yes sir, there was. Now what can I say; the train comes so early in the morning and so I thought...'

DSP Sharma slapped his potbelly. '*Jatinder*.'

'Sorry, sir, really sorry. I thought the team would come over on their own. I mean, they aren't milk-drinking tots, are they, sir.'

'Oye ban-cho, you didn't even stop and think for a minute that the message could be traced? I mean, who received and signed for the telex?'

'Myself only, sir.'

'Then?'

'Yes sir, sorry, I didn't think tha...'

'We could have sent some lazy bastards to receive the team. Now the two of us, hanging here like langoors.'

'Very sorry, sir. But I promise to make up for it. Please wait—I'll get some hot chola bhatura and tea for you. Or would you prefer some hot-hot puri-aloo?'

'I would prefer bheja-fry. Yours.'

The sub-inspector hung his head in shame.

DSP Sharma was satisfied with the duration of punishment. '*Achha bas bas*. Go get something nice and hot. What is the time?'

'Sir, your watch says twelve forty-five.'

'Well, this is great. Now I have to sit around and wait for another hour. And what are you staring at, hain? Take these useless garlands with you...Listen.'

'Passengers, meeters, and, greeters are, notified, this, that, two, nine, zero, four, down, Golden, Temple, Express, coming, from, Amritsar, to, Mumbai, Central, via, Beas, Jalandhar, City, Jalandhar, Cant...'

DSP Sharma rapped his baint on the thigh. 'Oh, no. She'll take ban-cho hours.'

'...Phagwara, Ludhiana, Ambala, Jagadhr, Saharanpur, Muzaffarnagar, Meerut...'

'You bitch.'

'...Ghaziabad, Delhi, New, Delhi, Faridabad, Mathura, Bayana, Shri, Mahabirji...'

'You computer bitch.'

'...Gangapur, City, Sawai, Madhopur, Kota, Bhawani, Mandi, Nagda, Ratlam...'

'I'll kill you.'

'...Dahod, Godhra, Vadodara, Borivali, and, Dadar, scheduled, to, arrive, at...'

'I'll ban-cho kill you.'

'...zero, six, hundred, hours, on...'

'Yes?'

'...platform, number, seven, is, now...'

'Yes, yes?'

'...delayed, further, and...'

'Oh, no.'

'...will, be, arriving, at, fifteen, hundred, and, thirty, hours...'

'No ban-cho, no.'

'...on, platform, number, seven.'

'No!'

'Any inconvenience is greatly regretted thank you.'

'Atithi devo bhava' should be replaced with 'Atithi dollar bhava'. Or 'Atithi hini bhava'. We have a yen for these things. If you say it quickly nobody will notice. Faster, they won't understand. Brrrr. These are some fringe fallouts of being an ancient culture with so many tongues and an equal number of wags that hypocrisy rolls effortlessly off. Like moss. Slurp. Euro. Slip. What is culture without a little vulture, yaar.

Scavenge, but dil se. Will go unnoticed. You hope. Lie to guests, hoping they perceive it as courtesy. Guffaw when they are flummoxed. Loud, roaring laughter to hide your own absence of etiquette. Speak in your foreign tongue in their presence—it is okay, these foreigners have no idea, only money. White foreigners, mind you. Black foreigners are beggars and drug peddlers. Khirki Extension is not a Windows update, silly.

We talk so much. We mean so little.

We promise so much. We do so little.

We count so much. We give so little.

Notice next time the donation boxes at checkout counters. A tambourine slapped repeatedly on the back of the thigh would rattle less. All coins. Some no longer in circulation. Some belonging to other Third World countries. A donation box is a dustbin. They even made the boxes transparent to shame us but we saw through their evil game. A foreigner in front rolls up a hundred-rupee note and stuffs it through the slit and we eat our fist in astonishment and anger. *Paise pedh pe ugte hain? Saala, firangi show-off.*

It is not because we are generous that we don't know how to say no. It is not because we are good at our work that we don't know when to end a discussion, when to leave or when to close a negotiation. It is because we don't know what goodies karma might deliver at the end of the next noun. Keep all options open so ad valorem and ad nauseum hang together. *Kisika kya jaata hai*. Killing with kindness is also good. It is the kindness that matters—see. Same to same. Say yes to all party invitations and finally decide where to go depending on which atithi and which devo will be there.

The propensity to say 'no problem' is directly proportional to the immediate benefits it may bring. If you don't measure the tent, you don't need to count the camels. One more camel? 'No problem'. *Solpa adjust maadi*.

'No problem' to tourists asking if they can visit Uttarakhand two months after the devastating floods because tourism is down.

'No problem' to a taxi ride to Jaipur that progressively picks up passengers until a few are hanging out the windows and counting the stars.

'No problem' to a dysfunctional water heater in a dysfunctional toilet because otherwise the German backpacker will check out and check into your cousin's quarter-star across the road.

Bless the relentless lethargy and inefficiency that compels us to say come tomorrow, next week.

Is there something especially wrong with us? No.

Is there something especially right with us? No.

Is there a common 'we' in a country of over 1.2 billion people? How do we build character without ego, pride without jingoism, energy without exaggeration? Jugaad, we haven't realised, is good for electrical repair, not relationships or building an economy. Or for an industrial take-off. But countless books have been written on the wonders of jugaad and we have read them all. We smile at our jugaad like proud parents smile at their accidental creation. One day soon, we will send a charpai into space. It will have solar panels tied to its legs with the same abrasive twine that its bed is made out of and Aladdin the astronaut will guide it expertly past the final frontier while he squats on it and sucks on a hookah.

Promote tourism, promote tourism, bring facilities like foreign.

'Kaisa laga, madam, room? It has a beautiful view of the lake and sunset when you draw the curtain.' You draw the curtain and are left admiring a loose brick wall plastered clumsily. The view of the lake is the print on the curtain.

The speed and the confidence with which you say it is what matters. In jugaad. It has given us the ability to think with our feet.

Over patiala, to a friend, tittering: 'You won't believe it, yaar, the firangan actually bought my story.'

'Mil jayega,' is the first thing you hear from the shopkeeper. You wait for ten minutes and then, 'Abhi out of stock hai. Arey Bunty? Note kar ley.' And Bunty removes the pencil stub from behind his ear to make a note of the thing you wanted, one that the shopkeeper had never heard of before. But no pencil stubs and oily hands when a white atithi comes calling. Then the whole shop stands up. '*Thanda ya garam, madam*?'

The road opposite the five-star is the most potholed. The way to a million-dollar farmhouse is never paved. The approach to a grand haveli is through a patli gali. Why? Because the lotus blooms in sludge. It is our national flower. Yes, we are like that. 'Andar say saaf hain, by God ki kasam.' Daily bath, no dry-cleaning.

We are so funny. Wish we could laugh at ourselves. Thoda sa, at least. At that brick wall of a sunset.

It is all very well to say 'atithi devo bhava' and 'dharmo rakshati rakshatah' to the next person, but do we really follow it? How often have you seen a packed train or a bus where someone offers a seat to the old and the weak? How often do we make way for an ambulance during rush hour—any hour? How often do we stop and say thank you to people who clean our homes and streets?

How often do we smile at each other in a day?

'Next!'

If the devil is in the details, so is humanity, courtesy, empathy, compassion and understanding. Why is it that foreigners pay more than Indians to visit the Taj Mahal? Is it normal for Indians to pay more than the Greeks, Italians and Americans when we visit their monuments? Small change, you'd say, but it is the small things that point to a character. Or the absence of it. Like being able to remember your atithi's name. Like being on time. This is no 'Arjunam uvacha' category of dialogue—it is more complicated than that. You see, the atithis have stolen all the Arjuns and we have all the answers.

And how do we come across as atithis when we leave our shores? There is a name for us among international carriers. It is called the IAS—Indian Assisted Service. You will see us at airports all around the world, being pushed in a wheelchair, wheeled to the duty-free shop where we will get up, walk around with a spring in our step, spend and then return to the chair without batting an eyelid. IAS—aiyoo, the irony.

It is a status thing, jumping the queue. '*Hum jahan khade ho jaate hain, line wahin se shuru hoti hai,*' is the one dialogue voted unswervingly one of the top ten Bollywood dialogues of all time.

People who keep quiet are not stupid. They are listening, watching, absorbing. Not necessarily judging.

There is no honour in an artificial hierarchy, no grace in servitude. Service is not servility. It is an attitude. It starts with self-respect. Stand straight. For a start. Maybe a spine will find its way eventually if you are humble enough.

We have formulated entirely new shrutis and mudras for welcoming an atithi. Soon we will market it as a new dance form. Hand gestures, feet gestures, face gestures. But in the end, what we really love is painting sunsets on walls. Embalming the truth and entombing the lake.

4

1976—Invisible Man

Warm sunlight bathed the valley and the houses that surrounded it. Pristine white smoke billowed from the chimneys of slanted roofs. Clear blue sky met fresh green pasture. Tall and strong pine trees broke through the mist and appeared to touch the few cottonwool clouds hurrying past. Horses grazed and children played around them, running excitedly after rabbits that wanted to be caught and cuddled.

A man lay cushioned over the flaming red and yellow leaves of a nearby chinar. Diagonal to him, resting her head on his chest, with her eyes closed, a contented smile on her face, was his young love, dressed in an intricately embroidered pheran and decked in jewellery that sparkled as it caught the sun. Bimla took one last look and then, with one swift run of her right hand, switched the month on the calendar to May.

Meanwhile, outside the mud and tarpaulin shack, the morning sun beat down in all its fury, forcing even the bloodied mongoose and the gaupicchaar to abandon their fight unto death and take shelter under the pitiful shadow of the lone kikar Shimmering translucent waves gushed from the scorched earth, robbing one of all sense of depth, making the kikar amorphous and trembling. And the loo, it howled at the full sun.

Only the vultures were appreciative. They enjoyed the abrupt coming and going, rising and dipping currents and acted dead in order to glide, only to come alive abruptly and plummet earthwards to collect in swarms around a carcass. An emaciated goat scampered across the area in an attempt to ward off a few overanxious vultures, raising a cloud of dust that welcomed Amma as soon as she emerged from the second mud and tarpaulin shack.

The sun hit her at once. She looked up to curse it but remembered it was a God and so stuck her tongue out and tugged at her earlobes. Hurrying across to the other shack, she tripped on the protruding root of a pipal stump. Now she did mumble a curse and, while dusting her sari and counting her bruises, noticed that one side wall was covered in sarkari posters. She was irritated by the vandalism of it—the posters seemed to have been pasted in a hurry. Amma could not read or write, and so could not understand what the posters meant. She could only appreciate their artistic quality—she liked a couple of them and many a time would even be thrilled that *her* walls had been chosen for defacement. But this collection appalled her. There was no figure or scenery, or a sunflower or even a flag—this one just had writing all over, that too in bold red. Amma could not know that it read *STERILISE AND LIVE LIFE*, and then in the next line, *HUM DO HAMARAY DO.* She went around the shack and angrily called out the name of her tenth child.

'Kalki?' she screamed, and then searched for the familiar response: the clang of a hastily dropped tin or a catapult, the frantic run of little legs. She paused and strained her ears, but other than the gargling drone of the loo and the brisk fluttering of a tarpaulin end, there was little else on offer. Livid, she butted the husk-and-cane door open and rushed inside.

Amma froze, then jerked back in response to what she thought was right in front of her—of all things, a snake charmer absorbed in his act, his cheeks puffed to their bursting point, swaying his 'been' and making imaginary infinity signs with his head.

Amma thought she was hallucinating—it must be the sun. But it was Bimla on her haunches, blowing air strenuously through a wooden pipe to resurrect the chulha.

Upon hearing the muffled drag of the makeshift door against the earth, Bimla paused momentarily and turned around. Through the dense blue smoke, she saw an imposing silhouette poised on the threshold, hands on waist, legs taut and apart, hair all over the place. Maa Kaali, no less. As the tears spread thin and her eyes adjusted, she realised it was her mother.

The silhouette approached, turning to flesh. Bimla hardened, her little palms wrapped tightly around the wooden pipe, the pipe clamped in between her teeth. Out of breath, she waited.

'Bimla,' cried Amma. 'Have you seen Kalki? I am going to thrash him.'

Bimla removed the wooden pipe from her mouth and gulped some spit.

'But, Mai, I thought he told you where he was going.'

'Why, where has the rascal gone?'

'Bholaji came running in a few minutes ago. Said he needed Kalki and four other musahur boys for the panchayat entertainment.'

'And you allowed him to go?'

'But Mai, Bholaji was adamant. He even snatched the slate chalk away from Kalki and his friends—they were all off to school, you see. I think it was Lokender and Chander and...'

'When did all this happen? Where was I?'

'Only a few minutes ago. All of them rushed to the Thakur well.'

'What did Bhola say about this, this entertainment?'

'Nothing much, just that it was a four-five minute job for Kalki and free lunch afterwards.'

Amma strode forward and caught hold of Bimla's ear, dragging her head along.

'You gadhi. Anyone walks in and takes my only son away and you just sit there blowing air?'

'But, Mai, I...'

'Quiet. Now don't stand here like a fool. Go and find out what's happening at the panchayat.'

'J-ji.'

'And listen—don't let yourself be seen. Hide behind the kiln and just observe. And any sign of trouble, you get back here—no, first run and fetch Baba, you understand?'

'Ji, Mai.'

'Go, now *go*. This mui Emergency has come twenty years too late, I am telling you. I'd have been the first in line for my *copper-T*, compulsory or not. *Go*.'

Bimla tiptoed out of the shack, then broke into a sprint, swaying and banking like a runaway bullock. Soon, she was at the kiln. She hid behind an unfinished fortification, its protruding bricks forming precise rectangular shadows that brought her some relief from the sun. She removed a loose brick and looked through the peephole. The panchayat was underway. She could see the panchas huddled up in a semicircle on the elevated platform by the Thakur well. Below them and spread all around were their subjects, squatting and fanning themselves with their turbans. The womenfolk were in ghoonghat and sat a fair distance apart. Bimla removed a second brick; now she could hear the conversations and the chit-chat clearly. But her brother was nowhere to be seen. Bimla pressed her face in to get a better look. She could finally make some sense of Badey Thakur's utterances, his thunderous voice sending a shiver down her spine even at this range. She listened.

At the panchayat, Badey Thakur was getting restless.

'Arey, Mahender Singhji, enough of chai-shai. Shall we wrap up this panchayat business, this heat is just too much.'

'Ji, Badey Thakur.'

'And will someone ever replace the gobar in this hookah?'

'At once, Badey Thakur. Arey Gajraj, you heard.'

'And wh...Arey, Panditji, looks like our entertainment has arrived. Are those the five boys my son had asked for?'

'Oh, they are here already? Ji, Badey Thakur, they are the ones.'

Badey Thakur was not impressed. 'They look tiny to me, pandat. Why Baldev, what exactly do you have in mind? Your last entertainment special with the bhangi kids didn't exactly set the house on fire, did it?'

'All in good time, father, please be patient. I give my word. You won't be disappointed.'

'I certainly hope so.'

Baldev tried some patter. 'Have heard a little about that boy on the right, there. His name is Kalki—same age as our Judev. Judev spotted him catching fish late one night in the Thakur pond. The little rat punched Judev in the face and shot off like lightning. This is going to be good fun.'

'Alright, then. Bring the boys closer, make them stand in line.'

'Yes, father.'

Badey Thakur shifted his attention to other matters.

'Arey, Mahender Singhji, Rajwardhanji.'

'Ji, Badey Thakur?'

'Bhai, what is to be done with this sterilisation business?'

'Hmm, it's a little tricky, Thakurji.'

'What is it you say, Rajwardhan?'

'I said it could be a little tricky, Badey Thakur. I mean, we do need to show the sarkari babu that we have carried out 200 voluntary nasbandhis—if we need that seed and fertiliser subsidy, that is.'

Badey Thakur let go of his hookah. '*Of course* we need it, Rajwardhan. Do you even know how much loss I incurred from the failed crops last year?'

'Absolutely, Thakurji. We are all with you on this. It's just that...'

'Just what?'

'Just er...'

'I will tell you, Badey Thakur, Rajwardhan's maybe feeling shy,' Mahender added in the awkward pause.

'Shy? Of what, Mahender Singhji?'

'Badey Thakur, there is no problem as such. We can have 200, even 400 nasbandhis. It's just that, er, do we, I mean, do Thakurs need also to participate in this?'

The pandit saw his chance. 'And if you allow me to speak, even pandits and banias too, Mahender Singhji. Please don't forget us.'

'Of course, of course, pandat. Yes, so as I was saying, Badey Thakur, our women are very scared of this, and so, too, are our men. Gajraj was telling me nasbandhi causes terrible after-effects in virile men.'

'So you mean…?'

'What I mean—*we* mean, Badey Thakur, is…can I suggest something?'

Badey Thakur sucked on the hookah robustly. 'Go on.'

'I have the last census records with me. It shows there are forty families of bhangis and twenty-four families of musahurs residing in our village.'

'Not in our village, Mahender Singhji, not in a thousand years!'

'No no, Badey Thakur, I meant residing on the outskirts. They are well away, you know that. Anyway, that gives us sixty-four families. Each family has at least two adults—that makes it one-twenty, not to mention the many girls and boys between twelve and seventeen. We are looking at no less than 200, 250 nasbandhis. No need to touch Thakurs, pandits and banias.'

'But would these people agree? Mother and father are alright, but what if they create trouble for the twelve to seventeen year olds?'

'You don't worry about it, Badey Thakur, that's our problem. No Rajwardhanji?'

'Indeed, Mahender Singhji.'

Badey Thakur scratched his stubble. 'Hmm. But we have to be smart about this. We'll start with a pay raise, reduced working hours, free dispensary visits, free school books, that sort of thing.'

'Pay raise, Badey Thakur?'

'Don't start panicking, Mahender Singhji, it's just a promise, what. Yes, it could work.'

Mahender Singhji thudded his fist into his palm. 'It will work, it must work, it *has* to work.'

'Leave it with me for a few days. Meanwhile, inform the doctor saab—the Thakur one, not that Pandey. Pandits are shaky at these things—no moustache, point two-two.'

'Yes of course, Badey Thakur.'

'Also, contact the sarkari. Get him to start preparing the subsidy papers. Make sure we get a hefty sum for all our troubles.'

'Yes, as soon as possible, Badey Thakur.'

Badey Thakur turned philosophical. 'This Emergency is good, I tell you. Trains are running on time, villages are prospering, population is coming down. *Talk Less, Work More.*'

'Indeed, Badey Thakur.'

'Alright, now enough of this serious business. Arey Baldev, what's going on? Is there something planned or not?'

Baldev hurried over. 'Yes Father, upon your command.'

'Yes yes, bhai, I haven't got all day.'

'Yes Father, at once.'

Baldev turned his attention to the boys. 'Hey, you lot. Look up. Face the panchas. Start with your jaat, your name, your age, your...'

'I said, Baldev.'

'Yes, Father?'

'Ask them to also tell us how many brothers and sisters they have, and their names. Kyon, Mahender Singhji? Make a note of their names. We'll get twenty volunteers straight away.'

'Ji, Badey Thakur. Excellent idea. *Shubh kaam mein deri kyon.*'

'Haan then, bhai, Baldev, resume.'

'Yes, Father.'

Baldev paced the rostrum with renewed urgency. Hands clasped firmly behind his back, head looking up, he roared at the line of pathetic little boys, a few of whom looked as though they'd faint any moment.

'*You*, your name is Kalki, no? You start first. Your jaat, name, age, and how many brothers and sisters you have. I said, *start*.'

Kalki shuffled nervously but managed to somehow overcome his terror. 'R-respected Badey Thakurji. I am a musahur. My name is Kalki. I am ten years old. I have nine sisters, all elder to me. Their names are Mala, Sarla, Bimla, Bela, Ganga, Jamna, Devki, Nandi and Kamla.'

'Next.'

'Respected Badey Thakurji. I am a musahur. My name is Chander. I am twelve. I have four brothers and six sisters. All sisters are elder to us. My four brothers are Ravinder, Dharmendar, Lokender and Inder. My six sisters are Bindiya, Parvati, Santoshi, Sharda, Gopi and Kajri.'

'These ones...are these your brothers, Chander?'

'Ji, Badey Thakurji.'

'Mahender Singhji, have you noted down all the names?'

'Yes, Badey Thakur. Just one thing—if that Kalki there is the youngest as he said, and ten, then according to me all his sisters should qualify for the voluntary programme.'

'Yes why not. They are old enough.'

'And the six sisters of this lot; they should, too.'

'Yes, of course. So, how many on the list already?'

'Ten, and eleven, and two parents for each—that's twenty-five, Badey Thakur.'

'How many musahur families did you say there are, belonging to our village?'

'Twenty-four, Badey Thakur.'

Badey Thakur was exultant. 'Wah. Achaa, now listen. Once we are done here, take Baldev and Ranbir down to their end of the village and get all the names on paper. Tell them Badey Thakur has arranged for free medicines and mosquito nets. And get that Thakur doctor by this evening and put a tent up near the dispensary.'

'Ji, Badey Thakur.'

'Well, good. Haan bhai, Baldev. Is this going to take till tomorrow?'

'Er, no Father…now listen up, boys. You have to play a game, nothing much. You will compete with each other for these—Panditji, please show them—these four rats with stones tied to their tails. The rats will be thrown into this well…'

'No-no…Baldev. Not our well, never. Rats are still fine, but these musahurs? Have you lost it, boy?'

'Don't worry, Father, after the entertainment the water will be purified with gaumutr, as Panditji here assures me.'

Badey Thakur looked suspiciously at the pandit.

'Pandat?'

'Ji Badey Thakur, there is nothing the gaumutr cannot purify.'

'Good. Continue, Baldev.'

Baldev rolled up his kurta sleeve. It slid down. He rolled it up again. 'Haan, so as soon as you hear the gun, you jump into the well. Don't worry—Misraji here tells me it is only forty feet deep. And the water is only nine feet. For the first round, we'll drop four rats for you five boys. The boy with the most number of dead rats to his credit at the end of four rounds will be the winner. We will also bet on you. Badey Thakur himself will decide the odds. If you please, Badey Thakur?'

'Well, Baldev, what a roundabout way of entertainment, hain. You sure have put some thought into it.'

'Thank you, Father.'

'You want me to set the odds?'

'Yes, Father, if you please.'

Badey Thakur scratched his cheek thoughtfully. 'Let me see now. Open your mouths, all of you.'

The boys did so.

'Good teeth, good teeth. Show you hands. Yes, rough alright. Hmm, I say ninety paise on Kalki, eighty on Chander and the rest… well, they look quite hopeless—make them all fifty paise.'

Baldev was ecstatic. 'Thank you, Father.'

'Now hurry up. This is taking too much time.'

Baldev nodded and looked up at the audience. There was a faint smile on his face, the smile of a confident ringmaster.

'Alright, brothers and sisters. Now's the time to place some nice bets...You there, yes, you. You, too? Certainly…Panditji, you? Certainly…on Kalki? Yes…and you, Mahender Singhji? On Chander? Seven rupees? Yes, you too sir, why not? Wait, sir…just a minute, let me note it down…Yes of course, and you too…'

Like cows at a cattle auction, the boys stood rooted and wide-eyed, the muscles on their bodies twitching involuntarily, failing even to dislodge the humble fly. Because they had no idea what was happening, what a bet was, what 'odds' were, their fear was not total. The bliss of the unknown protected them. But the signs were all of horror, and more.

Chander nudged Kalki with his elbow. 'Kalki, I think I can't feel my legs already.'

'Oh God, Chander, what's all this? I can't believe Bholaji would put us up to it.'

'What do we do, Kalki? Shall we make a run for it? I mean, we could...'

'Forget it, Chander. These people here—they'll chase and lynch us. And how can we even get through them?'

'What was that thing about naming our sisters?'

'Beats me. Some kind of threat, perhaps. Listen Chander, we just have to do it, understand? You *understand*?'

The boys began to drift away from each other a little. The youngest among them, Lokender, all of five, noticed a rivulet winding its way slowly from its source towards his two little feet. He hadn't even realised or felt the wetness over his legs, but now that he was aware, he forgot about the more pressing matter of life and death and began to worry instead about the ridicule his action may bring. He inched his foot out and rubbed the little pool in front of him into the mud.

Badey Thakur was getting restless. 'Enough now, Baldev. Stop all bets and get on with it.'

'Er, yes, Father. At your command, we can start the proceedings… how many bets, Panditji?'

'117, Chotey Thakur. Many have placed multiple bets.'

Baldev was rapturous. 'Good. Alright boys, to the parapet now. Bhola will help you. Bhola?'

'Ji Chotey Thakur, at once. Come, you lot.'

Kalki saw his chance. 'Bholaji, wait till my father gets hold of you.'

'Shut up, Kalki. Quiet. This is no time for talk. Even *my* head is on the block, you understand? Now get going and stand alongside, yes, good. Chotey Thakur, they are ready.'

'Good. The rats now. Panditji?'

'Ji, here, Chotey Thakur.'

'Yes, show them to the crowd and throw them in the well one by one.'

'Ji Chotey Thakur…there.'

'Great. Now listen up, you boys. Keep an eye out for the signal. You'll hear the gun go off for every round. Father, if you could please…'

'Yes yes.' Badey Thakur snatched the Enfield from Gajraj and raised it in the air, barrels pointing at the sun god. He fired.

'Alright boys, you heard the gun. Now go, go, *go*!'

The boys plunged one after the other into the well, making five distinct splashes.

Baldev rushed to the parapet and pulled himself up using Bhola's hand. He looked into the darkness and began his commentary, egged on by the rapturous crowd.

'They are in, they are all in, brothers and sisters. Looks like one of them—I think it was Lokender, the youngest—fell right on top of Chander's head...There's a mad scramble, I tell you. This is great...'

'Baldev, a bit louder—the crowd must know what's happening to their money.'

'Yes, Father…brothers and sisters, I can see the boys now…'

Meanwhile, down below:

'Chander?'

'Kaal-Kalki? Hain-Haan-uunhh!'

'Sorry! Hain-uunhh. Couldn't help it, Dharmender—you didn't spread out fast enough…where's Chander? Lokender?'

'Hain-uunhh. Hain-Haan-uunhh!'

'Chand...Chander?'

'Kalki, I am here. Where's Lokender? My brother, where is he?'

'Don't panic, don't panic. Listen, not much time, Chander, only four rats are in here. Means one of us will have to go without them—me. You *understand*? Let's do it. You *must*, for your brothers. Come, on the count of three.'

'Alright...'

While up above:

'Yes, brothers and sisters…Lots of thrashing…they look dazed… Lots of crying, too. Hey you, hear me down there? What's the story? They are there, the three of them. No Chander, no Kalki. This is too much. I can't believe my eyes. C'mon Kalki, you rat. C'mon Chander! Do it, you bastard...you can do it! Get my money, you musahur. Double it. Triple it! Get it. Get the rat...'

Badey Thakur was thrilled. 'Why, Mahender Singhji, this seems to have gotten the crowd excited. Look at them shouting and screaming. I tell you, the secret is always money. Get money involved and see them bastards wallow. They didn't sound as excited when I told these of my plan to buy three new tractors, did they?'

'No, they didn't, Badey Thakur. Your boy seems to have hit the bullseye with this invention of his.'

'He sure has, my good boy. I tell you, blood is after all blood, Mahender Singhji.'

'It sure is, sure is, Badey Thakur.'

'Now, let's listen in…what's the latest, Baldev? Louder. Louder, boy.'

But what Baldev couldn't bring to his shouting and screaming spectators was the tragedy that was unfolding deep within the darkness of the Thakur well.

'H-e-l-p.'

'Is that you Chander? C-h-a-n-d-e-r? We haven't much time. Listen carefully to me now.'

'We are all going to die, Kalki. Hain-Hain-uunnhhh, Haan-uunhh, haan-unh!'

'Listen to me, Chander, I can feel the rats. All four of them. The stones, I have felt them. Go under when I say. Then watch me carefully, don't leave sight of my hands. Take the rats. Put them in your brothers' hands. You understand? We haven't much time.'

Baldev did not stop with the commentary. 'Brothers and sisters. Kalki has gone under. Dharmender is thrashing his arms wildly…oye can you hear me in there? Stop that, you idiot. I can't see anything with all this sloshing. Wait. One of them is not moving…limp…completely limp…floating…mouth open…bloody nose…Lokender. But he is clutching a rat. He's gone, I think. Here comes Kalki…empty-handed…clutching air. Wah. What a game we have here. Bhola! I said, Bhola…throw in the rope. Get those bastards out.'

Inside the well, events had taken a terrible turn.

'No, Lokender, no. Lokender, open your eyes, Lokender, please, please, Lokender, look at me, I am Chander, your brother! Talk to him, Kalki!'

'I'll kill Baldev, I promise, Chander. I'll kill the bastard. I'll kill them all.'

'You'll do no such thing, Kalki. Listen to me. We have got to save Dharmender and Ravinder. We are next in line, don't you understand? *Don't you understand*? Take the rat from Lokender. What is done is done. Three more rounds, do you understand? Take his rat…draw his fingers open…oh my brother, my Lokender…'

'Listen, Chander, don't be stupid. We can't go on, just can't. Sooner or later, we are all going to die in here. We have got to think of something. Listen. I have an idea. The moment we climb out, we try to somehow...'

'They'll kill us. No, Kalki.'

'Listen, Chander. There *is* no choice, don't you understand? If we stay here, we'll all get killed. *Think*. It's our best chance.'

'I don't know, Kalki, I don't.'

'Listen, for God's sake.'

Baldev was getting restless. 'Hey, you. What are you murmuring in there? Shut up and climb up. Bhola!'

Bhola, with the permanent stoop he had acquired with the passage of time from having to always walk crouched in front of the upper castes of the village, now came bumping over.

'Yes, at once, Chotey Thakur...come on, boys...yes, that's it. Now tie that rope around, er, Lokender, tie it around him, I said. That'll do. Now come up slowly...there...put him down. You four stand in line here...Chotey Thakur? Done.'

'Good. Bhola, get the body removed. I really should...'

A squeak interrupted Baldev.

'Chotey Thakur?'

'Why, is that you, Kalki? Can you still speak? Even after this shameful performance? Yes, what is it?'

'You'll have to come and stand on the ledge here and see it. It's very big, Chotey Thakur.'

'What? *What*? Wait, I am coming...'

Baldev struggled up the parapet, his excitement getting the better of him.

'Yes, now what is it you wanted to show me...'

'*This*, you bastard.'

Badey Thakur saw it happen right before his eyes. For a few moments it was as though the world stood still.

'My son, my son. Baldev!'

Mahender Singhji rushed to the well, screaming in disbelief.

'Oh God. What has he done, the musahur. Badey Thakur, this way. Arey, Pratap, Judev, Raana, catch the bastard. Here, take Badey Thakur's gun. Let him not get away. Come, Thakur saab, here, use this stick to get up the ledge. Can you see Baldev?'

'Arey Baldev? Baldev, my son, can you hear me? Mahender Singhji, I can't see anything. I can't see him. Baldev? Say something, son. Mahender Singhji, get someone in there, quickly. Someone get him out, maybe he has fainted. He can't swim...oh God, he can't swim.'

'Don't worry, Badey Thakur...Arey Jaswant? You get in here.'

Jaswant dragged his feet. 'Me? But Father...'

'Yes, you. You good-for-nothing. Take the rope and go in...*now*.'

Badey Thakur watched Jaswant being lowered into the well. He clutched the hookah stem and brandished it as though it were a sword.

'I want him. I want that bastard Kalki alive, Mahender Singhji. Don't let anyone dare kill him...there he is, running away.'

'Yes, Badey Thakur.'

'My dear son. What harm did he ever do to anyone? He was only entertaining us.'

'Yes, Badey Thakur.'

'Now listen, Mahender. You gather a party and run over to his basti. Lock everyone of them up. Set them all on fire, you hear me? All of them. Forget the nasbandhi-vasbandhi. Just *get all of them*.'

'Ji, Badey Thakur—on my Thakur blood. I will shoot myself in the chest if there is a single musahur left alive by tonight.'

'Jump in, Jaswant, what are you waiting for? Let go of the rope... my son, my dear Baldev...he moved! He moved, Mahender Singhji, he moved, I swear he did.'

'I am so sorry, Badey Thakur; so, so sorry.'

Badey Thakur, his head shaking with rage, tears flowing freely from his bloodshot eyes, looked up and screamed, a terrifying roar, unheard ever before.

'*Kalki*. Today is the end of your world as you know it! Either you will live to see tomorrow or I will! It is the end of your world!'

'It is, Badey Thakur. It is.'

'He moved, Mahender Singhji, he moved. Baldev moved.'

What is the probability that you will be born a human being in your next life? How do you know you are a human being in this life? By the work you do, the money you earn, or the people who avoid you? There is no birth and there is no death. There is only suffering for those who cannot see a tribhangi in a bhangi, atmagyanam in gyanam.

What is the probability that the woman sitting opposite to you in the train is a goddess? Her legs are a little apart, her hair is all over the place, her eyes are bloodshot and there is Agni sitting next to her combing her hair in all her glory and fearlessness. Bloody Mary or Ma Kali?

Mimamsa. Swachhata. Bhiksha. Bhakti. Gyanam. Jigyasa. Daivikam. Netritva. Kaushalam.

Mala. Sarla. Bimla. Bela. Ganga. Jamna. Devki. Nandi. Kamla.

Mottled. Scarred. Broken. Blemished. Gnawed. Jarring. Defective. Negligible. Killing.

Jholi kab bharegi?

A long, long time ago, Greeks and Indians sat opposite each other, legs folded, asses on ankles. The kerchief was dropped and the qawwali commenced.

Calliope. Mimamsa.

Clio. Swachhata.

Euterpe. Bhiksha.

Erato. Bhakti.

Melpomene. Gyanam.

Polyhymnia. Jigyasa.

Terpsichore. Daivikam.

Thalia. Netritva.

Urania. Kaushalam.

Ennéa Moúses. Navarasa.

Ennéa Spóroi. Navadhanya.

Ennéa Planítes. Navagraha.

For every Greek rejoinder there was an Indian retort and vice versa. The clash of two civilisations was going to end in a tie. And then, an Invisible Man entered the arena. No one could see him, only feel his presence.

The Ring of Gyges, cried the Greeks.

Atman, replied the Indians.

But what is atman? Is it karma? And is karma a precise mathematical calculation of crime and punishment, credit and debit, male and female? Is it a natural process of seasons following each other as night follows day follows night, or is it an assembly line? The unnatural is for the unwise and the different, the dirty, the diseased is for those without drishti?

There is nothing unnatural in the world. *Nasti akrath krtena*—the uncreated is not created by an action, says the *Mundakopanishad.*

Krta—what is created or made; Akrta—what is not created, something real (vastu) that exists without being created. And the same vastu is presented in other Upanishads as satyam, truth. So much simpler to be ignorant and prejudiced, isn't it?

Yes, prejudices are comforting, like pasta and dal—you don't have to think. You can order without looking at the menu. *Satyam Shivam Sundaram* was quite a hit but flew over the cuckoo's nest. Nothing is born, nothing dies. Is, is all there is.

No worries if all this sounds like Greek or Latin or Sanskrit or Tamil. Language is your friendly foe in this game of hop, skip and jump. That square to the left is moksha. If you have language, you may wield power, but if you wield power, you don't need any language. Money speaks, wealth whispers. You can call people vermin and expect them to bow to your declarations just because you wield power. It is the 'bigger car' thing. It shows itself by the number of fountains you have in your garden, by the length and the breadth of your bookshelf in your drawing room. It shows in the way you stand in front of mountains and oceans or underneath the splendid vastness of a clear night sky.

It shows in the way you stand in front of humans you think are more powerful than you.

In the grand scheme of things there is no other. The vermin, the venerated and the vomit is you. In your bend is your bent. There is a distinct one in India, called the Indian crouch—rounded shoulders, heads down, repeating the last word that sounds important. Packing order, packed like sardines in a box. You don't exist, musafir, and neither does your boss. The *Chandogyopanisad* says, before creation, this world existed only in sat. Correct. Saturday. Since 'sat' existed before the creation of this world and your laptop and your neighbour's golf clubs, it includes time and is outside the concept of time. Eternal. Aparajit. Your atman is satyam. *You* are satyam. *Kun faya kun*.

So many of us still wonder why vegetarian cows that were fed offal turned 'mad'. What else can we do when we are so crippled by our own arrogance that we dare to interfere with nature? How else are we supposed to behave when we have no idea how that unknown part of our brain functions? No seriously, we must not blame ourselves. We are looking for ropes to tie the muses, the air, the fire, the atman, the invisible. A rope to tie the nas. Nasbandhi.

Sterilisation. The Emergency. The young and the old, the dying and the dead. We know about the dramatic suspension of civil and political rights across the country, but how much do we really know about what happened to people who were not human? They were a number, a quota, a quantity from a certain direction. It was an identity. I am sterilised, therefore I am alive. I can no longer reproduce because I am a bhangi, a musahur, a shudra, a paryan. Too many of us rats anyway. It was the miracle cure to get a ration card which could eventually, in the next life, lead to a passport. This life, universe, past life, energy, next-life quantum leap, but for the here and now, it will have to be a frog. Not necessarily in a well—a free frog.

In twenty-first century India, there are wells from which some men must not drink. There are homes where the underlings must not cast a shadow that precedes them.

Make a note to yourself to send a note to the sun to shine only on you.

In some parts of the country, women, children and men are massacred every day because they dared to or just happened to be standing on the wrong side of the road. Women are burned to extol unknown virtues and absolve society of some collective karma. Like one hundred jumbo jets crashing every day. Collective karma or human error? Collective stupidity or curse?

What, then, is the probability that nothing has started and therefore nothing will end? Maya is also the name of a civilisation. In this grand cosmic dance, we are all toys but some are made in China. So they must be destroyed. They are inferior and of poor quality and cannot go on forever like Duracell. Brahmin blood, Thakur blood, French bread, brown bread, universal dread.

The fear of the invisible is greater when accountability is higher. The fear of not mattering is heightened every time a bigger car, the fifteenth carpet, the sixth yacht and the fourth island is acquired. For it is the same people who say: what is all this—we come naked and go naked. This is karma.

By that token, we should all be walking around naked. Maybe some of us are. We are a land of over 1.2 billion visible and an equal number invisible. Satyam and asatyam?

We get enamoured by the visible revolutions. What of the hundreds of invisible revolutions that take place around us all the time? And within. Are they bloody, too? Do they wither away without reaching their ends?

Simon said silence like a cancer grows. But Simon was neither Greek nor Indian. He was just an out-of-work rhymester strumming his guitar and manufacturing melodies along with his college chum. So now we will be taught philosophy by college kids, huh. They will write *Iliads*; they will pen Upanishads, huh. Get away, man. You've lost your harmonica.

Silence like a cancer grows. It grows and grows and grows until it infects every last cell inside of us, and then it begins to ooze out like pus from our every pore, waiting to infect others. But this is where it fails, this is where the silent revolution meets its end. Because we have Tata Memorial. Followed by a stiff course of chemo to ebb this growth of silence. We make silence benign all over again.

What is it that you were doing for the last 5,000 years? Yes, good, carry on, carry on.

We can't see the invisible running. We can only hear their receding footsteps. Thank God, we say, thank God they are receding.

Everything you see will live after you. Now go and clean your street and post a selfie. Don't cover your nose. You are smelling elsewhere.

Only when the invisible becomes visible does the boy become a man.

Invisible no more. No more.

5

2004—The Naked and the Dead

'Hato, hato,' cried SP Kharbanda, slicing through the crowded platform with his baint.

It was an important day and his edginess was palpable. Ajay felt embarrassed at his subordinate's antics, more so, when he heard the whispered curse from a passer-by: 'Saala mamu. Look at him get his path cleared by that oaf.' He squirmed and decided to intervene.

'Arey Kharbanda, where's our car, bhai? These foot-overbridges never seem to end.'

'*...coming, from, Firozpur, going, to, Mumbai, the, nine, zero, two, four, Firozpur, Mail, via, Faridkot...*'

'Bas sir, only three-four minutes,' answered Kharbanda, his nose hair flipping in and out, now visible, now hidden, in step with his deep, beefy breaths.

'*...Kapura, Gangsar, Jaitu, Goneana, Kotli, Kalan, Budhlada, Bareta, Jakhal, Tohana, Narwana...*'

'You said that ten minutes ago.'

'*...Uchana, Jind, Julana, Rohtak, Ismaila...*'

'Bas, sir.'

'I hope you also understand my problem of the...'

SP Kharbanda was insistent. 'Bas sir, in a minute.'

'Ridiculous.'

The zigzagging became more frantic. 'Arey, move. Hut udhar...ji, sir, please come…'

The two eventually made it to the VIP car park. SP Kharbanda brought himself to a stop. 'Here we are, sir. Nice and open. Just give me a minute…oye. Arey, driver?'

While Ajay steamed his glasses and rubbed them with his handkerchief, SP Kharbanda walked a full circle around him, completing the first of the seven vows. Ajay realised Kharbanda's discomfiture and tried to help.

'I think those gentlemen by that paan shop might be the ones you are shouting for.'

'Haan, sir...arey, driver? Oye inspector. Yes, *you* there.'

Bidi, paan and gutkha were cast off at once as the coterie scrambled towards the epicentre. The inspector thought it fit to offer what, to him, felt like a reasonable explanation. 'Sorry, sir, we had just gone for a–'

SP Kharbanda exploded. 'Shut up. Ban-cho, is this what you are paid for? Haan?'

The inspector apologised, head firmly down. 'Very sorry, sir.'

'Saalon, I'll demote each one of you. And you—Kuljit. Kaminey, have you forgotten you were a do-paisa taxi driver once?'

Ajay tried to calm things down. 'Leave it, Kharbanda; let's just get on with it.'

'No no, sir, these ban-chos need to be taught a lesson.'

'I said, Kharbanda, you do realise, what I told you…about...'

'Oh, yes, sir...saalon, you are having paan, smoking beedi, when DIG saab here has to go for *soo-soo*?'

Ajay could not believe his ears. 'Kharbanda!'

'Ji? Oh. Sorry sir, I didn't mean to...'

'I said that's enough! Bloody chuck it all—I'll just take a taxi.'

'*Arey* no no, sir,' pleaded Kharbanda, his forehead embossed with wrinkles that resembled the ruts to a quarry on a rainy day. 'Here, please, get in. Inspector. Air condition *on*—full blast.'

Inspector Ghorpade slammed shut one of the back doors after Ajay had clambered in, and then ran around to open the other for SP Kharbanda. Look busy, he thought. '*Ji,* sir.'

'You and Ramesh and Omnath follow in the decoys.'

'Yes, sir.'

SP Kharbanda ducked his head through the window even though the door was wide open. 'Sir, shall I join you? At the back, I mean. Otherwise no problem, no problem, I'll follow in the decoy.'

'No, Kharbanda, please, get in. We need to talk—it's important.'

Kharbanda felt as though he had been knighted. The few and well-oiled tufts that were allowed to lengthen naturally on one side so they could be indentured and brought all the way to the other in multiple arches, those well-oiled tufts were no longer at their prearranged places, exposing the bald head. Kharbanda did the needful, then wiped his palm on the back of his trousers. 'Yes, sir…chalo driver—and not less than sixty, you understand.'

'Sir,' responded Kuljit the driver, in a manner befitting more an army major than a 'do-paisa' taxi driver.

With sirens blaring, the Ambassador shot through the heavy traffic, which had already been parted for it by one of the decoys.

SP Kharbanda continued where he had left off. 'I am sorry about all this, what just happened, sir. I really am.'

'Leave it, Kharbanda. And stop behaving like I am the home minister.'

'Yes, sir.'

'I think before we begin, you should know. The directive has come from the very top...can we talk safely here?'

'Yes, sir, absolutely. Driver, do you understand?'

Kuljit shouted through the Ambassadorial cacophony. 'Ji, sir, I am able to understand.'

SP Kharbanda was not quite sure if Kuljit's answer was to his satisfaction but he thought it best to say and ask less. 'He understands, sir.'

'Good. There's talk of president's rule in Maharashtra. You with me?'

'Err…'

'The directive is to—well—to *confirm* that the killing of Saane was at the Opposition's behest.'

SP Kharbanda acted as though the air had finally been cleared. 'Oh.'

'Personally, I am quite pleased that this Saane was cleaned up.'

'Yes, sir, me too. He was a real bastard. Saala.'

'You might not be aware of how extensive his...'

'Believe me, sir, it is no secret. The bastard was all set to give away thousands of hectares of agricultural land for all this SEZ-Ves-EZ tamashaa.'

'All that and...'

'Imagine, sir, how much he must have made in the deal.'

'Yes, now we...'

'And here we are, not sure whether we'll be transferred to Leh or Ladakh next.'

'Well, anyway, to come back to...'

'I tell you, sir, we are wasting our time in this force. Politics is the real deal, Sirji.'

'Well, Kharbanda, if we could...'

'Sometimes I think I should go back to my pind and...'

'Kharbanda!'

SP Kharbanda bit his lower lip. 'Oh, sorry sir, sorry.'

'Yes, so as I was saying, once my team's job is done, the case will be transferred to the CBI. You see, Kharbanda, this is a masterstroke.'

'I don't get what...'

'The centre doesn't want the CBI first up. They know the Opposition in Delhi will start crying foul—the CBI is this...that, a puppet, pawn. You get me?'

SP Kharbanda scratched his stubble, a greyish-black tinge that was threatening to take over the face and neck. 'A little, sir.'

'So now *we* do the dirty work, we furnish proof that Saane was done in by the Opposition, and once we have done this, once we have wiped the shit, IG saab will simply wriggle his ass and pull the flush.'

'Sir?'

'Arey hand over the file to CBI, I mean.'

'Now I get you, sir. The ban-cho minister-jaat, sir. Oh, sorry, sir.'

'Arey relax, Kharbanda. In fact—just between you and me—the IG has been promised a plum post once all this is over.'

'Must be, sir.'

'The real aim here is to deploy president's rule.'

SP Kharbanda enquired, childlike. 'But why, sir?'

'Arey bhai, how do I know. These things don't filter through to our in-trays, what. There must be a pucca plan. So, now you are completely in the picture, I hope.'

'Yes, sir.'

'So can we begin? We haven't much time, you understand.'

'Yes sir, I'll start from the very beginning.'

'And be brief—speaking of which, I am again reminded of my… thirty-five minutes gone already, Kharbanda.'

'Bas sir, in three-four minutes. We have…yes, we are past Naoroji Road.'

'Good. So tell me.'

SP Kharbanda shuffled his bottom on the deep cushions of the back seat, sinking a little deeper. 'Yes, sir. I'll be brie…I'll start. Your mission is accomplished, sir—even before you have made your hands dirty on this case.'

'Go on.'

'Indeed, Saane saab *was* killed through a supari. A fellow named Kitla, an underworld gang member, he cleaned up Saane. One shot. Here—between the eyes. Unfortunately, before we could determine that Kitla was the man who did this, the bastard was washed and dried in a police encounter. We...'

'An "honest" police encounter?'

SP Kharbanda pinched his Adam's apple. 'Yes, sir. God promise.'

'Carry on.'

'We apprehended a sleeper. From his mobile we discovered that he—Dev is his name—was in regular contact with Kitla.'

'If he was a sleeper, why was he in regular contact?'

Ban-cho. *Didn't think of that, did I*, thought SP Kharbanda. 'Err, sir, the regular contact was in the last three-four days only.'

'You and your three-four days. Anyway, go on.'

'So this is where the investigation is at present. We can prove that Dev was in regular contact with Kitla. Kitla belonged to the Mitoo gang and was killed in an encounter. And lastly, sir, the Mitoo gang is on the payroll of the Opposition—I mean the ruling party here but the Opposition in Delhi—of this we have solid proof. So there.'

'All well and good, but how do you know Kitla killed Saane?'

'Sir, this is where the story gets a little complicated.'

'Don't worry, let it get complicated.'

'Err, yes, sir. Sir, to answer your question, very simply, this is presently a conjecture.'

'Conjecture? A bloody conjecture?'

'But a very good and concrete one, sir, believe me. Please hear me out.'

'Go on.'

'Unfortunately, Kitla wasn't there to confess as he was cleaned up a day before Saane was found. But—and here is the crucial fact—this fellow Dev, he was caught red-handed when he was trying to retrieve Kitla's mobile from the murder scene. Now why would Dev do that?'

'Yes, why would he?'

'Precisely because Kitla—the ban-cho monkey that he was—dropped his mobile while he was popping off Saane. He soon realised this and asked Dev to go and get the mobile from the spot. It all adds up, sir, I have double-checked, triple-checked.'

'Hang on, hang on, hang on. Has Dev confessed at all?'

'Err, not yet, sir. You see, he resisted arrest with some force—my sub-inspector was nearly chopped up. So naturally during the arrest, we had to use force as well. Bastard won't be able to speak for at least a month now.'

Ajay threw his hands up in the air. 'Well, that's just great, Kharbanda. Ban-cho, how am I going to make all this waterproof without a spoken confession?'

'But sir, he signed the confession papers.'

'Not good enough, Kharbanda, you bloody well know that. When this Dev is able to speak—tomorrow, the day after, in a week—what if he denies everything he supposedly confessed to?'

SP Kharbanda was thinking furiously of some reply. *It can't go all wrong now, he prayed, it just can't.*

'Arey speak up, Kharbanda—throw some ideas at me.'

A brainwave reached the deserted shore. 'Sir, this one month time I am absolutely sure of—I'll wage my ban-cho *VIP* on it. I have seen his condition.'

'What do you mean?'

'Err, not good, sir. A miracle if he can eat anything more solid than dalia for a month.'

'Where are you going with this?'

'A month is a long time, sir. In a few days the case will be the CBI's headache. No?'

'Well, that's true...'

'And they'll scream hoarse how they have cracked this case—peddle this Dev story also?'

'Yes…'

SP Kharbanda was ready with his closing argument. 'So? If they find their main link in the case has started to bubble up from his ass, well, it's their headache then, isn't it?'

'Yes, you may have a point after all, Kharbanda.'

Ban-cho Kharbanda, you are a genius, thought SP Kharbanda to himself.

'Well, just make sure Dev doesn't open up during this next month.'

'That I promise.'

'Good. Just one more thing.'

'Ji, Ajay saab?'

'You said, about the body—one clean shot?'

'As a whistle, sir.' SP Kharbanda went on to demonstrate the euphemism.

'I'd like to see the body.'

'But sir, there's no need. I have personally seen it. It's an open-and-shut case. The autopsy report says so, too. Point-blank. Forehead. *Dhamaak*.'

'Nonetheless, it is important that I see the body.'

SP Kharbanda was fighting for his life. He tried one more time. 'But sir, really, why should you go out of the way? I will prepare all the papers. You can be back in Delhi tomorrow.'

But Ajay was unyielding. 'Kharbanda, I have been in this business far too long to make sure shit doesn't land at my doorstep. Don't mind my saying so, but I wouldn't flinch one bit if the blame of a botched-up investigation were to all fall at your end. But not at *my* doorstep, no. You get me?'

SP Kharbanda exhaled in defeat. 'Er, as you say, sir…arey, driver. Take a U—we are going to King Edward Memorial Hospital morgue.'

'Sir?'

'KEM. In Parel. Tata Memorial ke paas. Take the Lalbaug flyover.'

'Ji, saab.'

Ajay thought it fit to cut in. '…And one last thing, Kharbanda.'

'Ji, sir?'

'Ask the driver to pull over by that postbox—enough is enough. And switch that ban-cho siren off.'

'Oh. Of course, sir. Driver.'

The car screeched to a halt. Ajay extricated himself from the thick padding and walked hurriedly towards the postbox, dismissing the stirred-up dust with a wave of his hand. He looked in all possible directions and proceeded to vandalise public property. Done, he shook the last drop away and turned around, surprised to find SP Kharbanda so close to the action.

'Shall we, Kharbanda?'

'Shall we what, sir?'

'Have tea with bloody Saane, is what.'

'Oh, yes, sir. Driver?'

'Ji, saab.'

The procession was underway once more. The silence was broken from time to time by the squealing springs of the back seat. Ajay shifted his position a little. 'How much further, Kharbanda?'

'It's just here, sir, just next to the Grand Mumbai Food Court.'

'Well that's convenient—for the customers, I mean.'

'They serve very good vada-pav, sir—you should try some while you are here.'

'Maybe after we are done at the morgue…'

'Er, I think we are there already…arey driver, park by the side entrance and leave the AC on. Full blast. Come, sir.'

Once again, Ajay had to squeeze himself out of the car. He made a mental note to circulate a memo demanding that the padding in lal-battis be sheared down to half its tog value. SP Kharbanda had hopped out already and was holding the entrance door open for DIG saab.

Ajay inspected the building like an unsure tenant. 'Chalo, chalo, we haven't much time.'

SP Kharbanda was most welcoming and considerate. 'After you, sir.'

Once inside, the officers took one breath and wished immediately that they hadn't. The air was thick with formalin of nineteenth-century vintage.

Coughing and gasping, SP Kharbanda hollered. 'Arey is anyone there? Hello. Arey bhai, I said hello…'

Ajay cleared his scratchy throat. 'Typical. Must have gone for paan.'

'Very likely, sir. They must think no one can slip out.'

'Shut up—and find out.'

SP Kharbanda was a touch disappointed at the roasting. 'Y-yes, sir…Oye hello.'

Hearing the commotion, a cadaver moonwalked from the booth next to the hallway. It was clear that besides an occasional bribe, the man took no nourishment. The eyes had sunk in completely and the cheekbones would have merged with the cranium had they progressed any higher. He wore a heavily soiled vest, and underneath, even more heavily soiled khaki trousers. He was either a morgue keeper or a mechanic, or both. Ajay started counting the ribs.

'Yes yes, coming,' said the man as he snatched his shirt from a hook and commenced the rather painful exercise of wearing it. 'Oh. Kharbanda saab. What brings you to our maikhanaa?'

'Well, Patankar, keep your chatter to yourself. This is DIG Ajay Biswas…'

The man had a name after all. Patankar stopped buttoning up his shirt midway and stood to attention, which was, in his case, a loose interpretation of the phrase.

'Oh. Welcome, sir. What would you like. Chai? Some soft drink? Arey Tiwari?'

Ajay couldn't look directly at Patankar as much as he tried. Instead, he addressed the next stage in human evolution. 'Please can we get on with it, Kharbanda?'

'Y-yes, sir. Arey Patankar, saab wants to see Mr Saane.'

Patankar seemed delighted. 'Sure, no problem. He was due back to his family this afternoon but they haven't turned up yet. Please follow me.'

Kharbanda noticed a floating straw and decided to clutch at it. 'DIG saab has a very busy schedule. If it isn't possible, then…'

'No, no, it is. The family can wait, no hurry for them. Arey Tiwari, find the Saane file and bring it to Room 4.'

Patankar led the two officers through the hallway and into a large hall. He continued to limp forth, providing ample time to the officers for a look around. Ajay was surprised and relieved—there were no dead bodies strewn about as far as the eye could see. *Patankar must be leading us to a temperature and humidity-controlled room, with an operating theatre-like overhead lighting, with large drawers-on-wheels that could be pulled out from the walls, just like in the movies,* he thought.

Room 4 came into view. Patankar pushed open the doors.

It was as though Ajay was run over by a truck made wholly out of foul smells. 'What th...Open the windows. Teri maa ki...What's with...oonh-hoon, behn ki...what's with all this water, ban-cho?'

Patankar thought it proper to warn: 'Careful, sir—with that one on the floor.'

SP Kharbanda wore an I-told you-so expression. 'Sorry sir, but I told you so. There was no need.'

'Shut up. Patankar, what's with all this mess?'

'Arey saab, power goes off ten to four. The only way is to keep the bodies on ice slabs that are supplied every other day.'

'Man, this is disgusting. Don't you have an exhaust? And where is Saane?'

Patankar stooped to clutch his knee and started to limp away efficiently. 'Ji saab, it's at the end, the VIP corner…here, saab.'

Ajay was shocked beyond belief. 'Oh God, Kharbanda—the body has nearly decomposed. I can't make out whether it is Saane or not–'

'Yes sir, this ban-cho morgue has always been like this—bas naam ka King Edward. But for that massive mole by Saane's nose it is now impossible to...

'Yes, quite right. What a massive mole.'

'Not very photogenic, was he, sir?'

'Shut up. Can you turn the body, so that he is looking up?'

'Ji, sir.' SP Kharbanda wedged his foot between the fast-melting ice slab and Saane's love handle and booted the dead politician over, something possible only with a dead politician.

'Bloody hell—some point-blank, this.'

'Ji, sir.'

'...hang on, hang on, hang on.'

SP Kharbanda was doing just that, for dear life. 'Yes, sir?'

'Hand me your baint, Kharbanda.'

'Sir, if you don't mind, please don't touch the body with it. It's Kashmiri willow, got it especially...

'Shut up. I'll get you another one.'

'Ji, sir.'

Ajay poked and prodded. 'Hm...here...and here...do you see this, Kharbanda? Patankar?'

'What is it, sir?'

'You mean, Kharbanda, you can't make out?'

'No sir, what?'

'His neck is broken. And the right shoulder, here, is dislocated. And do you see that stab wound below the lung? And look at the way his lower leg bends upwards—how can it be? Show me the autopsy report.'

Tiwari, who had arrived unnoticed and had been dipping and ducking his head for a better view of the proceedings, now handed over the file to Ajay, drawing open the laces with a flourish. 'Here, sir.'

Ajay glanced through the tea- and pickle-stained pages, each one duly signed and dated by a gazetted officer, that forever-hunted but rarely sighted animal. He studied the concluding paragraph on the last page with the care it deserved, for the sake of the Shakespeare who wrote it. He began counting on his fingers the number of times the word 'vide' appeared, but soon ran out of digits. Hmm... Kharbanda?'

'Ji, sir?'

'It is clear that Saane fell from a height. And he was probably stabbed, too. But the autopsy report doesn't mention these injuries at all. Was Saane shot *after* he was dead?'

SP Kharbanda decided the best option now was to hang his head in shame and wait for the storm to pass, something he had learnt from DSP Sharma, who, in turn, had learnt it from Sub-Inspector Jatinder, who had learnt it from his younger brother just before he was thrashed with a cricket bat by his father.

'Kharbanda?'

'J-ji sir, er, sir please, hear me out...'

'No wonder you didn't want me to see the body.'

'No no, sir, you misunderstand...'

'Ban-cho, you were taking me for a ride, haan. *Why?* I want to see the crime scene. How far is it?'

'Sir, but...'

'Kharbanda!'

'Close by, sir—Lalmatti Gardens, behind Bombay Presidency Golf Course.'

'And whereabouts is that?'

'Chembur, sir.'

'Let's go. And I'll sort *you* out in the car.'

'J-ji, sir.'

Ajay strode out with such a look of guaranteed apocalyptic reprisals for his subordinates that SP Kharbanda began to mentally draft the first version of his will. Patankar and Tiwari were nowhere to be seen—they had presumably crawled back into the formalin tank they had emerged from. Down but not out, SP Kharbanda manufactured a long jump and resurfaced in front of Ajay just in time to open the entrance door. Following Ajay to the waiting car, he struck the bonnet with his baint. 'Driver! Lalmatti Gardens.'

'Ji, saab...and decoys?'

SP Kharbanda turned around and thought it best to take a second opinion. 'Sir, he is asking about decoys.'

'Decoys ki maa ki. Let's *go*.'

'J-ji, sir.'

En route, when he thought things had calmed down a little, SP Kharbanda tried one more time. 'Sirji...'

Ajay was unmoved. 'Not *one* word from you, Kharbanda—not *one*. Just let me know when we are there.'

Kuljit, meanwhile, was hunched over his steering wheel, habitually changing into higher gears at low speeds, further adding to Ajay's annoyance. He rolled down the window and spat out an elaichi.

SP Kharbanda decided that the minute of silence that had passed was an appropriate enough gap for him to try his hand at a grovelling apology again. 'Sirji...'

Ajay looked up, and pretended his pineal gland was about to flare up a third eye. 'You open your mouth again, Kharbanda, and you'll get it.'

And so it was back to watching the world go by for the distraught SP Kharbanda. If he were in a less sombre mood he would have tonked Kuljit behind his ear for making the world go by so slowly. Fifth gear at forty meant you were never sure if the hum being generated under your backside was through your own efforts or the car's.

Ajay was getting impatient. It had been close to three-quarters of an hour since they had left King Edward. 'Well? How much more?'

'Not long now, sir, maybe three-four minutes.'

'Great. Tell me, Kharbanda. How long does it take for the earth to spin one rotation on its axis?'

'Er, twenty-four hours, sir.'

'Really? I thought it was three-four minutes.'

'Sir?'

'And for the earth to go round the sun?'

Kharbanda couldn't make head or tail of this bizarre line of questioning, but he was thankful he still remembered his fifth grade science lessons. '365 days and six hours, sir.'

'You sure it's not three-four minutes?'

'Positive, sir.'

Kharbanda firmed up for the next question. Here comes one on Pluto.

Ajay brought things down to earth. 'So are you going to tell me why Saane was shot *after* he was dead?'

'Sirji, please, you can do anything—fry me in boiling oil, throw me to the gharials—but believe me when I tell you that this is all that DSP Sharma's doing.'

'I don't care. This thing will shake your testicles off you—I'll make sure of that. Bastard, lying to me. On my bloody face. Driver. How much longer?'

Kuljit slowed down to negotiate a speed bump, refusing to shift from third. It was a toss-up whether it was because of the car or a genetic predisposition that he stuttered a reply: 'B-bas, saab, w-we have reached. I'll park for you here, sir?'

Ajay couldn't wait to get down. 'Yes yes.'

After he had done so, he noticed the forlorn SP Kharbanda still staring blankly out the window at a lamp post.

'Well, are you going to get down or you want to be bloody pushed?'

'Y-yes, sir.'

'Come on then, dammit. And I take it you have personally seen the spot.'

SP Kharbanda pulled up his trousers. 'Yes, sir. Only this morning...'

'*This morning*? Saane has been dead for three days. You donkeys don't surprise me anymore.'

'Er…please follow me, sir.'

'Keep talking, keep talking…'

'Sir, what can I say? You are in a position to strip me naked in the market, sir.'

Ajay stepped on the elevated footpath that looped the great expanse. 'That I will, I promise you.'

'Sirji, you know very well how it is.'

'No, I very well don't.'

SP Kharbanda slowed down a little. 'The pressure got to me, sir. The pressure of giving results to the Dilli team.'

'You are a bunch of bloody jokers, you know that?'

'Worse, sirji, *worse*. I am at fault—I myself acknowledge that.'

'Oh. How grateful I am to you for that—sirji.'

'I'll give you nothing but the truth now, sir. *I* told Sharma to shoot Saane.'

Ajay stopped in his tracks.

'Why, you bastard, *why*? Was he trying to get you transferred; was he doing some hanky-panky with your wife?'

'No no, sir, not like that. I told Sharma to shoot Saane—the *dead* Saane. There was no time to investigate. The team would have wanted results. We already had a bona fide story of an encounter—that Kitla ban-cho.'

Ajay shook his head in disgust. 'I tell you, man...'

'On such occasions I have always relied on my sixth sense.'

'Well that's great—exactly what's prescribed in the police manual.'

'I thought a good story would be to mix Kitla with Saane. Admit it sir, you yourself liked it.'

Ajay couldn't believe his ears. 'You ban-cho, Kharbanda. Now you are blaming me?'

'No, sir. I am only saying that everyone would have believed.'

'Wah, Kharbanda. So now the job of the police is to make stories up, is it?'

'I am completely at fault, sir—hang me if you wish.'

'You be sure of that, Kharbanda, you be sure. Ban-cho, making stories...now why the shit are we going around in circles?'

'Bas, just near that champa, sir, can you see? By that bench.'

The men reached the park bench. SP Kharbanda was tempted to take a seat but decided wisely to wait and watch if DIG saab did so first.

Ajay tapped the armrest with SP Kharbanda's Kashmiri willow baint. 'Is this where? Behind this bench?'

'Yes, sir. To the best of my knowledge, the body was in the bag when it was discovered.'

'To the best of your knowledge? I admire your nerve, Kharbanda.'

'Thank you, sir.'

'Shut up. *Shut up*.'

SP Kharbanda felt giddy.

Ajay, meanwhile, had set the wheels of his brain in motion. 'The body was found behind this bench. Add to that the fact that Saane's bones were all broken. Well, it doesn't take an Einstein to conclude the bastard fell from above and probably rolled over a little to rest here...look up, Kharbanda. Saane obviously fell—or was pushed—from the top of this cliff here. What's on top, there?'

'Sir, it must be the golf course. You see there those carved-out stairs?'

'What are we waiting for, then. Your baaraat?'

'Er, yes, sir, please follow me.'

Ajay felt he needed to fill up the silence in the minutes it was taking them to climb the stairs. 'What a force, man, what a force, I tell you. I mean, you guys came here and obviously you knew at once that Saane must have fallen from a height. But you'd rather not move your lazy asses and do a bit of investigating…'

He took a breather at the fifteenth step and recommenced. '*That* you leave to a senior officer from Delhi. And I can guess why. Because *I* am a crazy enough ban-cho to see things for myself. Most would only be too happy to take your word for it—grab the reports and go back to Delhi. And I haven't even come to how you ban-chos managed to fabricate the autopsy report.'

Ajay grabbed at his knees and interrupted himself to ask, 'How much more, Kharbanda?'

'Sir, only three-four more steps…'

'Just as I suspected.'

'Sir?'

'Shit, the picket seems to be locked.'

'No sir, look, just a piece of wire holding the gates. Please follow me…'

The men went past the rickety gate and found themselves standing on top of freshly cut and watered grass.

SP Kharbanda was impressed. 'Looks like a lawn, sir.'

'Green. It's called a green.'

'Yes, sir. Very green it is, too.'

'Amazing. The monkeys haven't even bothered to put a fence or a rope.'

'Plain stupid, sir. Anybody can topple over easily.'

'Well not anybody, Kharbanda. Saane himself.'

SP Kharbanda went over to the edge and had a quick look. 'Yes sir, looks very likely. What a fall.'

'Chances are he didn't feel a thing and was probably unconscious. Look. The grass here is a bit scuffed.'

'Yes, sir.'

'But what was he doing up here? Let's check at the club if he had signed up for a game. Wednesday, wasn't it?'

'Ji, sir, the body was found Thursday morning.'

'It says seventeenth hole here. The clubhouse must be nearby...'

'Yes. This way, sir,' said SP Kharbanda, walking a step behind Ajay, but without a golf bag.

The clubhouse was impressive, if a little out of date, given that hardly anyone in Mumbai was now on familiar terms with a smoking chimney, or for that matter, heavily ivied, louvered windows.

If all this had left SP Kharbanda a little overawed, he did a good job of hiding it upon reaching the reception area. 'Arey ban-cho someone there? Oye ganduon, hello.'

A young man, looking as though he had just stepped out of his boudoir, appeared from nowhere, as is generally the norm in select establishments. 'Good evening...but how did you come through that way, if I may ask?'

SP Kharbanda was in no mood for manners. 'Never mind, ban-cho. Are you the receptionist?'

The man investigated his fingernails and blew air at some of them. 'How very rude. First tell me how you came in from there. The club is closed today.'

'Oye ban-cho, don't get cocky with us. I am SP and sir here is DIG.'

The haughtiness evaporated quickly. 'Oh. Sorry, sir. What I meant was...

'Never mind what you meant. Is this the way to talk to people, haan? This is a clubhouse, not Vidhan Sabha, ban-cho.'

Ajay wanted a quick death. 'Uff.. Leave it, Kharbanda. We have a job at hand, damn it.'

'Er, yes, sir...listen, we want some information.'

The receptionist was all good manners. 'Please, sir, anything.'

'Show us your entry register—check for Wednesday last.'

'Here, sir...'

'Everyone who comes in has to enter his name?'

'Yes, sir.'

'Hmm. Sa...Saan...Sa...Saane. Sir, Ajay sir. Here it is.'

Ajay came forward. 'Show me.'

'Here, sir. Saane—signed for a game. A set of left-handed clubs—says 6.30.'

SP Kharbanda looked up from the register. 'Till what time is the last round accepted?'

'4.30, sir.'

'Why has this person signed for a game as late as 6.30 then?'

The man pulled the register in his direction. 'Er, sir, let me see...'

SP Kharbanda wagged a finger. '*Oye saaley*. Don't try and mess with us.'

'Kharbanda, please!' cried Ajay.

The receptionist glanced at the entry, trawling his forefinger slowly under each line. 'Er, yes sir, this here has been signed by Mr Saane. Life members have a free hand. Saane sir was also a member of our executive board...sir, if my job here is done, can I...'

Ajay broke in. 'Wait. Was anyone with him on Wednesday evening? Were you at the counter that day?'

'Er, no sir. Actually, there's no way to tell—by the register, I mean. Members come in and sign it by themselves. Mr Saane must have done the same, by habit.'

'And if he had a guest, would he have signed up for him, too?'

'Probably not, sir.'

'Did you see Mr Saane that evening?'

'No, sir.'

'You sure? Wait—did he ask for a caddy?'

'That I'll check, sir—in the caddy register.'

Ajay drummed the reception desk with his knuckles. 'You do that.'

The man brought out the caddy register from under the counter. He licked his thumb and flicked the pages. 'Now let me see...Wed-nes-day...Wed-nes-day...no sir, no caddy has been signed in after the last bell—that's 4.30. Looks like Mr Saane didn't ask for a caddy.'

'When was the last time—before Wednesday—that Saane came in?'

'I saw him come in and play a round last month, sir.'

'Was he on his own?'

'No sir, he was with Mr Thapar, chairman of Credence Group.'

'Yes yes. Were they here long?'

'They played a full round, sir...I really apologise but I have to close up, sir...'

'Yes, nothing further. But SP Kharbanda here will need to have a look at that register again…also, Kharbanda, you make a list of all those who came to the club on Wednesday.'

SP Kharbanda protested feebly. 'But there will be hundreds, sir.'

'I don't bloody care if there are thousands.'

'Y-yes, sir.'

Ajay turned to the receptionist. 'Thank you—your name?'

'Raghav Kathuria, sir.'

'You have been here long?'

'Nine years.'

'Good. Raghav, Kharbanda here will be in touch in the coming days, alright?'

'Sure, sir.'

'Come, Kharbanda, let's go.'

SP Kharbanda braced himself for the journey back. A swig or two of the free stuff would have been handy. *If only I was the senior here,* he cursed. 'By the same way, sir?'

'No. Ask the driver to meet us at the clubhouse entrance.'

SP Kharbanda drew out his cell phone from its holster in a flash. 'Yes, sir, one moment…hello? Arey Kuljeet? Where are you? Come to club entrance. Yes, main gate, main gate; you understand?'

'Come, Kharbanda, let's wait outside.'

'Ji, sir.'

The men passed the glass-and-metal doors and waited by the side of the vine-covered porch. Ajay looked around vaguely as he spoke. 'Not much to go by, no Kharbanda? I mean, what was that bastard doing playing golf at seven in the evening?'

'Ji, sir.'

'Here's how I look at it. Obviously, Saane didn't suspect anything untoward might happen. He could have come along with a guest and not signed him up. Quite likely a business meeting. This guest could then actually be the one who polished off Saane.

'Very likely, sir.'

'I mean, think about it. The fellow just needed to push Saane off the seventeenth green, that's all.'

'Very likely, sir.'

'What very likely, very likely?'

'I mean, sir, this is great. You are like Sherlock Holmes.'

'But *you* are the bloody Sir Arthur Conan Doyle, aren't you? *You* write all this stuff, no?'

'Sir, sorry. You are still angry about all that...'

'No, no, no. I want to garland you—for making me run around like a monkey.'

Take it like a man, Kharbanda, this too shall pass, the SP said to himself.

'...but you know, Kharbanda. Something within me has quite enjoyed this, this adventure, investigation, whatever you may call it. Somewhere, hidden beneath those mountains of reports and files and committees—somewhere there, a young and dashing Ajay Biswas, IPS lurks.'

'I knew it sir, I knew it.'

'Well, I am not *that* angry with you now.'

SP Kharbanda grinned. 'Thank you, sir. And, er, if you have cooled down a little more, may I also suggest something?'

'Now what. You killed Saane's dad, too?'

'No no, sir. You *na*.'

'What, then.'

'Sir, this golf-woalf investigation is fine, it really is. But, sir, in the end, where is it leading to, you tell me? By your brilliant deductions all we know now is that a ban-cho killer is at large. So, in three days time, what will you tell the CBI—that the killer is at large?'

Ajay showed interest. 'Go on.'

'Will your IG and your home minister be satisfied with the report on their table that says the killer is still at large? Where will they slap the president's rule then—on my ass?'

'*Oye saala*. Bastard, Kharbanda, you are an evil genius.'

'Thank you, sir. But if we go by what *really* happened—home minister, CBI-she-BI, you, me, that ban-cho Sharma—all are happy, sir. No?'

'Kharbanda, this is good. And you will take care of everything? That fellow Dev? The autopsy report?'

SP Kharbanda bowed like the Air India Maharajah. 'Sir, please, you insult me. It is my holy duty.'

'But if word gets out. If I hear *one* word...'

SP Kharbanda wanted to prostrate himself before Ajay. 'Over my dead body, sir, over my dead body.'

'And you will continue to investigate the case? Even when I am back in Delhi?'

'I promise. On Saane's dead body, sir.'

Ajay was exultant. 'Well, what can I say, Kharbanda? You have more than redeemed yourself.'

'All because of seniors like you, sir, who have so much faith in me.'

'A formal commendation would be in order—I'll see to it.'

This was Dussehra, Diwali, Holi and all the rest of the three thousand seven hundred and twenty-two festivals coming early. 'You are just too kind, sir. Really, I mean it.'

Ajay waved his hand but expected to hear more of the praise. 'Oh come off it, Kharbanda.'

'I pray to Sheronwaali Maa that you become IG soon, sir. And over here we have Siddhivinayak, too—very powerful, sir. The two rats outside.'

'Arey leave it, Kharbanda.'

'Come sir, the car.'

They are generic but they have a national patent. Usually inert, they occasionally swing into action only to be pulled down by the weight of their own contradictions and confusions. Generally large, they manage, however, to slip through cracks and crevices, taking with them entire buildings complete with documents and cupboards.

Here now, gone now.

Susceptible to grease, the patent used to be called Pandeyji or Chaubeyji; strangely, never a Srinivasan. Then Chulbul entered the vocabulary and changed the landscape forever. Out went whatever reason remained.

The Chulbulisation of the Indian police force has happened over years. If glasnost and perestroika can enter the language, so can Chulbulisation. If we can raise a sabzi-mandi jugaad to the level of international negotiations, why can't we accept that Chulbul is the way we police ourselves and that the world might as well learn the ropes? Why blame chul when we bull?

I Chulbul.

You Chulbul.

We Chulbul.

They Chulbul.

Bolo kitne Chulbul? *Bolo, bolo. Bolo na.*

Chulbulator, terminator, calculator, tabulator, later, later—come tomorrow. Vision: myopia. Mission: don't know. But who cares. This case is anyway going to self-destruct in five seconds. 5, 4, 3, 2, 1... Find the file. Find the file!

The country's best-kept secret is a question the guilty ask of Chulbul: what do you want? Since the wanting is directly related to the wanter and the wantee, Chulbul is often a middle person. This is unhelpful. Years of not knowing which leg to stand on or, for that matter, whether to stand, sit or crouch has affected Chulbul's posture. Tight pants don't help.

That is not all. Chulbul is often asked to lie, un-lie, lie again, distort and look the other way. In the interest of survival and upgrade, Chulbul has a permanently tentative language which is servile, all accepting, all knowing, all unknowing, here and there, everywhere and nowhere.

It follows naturally that Chulbul's method of work suffers. In most cases, Chulbul will arrive at a crime scene and ask the people present for gossip, which will then be reported as evidence. How often have you seen or heard of Chulbuls interrogating the victims as if they were criminals? That's because Chulbuls are forced to lead a life of crime and sleaze—that is what they see all around them.

All Chulbuls belong to the Chulbul Party of India. We see a Chulbul accepting a bribe of hundred rupees. We report that to a higher authority, little knowing that they are also Chulbuls. Everyone's a Chulbul. Chulbul is really a politburo hydra.

But it is not Chulbul's fault. Not at all. For this is a Chulbul country, a Chulbul civilisation. To make stories comes easily to us. Hardly ever is Isabgol required. Ours, after all, is a land of stories. Bad stories, good stories, true stories, concocted stories…heck, we heard stories even before we were born. All Chulbuls are Abhimanyus and the thana is Chulbul's womb, where, legs on table, exhaling noisily over garam chai, he hears and makes stories. Most of them are forgotten after a hearty laugh, but some get into files and become the truth, the absolute truth and nothing but the truth. Hearsay splits into two words like atomic fission. Hear. Say. The witness heard it. The victim said it. Enough for the gavel to be brought down. Dhara such-and-such ke tehet…three, seven, ten, fourteen years—the quantum doesn't matter—what matters is that we the Chulbuls managed another 'victree'.

Arey yaar, sunn na! Bahul saal pehle…

We might be malnourished but we tell great stories. Our umbilical cord only fed us stories, not micronutrients. And that is why we are all eternal, that is why we subscribe to the legend of Chulbul, right from the time we enter stark naked to when we exit dead.

6

1977—Midnight's Children

The train pulled up with a backward tug, taking everyone by surprise. Army-fatigue-covered trunks tumbled from the doddering heads of coolies. Passengers struggled to hold on to the railings, opting to pass along their suitcases to strangers in nervous trust. Toilet doors swung open and shut, revealing huddles of ticketless passengers. Smokers relishing their last wholesome drag panicked for some purchase as the vestibules they were standing on swayed wildly. Men with datuns wedged in their mouths jostled with bare-chested men saronged in tartan gamchhas to win the race for the exits. Agitated crowds collected at all doors, wanting to get down, wanting to get in. That it was a three-minute stop at the Mughalsarai Railway Junction didn't help matters.

Clasping the corrugated wooden handle of his tea canister, Kalki managed to slither in unnoticed. He conquered the compartment passageway, foothold by foothold, and howled.

'Chai…e….chai….e…'

'Arey chotu, a chai here, quick,' motioned a man while scratching his belly that had managed to iron out the ribs of his sleeveless 'dora'.

'…*Kindly pay attention! Coming, from, Rajender, Nagar, going, to, Kalyan…*'

'Ji, saab.'

'Arey, listen. Two teas here too, jaldi.'

Kalki juggled the kullarhs deftly. 'Aaya memsaab, bas one minute,' he cried while pouring tea from a good height to work up some froth.

'...*the, two, one, four, two, Babu Rajender Prasad Super Express*...'

'Arey Chotu, how long does the train stop at Mughalsarai?'

'Bas three minutes—arey, there you go, saab, it's moved.'

The train jerked free and went into labour. It grunted, it pushed, it pulled before at long last, it picked up speed.

'...*via, Patna, Ara, Buxar, Mughal, Sarai, Satna, Jabalpur, Bhusaval, and, Manmad, is*...'

Canister dangling like a pendant from his neck with the help of a doubled-up naada, the kullarhs stacked up cosily inside his vest, Kalki made a run for the exit. A minute later he stood at the threshold, not bothering in his daring to grab hold of the door railing. His composure belied the speed of the train.

Scanning the platform, he spotted his friend Karim.

'Arey Karim. What are you doing here?'

Noticing Kalki, Karim burst into a run, laughing and flailing his arms, his strides getting shorter and comical as the train finally caught speed.

'Oye, Kalki. Get down, saaley.'

'...*now, arriving, at, Mughal, Sarai, at, platform, number, one, thank you*...'

Without a thought, Kalki jumped off the train. Soon, he dampened his jog, catching Karim's shoulder in the process. 'Saala...that was cutting it close, Karim.'

'Listen to me. Rajdhani just passed by teen number. I saw the pantry clearing the bins—all that machhi and bhaat.'

'Rajdhani, you said. Bound for Howrah?'

'We need to hurry. Teen is Raju's area.'

'I know that Raju saala—nothing escapes his ugly mouth. And if it is Rajdhani, forget it.'

Karim held the canister close to his ear and shook it. 'Chai all gone?'

'No, yaar. With a three-minute stop, I can't cover more than one bogie. And I have been alloted a freight train platform. I mean, who decides on this division, haan?'

'Arey, all this is handled by the coolies and the stationmaster himself, saala. You and I are small flies, brother.'

'All evening I have managed only six rupees. Minus the cost of kulhars and what are you left with? And now my night shift starts on ek. It can't go on like this. I simply have to move to a different platform.'

'Let me see what I can do, Kalki.'

'Pucca?'

'Haan yaar; now hurry or there'd be nothing left for us. Arey Kalki, I just remembered—Bansilal had asked me to go look for you.'

'When?'

'An hour ago. He sounded angry. But it's still ten minutes till your shift, isn't it?'

'Arey, you don't know, Karim. Saala, *one* minute late and I get docked half my wage.'

'Come, let's take the tracks—overbridge will delay us.'

The boys jumped from the platform ledge and scurried across the tracks, taking care not to land their feet on the putrefying filth discarded from the trains and platforms. They avoided the sleepers and kept to the rails, steadying themselves with outstretched arms like condors in flight. Abruptly, Karim noticed some movement.

'Look. There's Raju and his dogs. What yaar Kalki—all because of you.'

Kalki picked up a rock and hurled it with all his might. 'There they go running behind the yards...oye saalon. Come back, you thieving dogs.'

'Bastards. They seem to have finished off nearly everything.'

'Wait, don't lose hope; let me see now.'

Kalki rummaged through the heap of discarded food. 'Can't make out any fish.'

'Dhutt. Arey dhuttt.'

'What is it, Karim? *What*?'

'Rats. Saala, can't even have one meal in peace.'

'Don't take it out on rats.'

'Why. You related to them?'

'Leave it.'

'No no, tell me na. You want to marry one. Is that it?'

'Don't push it, Karim.'

'Achha na, I was only joking. I love rats. No seriously.'

'Come away, there's nothing here. Those dogs got away with the best bits. Maybe the next Rajdhani.'

'Haan yaar...'

'...*kindly pay attention! Coming, from, New, Delhi, going, to, Cuttack, the...*'

Kalki tossed away the mango peel he had extracted from the heap. 'Karim bhai, hear that? That's Behrampur coming in on ek. It's time for my night shift at Bansi's—he'll kill me. Chal, I'll see you at school tomorrow.'

'To hell with school.'

'Come on, don't say that.'

'What "don't say that"? I'll be selling mugs and chain locks and nail cutters till I die—it is my fate.'

'Our fate is not in anyone's hands.'

'Not in anyone's hands. So you like it when people throw your salary at you from moving trains, is it? You like shooing away rats to get to your lunch and your dinner, hain? Saala bastard, not in anyone's hands...'

'Enough of your bakwaas; look, I am off.'

'...*two, three, zero, two, Barhampur, Express, via...*'

Karim caught hold of Kalki's hand playfully and swung it. 'Come, I'll accompany you to ek. My shift on aath doesn't begin till ten.'

'Hurry then or I'll lose half my wage.'

The boys walked alongside each other, Kalki on the rail and Karim hopping and skipping the sleepers. Karim picked up a stone and lobbed it high up in the air. He ran forward to catch it.

'Haan, haan. What's a one day wage, yaar?'

Kalki clucked his tongue. 'Saala. You have your mausi to buy you your schoolbooks. Maybe you should tell her to buy some for me too next time. That way I can forego the night shift and sit on my ass all day like you.'

'...*Kanpur, Central, Allahabad, Mughal, Sarai, Gaya, Parasnath, and, Dhanbad, is, arriving, at, Mughal...*'

'You think mausi's generosity comes free? *You* take my place tomorrow onwards, bastard—let me see *you* carry forty buckets full of shit from the cowshed to the gobar-gas plant every morning. Saala.'

'Achha yaar, leave it. Remember what the *Gita* says: "Do your job, don't worry about the fruits".'

Karim made Kalki slow down by catching his wrist. 'Who is *Gita*? Your night-shift company, is she? Good-looking, is she? Is she?'

'*...Sarai, at, platform, number, one, thank you...*'

'*Gita—Bhagavad Gita*, you stupid...'

'Oh. And anyway, what's new in what it says, hunh? We *are* only doing our jobs, aren't we, and we have never gotten close to as much as a half-eaten apple—wrinkled guava maybe...'

Kalki slapped his forehead. 'No, you brain-dead son-of-a-mule. Fruits, meaning, not "fruits" but reward, benefit. You understand?'

'Saala. Give me *real* fruits any day.'

'Bas, enough yaar. No point telling you anything.'

'And anyway, where have you been getting all this gyan from, haan?'

'Arey, Bansilal's stall is full of such books. *Gita, Ramayan, Quran, Mahabharat*—you name it.'

Karim smiled as he hauled himself up the platform ledge. 'Oh. So now you have become a panditji.'

'Achha yaar, enough. Now give me a hand...'

The boys stood on platform one, inspecting their whereabouts like two soldiers dropped behind enemy lines. Kalki scratched his head. 'Oye, what's the matter? Number one looks deserted. And who is that fat dog with one arm longer than the other?'

'Why, that's Bansilal, you fool. And by the looks of it he is carrying a gun.'

'That's not a gun, you mule, that's a fly swatter.'

'I am sure he'll use it like a gun on you. Anyway, happy night-shifting, see you sometime tomorrow.'

Kalki shouted after Karim. 'Not *sometime*, saaley, early morning. School—understand?'

But Karim was already a fair distance away, refusing to look back. 'Didn't hear you. Goodbye, Kalki.'

'Saala,' mumbled Kalki, shaking his head. He consulted the platform clock and calculated he was five minutes late—acceptable given the time. But then again, the country was in a state of Emergency. Five minutes were five too many. His thoughts were interrupted rudely by a near collision with the behemoth that now stood right in front of him.

'Oye, Kalki-ke-bacche. Where the hell have you been?'

'Good evening, Bansilalji. What happened? You look like you are in a bad mood.'

Bansilal reached for Kalki's ear. 'Saaley kuttey, how dare you.'

'Ji?'

'I said, langoor ki aulad, how dare you talk back to me like that?'

'...'

'That's better. Keep that trap shut—you should know who you are talking to, you understand?'

'Ji...'

'Again!'

'...'

'Didn't hear you. You said something, boy?'

'...'

'Sure you didn't?'

'...'

'That's good. Now listen—Yes...where was I. Yes, where were you? Aren't you late? Haan?'

'...'

'You don't understand the value of time, hain?'

'...'

'By my watch, you are seven minutes late.'

'But saab, I...'

'Haan? Haan? Didn't hear you...'

'...'

'There are boys who will work better for half the money I pay you. But I say, *no*. I say I am a kind man, I'll help this rotten bastard trying to make something of himself. Listening?"

'...'

'I say, "Go on, get lost. I already have my little Kalki musahur." That's what I tell them. And what do I get in return? Do I get some respect from you? But for me, you'd be picking and eating shit from the tracks. Do you understand me, boy?'

'...'

'I let you read all the stall books, no extra charge, no pay cut. You try and read such good stuff from a library, they'll fleece your little ass. But I say, "Arey Bansilal, think of the punya you earn from this". *Who* will even look at you, let alone help you go to school, haan? Didn't I write a letter of recommendation for you? Didn't I write that Kalki is a very intelligent boy and that he has read all my stall books, haan?'

'...'

'Who else would you have got that letter from? A coolie? From that bastard Raju? And what would they have bragged about you—that you can pour a cup of tea in a kulharr without spilling a drop?'

'...'

'Are you listening, boy, or am I just talking to myself?'

'...'

Bansilal formally lifted his gag order. 'Oh. Yes, you can respond now.'

Kalki opened the floodgates. 'I am so sorry, Bansilalji. Cut my head off and put it on display at the stall if it ever happens again. It was all the fault of the platform clock, Bansilalji.'

'I am listening.'

'Please don't even think of paying me my wage for tonight.'

'I wasn't anyway...'

'You have been like a father to me, saab, what more I can tell you.'

'You can tell me more.'

'But for you I couldn't have even dreamt of going to school. You are like a god to me.'

'Carry on.'

'I cannot apologise enough. I have a valid excuse, but saab, in reality, no excuse is valid enough.'

Bansilal was pleased by this. 'Good, I like that.'

'It is my weakness. It has always been my weakness, the desire to show off.'

'Accepted, accepted...'

'I must ask you to trust me as you have never trusted me before.'

Worry lines started to form on the fat man's forehead. 'Wha–, what's going on...'

'I belong to the world…'

'All that's fine, but...'

'I am an imbecile. I see only half the picture.'

'I am glad you have seen reason but...'

'It is the brain, the little grey cells on which one must rely. One must seek the truth within, not without.'

'Why, that's good. I mean, the way you have put it...'

'In that case I shall require four weeks' wages in lieu of notice.'

'What?'

Kalki ducked his head and squeezed his tongue out. 'Arey sorry, saab, forget the last bit.'

'Why. W-what's going on? Is there—are these some lines you have picked up from...'

'Ji, saab, from my partners Hercule Poirot and Miss Marple.'

'Why, you bastard. You making fun of me?'

'*…Kindly pay attention! Coming, from, New, Delhi, going, to, Dibrugarh, the…*'

'I *knew* you'd like them. You have that reader's eye—ear.'

Bansilal was pleasantly surprised. 'Do I?'

'Sure you do. Why else do you think Wheeler & Sons have kept you in charge of their stall for the last fifteen years?'

Bansilal puffed up his chest a little. 'Yes, I see what you mean.'

Kalki was unforgiving, certain that sarcasm was lost on Bansilal. 'They can judge a man's intelligence, his interest in literature, in fiction, in crime…'

'*…two, four, three, six, Dibrugarh, Rajdhani, via, Moradabad, Bareilly…*'

'You think so?'

'Of course. You have educated so many travellers, saab. It has been your gift, your contribution to humanity.'

'Now don't stretch it, boy. That's not a line from a stall book, now is it?'

'Arey saab, you are too modest. You don't know what the world thinks of you.'

Bansilal agreed. 'Well, I can guess sometimes, but...'

'Leave it na, saab. Let bygones be bygones. As I was saying, from today I'll redouble my efforts in your service.'

Bansilal pinched Kalki's cheeks, first one then the other. 'Kalki, you are a good boy. I am happy to have bought you from Deodhar. You are the best investment I have made in years. Worth every paisa.'

'*...Lucknow, Varanasi, Ballia, Chhapra, Hajipur...*'

'Arey saab, leave it na.'

'No, I am telling you it is true.'

'Arey saab, why make fun of your humble servant.'

'Arey ban-cho when I say it is true, it means it is true.'

Kalki scratched his head. 'Er, then saab, about today's wage...?'

'Achha achha saaley, I won't cut it.'

'Saab, there is only one of your kind.'

'That there is.'

'*...Barauni, Katihar, Kishanganj, Jalpaiguri, Cooch...*'

'I mean it.'

'Bas, now don't push it. You know I only mean well when I scold you.'

'*...Behar, Alipurdaur, Kokrajhar, Bongaigaon, Guwahati, Lumding, Diphu, Dimapur, Mariani, and, Tinsukia...*'

'Of course, saab.'

Bansilal gave Kalki a gentle push. 'Now get in or customers will think the stall is empty.'

'Ji. You first, saab.'

Bansilal shook his head slowly. 'Alright, alright...saala. But you are alright, Kalki.'

'*...is, running, seven, hours, late, from, its, scheduled, time, of...*'

'Thank you, saab.'

'Enough now. Let's get some business rolling...haan, yes madam? Can we help you?'

'*...arrival, and, will, arrive, at, Mughal, Sarai, at, zero, five, forty, hours, on, platform...*'

A young woman, wearing an ill-fitted blouse safety-pinned to a heavy sari, shuffled her feet by the magazine racks nervously. She raised her arm to reveal it half-hidden by maroon bangles that fell against each other. The half that was not hidden was hennaed intricately. Her hair parting was daubed with the brightest of red sindoor. En route to her honeymoon, this was perhaps the first occasion when, coaxed by her husband, she had ventured out on her own to explore the workings of the world. She stretched a hand out, uncertain where to point it.

Bansilal tried to be encouraging. 'Anything in particular? Arey, Kalki beta, please show madam the latest magjeen-shagjeen.'

'Yes, sir…here, madam. Here's the latest *Women's Era, Stardust, Illustrated Weekly*—or would you want *Griha Shobha*? *Nootan-kahaniyaan*?'

The woman pointed accusingly at a magazine. 'Is that the latest *Filmi Kaliyan*?'

'*…number, four, Thank you…*'

'No madam, latest comes tomorrow by Rajdhani. This is last month's…have you read it, but? No? It has the latest on the Rakhee–Neetu Singh tiff. We'll give you forty percent off—no saab?'

Bansilal nodded approvingly. 'Yes yes, why not.'

'Okay, then. That *Filmi Kaliyan*, and that *Griha Shobha*.'

'That'll be seven rupees, madam.'

'Here.'

'Thank you…come again.'

The woman snatched the magazines from Bansilal's hands and hurried out of view. Bansilal gave a knowing smirk and fell back on his stool. He took the fly swatter and sliced the air a few times. Turning to Kalki he asked, 'Oye, Kalki? Ban-cho I didn't know Rakhi and Neetu were tearing their plaits out?'

'Arey saab, who cares. *Filmi Kaliyan* got sold na? Bas.'

'Saala. You'll get me into trouble one day.'

'Why, saab? Will Rakhee aunty and Neetu didi get down from Kalka Mail with brooms in their hands and come looking for our stall?'

Bansilal spotted another customer coming their way. '*Quiet.*'

This time round it was a middle-aged man, wearing spectacles thick as the bottom of a goli-soda bottle. He brushed away an imaginary speck of dust from his dog-collared shirt, which stuck to his upper body like a swimsuit. Unconcerned with his fashion statement, he joined his thumb and forefinger and placed them right under his beaked nose. Then, smoothly, he broke the two-digit formation apart, running each along his handlebar moustache down to the last bristle. He repeated the procedure and said: 'Arey bhai, listen.'

'Yes, sir...Kalki beta.'

'Yes sir, how may I help you?'

'Arey, you have that latest one by Agatha Christie?'

'Which one, sir?'

'Arey, that latest one. Can't remember the name, it's on the tip of my tongue. Arey, you know the one na—she came out with it only this year.'

Kalki tilted his head forward a little. 'But sir, didn't you know? The queen died last year. It was in all the papers...'

'Which queen? Who died?'

'Agatha Christie, sir, the queen of crime.'

The man was taken aback. He removed his glasses. 'Oyay chhotu, saaley—you making fun of me?'

'No sir, I was only...'

'What "I was only"? What is this stall? Who is the proprietor?'

Bansilal came off his stool. 'What…? Yes sir, it is me, Bansilal. Why, what happened, sir?'

'Ban-cho I'll complain to your headquarters. Give me your full name.'

'Arey sir, no need to get this angry. Please, let me handle this. Kalki! Apologise. Right now.'

'But saab, I...'

'I said, apologise to our respected customer here right now.'

Kalki turned to the man and bowed. 'Sir, Bhagwaan-ki-kasam, Dharti Mata-ki-kasam, my intention was not what you think. I was only trying to second-guess what book you were looking for. Please, I apologise, from the bottom of my heart.'

'Yes, alright. Better be careful next time. Now, what was I asking for.'

'About her latest, sir. Yes sir, in that case you want *Curtain: Poirot's Last Case*. Excellent choice, sir, if I may be permitted to say so.'

'Yes, that's what I wanted in the first place.'

'Yes, sir, here it is—*Curtain*. Sixteen rupees, fifty paise.'

'Here, take the money...Any good, this? Well, how would you know.'

'Indeed, sir, if I may be allowed to say so, it is excellent. Madam Christie wrote it forty years ago, almost during the same time as her *Murder in Mesopotamia*, but it smells and feels like Poirot is at his best.'

The man gaped in wonder. 'Arey Bansilal, who is this boy, bhai? How is he speaking such good English, hain? And *smells. Feels.* Hercule is his chacha or what.'

Bansilal added his two-penny. 'Arey saab, you will cry buckets at this poor boy's story.'

'Some other ti...'

'He ran away from his village last year and landed up at Mughalsarai. I took pity on him and gave him this job. He is very intelligent, saab, even goes to school every day. He has read *all* the books we have stocked here. Backwards. His favourites are of course Agath...'

The man cut Bansilal in mid-flight. 'I don't have time, boss—train's about to leave.'

'Some other day then...Arey, Kalki beta, go on na, whatever you were telling sir.'

'Ji, saab. So as I was saying, your choice is perfect for your travel to—Cuttak, is it?'

The man looked suspiciously at Kalki. 'What is it to you? I may be going anywhere.'

'No no, I was just asking so I know how much time you have at hand, sir—to finish the novel, you see. Well, anyway, it is sure to keep you awake all through your journey.'

A chin was scratched. 'You think so? I mean, Agatha's lost her touch recently, no?'

'You might be right there, saab—about the late madam, but this was written almost forty years ago.'

The man clearly felt out of depth. He pretended otherwise. 'Ah, I see what you mean.'

Now there was no stopping Kalki. 'What a story, saab, *what a story,* I tell you.'

'Yes yes, no need to...'

'Captain Hastings goes to see Poirot for one last time. Poirot is very sick—in a wheelchair.'

'Yes, well, enough...'

'Poirot tells Hastings there's a murderer in the house and that he will refer to him only as X.'

The man tried to cut in. 'I said, listen boy, that's...'

'This X was not a suspect in five previous murders, but four of the five suspects in those murders are dead.'

'Oye, listen, I said enou...'

'Remember, sir, a fellow named Norton. As you read the *Curtain* tonight, you'll find that Poirot has di...'

'Oye, you little ban-cho. Stop! You bast...'

'But before the great man has left us, he leaves Hastings with some clues. A copy of *Othel...*'

'Right, that's it, ban-cho. Saala, come here you bastard, you are not listening...'

Kalki emerged from his trance. 'What…What, sir?'

'Ban-cho, you are telling me the whole plot. You think you can get back at me like this, haan?'

'Arey no no, sir, you misunderstand. I was just trying to spruce up your interest in *Curtain*.'

'Saaley, to hell with your curtain-shirtain...Oh ban...Is that? That's my signal.'

'Arey saab, wait.'

The man waved his fists. 'You bastard, I'll see to you next time. And you too, Bansilal.'

'…*Kindly pay attention! Coming, from, Firozpur, going, to, Dhanbad, the, three, three, zero, eight, Gangasatluj, Express, via, Firozpur…*'

'Sir, believe me I was...'

'…*Cantt, Mallanwala, Khas Makhu, Lohian, Khas, Malsian, Shahkht…*'

Bansilal pleaded with the man, now darting his way around stray dogs and tin trunks. 'Sir, please.'

'…*Nakodar, Nurmahal, Bilga, Phillaur, Ludhiana…*'

Kalki and Bansilal looked at each other. The background station hum was shattered by belly-slapping laughter.

When both had recovered, Bansilal said: 'Abey Kalki, I could hardly wait. Look at that bastard running for his coach. Saaley, you want me to go bankrupt? Is that it?'

'...*Dhandari, Kalan, Sanahwal, Doraha, Khanna, Govindgarh, Sirhind, Rajpura, Ambala, Cant...*'

'Arey saab, just the opposite.'

'...*Barara, Jagadhri, Saharanpur, Roorkee, Najibabad, Nagina, Dhampur, Seohara, Moradabad...*'

'How so, my little Kalki musahur?'

'Arey saab, this pirated edition has seventy pages upside-down and twenty missing.'

Bansilal instinctively swatted a fly on the face of an annoyed Shatrughan Sinha. 'What?'

'...*Rampur, Bareilly, Pitambarpur, Daryabad, Patranga, Rudauli, Sohwal, Faizabad, Dev, Nagar...*'

'Yes. I found out the hard way. The bastards who do this...I had to hitch a ride all the way to Patna to get to a good copy of *Curtain* and read the end of the story.'

'...*Ayodhya, Goshainganj, Akbarpur, Malipur, Bilwai, Shahganj...*'

'You *are* something, boy. I tell you Kalki, you are something.'

'...*Kheta, Sarai, Mihrawan, Jaunpur, Jalalganj, Khalispur, Babatpur, Varanasi, Kashi, Mughal, Sarai...*'

'Saab, about my daily wage...'

Bansilal flicked the dead fly off Bihari Babu's face. 'Yes yes, in my appreciation of your service, I'll give you not money but that very ban-cho *Curtain*—the one in your hand.'

'...*Saidraja, Bhabua, Road, Kudra, Sasaram, Dehri, Gaya, Hazaribagh, Gomoh, and, Tetulmari...*'

'But saab...'

'Final it is, bhai.'

'Saab, please...saab...yes, madam? You want? *Manorama*?'

'...*will, arrive, at, Mughal, Sarai, at, twentythree, twenty, hours, on, platform, number, seven, Thank you.*'

Bar bar din ye aaye, bar bar din shit laaye; tum karo safai roz ye meri hai arzoo. Happy Burday to you! Happy Burday to you! Happy Buuuurday, dear Marga-r-i-t-a, Happy Burday to you.

Wake up, wake up, children. It is midnight. The clock has struck, the mouse and the scavengers have run out; hickory, dickory freedom. Say your prayers to Bapuji before you leave. Chapter and worse.

Chalo, chalo, jaldi, jaldi. Time and tide wait for no child. Neither does open defecation. Ram, Rahim, Vasudha, Josephine, Leyla, Kalki! Chalo, chalo, time to pick up the tatti. Easier when fresh—doesn't mix with the dog and bull shit that follow a little later. Now pay attention. Be attached to your work, which is picking up shit and not the fruits. And certainly not the money, because money can lead to a landfill. You don't want vultures circling over you, do you now? Embrace your destiny with pride. Nishkam karma. In the eyes of God, we are all equal. Karmanye Vadhikaraste—no to the fruits, no to the fruits, you bhangi. The attachment has to be to the duty. Pick up shit in this life so maybe, just maybe you can pick up a human existence in your next. Imagine being human—ooh!

Haina, bolo bolo. Kalki ko potty se, potty ko Kalki se, pyaaaar hai, pyaaaar hai.

Now, now. Please stick to your task. Children between four and seven—you clean the latrines, go on. Your hands are smaller and more nimble to scoop the poop. And don't touch anything you are not supposed to. You must not steal. It is very bad to take what is not yours. God is watching and keeping notes, especially over the scum. Because scum is like the disease that can spread unchecked, unlike the creamy layer which is like cream and has to be spread carefully. There's never enough to go around, see. Cleanliness is next to godliness and godliness begins with not being a petty thief who steals toothpaste, you hear! Creamy layer only steal cream, not chappals. Chi.

Damn. Toilets are being built, so sad. No more open defecation. Business will go down the drain. Seminars must be held on the importance of open defecation as a business model for an economy that is perpetually orange. What? Yes, yes, forever taking off—neither green nor red. Forever orange. What will the scavengers, those little children we pretend don't exist, eat? Our children, mine, yours. Born dead—dead right. But they look so happy.

That's the beautiful thing about India. Even the poorest of the poor, the Nelson and Gina, the pavitra and the paapi—they all look so happy. Their eyes are sparkling and effervescent. Yes, with temperature—fever. No, no, they are glowing with joy. Poor people are so happy with so little. It is the rich who are difficult. Never happy. In the favelas and townships in Mexico and South Africa, you would be stoned for driving a Lambo. There, Ferrari red is bloody red. But India is truly a free country where you can do what you want. Children will run alongside in delirium, breathe in your exhaust. They are so kind they won't even scratch your car. Freedom. Weep. Freedom sweep.

Haina, bolo, bolo.

Like that, we are very brilliant. Even our poor children are clever. Lack of opportunity. What to do? They breed like rats, these poor people. But see how they MT—multitask. After cleaning the latrines, some of them have graduated to washing cars. And those who have the misfortune of being able to read can be paper boys. Not girls. Because the borrowed cycle is gents only. See, it is a little difficult. Young girls have no underwear so can't ride a gents' cycle—you have to be sensitive to these unseen challenges in the context of the poor and very poor in India. It is not the same thing as being wretched in Brazil. *Obrigada, nagada, nagada.*

We see them everywhere. MTing. Carrying school bags heavier than themselves to accompany their master's vice. Running back and forth like rats between errands—tailor, mochi, vegetable chopper, dhobi and in some cases, homework doer. *Punkh hote toh ud jaati re*...but right now being a punkhawallah would do. Chop chop. Work those arms, little girl.

No need to get any health insurance or pension or for that matter, anything that even distantly resembles a right. We boast that we give them our used clothes and our leftover food. They would be dead without us, no? If they take a day off, we complain about how there's no one to walk the dogs, make tea, unwrap biscuits, bring water, turn on the switch, sharpen the pencil and close the window.

We don't say they actually help our children do their homework. That would be too much. After all, we found her in Dhanbad on a railway station with lice in her matted hair and nose running like the Ganga. If it had not been for us, she would have become a prostitute. She can thank her stars. We have bought her binoculars and nail polish. So she can feel a little sophisticated. Also perfume from Sarojini Nagar and Stayfree from Khan Market. So she stays free. And—and—to-and-fro train fare for her to visit her village every two years. Last year, she even accompanied us to our VIP box at a T20. Good karma. Now she wants to go by plane. See, next she'll ask for Ray-Bans and Victoria's Secret—these people are really quite greedy.

We'll write about you. Observing poverty, hunger and disease is lucrative. It is the stuff of grants and theses and trips to Scandinavia. No worries. Our pickers of night soil and rags, eaters of banana and mango peels will always be there, generation after generation, to tick off the boxes. Looks good on a biodata. Sorry, sorry, CV. Biodata when talking about a ragpicker or a shit collector is really being unkind. Extracurricular activities: Worked for a week in a slum in India where there was no electricity, no 24/7 hot water and no private toilet. And gawd, were the children dirty. But I survived and here I am working for an investment banker.

Haina, bolo, bolo.

There is always a karmic distance to maintain between the lives of the wretched and the rich. Wretched, rich. Wretched, poor. We do so much for them. But what have we done for ourselves? To free ourselves from the tyranny of ordinariness?

And then, suddenly, one crosses the road. Goes from here to there and from there to here. Like a benevolent cuckoo that laid eggs in a crow's nest. Someone who decides to give karma a miss, leaving everything with just a heart and a dream for a compass. Someone who questions all, trusts all, questions nothing, trusts nothing except the now and the here. *Apna haath Jagannath.*

The one who dares will be individually feared and collectively condemned. The one who dares to seek knowledge and live life in a 'non-karmic' way will be damned. Oh, the joys of inverted commas—a great escape. First we will pretend it is not happening. So will the interloper. In India, everybody lives outside the law anyway. Everyone pretends. The poor, the rich, the middle—we all pretend. Survival is pretence.

Campris?

What a splendid marketing tool. Better than the church that has the world convinced it is 2,017 years old. *Immaculada.*

Who are these children? Do they know they are children? How, if they have never had a childhood, never really stolen food from the kitchen or swung a bat to play? How are they children if they have not felt the warmth of a mother's bosom, her smell and her fragrance, the transmitters of culture and traditions, the neurons of character construction and destruction? Did you ever steal ghee, bhangi boy?

How do you know you are a child if you have never cried over a whim or a fancy? How do you know you have arrived even if you have had the best of education? How do you know the other children of midnight don't think you are one. Say it! Are you the one who escaped or the one who got entangled?

It takes eight minutes for sunlight to reach us. And forever for the sun to rise.

But the son also rises. Didn't the father say so— '*He will rise!*' Maybe your own shadow is upset with you.

So are you midnight's child? Say it! Before you rush to die.

7

2004—The Heart of the Matter

Tell her. Tell her. Now. Tell her now, you fool. You waited fifteen years. You stayed up all night yesterday wondering what you will say to her when you meet her at the platform. And now you are tongue-tied. Damn it. I don't know what to say. We have been quiet for ten minutes. This is getting awkward. Go to hell. Why doesn't she say something? Maybe there is no need. Maybe she can read me. Rubbish. She thinks I am an idiot. I am. Am I? So where do I begin. That's a stupid line. Start with something trivial. What is trivia? Relax. Select. Take it easy. What take it easy. She is pretending to be calm. She is acting normal. She can read me. She came all the way to Mumbai just to read me. She is waiting for me to make a false move. How can she act so normal after what happened between us? It's a set-up. Shut up, you idiot. She is Aparajita, your Api. If she can act, so can you. So act. Pretend. Save yourself. Say something.

'Certainly crowded today,' said Akhil, breaking their silent climb up the stairway.

'It is,' replied Aparajita.

What was that, asshole. It is a train station. Train stations are crowded. Shit, I can't do this. Maybe when we reach the guest house I can talk to her. Impossible to make any sense here. The whole damn world is watching us. If you keep postponing, tomorrow never comes. Why? Why are you behaving like this with her? Start with something else. What? Tell her how you refused to take a PhD student last year because her name was Aparajita. I can't tell her that, you jerk. Okay, then. Tell her you have thought of her every single minute of every single day of every single year for the past fifteen years. That sounds cheesy. Anyone can say that. Then go to hell. 37…38…53…I am counting the steps. She belongs to another man. I will keep counting the steps.

Tell him. Tell him. This silence is awful. I am walking with him. With him. Good lord, him. I am going to keep it simple. I can't say it here, so be quiet. Why on earth does he not say something? Maybe he feels nothing. I know that is not true, but then what do I really know? Tell him the damn truth, the damn truth. That I came just to see him. That I wanted to see him. But why did I want to see him? Do you know that? No, I don't. How can I? After all that happened between us. Tell him you stopped caring about your life, tell him you take each day as it comes, that you breathe a sigh of relief once it is behind you. Tell him you don't care, that you are like the wind, you drift and you reach places you don't want to or care about. Tell him you miss him but you fear telling him that. Tell him the truth. But I can't, and besides not now. The whole damn world is watching us. And what will he think, what will he say…you are married and he will think you are nasty to still have such thoughts about him. But this is your chance to tell him, yes he will think…gosh, why is this so difficult? I thought I had smiled my way well through the nervousness. Yes, I thought I was brilliant, wasn't I? I smiled when all I wanted was for the earth to open up and take me in. I laughed, I cracked jokes, when inside, I was hurting. But why was I hurting? Oh God, this is unbearable. Isn't he the reason for your coming to Bombay? Go on, be honest. Well, let him say something first. He should start, yes he should. Let him say something first. Oh that's so typical of you, you fool, you coward. Listen, you must say something now now. Now.

'Arey here, give me that suitcase,' said Api, clearing her throat.

'…*Kindly, Pay, Attention! The, Six, Zero, One, Zero, Mumbai, Mail, from…*'

'No, it's fine,' said Akhil, relieved the tension was broken at last.

'Listen Akhil, it's no bother really. I'll take a taxi to the guest house.'

'...*Chennai, to, Mumbai, Central, Via, Trivellore, Arakkonam, Tiruttani, Puttur, Renigunta, Koduru, Razampeta, Nandalur, Cuddapah*...'

'No, I told you na, it's a day off for me.'

'...*Kamalapuram, Yerraguntla, Muddanuru, Kondapuram, Tadipatri*...'

'Alright. But aren't we going in the other direction?'

'Relax, Api. I have escorted many women from platforms to guest houses.'

'...*Rayalcheruvu, Gooty, Guntakal, Junction, Nagarur, Adoni, Kupgal, Kosgi, Manthralayam, Road, Matmari, Raichur, Krishna, Narayanpet, Road*...'

Api stopped in her tracks. 'I say, Akhil.'

'...but none as beautiful as you.'

'Watch it. You don't want to be escorted from the platform to the police station.'

'...*Yadgir, Nalwar, Wadi, Shahabad, Gulbarga, Ganagapur, Road, Dudhani*...'

'Just what you would expect from a police memsaab for all your troubles.'

'Achha Baba, enough, na. I know you can flirt.'

'...*Akalkot, Road, Hotgi, Solapur, Junction, Mohol, Madha, Kurduvadi*...'

'Thought you'd forgotten...Arey coolie. Is that St George Road gate still open?'

'...*Kem, Jeur, Bhigwan, Daund, Junction, Pune, Junction, Khadki, Lonavala*...'

'It is, saab. Closes only after five.'

'Thanks. Come, Api, we'll take a shortcut to the car park.'

'...*Karjat, Kalyan, Junction, Thane and Dadar, is, arriving, at, platform, number, Seven, thank, you*...'

'I am after you...'

'Behind you, Api, *behind* you.'

Api smiled. 'One and the same.'

'So, back in college, were you behind me, or after me?'

'Neither. *You* were after me.'

'And then I looked back and you weren't behind me.'

The witticism backfired. Akhil tried to smooth over the thing. 'Joke. Arey joke, yaar.'

'Really, that's not funny, Akhil.'

'Achha sorry, bas. Leave it na, boss, come on.'

The two squeezed through the side exit and were accosted right away by touts. But they were seasoned at this—the trick was to keep walking. For a moment, Akhil lost sight of Api, who, understandably, had attracted more of the swarm. He managed to catch her by her wrist and pull her to safety. Akhil located the attendant carrying a wire loop overflowing with key bunches, swapped a ten-rupee note for his car keys, and together with Aparajita, navigated his way through the impossible mess, made more impossible by cars in neutral parked bumper to bumper in multiple rows with just about enough space to get through.

'You can let go of my wrist now,' said Api, smiling.

'Oh, sorry. I didn't even notice,' said Akhil, embarrassed, as he put down the suitcase and shoved a car away using his backside.

'Hahh...so, here we are.'

Api couldn't help the look of astonishment. 'Hang on a minute. And what in heaven's name do we have here?'

Wiping the sweat from his face and neck, Akhil looked at Api. 'What?'

'This. A *Fiat*. You must be joking.'

'Why, what's the problem? You allergic to Fiats?'

'Listen sweetheart, tell me if they aren't paying you well. I am sure you are well qualified for a constable's naukri. I'll talk to Ajay—constables earn a packet these days. I know of one who drives a *Honda City*...a Fiat.'

'Listen, my apsara. I own this dream car by choice, for your kind information. I mean, what's wrong with it?'

The flirting, the bonhomie. Sweetheart. Apsara. It was obvious to Api that both she and Akhil were trying desperately to overcome their unease. She plodded on. 'Dream car? Ekdum mad.'

'Leave it, yaar. Come, get in. Or would you like to sit in the back? Whatever suits you, memsaab.'

'No no, I don't want to be leered at through the rearview mirror. So, did you buy this or was it excavated?'

Akhil pulled the door open for Api, then made his way back to the boot. Placing the suitcases by the stepney, he flicked the supporting hook loose, and after a couple of mock drops, let go of the lid. 'Forty thousand, I paid, for my wife.'

'Your wife.'

'Padmini.'

Akhil turned the ignition, and then again, this time narrowing his eyes as though saying a silent prayer. Padmini grunted to life with reluctance. In celebration, he revved the engine.

Api gave out a chuckle. 'Namaste, Padminiji.'

Akhil noticed Api fanning herself with the end of her pallu and reached over to his left to twist the rhino horn of the vent window; it swung out half-heartedly.

'Thanks,' said Api. 'Ab chaliye, Padminiji. Your hubby is all set to be led by you.'

'I am her second husband. But the first one only had good things to say about her.'

'Oh. Passed on, is she?'

'Respect a man's choice, will you? I mean, thankfully—I was about to land up with Premier Aparajita, or was Aparajita the first name? I can't remember. Well anyway, some get Padminis, some have to make do with Aparajitas.'

Akhil was looking straight ahead but he knew already that the joke had misfired. This was to be expected. It was too much for the brain to manage—anxiety, nervousness, anger, irritation, happiness, joy, pretence. Some steam was inevitable.

'Really, Akhil.'

'What?'

'No really yaar, this is not done.'

Akhil pulled over to the side. He looked at Api. 'Arey, a joke yaar.'

Api, knowing Akhil's condition, didn't really mind the joke but pretended otherwise. 'Not done means not done.'

'Come on! What happened to your famous sense of humour? Oh, hang on, sorry, that was me.'

'Now, can we please make a move? Or should I do an aarti of your dear wife first?'

Akhil smiled and turned away, relieved. He honked to scare away a few stray dogs that had come sniffing, and continued onwards on their journey.

Api was relieved, too. This jumpiness from both of them was palpable. Perhaps, she thought, it was to be expected—seeing each other as they were after fifteen long years. She tried to lighten up. 'You *are* mad. And judging by the present condition of dear Padmini, probably a wife beater, too.'

'That's slanderous—I could never. It's just that every now and then my Padmini thinks she has had enough of me, drifts and veers towards other men...'

'By other men you mean Qualises, Santros, Ambassadors…'

Akhil nodded his head. 'Precisely.'

'She's a swinger then, is dear Padmini.'

'Well, at least one of us is.'

'I don't blame her.'

'Well anyway, so that's the explanation for her nicks, chips, dents…'

'Broken backside—sorry, bumper.'

'Dark spots.'

'Twisted axle.'

'Busted taillights.'

'Ruptured exhaust.'

'Cracked windshield.'

'Smelly glove box.'

'Defective tachometer…smelly glove box? Oh come on, that's too harsh. She doesn't smell.'

'This foul smell must be your doing, then. Sorry, Padmini, sorry. I thought the wife was to blame.'

Akhil laughed. 'So often the misunderstanding.'

'So, met anyone from Padmini's family?'

'That's the great thing about her—no obnoxious in-laws.'

He had done it again. 'Shit, sorry, listen, I didn't mean…sorry yaar, really, Api. Got carried away with all this stupid nonsense, you know. Really, I am sorry, okay?'

Api looked out the window. She knew she had to be ready to drink all the poison. She closed her eyes and then opened them again, ready to take it all.

'I said sorry na. Please, Api, now forget it. You want a Gold Flake?'

Akhil plopped the packet and the lighter in Api's lap and snatched open the ashtray from the dashboard. Api lit two cigarettes and jammed one in Akhil's mouth. Only a second later did it dawn on her that she had acted absentmindedly, a reflex coerced by memories, of years long past. Akhil realised it, too, but pretended to overlook it. He nursed a hearty drag, then let the smoke seep out slowly from the nose. 'Thanks…'

No one spoke for the next few minutes. The silence was unbearable. It got to Akhil first.

'Hey, Api yaar, I said sorry na.'

'Haan? No no, nothing…'

'Come on yaar, we are meeting after fifteen years. Put it down to the, down to the…*insufferable excitement* of seeing you again.'

Api smiled. 'Achha yaar, forget it. Forgiven.'

'That's like a good friend. We are friends now, no Api?'

'Yes, why not?'

'Why not.'

'So…'

'Listening…'

'Does your Padmini...'

Akhil smacked the steering. 'Not again yaar, Aps, please—enough of Padmini for a day I think.'

'I was about to say, does your Padmini sing, too.'

'Like a koyal.'

'What's stopping her, then?'

Akhil stole his eyes away from the road for a moment and rummaged through the glove box. 'Why not. What would you—is there a song you have in mind you want my Padmini to sing?'

'No, we'll go by her husband's choice.'

'As you please…'

Akhil got hold of a cassette and used his teeth to flick open the cover. He pushed the cassette into the music system.

'*...Aa jaao tadapte hain armaan...ab raat guzarane waalee hain...ab raat guzarane waalee hain...*'

'Good God. I didn't even know this was available on tape.'

'*...main row-oon yahaan, tum chup ho wahaan...ab raat guzarane waalee hain...ab raat guzarane waalee hain...*'

Akhil adjusted the volume. 'Course it is.'

'*...chaand kee rangat udane lagee…wo taaron ke dil ab doob gaye... doob gaye...*'

'What has become of you? The world has moved on you know, Mr Devdas.'

Akhil contorted his face to bring out the *Devdas* look, and broke into the translation, placing a hand on his heart for added effect. 'Yes, *but I still ache for my beloved…when the night is passing by…*'

Lata, unconcerned, continued with her mesmerising. '*...hain dard bharaa bechain samaan...ab raat guzarane waalee hain...ab raat guzarane waalee hain...*'

'*…and I still cry here…while you are silent there…*'

Api raised her eyebrows together with a reproachful smile. 'Who, me? I think your love for Padmini has affected you irreparably. Sorry Pads, but I think it is time to look for a two-legged wife for my Akhil—not a four-wheeled one.'

'*…is chaand ke dolay mein aaee nazar...ye raat kee dulhan chal dee kidhar…chal dee kidhar...*'

'You think so?'

'In the little time I have spent with you today, I *know* so.'

'*…aawaaz toh do, khoye ho kahaan...ab raat guzarane waalee hain... ab raat guzarane waalee hain...*'

'Then can I please have one with a spacious boot?'

'Akhil!'

'…With those large, wondrous, calf-like eyes that my Padmini has.'

'Padmini has calf-like eyes? Oh, stop it now.'

'...ghabaraake nazar bhee haar gayee, takadeer ko bhee neend aane lagee...neend aane lagee...'

Akhil threw his head back and laughed. 'Just one last thing while we are on the topic. So, you are going to be on the lookout for me, I take it?'

'You leave me with no choice. It's either this or watching my Akhil descend into complete and utter madness.'

'...tum aate nahee, main jaaoon kahaan...ab raat guzarane waalee hain...ab raat guzarane waalee hain...'

'*My* Akhil?'

'...'

Just a minor misfire this time, thought Akhil cheerfully. 'Good. So I can stop my own search then.'

'You mean you had put in your application at Rishtey hi Rishtey, twenty-eight Raugarhpura? I knew it!'

'Not yet. But I'll take a pass now.'

'...Aa jaao tadapte hain aramaan...ab raat guzarane waalee hain... ab raat guzarane waalee hain...'

'So. What kind of woman would you want as your wife? Turn that prehistoric gramophone off, will you?'

'...ab raat guza...'

'Sorry, what was that?'

'I asked, what kind of wife...'

'One not like you; sorry, like you; sorry, not like you.'

'Decide, man.'

'Seriously? You want to know? Or rather, you don't know?'

'How would I, Akhil?'

'Indeed, how would you.'

'...'

Akhil tried to think of something witty, but in the end, could only muster a meek 'So...'

Api replied in equal measure. 'So...'

'Shit, listen yaar Api, this is getting a bit sil...'

Api saved the day. 'Arey Akhil, are you in touch with any of the buggers from college?'

'Off and on. Most of them married now, with kids. Some divorced...'

'Ya? Like who?'

'Remember Gaurav Batra? Drinks man at Stephen's–Hindu basketball matches? Presently teaches at American University.'

'Which one?'

'No, American University, as in Delhi University.'

'Oh…and Anupam?'

'Was trying to communicate with some Nicobar tribes last I heard.'

'Fat Bugga?'

'Runs a start-up in San Fran; calls it 3.1417—for pi. Typical.'

'Any sweetie pie for him yet?'

'No, but apple pies, lots, judging by his love handles.'

'And what of the ladies?'

'What of them?'

'Anyone you are in touch with?'

'Rupali joined the UN as a translator, and Piya pitched her tent on the banks of Narmada along with Medha. And of course, there was this one woman who sought secure pastures and married an IPS officer. Now who was that, I wonder.'

'Shut up.'

Careful now, Akhil warned himself. '…Busy travelling with her entourage of maalis and dhobis and aayaahs to all sorts of hill stations.'

'What absolute rot.'

'Hob-nobbing at IHC, IIC, Gymkhana, even shady circuit houses.'

'Nonsense. We got admitted to Gymkhana only last year.'

'Admitted. Sounds like a hospital. Hope your vaccinations are up to date.'

'Ha-ha-ha, very funny.'

'But tell me, seriously. How do you guys spend your time?'

'Well, my dear husband keeps himself busy in matters of the state.'

'Nabbing pocket-maars, twiddling the ears of roadside bhelpoori-waalaas, that sort of thing.'

'Stop it. And yours truly...'

'You were once.'

Can't help it, can you, you smart little twat, moaned Akhil, and hung around, like a child caught with his hand in the cookie jar, for the outcome of this current stupidity.

Thankfully for him, Api carried on. '...and yours truly supervises PhD students on a foreign language—and writes some treatise occasionally.'

'Ya? What was the last one?'

'An exploration of the possibility of the presence of elements of stream of consciousness in the poetry of T.S. Eliot.'

'What in God's name?'

Api rushed her hand to steady the steering wheel. '*Watch it*—with that scooter.'

'Sorry. What was it—stream, something, something...'

'Consciousness.'

'And people think we scientists are the crazy ones.'

'Count them—you'd find twice as many psychotic writers as scientists.'

'So you keep away from IPS-memsaab kitty parties then, I take it.'

'If you are interested, there are some very pretty IPS-memsaabs floating around—recently single.'

'I am alright with my Padmini, thank you.'

'No, really. Nice bumpers, too.'

'Leave it na. So...given any demonstration of your anarchist tendencies lately?'

'Protested over stuff, you mean? Nothing much. But did lead a morcha to the Crime Against Women Cell recently—was tear-gassed.'

'Nasty.'

'All this while, haven't really asked you about your life.'

'So ask.'

'Well, how's life?'

'Good.'

Api gave a pleading look. 'Akhil. Tell na.'

'What's there to tell yaar? Research and teaching keeps me busy...'

'Just busy? Or very busy?'

'There are days...but you know, being in this profession—if you can call it that—it gives you room to think about a lot of things... what people in other jobs don't bother straining their brains on; a different perspective on things, the way the world works...science is a bit of a back-room thing, it slips in quietly.'

'Tell me—is it frustrating?'

'Sure it is. But then again, it's a little different from you guys—the arts, I mean.'

'Like how?'

'Okay. For example, you read a great book or admire a great painting—what do you feel immediately afterwards? You say to yourself: Wow. Fantastic. How could this person write so well, paint so well?'

'Yes...'

'But you know, when *I* see a great work of science, when it comes out in the open, you know what I think? I think: Shit. Bastard. Why the hell didn't *I* think of it.'

Api asked in all seriousness. 'You do?'

'Yes, and *there's* the difference. A part of me feels gutted. I go into self-ridicule. I start analysing my frailties. I am sad for days. I shouldn't be but somehow I manage to...I am telling you the reality. Of course, in public...'

'So you get envious, resentful, jealous, self-obsessed...'

'No, it's not that, it's not in a bad sense at all. I feel...I lost out—but in a good clean sense. When Mullis came up with PCR—you know, the guy who got the Nobel. Polymerase chain reaction.'

'Used in DNA fingerprinting, right?'

'Yes...well, when I first heard of it I felt gutted. All the reagents, the DNA, the polymerase, the primers, they were at hand. And such a simple idea. Why couldn't *I* think of it, too? And guess where the bugger was when he got the idea? Stuck in a traffic jam in California, with his girlfriend.'

'Ah.'

'So that's the beauty of it. Science is a wholly individual exercise. And it works in small steps. I mean, you never see a writer with a brilliant idea writing a book that's *one* page, do you. But here, it is that one page, *one* line idea—that spark—is what matters. And when you see someone get that brilliant idea, you feel good for the dog but bad for yourself.'

'Yes, I see what you mean.'

'With you guys, it never happens that a writer curses himself for not writing the exact masterpiece he just read, cursing that the whole English language was at his disposal, too.'

'True.'

'You guys admire it—the masterpiece, but you don't feel bad about yourself.'

Api couldn't agree more. 'Yes...'

'And this can be disconcerting. You see, at the core is the...'

Api looked out the window, at the millions of small shops claiming to sell everything from a screwdriver down to a screw. Everyone left to fend for themselves, everyone fending for themselves.

'I am boring you.'

'No no. So you must feel lonely...'

'It can get mundane at times. I would have preferred being a theoretical scientist. All you need is a little paper and pencil—no equipment, no reagents, you know, not dependent on grant agencies, the bureaucracy. But what's the point of doing science here anyway, haan? Look at the state of our country. I mean, how can I hide myself in my lab and forget all this...damn thing gets to me at times. Anyway, I am quite philosophical about it.'

'Are you now. Akhil the philosopher. So, philosopher saab, tell me about your social life.'

'First you. What's your story?'

Api stayed silent for a long time. Then, slowly, measuring her words, she said, 'Do naphthalene balls have a story?'

Instinctively, Akhil wanted to ask what she meant, but held back. They drove in slience for the next ten minutes.

Akhil said, 'That made me think, Api.'

'Sometimes a single sentence is enough.'

'I am sorry.'

'Imprisoned in a cupboard, slowly, without telling anyone, without showing it, the naphthalene ball gets smaller and smaller. And then it disappears, even the odour, the scent, all traces.'

Akhil stole a glance at Api.

'That's my story.'

'Not very different from mine, then.'

Api tried to cheer up. 'Don't be silly. Your turn. And please, for my sake, something more than just one sentence.'

'There's nothing really to tell.'

'Come on, that can't be.'

'It is either the lab or the flat.'

Api poked one more time. 'No friends, et cetera?'

'I keep myself busy, though. I do my little bits here and there, you know.'

'So…all in all, after hearing the defence of Muzrim Akhil Sukumar, I have come to the conclusion the muzrim must urgently be fixed up with a beautiful, understanding...'

'Leave it, Api. I am okay as I am. Why ruin someone else's life?'

'What makes you think you will ruin her life?'

'What makes you think I won't?'

'I detect some bitterness...'

Akhil exploded. 'Bitterness? *Bitterness*. Look at my best friend. The bugger hasn't even bothered to see me for fifteen years. He's been in some other Brahmaand all this while.'

'Come on yaar, you know it's not like that. We have been...'

Akhil knew he was losing it but he couldn't stop. 'And what does he have that I don't? Oh yes, he has Aparajita. *My* Aparajita.'

'Akh...'

'The Aparajita who made ten promises and seven vows behind the college chapel. The Aparajita who herself was vanquished by the rules of this society.'

'…'

'It's funny how Aparajita means the one who cannot be vanquished. It really should be the one who bloody choked.'

How far is too far. How much more can you stretch a man's endurance before you break it into a million pieces, before the thrill of I-can't-care-less grips you.

'Look, I am sorry, Api. I don't know what came over me. This is stupid...'

'No, Akhil, it is my fault. I somehow imagined time would have covered up all those terrible...'

'Guess I turned out to be a little more difficult to cover up than time had imagined.'

'Coming to Mumbai was a mistake…'

'No, don't say that, Api, don't. Don't make that face, Api, don't cry now. I had promised myself I would behave, that I would try and wipe off the past, but looks like I couldn't do it. I tried—could you at least not grant me that? Fifteen years of loneliness, of silence...'

'Akhil…'

'Fifteen years of hate, anger, sadness, disgust, I kept it to myself.'

'My Akhil…'

'Could you not overlook my crime, just this once? I mean it when I say that I am very happy for you, and of course for your bastard husband. I really mean it.'

'I know you do.'

'So forgive me.'

'Of course, sweetheart.'

'And don't call me that.'

'Th-ha. Okay.'

'Thank you.'

Api looked at him adoringly.

'Do you realise, Api, that all this while my Padmini has been listening quietly to our conversation?'

'No never, no Padmini, please! She is the root of all our troubles.'

'Women usually are.'

'That's not how you thought when you wrote that poem in my honour, did you, Devdas ji?'

'Which one?'

Api smiled. 'You mean you wrote more than one?'

'Well, how else can one do justice to your immense beauty?'

'Shaawd-upp.'

'Ya, I remember. Goddamn cheesy it was, too.'

Api protested. 'Hey, I thought it was beautiful.'

'You did? You should have said so at the time.'

'Well, you know how girls were back in those days—stupid, timid, petite…'

'Two outta three ain't bad.'

'Very funny. You remember that you wrote a poem, or you remember the poem itself?'

'What do you think?'

'I don't believe you.'

Akhil shook his head mockingly and cleared his throat. 'Aps, Aps, Aps. *For my nights that gently sleep...*'

'No way. No bloody way.'

'*...Are awakened by the light of your morning*
And my eyes that gently weep
Are opened by your whispers that say nothing
Is it your smile or your frown that kills me
That I cannot decide
Is it my pleasure or my pain when I see you
That I cannot hide
I can't recall the time you were gone
Is it a week, a month, a year
I can't forget your last words
To yearn, to ache, is to fear
There was that night, there was that rain
There were your arms, there was your grip
There were your locks, twisting in the wind
There was your smell, there was your lip.
And the night came again, so did the rain
But the arms were gone, so was the grip
And the locks, those locks, away they sailed
But your smell remains, as does your lip.'

Akhil looked triumphantly at Api. 'What? What are you looking at? You thought I'd forgotten it, did you? I wrote it. What is astonishing is that *you* remember it. Or do you?'

'Why would I forget it...how could *I* have forgotten it?'

'I don't know—too many reasons.'

'Never enough.'

'Gratified.'

'...the horror—the horror.'

Akhil stole a glance at Api. 'What? What horror?'

'No, Professor saab, I meant the horror—the horror that you remembered it.'

'What is so horrible about that?'

'No, it is horror in a nice sort of way—like astonishing, oh-my-God oh-my-God. Understood, budhoo?'

Akhil looked a little lost.

Api smiled. 'Heart of Darkness...Conrad...No?'

'Don't know what you are on about.'

'No, the phrase "the horror, the horror", taken from Conrad.'

Akhil wore the expression of a Tamil boy lost in a Latin class. He ducked his head out and noticed they were on Pedder Road.

Api was laughing. 'You mean…good lordy. You mean it has only ever been sulphuric acid and ammonia and benzene and salt and pepper?'

'What's so funny?'

'Come-awnn. You are talking to a lecturer in English, my test-tube loving primate—and you tell me you haven't read a single word that wasn't your silly chemistry?'

'Well, you are talking to an assistant professor in chemistry, my vilaayti mem—ever heard of Grignard Reagent? No?'

'*Ulysses*...No?'

'Diels-Alder Reaction...No?'

'*Catch-22*...No?'

'Swern Oxidation...No?'

'*Slaughterhouse-Five*...No?'

'Wittig Reaction...No?'

'*The Great Gatsby*...No?'

'Schotten-Baumann Reaction...No?'

'*Animal Farm*...No?'

'Yamaguchi Esterification...No?'

'*Lolita*...No?'

'Wolff-Kishner Reduction...No?'

'*The Grapes of Wrath*...No?'

'Reformatsky Reaction...No?'

'*Under the Volcano*...No?'

'Ullmann Reaction...No?'

'*I, Claudius*...No?'

'Fukuyama Coupling...No?'

'*A Clockwork Orange*...No?'

'Rosenmund-von Braun Reaction...No?'
'*To the Lighthouse*...No?'
'Rosenmund Reduction...No?'
'*A Portrait of the Artist as a Young Man*...No?'
'Baker-Venkataraman Rearrangement...No?'
'*Deliverance*...No?'
'Clemmensen Reduction...No?'
'*An American Tragedy*...No?'
'Cope Elimination...No?'
'*As I Lay Dying*...No?'
'Dess-Martin Oxidation...No?'
'*The Joke*...No?'
'Mitsunobu Reaction...No?'
'*Native Son*...No?'
'Arbuzov Reaction...No?'
'*The Good Soldier*...No?'
'Doebner Modification...No?'
'*Henderson the Rain King*...No?'
'Eschweiler-Clarke Reaction...No?'
'*On the Road*...No?'
'Heck Reaction...No?'
'*The Postman Always Rings Twice*...No?'
'Favorskii Reaction...No?'
'*Appointment In Samarra*...No?'
'Finnegans Wake...No?'
'*A Passage to India*...No?'
'Friedel-Crafts Acylation...No?'
'*The Alexandria Quartet*...No?'
'Grubbs Reaction...No?'
'*The Way of All Flesh*...No?'
'Hofmann Elimination...No?'
'*Light In August*...No?'
'Cannizzaro Oxidation Reduction...No?'
'*The Wings of the Dove*...No?'
'Horner-Wadsworth-Emmons Reaction...No?'
'*Tender Is the Night*...No?'
'Hunsdiecker Reaction...No?'

'*All the King's Men*...No?'
'Meerwein-Ponndorf-Verley Reduction...No?'
'*The Bridge of San Luis Rey*...No?'
'Michael Addition...No?'
'*Go Tell It On the Mountain*...No?'
'Iwanow Reaction...No?'
'*Lord of the Flies*...No?'
'Kochi Reaction...No?'
'*A Dance to the Music of Time*...No?'
'Nozaki-Hiyama Coupling...No?'
'*A Bend In The River*...No?'
'Oppenauer Oxidation...No?'
'*Death Comes for the Archbishop*...No?'
'Overman Rearrangement...No?'
'*Ragtime*...No?'
'Mannich Reaction...No?'
'*Angle of Repose*...No?'
'Passerini Reaction...No?'
'*The Catcher In the Rye*...No?'
'Pechmann Condensation...No?'
'*Of Human Bondage*...No?'
'Wurtz Reaction...No?'
'*A Farewell to Arms*...No?'
'Sharpless Epoxidation...No?'
'*Lord Jim*...No?'
'Sandmeyer Reaction...No?'
'*The Prime of Miss Jean Brodie*...No?'
'Wenker Synthesis...No?'
'*Kim*...No?'
'Staudinger Cycloaddition...No?'
'*Winesberg, Ohio*...No?'
'Tamao-Kumada Oxidation...No?'
'*Sophie's Choice*...No?'
'Woodward cis-Hydroxylation...No?'

Can't trust her. Wears short skirts, smokes, drinks. Goes out with boys. Comes home at odd hours. No character. She was also seen buying tampons. Why would an unmarried girl buy tampons? Also beer. Pretends to listen to Indian classical music so she can fool us. Outside she does Bollywood dance. Don't trust but verify. It is our aadhaar.

He is a good man. Always obeys his parents. Only social drinker. No bad habits. Had some girlfriends. It's normal. After all, what is there? He only exchanges books and music with them. At least it proves he is not a homosexual or a transgender. Thank God. At the right time we can find a nice girl for him. From a good family. Trust but verify.

Indians don't have sex. Especially the men. Beef outside is okay, not in the house. Foreign cows are even better. Foreigners like the *Kama Sutra* because they begin from a very young age. In South India, we have Syama Sastri—music, music, divine music. Love? What has love got to do with anything? What has love got to do with marriage? What has marriage to do with sex? What has anything got to do with anything in a culture where every relationship has an accepted name? Wife, daughter, mother, sister, cousin sister, cleaning lady, pati, aunty. Woman? Okay, how about lady? No? Okay—cook and caretaker.

Beware of the single, unattached woman. Something must be wrong with her. How can she be good-looking, educated and single? Has the three-body problem ever been solved? One can understand if she was ugly or had buck teeth. Maybe she has a thyroid problem. Must recommend her to a good specialist—he will sort her out.

In a society where it is difficult to tell the difference between misogyny and patriarchy, the best trick in the book is to blame the woman. In a country where millions of women have spent entire lives protecting the reputation of the family, who gets to throw the first stone at Magdalene There is not a single woman in any part of the world who has not been a witness to or been a victim of violence and sexual harassment—from rape to thrashing, from starvation to ostracising. How long can we take this? How long can a woman remain unwoman so society can accept her? Intellect, in the absence of social choices, is falsely primed but when a personal decision has to be made—like picking a life partner—multitudinous variables kick in. Blackmail works.

When it suits us, women are worshipped and revered. When it suits us, women are indulged in, admired, and even treated as equals. When it suits us, we praise women who destroy their bodies and souls because suffering builds a woman's character. When it suits us, she is playing victim. When it suits us, it doesn't suit us. And when it doesn't suit us, she must be a prostitute. Not a devadasi. Yallamma! A prostitute.

When it suits us, we'll even borrow a pinch of clay from where whores live to shape a Goddess.

When it suits us.

How can you love when you have not been loved? How can you occupy your own space when you have been occupied by others? How can you even begin to feel like a child, a daughter, a young woman, a lover in a country where the first time most women encounter their sexuality is either through abuse or disease? How can you even begin to understand that every relationship has a place, a time and a border, when every space is violated and turned upside down?

Akhil and Aparajita fell in love. Serves them right. Only in English do people 'fall' in love. In Hindi, they don't. In Hindi we say, '*Mujhe tumse pyar ho gaya hai*' and not '*Main pyar mein gir gaya*'. See? And therein lies our culture. Equal-equal, same-same. Everything can be said behind the temple. The arangetram is on the stage, but the classes, the shrutibhedam is at home. In the afternoons. When you grow up, you will understand what women mean when they say, 'In the end he will come back to his family'. You will understand after you get married why that cleaning lady was asked to leave. She jumped on the master of the house. And she was "pet sey". So she was shipped off to some back-of-the-beyond hamlet with a little money never to be heard of again. That's how we treat our women. That's how Indian women treat other Indian women. Generally. That's how women opposed to such practices also learn to keep silent. Not all, but most. Choice is a luxury.

You have to be cultured to understand that violence against women is part of human history. Historically, armies have killed the men and raped the women. That is why in some cultures you can have four wives. Because all the men are dead and who will keep the production neé progeny going?

That is the heart of the matter. That is how victors write history. That is how the strong in a family tell stories. There will always be a loose woman in every family. You see, India is a great civilisation. We live in many centuries. Our women understand this. That is why there is no place like India. For women. And that is why there is no place for women in India. Everything depends on what you are dealt.

Have you ever fallen in love? Did you tell him? Or did you just keep your feelings to yourself because you were confused and kept muttering: *'Is rishte ko kya naam doon*?'

Or you want to let him slip by only to see him after fifteen years? Yeah, we can arrange that, too. What's the matter with you—you have no heart?

Darpok!

Kai rishton kay naam nahi hotey—the very universe that frightens you makes you think like this. It is okay to be different. It is okay to be of a different level of culture. It is okay to be childlike and philosophical at the same time. These are all but manifestations of the atman. Of that, there is only one. Atman wearing skirts is also acceptable as is the one wearing pink-striped shoes.

8

1984—Nineteen Eighty-Four

'Now imagine you are stubbing a cigarette,' shouted someone amid the cacophony that engulfed a first-floor room in Allnutt North.

'Y-yes, sir,' mumbled both Akhil and Ajay, addressing second- and third-year students of St Stephen's College, New Delhi.

'Good. Now imagine you are rubbing your back with a towel held stretched between your hands,' barked another as a cigarette switched toes among the seniors.

'Sir, like this?' asked Ajay.

'Haan ban-cho, like that. And don't question your senior—*ever*.'

'S-sorry sir, didn't mean...' apologised the petrified fuchha.

Akhil, meanwhile, had continued to stub the imaginary cigarette, his performance now reminiscent of a disinterested factory worker tucking his 400th Dunlop tube into a cycle tyre.

'*Now*,' snarled one communist-looking senior, 'Now, yes,' struggling to make sense amid peals of thigh-slapping laughter. His friend, also on laughing gas, took over. 'Yes, now wipe and stub at the same time,' he demanded. 'Wipe and stub, wipe and stub.'

Akhil and Ajay followed the sacrosanct decree in the throes of guffawing and convulsing. The belly dancers wiped and stubbed, wiped and stubbed, with stoic expressions on their faces, not daring to look directly at their commandants, but stealing glances at each other as if to say, 'Saalon. Our turn will come, too, you'll see.'

The unusual dance lasted a few more minutes until one of the seniors took pity on his friends, who by now resembled Hare Krishna hippies hallucinating before their maharishi. 'Okay, bas, bas,' said the kind man. '*Chhod do saalon ko, yaar*,' proposed another. Akhil and Ajay looked at this God incarnate and thanked him with their watery eyes.

'Haan yaar, enough of these two,' said a third. 'Bastards don't know even *one* dirty song, not one. How will they survive until the freshers' night, man?'

The reference was to the celebratory night to be held a fortnight later, which formally marked an end to ragging. For Akhil and Ajay, this night seemed a good hundred years into the future.

'Thank you, sirs. Really, *really,* thank you,' they blurted and started for the door.

One lord rose and hailed them back. 'Not so fast, saalon,' he said. 'You need to visit room A-8. A bastard called Kha-khao lives there. Taekwondo champion. Chinky. Once ate a dog with butter naan. What was the name?'

'Kha–, Kha-khao, sir,' said Ajay, about to faint.

'Yes, Kha-khao. So you two, you go to Kha-khao and get his intro. Other intros will follow after you have got his.'

By intro, this peer of the realm, meant Introduction—that prized possession of a senior's name, the harbinger of relief from ragging.

'Y-yes, sir,' stammered Akhil.

'Then run, babes, run. I want you knocking at Kha-khao's door in two minutes flat. Now *shoot.*'

Akhil and Ajay bolted like the proverbial horse with a jalapeno embedded in its posterior. In preparation for what was to follow, the moon slipped under a grey cloud, just as the two lambs, desperately short of breath, knocked at the slaughterhouse door.

'Who is it, bey?' came a terrifying voice from inside.

'Sir, Akhil and Ajay,' bleated the lambs, knees jangling.

'Who? Louder.'

'Sir, Akhil and Ajay.'

'Oh, ho ho. Come in, come in. Who sent you?'

No one knew whether Kha-khao was the first name or a surname, but it was clear from the first glance at him that the man needed as much 'introduction' as a lion in his lair. There was also an uncanny resemblance between the two species, down to the ruffled mane, that Kha-khao caressed forebodingly from time to time.

'I asked you a question. And I don't like repeating myself.'

'Sir, Laddu sir and Ahirwal sir.'

Sprawled on either side of Kha-khao were two of his chums. Both looked distinctly non-mammalian. One was flipping through *Debonair* while the other was trying ever so carefully to pry open glued pages of *Penthouse*. They looked up.

'Oh-ho-ho-ho. Freshers, haan. Fuchhas.'

Akhil realised he was shaking despite holding himself together. He investigated and discovered that in fact he was *being* shaken by Ajay standing adjacent and vibrating like a tuning fork. He inched away a little. 'Y-yes, sir. Fuchhas.'

Kha-khao drew them in. 'Come, come. Stand over there. Close your eyes, both of you.'

'Sir?'

'Are you deaf?'

Ajay was non-committal. 'No sir...yes sir.'

'Good. Now tell me—first you...Akhil you said, no? Ya, tell me how many of us are here and where we are from.'

'Sir?' interrupted Ajay.

'Shut up. Did I ask you? What was your name, again? Ajay? Ya, take that chair, put it by the wardrobe, get on it, climb up the wardrobe and go hide yourself on the top shelf.'

'Sir? But...'

'*Now*.'

'Ye-yes, s-sir.'

Ajay dragged the chair by the wardrobe and paused for a second. He looked at Kha-khao, and, without pausing this time round, leapt on to the topmost shelf like a gazelle. He rolled himself up and pulled the panels shut.

'There, that's good. One less bastard for the time being...Oye. Oye, saaley. Can you hear me in there?'

'Y-yes, sir...just about...'

'Good. Now you—lover boy. Akhil, haan.'

'Yes, sir.'

'Were your eyes shut all this while?'

Akhil had followed the order to such an extent he was beginning to see a galaxy of round black atoms merge and fritter away, and then merge again. 'Yes, sir. Can't see a thing.'

'So now. Tell me, how many of us are here and where are we from.'

'Sir, in this room?'

'No, in the ladies toilet, chutiye.'

'Y-yes, sir. There are three seniors and two freshers in the room—one is in the wardrobe.'

Kha-khao threw his head back and growled. 'You enjoying this?'

'Completely not, sir.'

'Good. Carry on.'

'Yes, sir. I think the sir on your left might be from Madras.'

Kha-khao turned to his left and slapped a thigh—not his. 'Abey kallooo, see. Even the fuchhas can guess where you are from. I *told* you, *Fair & Lovely* works only on chicks, man.'

The man from Madras chose his word very carefully. 'Bastard.'

Akhil, who by now had turned into a brown Rutherford, witnessing as he was bombardments of beta emissions, continued in the same breath. '...And sir, I think the person on your right is from Bihar.'

Kha-khao now turned right and punched an upper duodenum—again, not his. 'Oye Harry. See that? You got to change your appearance, man, if you want to look decent.'

Harry was plain and simple. '*Bhosdi ke, tu toh gaya.*'

Akhil was beginning to enjoy Kha-khao's sardonic sense of humour. He made his next move. 'And sir, I think you are from China.'

The silence that descended on the room was of library thickness. It was shortly broken by equally thick, and ill-made, vocal cords. The men who had earlier been pigeon-holed as Madrasi and Bihari now turned apoplectic. 'Oooh-hooo-hooo-hoo. Saala. Now what do you have to say to *that*, you *chinki* bastard?'

Kha-khao snatched the Che cap from his head. 'China? Did you say China, you bloody bastard? I'll kill you.'

Akhil, eyes still tightly shut, was shaking like a leaf. 'S-sor-sorry sir, I may have made an error of judgement, please forgive me...'

'Saala. Error of judgement. Where did you learn to talk like that, boy? China...Saala. You have had it now ban-cho, you are history. Oye, you still in there? Isn't your friend history now?'

Ajay hoped the lizard wouldn't enter his socks as he replied. 'Y-yes sir. Doesn't look good for him...'

Kha-khao flexed his muscles and sundry ligaments. Akhil couldn't see this frightening sight but he could hear it. 'Bastard. Haven't you seen anyone from Manipur before, haan? China.'

The pleading in the voice tried to convey what the eyes couldn't. 'So sorry, sir. In fact, that's what I wanted to say—Manipur.'

'You think Manipur is in China?'

'No, sir, I...'

The man from Madras intervened, having rearranged his shape after all that hollering. 'Arey leave it na, yaar, enough KK, man.'

Kha-khao relented. 'Hmm...so you bastards know who I am?'

'Yes, sir.'

'Who?'

'Kha-khao, sir.'

'Who told you?'

'Laddu sir.'

'What did he say?'

'He said, now we must go to Allnutt South and get Kha-khao's intro.'

'And what did you say to that? Didn't you know Kha-khao gives his intro last?'

'Yes, sir, we had learned of this. But Laddu sir was adamant.'

Kha-khao asked with all humility: 'You know of my claim to fame, then.'

Akhil tried hurriedly to remember. And then it struck him he could never forget it even after a botched-up lobotomy. 'Y-yes, sir. You are the inter-university taekwondo champion. You, er, also punched a dog dead once, who was barking outside your door one night.'

'Just that?'

'N-no, sir. Then you ate it, sir. W-with butter naan.'

Harry slapped Kha-khao's arm playfully. 'Arey, Kha-khao, leave it yaar. The kid's peeing in his pants, man—and the one inside the wardrobe must be shitting...Oye saaley, you still in there?'

'Y-yess, s-sir, very hot here...'

Kha-khao ignored the cry of discomfort. 'Haan, so Akhil beta, you can open your eyes now.'

'Thank you, sir.'

Perhaps the same sensations that overwhelmed Akhil may also have struck the drifting amoeba the moment God said, 'Let there be light.' He would never again look up the word 'brightness' in the Concise Oxford, that much was sure. Soon, the imposing figure of Kha-khao came into view, together with two less imposing ones.

It was as if Kha-khao was waiting. 'Feel better? Arey, where has your lover gone? Arey, he was here only na, a minute ago.'

'Er, he is in the wardrobe, sir.'

'Really? Oye. You still in there?'

Ajay could not make out in the near darkness whether the noxious fumes cauterising his nose hair were coming from Kha-khao's underwear or his boxing gloves. 'Yes, s-sir; it's really quite hot in here...'

Kha-khao, as his taekwondo partner would swear, could be a little unforgiving at times. 'No one asked you for a weather report, ban-cho. Achha Akhil—Akhil what?'

'Akhil Sukumar, sir.'

'What time is it?'

'Zero seven hundred hours, sir.'

'Zero seven...what?'

'Sorry, sir, 7 am.'

'You trying to drop a hint with this zero seven hundred shit? You tough? You acting tough on Kha-khao?'

'No no, sir, I am sorry. It's a habit, sir. I am from the Ramakrishna Mission Ashram School, sir. In Bhopal.'

'I don't care if you're from Jhumri Talaiyaa. What has it got to do with your zero seven shit? Your dad's in the army or what? He is posted there?'

'No sir, I...'

'Then? Your mom surely?'

'S-sir…'

'*Speak up*, zero seven hundred.'

'My parents are no longer with me, sir.'

'Why? Where have they gone leaving their darling son behind?'

'They are no more, sir. I am an orphan.'

'Shit—sorry, man. I didn't mean...'

'It's alright, sir.'

'And what course are you reading here?'

'Chemistry, sir.'

'Marks in twelfth?'

'Ninety-six percent, sir—physics, chemistry, maths, English, English elective.'

'SC/ST quota?'

'No, sir, no quota.'

'What are you—a brahmin, khatri, bania, what?'

'I am an SC, sir. From the Chamaar caste.'

Kha-khao was now showing his other side. 'So let me get this straight. You got ninety-six percent PCME—and without quota.'

'That's correct, sir.'

'You some sort of genius, boy?'

'No way, sir.'

'Why chemistry?'

'I had applied for English, sir. But during my interview, one of the sirs told me his driver's English was better than mine.'

Kha-khao sent his hip flask flying in the general direction of the wardrobe. Inside, Ajay thought a crude bomb had gone off. 'Bloody bastard. Who was it?'

'Don't know the name, sir.'

'Saala. Bet he got jealous of you.'

'No sir, I didn't mind. My English really isn't very good. But I want to improve.'

'You are alright kiddo, you are fine. What time is it, Aks? We'll call you Aks. Is that alright?'

'Yes sir, 7.20 am, sir.'

'Have you slept at all since last night?'

'No, sir.'

'Are you sleepy? I am sure your partner must have slept off in the wardrobe by now…oye. You still in there?'

Ajay had suffocated a long while ago. Now he was dying. 'Y-yes, sir. Sir, it's really hot in here now, sir, please...'

'Okay, okay, you can come out now.'

'Thank you *so* much, s-sir…'

Ajay could have discussed fresh air with Sir Edmund Hillary. He sucked in so much of the stuff his lungs started knocking on his ribcage. 'Thank you, sir.'

Kha-khao appealed for a vote. 'Arey Harry, what shall we do with these boys now?'

'Arey leave them, yaar. It's enough, man—the bastards have earned it, especially this one.'

Kha-khao agreed, a first for him. 'Haan, so Akhil and Ajay.'

'Yes, sir.'

'How come you two are running around as a pair?'

'Sir, we are room partners.'

'Number?'

'A-101, sir.'

'And where are *you* from? Ajay what?'

'Ajay Biswas, sir. I am from Calcutta, sir.'

'Why are you from Calcutta?'

'Sir?'

'Didn't you hear me the first time?'

'Sir, because I was, er, born there.'

'Ya ya ya…which course?'

'History, sir.'

'What does your dad do—does he play the harmonium?'

'Sir, he is IG, Central Reserve Police.'

'Currently posted where?'

'Sir, in Amritsar.'

'Visiting Jalianwallah Bagh?'

'No, sir. He was part of Operation Blue Star.'

'Bloody hell—the one that just got over?'

'Yes, sir. He was in charge of crowd control.'

'Did he kill anyone?'

Ajay was not sure where all this was going. The wardrobe looked inviting. 'No sir, not to my knowledge.'

'So he tells you every time he kills someone.'

'No, sir.'

'Then?'

'Sorry, sir. I meant, I don't know.'

'Hmm…why are you reading history here?'

'Actually sir, my dad also read history here—class of '61.'

'So? Is this like some Bong family tradition—you got to do what your dad did? Don't get haughty on me, ban-cho.'

'No sir, I didn't mean...'

'Shut up. Will you take the UPSCs?'

'Er, that is my dad's plan, sir.'

It had been a full three minutes since Kha-khao had turned red with anger. He consulted his watch. 'I didn't ban-cho ask about your dad's plan, bhosdi ke.'

'Y-yes, sir, I might take UPSC.'

'Why. What's the connection of UPSC with history ban-cho?'

'No connection, sir.'

The man from Madras had had his fill. 'Arey, KK, it's enough for today, man. Leave it yaar. I'm off.'

Kha-khao agreed. The end was near. 'Ya, alright. Ajay? Shut up. No one's interested why and where you are from.'

'Yes, sir.'

'Question is, are *you* interested in getting KK's *intro*?'

'Very much, sir.'

'And you, Akhil?'

'Tremendously, sir.'

The three seniors got up and took positions. The man from Madras spoke first. 'Well, Mr Sukumar, Mr Biswas…'

'Sir.'

'It was a pleasure meeting you. I hope the feeling was mutual.'

'Yes sir, it was.'

'I am APD, Arun Parinjarekara Devanathan.'

'Sir.'

The man from Bihar was next. 'And I am MPB, Mahendra Pratap Singh Bhusrri.'

'Sir.'

The man from China followed. 'And gentlemen, I am Kha-khao.'

'Sir.'

'Now buzz off, you two. And any problems, come straight to me. You understand?'

'Yes sir, thank you, sir.'

'Or better, tell any senior bothering you that you have Kha-khao's intro in your jhola.'

Akhil could have cried. 'Fantastic, sir. Feels so good.'

'Stop auditioning for Cinthol and get lost.'

'Thank you, sir.'

The boys emerged from Kha-khao's den like hippies out of Kathmandu, not sure of love, life and the universe any more. Ajay set the debriefing in motion. 'Shit. Bloody I am exhausted, man—you Akhil?'

'Can't even walk. How was it in the wardrobe?'

'Saala. Bastard, Kha-khao. I'll put in a written complaint to the princy...'

'Just leave it, yaar. In fact, I think we got away lightly.'

'Bastard—*you* got away lightly. You couldn't have lasted in that hovel for more than five minutes—all his unwashed clothes, the stink.'

Akhil smiled. 'I have been stuck in worse places, much worse.'

'Ya? Like in Kha-khao's ass?'

'Arey think of the positives—we managed to get Kha-khao's intro.'

'*You* can stuff his intro where I think, man. I'll take him on. This is not the end, I am telling you.'

'*Arey, chhod na*. This is a tradition—you'll do the same to fuchhas next year, mark my words.'

'That much is true. What's the time, army major?'

'Zero seven hundred thirty hours, sir.'

'Hey, I was listening to your conversation with that dog Kha-khao. It's great to have you as my roomy.'

'Likewise, yaar.'

'You are a genius, you bastard. It must have been so tough.'

'Arey no, man. Can I call you man?'

'You can call me a bastard, a ban-cho, a dog, a man—anything—but not Biswas. Reminds me of one gora teacher at my school—Mr Biswas this, Mr Biswas that; bloody half the time I thought it wasn't me but my dad at school.'

'Which school?'

'Lawrence School, Sanawar. Anyway, listen, Aks—I like that—Aks. Ya listen, I think it's too late now to have breakfast. Why don't we go to the assembly directly, haan?'

'Sure, can't be late for the first one.'

'Come then, the hall's only a minute from where we are.'

Ajay continued his lament as the two made their way to the assembly. 'All my life I have been a prisoner of this assembly shit. I don't know what dad saw in this college, yaar. The place reminds me of my damn school.'

'I heard what you told Kha-khao. Your father's a Stephanian, too.'

'Arey he's got it all worked out. Sanawar, Stephen's, history, UPSC, IPS. Maybe a nice Bong girl. Maybe two kids as well…'

'That's great.'

'What shit. What about you? You have always been in Bhopal? Any brothers, sisters…'

'No. I am on my own.'

The assembly hall came into view.

Ajay stopped in his tracks. 'Shit—Amin sir, at the entrance.'

The young men found the entrance to the assembly hall guarded by none other than the legendary Professor Amin, a man who had rewritten history. His defence was that the scholars before him were so bad they had left him little choice. 'Morning, morning. Late on the first day?' he remarked, pouncing on Akhil and Ajay.

'Morning, sir. Very sorry, sir. There was a line for the toilets,' said Akhil.

'I believe you, I believe you…and your name is...'

'Akhil, sir. Akhil Sukumar—first year chemistry.'

'Good. And about you I know, young man. Ajay Biswas. Taught your father. Can't say he learned much—made for UPSC, he was. Like father, like son, I take it.'

Ajay looked around for the wardrobe. 'Er…'

'*Chalo, chalo, bhai*. You are already five minutes late. Principal saab is about to begin.'

'Yes, sir. Sir, where do we...'

'You can't get to your seats now. Maybe find a seat in the English first year section…there—you see?'

'Thank you very much, sir.'

The lads began making their way through a sequence of protests and outstretched limbs. Meanwhile, up on the dais, someone bearing a close resemblance to the pope was trying to get his message across through the collar, the hand-held and the podium microphone, thinking mistakenly that only one of the three was functioning. The result would have made Moses proud. *'And may I now request our principal saab to say a few words of welcome to our first year students? Sir, please.'*

Akhil and Ajay found two empty seats in the English section and sat down, pretending at once to be the sombre and interested audience, as first-year students were expected to be.

Principal saab, meanwhile, had taken possession of the three working microphones. He began in the customary Indian way, by thanking everyone he ever knew and sparing only the cleaning lady and the chauffeur.

'…Thank you, Clement saab, vice-principal saab, the dean, the honourable bishop, Heads of the departments, my colleagues and friends. I shall call you friends, because that is precisely who you are—friends. But who is a friend? Is he someone who will stay silent while he sees you doing more harm than good? Is he to keep quiet while he sees you do immoral, unworthy things? In other words, is he supposed to be a comfortable pillow for you? Throw it away when you don't like it anymore; when it has become hard and difficult, no longer soft and silent? No. I am not that sort of a friend…'

Ajay was beginning to lose interest. 'Arey Aks, this'll go on for an hour, man.'

Before Akhil could agree, pat came a rap on the knuckles from a young woman seated next to them. 'Shhh! Quiet, you two.'

Ajay ignored the put-down and consulted his watch. 'What rotten luck.'

Principal saab, as it transpired, had no intention of looking at his watch. '*...and as long as you are Stephanians, you shall adhere to a code. A code of honour, a confidence to do things as they should be done, without fear of reprisals or retributions...*'

Ajay, his mind sufficiently far removed from the chatter of codes of honour, reprisals, and retributions, now remembered something important. 'Listen, Aks. Bastard, did you lock our room?'

'Saaley, I thought *you* did.'

'Shit, ban-cho. My priceless laal-mirch pickle that mom gave...'

'Shh!'

Seeing the woman about to lose her cool again, Ajay thought it an opportune moment to get the introductions over and done with. 'Sorry, sorry. Hi, I am Ajay—history and he is Akhil—chem.'

'What the hell are you talking about?'

'And you are?'

'Aparajita. Now shushhhh!'

'Aparajita what?'

Principal saab, meanwhile, was giving Nietzsche and Kant a run for their money. '*...You may learn, when you further your education beyond this college, that there were better teaching methods available, that there were better books, that there were, indeed, better teachers. But then, you will also realise, that to better your education was not our aim to begin with.*

Education is a very abstract thing. Is it improvement or is it refinement? Is it enlightenment or is it indoctrination? Is it information or is it guidance? I shall ask of you the answer on your last day here.

And finally, I am a terrible stickler for a few things. Attendance—minimum of eighty-five percent before I allow you to sit for your exams.

Then, I have laws: You shall respect your teachers. You shall call a sweeper by his surname, and you shall put a mister in front of it. You shall address the college gyps as sirs. You shall attend the assembly every day. You shall form orderly queues. You shall not play in the lawns. And for those of you staying in the residences—not hostels, mind you—you shall sign the night register. You can complain about the mess food, but only through the written word.

I shall be watching you. Closely.

Look up, all of you. What do you see? No, don't say a fat, middle-aged, bald man going on and on about morals...I meant look up on the wall above. Yes, the words: "I AM THE LIGHT OF THE WORLD; HE WHO FOLLOWETH ME SHALL NOT WALK IN DARKNESS BUT SHALL HAVE THE LIGHT OF LIFE".

Jesus was—is—the light of the world. You may follow him, or you may not. Either way, presently, it is my job to lead you out of your darkness.

Thank you...Now, Clement saab, if we may proceed to the dining hall?

The discourse must have been soul-stirring, judging by the speed with which students sprang up from their seats and rushed out.

But Ajay had not forgotten his one single aim in life. 'Aparajita what?'

'Aparajita Balasubramanian. Now quiet.'

Ajay heard Robindro Shongeet.

What was their first interview like? Did they fail? Did they pass? The were probably thrown out. Both of them looked so untidy, like drunkards or bouncers. Neither Jack (Nicholson) nor Gérard (Depardieu) were blessed with good looks. And Richard (Burton) didn't even finish school. Aiyoo. And, if Amitabh (Bachchan) had applied for a job, he might have been a lower-division clerk. All their CVs would have been rejected, at the hechaar level. In the unlikely event of an alert hechaar, compliance would have dropped from above, to be pulled and placed in front of the nose to ensure breathing. Breathing is prohibited in certain areas. Cheating is not.

And as you walk out of the gates of this grand institution, you shall be carrying the weight of not just your golf bags, you shall be carrying forth a tradition, a belief, an era, a civilisation—the hopes and dreams of millions of slaves and black people who built that house we call White. *Wah, la vie est belle*!

As you, only you, the purebred among the thoroughbred know that you can tell an aristocrat from a distance—it will always be a person who boils his or her ice cubes. That kind of purity is only perceptible to the rarest of the rare, the clearest of the clear. No IIT, MIT, LSR, Oxford, not even an LSE. This Jack had so many Jills. And that Gérard fellow could only afford a bicycle. One of them speaks English with a French accent and the other looks scary in any language. As for Richard, so many marriages—untrustworthy rascal from the word go. A coal-miner's son can never be a don. A true dawn, a breath of fresh air, a torrent of words can never flow from gutters where rats live.

That is what education in the best of the world's institutions does to you; you can open windows and doors for the rest of your life. You will all look alike, speak alike, like alike, dislike alike, dream alike, marry alike, bear children alike, who will marry alike despite their likes and dislikes. They will all play golf, drive similar cars and, despite being called weekend vultures for wanting to play golf with an unknown rich man so you can access his money, they will continue oblivious to the comedy. Life is a comedy, especially when it is visible to some and totally invisible to some of the cast of characters. *Allez*, it's much more of a comedy especially in India where we go through so many funny contortions to hide our real selves.

Say what is not asked. Ask what is not said. Make up the rest and then complain that you are misunderstood.

So try this. Ask any middle-class Indian a simple question: So, what do you do? Nine out of ten will tell you where his father got his degree. *My father is an IITian*. So try again: So, what do you do? *My father also went to IIM*. Mother? *She, too; a gold medallist*. But sacrificed her career so she could speak about it for the rest of her life. So, what do you do? *I have lived all over the world, worked in private equity and BFSI, and now I am taking courses on how to write my CV*. So what do you do when you meet Attitude and Entitlement with a big A and E?

By this time and stretch, Jack, Gérard and Richard would have been thrown out, dirty clothes and body odour included. People would have laughed at them. No CV, no manners, but boy, do they have Attitude. Would you have given Jack and Gérard a second look if they had walked into a party? Would you have noticed them on the street? But when these two cuckoos appear on screen, they transform not just themselves, but also the audience. The world's best lawyers did not go to Yale and some of India's top CEOs are graduates from REC Tiruchirappalli and 'behenji' colleges. Many of them went to Minnesota, Navodaya Vidyalayas and Anganwadis. Some didn't even go to any school.

What makes you a human being? Bonding in a building or plain and simple bonding with life in all its beauty and stench, grandeur and stupidity? Of daring to open all doors and windows with the courage and humility of your own hands or hanging on to non-existent coat-tails? Gas, where everyone is a CEO, an advisor, a consultant, an image guru, a value-adder—there are even classes that teach people a subject titled 'social climbing'. Heaven must definitely be a boring place.

Life is a CV. There is little glory in imitation, especially the kind that herds together for want of courage couched as parents expect, society wants, neighbours say, cousins went, father did, mother wanted, grandparents prayed. Yes, we are all born without a net. The lucky among us get to decide how and what we want to trap ourselves in and the kinds of crutches we want to build, for others, so we can be free.

Try trapeze.

We all write our CVs together—in fear. Fear of finding out that life invites you every day to meet yourself. Jack and Gérard and Richard and Amitabh must have figured that out differently and together. Life is a stage and not everyone is a stooge.

1984 was written in 1948.

9

2003 – Such a Long Journey

With his legs perched on the wrought-iron balcony railing and his eyes scanning the unspoilt beauty of the Cornish coastline, Mattyboy was forced to contemplate life and its rewards.

'Blimey Maai,' said Matty out loud. He recalled the last time similar circumstances had thrown him in the lion's den. He was on his honeymoon, strolling around a beach in Phuket with his arms around his missus, when he looked up at the stunning full moon and the way it was slipping in and out of clouds, and felt something inside him stir. Something disturbing. Words. *Oii. Watchii. Naugh becomin' a sissy bleedin' poet now, aa ya,* he had said to himself and gone on to press his missus and pull her down on the sand.

'Fooh. That woz nice, wannay,' mumbled Matty as he fetched his legs down. His thoughts began to wander. The open blue sea, the frothy waves, the cawing seagulls, the warm afternoon sun, his kids shouting and making sandcastles—everything receded to form a backdrop while Mattyboy walloped his head and shut his eyes. *Bleedin' cow. Now wayaa's she 'idden me season tickee... think.*

Matthew Dearlove was twenty-six years old and worked at the passport office in Croydon. He was born and brought up in the east end of London, and there goes a story that he was snatched from the cradle within minutes of his birth by his granddad and whisked away to Upton Park for the West Ham–Newcastle Cup semi. 'Ammers till I die' was the family motto. Matty grew up on a staple diet of *Steptoe* and *Delboy* and *Eastenders*, and made many friends along the way, all of whom had also grown up on a staple diet of *Steptoe* and *Delboy* and *Eastenders*. His best friend was Johnnyboy, who had decided to settle in a remote place off the Cornish coast called Truro, and in whose balcony the holidaying Matty was threatened with contemplation.

Johnny was a graphic designer, and on working days—while back in Croyden—Matty multitasked and picked BLT remnants from his teeth with the sharp end of a matchstick even as he scanned with narrowed eyes an anxious Ghanaian asylum-seeker—Johnny went fooling around Truro town under the pretense of getting fresh ideas: 'Fresh new idears maai, no-wough-a-meen.' His employers strained their ears and raised their antennae but failed most times to know what Johnny meant. 'Giss on, you cockney bh-astard,' they exhaled out of earshot.

To sum up, both gents were happy and content with their lives, although it pained Johnny to have to watch his beloved West Ham United on Match of the Day while Matty got to see them ringside every Saturday come rain or shine—before his missus hid away his season ticket, that is.

'Goddam silly cow,' muttered Matty.

The balcony door slid open and out came Johnny, dangling what appeared to be two beer bottles.

'Iyaa—try this local stuff.'

'Ta mayt, cheers...Oooooaaa. Wough the bleedin' el was *that*,' cried Mattyboy, spitting his mouthful of the bottle's contents like an angry gargoyle on a pouring day.

'The local Cornish bollocks.'

Matty continued with the spitting. 'Luddy el, Jonnyboy. Heh. Come back, son.'

'Nough-aaf mayt, nough-aaf.'

'Me serious, you wankaa...Aamin, a hundred miles 'way from civiliezayishun, least you expect's a good bleedin' beverage, innit. Bloody savages.'

'Tell me 'bout-ee, git. As it is, the rub-a-dub downs the clangaa by effin ten.'

'You kiddin. What *is* this plaaice?'

Johnny answered reassuringly. 'Still England maai, still queen mum's pad.'

'Effing el, Johnny. Well, 'pose the barmaids make up for it, aye. Aamin, phwoarrrr, aye.'

''Pends on yer orientaishun. Half the cows 'round eyaa look like bleedin' geezaas.'

Matty thrust his pelvis out and his crooked elbows back and repeated the workout a couple of times. 'Djugo for those ones, then.'

'You oal tossa.'

This time around, Matty straightened the elbows and dug his hands in his pockets. He crossed his legs at the shins and struck the ballerina pose, reclining gently on the Victorian ironmongery. From the town to the gown is a short journey. 'So...howz the muppets of Truro treatin' ya?'

Johnny took a swig of the Cornish medicine. 'Doaneven bauver askin', maai. This design company I work for...'

'Sanders, intchya?'

'Yiah, well tis a load of bollocks. Bleedin' expect ya to work ya bum off all dee long. An' tossas 'round iyaa dunno footy, no clubbin', no chicken tikka masaala bleedin', too. I telya maait, 'tis quite a jump from good oul Le Bow.'

'Howz the missus an' kids takin' it, then?'

'Not too bad, not too bad. But djyou know what they's like mayt, innay. Delia-bloody-Smith, long walks, 'ome early, telly—that sough of girlie thin'.'

Matty commiserated. 'Yaa maai, tell me 'bau-ee. Me bird hid me 'ammers season tickey some-wiah the other nigh—the one we'd gough-un together, 'member?'

Johnny swallowed a mouthful and waited for the poison to go down. 'Nouuu.'

'I know, mate. Said, nuff of footy. That I gaugh-oo change me life; take the kiddies out on weekends, eating out—that saugh-a stuff.'

'You poor plonka.'

'An' that's naugh-it, maai. She says, says is time to change the loca'ity, too. Says it's too down-markay 'n like.'

Johnny shook his head. 'Doanno 'bout you mate but that's just ou of audaah.'

'Aamin, can't take the Del boy outta me now, can-ya?'

'So, what did ya tell'er.'

'Shiftin, we are, month's time. Croydon.'

'Bend down, didjya.'

Matty tried to defend himself. 'No mate. It's quite sensible too innee, with me passport office nearby and Rubics, too. Woan change me club though, tould'er. 'Ammers till I die mate, yaa.'

'Yaa, mayt, buh-waugh-now.'

'Wadj-ya-meen?'

'Aamin, with the kids-cool an' all.'

'Me in-lozz, inni—bless'em—stay stone's throu from the new 'ome.'

The psychoanalysis was going nowhere. Johnny consulted his watch. 'Good, good…listen, Matt, dijya ever tell yer Chrissie 'bout our li-aa conversaishun the other nigh'?'

'Why, what's Say-raa been tellin' ya. Carpet bombin' like, izzi.'

'Nough reely, nouu. Buh-ya-no how tis like don't ya, maait. Aamin, she's been actin' a bit straaingely laytly, if ya know wough-aa-meen.'

Matty came closer. 'How so, mayt?'

'Well, there woz the dog 'n bone aa ceived one nigh, just as I was 'bout ta leave office—could've sworn that was me missus breathin' down the receivaa.'

'You're just para maait, just para, atsawl.'

'I swear she's got an inklin'. 'eemen do maait, sixth sense an' all… neeway, sure you didn't mention a thing about me seccy to Chrissie—'cause they *do* talk on the phone, I tell ya maaiy—missus and yer Chrissie—au-wayz on the founn, they are.'

'No mayit, calm down will ya? Told ya, didn't say a word to missus. Anyway, aagough plenti on me platter too, if you no-whattameen.'

Johnny punched his friend playfully. 'You little bastaa. Well, you gonna tell me boutit or nouugh.'

'All in good time, Johnny boy.'

'Commawn you stinkin' plonka, out with-ee.'

'Tis a nice 'ittle Paki bird at the passport office, maait.'

'*No*. You geezaa.'

'Wears the—wough-ya-call-ee, *Ji-*, *dhi-*, *hijab*…Looks good on'er—if you ask me 'onest opinion.'

'Well, I *am* asking your honest opinion, you dirty li-ul basst. 'King-ell, Chrissie don't know-nothin' 'bout-ee?'

'Course she don't, you plonk.'

'But how can ya see'er? Aamin she covered faum ed-to-toe in a bed sheet an'all…'

Matty tried to enlighten Johnny on the subtleties of Islamic headgear. 'Why, you ignorant lill bastud. A hijab—don't mean a bed sheet, you plonka. Just covers her head, 'atsall.'

Johnny raised his hand in apology. 'Sorry maait. Don't knou the luddy difference, now do I.'

'Yaa, how could ya. Aamin, your seccy don't wear a hijab, does she? Just a fat, lumpy, middle-aged jersi, intshi?'

'Shut-ee, you wankaa. She ain't lumpy, and she ain't middle-aged naaither.'

'Awe-rye, awe-rye. Touched a raw nerve, did I? Did I? Way-yaa. They-yaa.'

Johnny tried to avoid being smacked on his family jewels. 'Piss off, you wank...'

'Shh, quiet! The kid's comin.'

Matty switched to something more academic in a flash. 'So, aa-ahem…what kinda graphic design jobs do ya get 'round-iyaa?'

'Nothin' much, maai...'

A sporty, ginger-haired, baby-faced little girl came running in and tugged at Johnny's denims. 'Dad. Uncle Matt.'

'Yes princess?'

'Mum's callin' both of ya.'

'Awe-I, daalin'. Come Matt, let's see wauz bin brewin' while we've bin chattin' iyaa.'

Matty leaned out beyond the railing and shouted for his kids. 'Andeyeeeee? Maggieeeeee?...Comeon in naaow, you ear?'

The children sprinted over and collected under the balcony. 'Oh Dad, but we've just started. Maggie's thrown me a challenge—fastest to that bowut'n back. You carry on, Dad. We'll follow in a minute—honest.'

'Awe-righty then, just ten minutes, awe-I.'

'Right-o, Dad.'

Johnny picked up the half-full beer bottles, noticing for the first time the Teutonic lettering on the label. 'Kem on then, princess—lead us to where the ladies are, woanchya?'

'You go in, Dad. I'll come along with Andy and Maggie. Please?'

'Aouuright, but no goin' niya the pier. And ten minutes sweetheart, oukayeee?'

'Thanks, Dad. Byee.'

'Bye, darlin'...Come on'en Mattyboy—and listen mayt, 'member wough I toldjya.'

Matty tapped his nose. 'Mums the word, son.'

'Gudi-gudi-goood. Come.'

The gents made their way in, sliding shut the balcony door behind them. They skipped down the spiral stairwell humming and whistling as they went to meet their better halves in the lounge below.

'There. There's the two of ya,' said one better-half. ''Ave been shoutin' 'oarse all this time. Where whirr ya?'

'Evenin' layidies. Have been showin' Matt 'round the pad. He seems to like-ee, inni Matt?'

Matt chipped in while eyeing Johnny's football figures collection. 'Yaa—you've gaugh a nice thingy iyaa, Say-raa.'

'Think souugh?'

'Tis like bein' on a 'oliday all ear long, inni.'

'Telit to John, iyaa. Haven't been on an 'oliday for months.'

'You don't need to now, doouya?'

'That's what *he* bleedin' keeps sayin.'

Johnny protested playfully. 'Wough-me?'

The women giggled. 'Nee-way, come in boys. Coffee. Tea.'

'Tea please, Chrissie. Sou. What'ave you-oo hens bin up to, 'en? Hope Chrissie's not given waai too many secrets, have you, Chrissie?'

'As a mat-aah of fact, was just mentionin' to Say-raa bout the fay-yaa you've been 'avin' backin Croydon.'

Matty felt a bit dizzy. 'What. Oyee!'

'Just kiddin', daalin'.'

Matty changed the topic swiftly. '...Anything good on the telly, girls? By good, aamin footie.'

'You wish, lads.'

Johnny extended his right hand, revealing St. George, a werewolf, a mongoose and a snake, all busy in the process of killing each other, in that order. The rest of the emotional scene would have come into view had he removed his T-shirt and lowered his trousers. 'Give us the 'mote, luv.'

'Stay away, *you*,' said Sarah smacking Johnny's hand away. 'Now, let's see...'

'...The...hyeenaa, has found, his prey...'

'...No, that's not what I'm asking minister...'

'...Three!...and the next number is...'

'...Oh gaawd. O-my-gaaad. Now that's aa hooge punch by the underta...'

'Neville!...now to Giggs...Keane...now to Van Nistelrooy...three men back...Van Nistelrooy! Oooh, fingertip save, that...'

Both Matty and Johnny jumped. 'Ya. Ya, that's it. *Stay,* Say-raa.'

'You wish, lads. Aren't you ev-aa fed up of-ee. Aamin Des Lynem's all fine, but...'

'...This whole business of overcharging...'

'...Are you saying, then, Sir Rupert, that the House of Lords...'

'...Well, there's my lad. Two balls left, just two red ones, ladies and gentlem...'

'A singer...a pop star...and now an activist...'

Sarah couldn't believe her ears. 'Blimey, George Michael. Chrissie. That's Jorji on Hardtalk. Hurry up, luv.'

'...but just how is he...'

The lads gave out a collective groan. 'Oh, no.'

Sarah was festive. 'Oh, yes. The- zappa- 'as- found- its- prayee. Didjya know Johnny, I had a huge crush on George back in them days...Chrissieee. Are you coming daalin'?'

'...George Michael, a very warm welcome to the progr...'

'Really. That's strange. I thaw even aar Mattyboy, too...'

'Thank you. Nice to meet you Tim.'

'Shut it, you tossa.'

'Why Iraq? 'Cos it's fashionable?'

Chrissie came thundering in, 'Shh. Easy now, you two…Iyaa, take your cuppa and be quiet.'

'Oh God, no. I have absolutely no desire to be here today. I've got absolutely—I'm really reluctant to be here.'

Johnny protested. 'O come-awnn, ladies. We can't sit through this now, can we Matty? Not after what the bugger did to me hand that nigh.'

'*Why?*'

Sarah asked, eyes glued to the TV. 'What bugger? What hand?'

'Simply because—in all honesty, I was kind of first out of the trenches...'

'Dinchya knou? *That* bugger. George bloody Michael, you muppet.'

'…in terms of entertainers that were going to get behind something which would divide—which at the time was so divisive...'

Sarah swung round, open-mouthed. 'You've met-im? Nouuu!'

'…that if you're approaching a subject as divisive as Iraq was six or eight months ago, then...'

'Well, not exactly. I wozat Earl's Court when the plonka was strumming his guitar an' all, innay.'

'…then you're taking a big risk as an entertainer; because you're going to...'

Matty objected. 'That woz ages ago, you bugger.'

'…alienate a lot of people, and I did...'

'Yaa, but it's fresh Mattyboy, fresh as a bleedin' daisy, I tell ya.'

'…very, very quickly. And I was completely pilloried...'

'Why, what did he do, dear George?' asked Sarah.

'…really for having the audacity to be a pop star...'

'Bugger tould everyone to raise their arms an sway'em left an effin' righ—like this...'

'…who's in the mainstream, as opposed to a rock star...'

'And you refused?'

'…or, you know, some kind of protest singer.'

Johnny gave Matty a dirty stare. 'No, you stewpee, wankaa. It was quite a sight actually, 'til some plonk-head near us propoused we click aar lighters on, too...'

'But there's no such thing as bad publicity, is there?'

Matty now looked very fascinated. 'Say-raa daalin', this is interesting luv, coodjya lower the volume please, hen?'

'There is...'

Sarah did so grudgingly. 'Jus-a bit, then...There, is that oakayee?'

'Particularly if your record sales are falling?'

'Ta luv, that's fine. Ya, so wayaa woz u, lie-aa lamp.'

'Did you see my publicity? Did you see...'

Johnny continued. 'Well, it got me too, the lietaa bit, aa-min. And then—it could only've been a couple-aa minnets—me bleedin lighter blew in me hand.'

'...any of it? It was absolutely dire. And I'd like to add—I have absolutely no...'

'Jesus.'

'...my record sales are not falling...'

'Nough-aaf, maai. Ended up in the burns ward at St George's, I did.'

'...I released two singles six years after my last album. And my fans are now thirty-five, on average...'

'Wough. He was so kind as to take ya to his 'ospital? That's so typical of him, that George.'

'...right? There was a piece on Channel Four about three or four months ago...'

Johnny punched Matty in the stomach. 'No, you stupid plank, stop taking the piss—it ain't 'alf funny, you git.'

'...where an artist was challenging Woolworth's because they were not stocking...'

'Awe-i, awe-i, Jonnyboy. So waugh 'appened, then?'

'...their records, and so they had a representative of Woolworth's on...'

'Couldn't use me left hand for a week, that's waugh 'appened.'

'...and this woman said, well we've done our market research for Woolworth's and...'

Matty asked in all seriousness and with suitable gestures: 'So, how didjya—aamin—you no-whataamin...Black n' Decker—right hand then, was it. Faugh a houul week?'

'...we know that the singles market of two-thousand-two is teenage girls...'

'You stewpee git, shut-ee.'

'...between the ages of twelve and—no eleven and twelve, that was as wide as it got—eleven and twelve! The only reason...'

'Nuff lads, *quiet.*'

'...I have to release singles, as someone with an audience of thirty-five plus...'

'Ya awe-i, take it easy girls. We nouu you fine-im lovely, now dountchya?'

'...is that if you don't release them as a single in Britain...'

'Very...listen, Johnny, just please find out 'bout them kids.'

'...you can't get them on the...'

Johnny waved his hand, picking up the thread where St George had just speared the werewolf with the sharp end of a flagpole. 'They're busy playin' on the beach.'

'...radio. I don't want to compete with, you know...'

'Well they've been out a long time, inni. Please, Johnny.'

'...pop idol and the carious young people...'

'Ya awe-i...Andieee? Maggieeee?'

'...in the charts that are roughly half my...'

'Not from iyaa, Johnny. Loudaa, they can't ear ya.'

'...age right now. I'd rather just release my albums...'

'Awe-I, awe-i...'

Johnny went reluctantly and opened a French window.

'But you say you're happier to have a big debate than a hit single. Really?'

'...Andieee? Oiii. Oiii!'

'Absolutely.'

'I said, oiii!'

'You must be the only one in the business then.'

Andy looked up from his sandcastle and ran towards the house, screaming and shouting. 'Uncle Johnny, look what I found.'

'I think I probably am. I think...'

Matty heard the commotion and joined Johnny at the door. 'Whaugh. Wayaa. Wayz Maggie. Look, din-I warn ya. Din-i? Aye?'

'...I probably am by now. I've had twenty years...'

'No dad, you doan understand. I've found this—a bottle.'

'...of this business. I'm never on the television...'

Sarah, who could hear everything from across fifteen feet, barked. 'You lot. Come iyaa.'

'...never. I never do TV...'

Andy trotted over, followed shortly by the keyed-up pair of Maggie and Clare. 'Hi, Mum. Hi, Aunt Say-raa.'

'...I'm phobic about cameras. I...'

'Hi, boyz'n'gulls. What's that in your 'and 'en?'

'...have no interest in promoting my music beyond making videos.'

Andy was beside himself with excitement. 'A bottle.'

'But you never protested at the height of your fame, did you?'

Johnny and Matty joined in. The children were clapping their hands and jumping up and down. Matty ruffled Andy's hair. 'Show us a minnet.'

'Well, of I didn't. I was nineteen, twenty, twenty-one. What...'

'Ear, dad.'

'...were you doing when you were?'

Matt inspected the bottle carefully. 'Looks like a baugh-ul, Jonnyboy.'

He shook the bottle and put his ear to it. 'Luddy 'el, Jonny, it's got some sort of paper inside...Co-blimey—a message.'

'A lot of people at nineteen, twenty and twenty-one were on the streets marching, weren't they? Against Vietnam, for instance.'

Johnny cried out with all sincerity. 'Sweet Jesus.'

'Yes, I know, but I was too young for that. This is my time.'

The ladies, who had only momentarily been distracted by the bottle and had turned their attention back to dear George, now demanded some quiet. 'Shh. Hush, you two.'

'There have been other wars since, haven't there?'

'Chrissie, Say-raa, you've gotta 'ave a look at this thin' iyaa. An' daalin, switch the plonka off, will ya?'

'This is my time. I do understand what you're trying to say. But the fact is...'

'Awe-eye...'

'...I really have no concern about being accused of needing...'

Chrissie switched the telly off and plopped the remote in Sarah's lap where it promptly got lost in the many folds. She turned dejectedly. 'There...'appy now?'

'Ta, hen. Now look.'

'Wough. Wough-is-ee. Just a bottle, innit.'

Matty was trying to uncork it. 'It's gaugh somethin'…Iyaa, lemme jus...'

'Careful Matt, you'll break-ee. Iyaa, waugh-uz it say on top. Old Monk...rum.'

'Where's it faum-en?'

'Made in India. Blimey, maai.'

Johnny was stunned. 'The bleedin' thins come up iyaa, all the way from thiyaa?'

'Looks like, inni. Lemme uncork-ee…Jesus, seems to be stu– gosh it's tight, maai.'

'Careful, you git.'

''Bout to, 'bout to…Aaaaa—dunn-ee.'

Johnny took possession of the contents. 'Blimey. There's sheets maai, luddy tons-of-um.'

'Say-raa, Chrissie. Iyaa, 'ave a look at this stuff. Luddy, all the way fawm India.'

'Waugh-iz-ee?'

'Well, cow, tis a message, inni.'

'Mathew. Language.'

Matty apologised. 'Sorry, luv. Aamin, you've gaugh-oo see this… Where didjya getit fawm, Andy?'

'From the sea, Dad. I was runnin' up to touch the boat when this thing hit me ankle. Read it, read it, Dad.'

Johnny nudged Matty with his elbow. 'Ya, waugh-uz-ee say, Matty....Nough a recipe for CTM, aa-hoap.'

'Bettaa. Iyaa, listen t' this...*Mumbai…Thursday, eleventh March, nineteen ninety-nine*…Blimey, duzzat mean tis taken fo years to get iyaa?'

'I'll be damned. Jesus.'

'God almigh-e.'

Matty shouted everyone down. 'Lisonn...*This may take a while to reach you. In any case, you will be the first to learn of when, how, and why, I murdered the 'Pride of Bombay' Mr Ramrao Apte. Let me begin with the answer to the first ques...*'

The men looked at each other.

'I said, sweet bleedin' Jesus.'

'Effing el, Uncle Alb. What the...'

'You gau-oo be kiddin' me. Mother of God. Effin'...Didjya hear that? Aamin...'

Chrissie cut the slang procession short. 'Johnny. The kids! Language.'

'Sorry, luv. But didjya...'

'Andy. Maggie. Clare. Out. *Now.*'

'No Mum, please.'

'The beach, I said. Now. Mathew?'

'Yeah, kids. Mum's right iyaa. This ain't no kid stuff, this.'

'But, Dad...'

'Pleaz, the beach, kids. We'll call ya in when we're dun ear, awe-I.'

Andy stuck his lips out and dragged his feet. 'O, this is soooo unfair.'

'I knou, I knou. The beach, kids.'

Heads down and shoulders slumped, the children made their way slowly out the doors.

Johnny breathed a sigh. 'Phew. Go on then, Matt.'

'Awe-I...*to the first question: when? This morni...*' Matt paused and looked up. 'Good sweet Lord, I said.'

'Carry on, you git.'

'his morning. Ten-thirty. Presidential suite. Hotel Taj Mahal. So, the complete...'

'Stop it, Matt. This is getting too much,' Sarah interrupted.

'Yaa, Chrissie's right iyaa. Too weird is this.'

'O come-awn, Say-raa; be a sport, hen. This is grayit. Carry on, Matty.'

'...complete answer to the first question: I killed Ramrao Apte on Thursday, eleventh March, nineteen ninety-nine, at ten-thirty precisely—I confirmed. To the second question: how? I arrived at the Taj at nine sharp...'

'Listen fellas, this is perverse!'

'O come off it, Chrissie. It's no such thing. For all you know, some Paki...'

'Mathew!'

'Sorry, luv...didn't mean no harm…Maybe some Indian geezaa in Brighton roat it as a bee-aa-fun and threw the Aristotle in. Come-awnn luv, be a sport now.'

'But still...'

Johnny behaved as though the matter was settled. 'Ya, ya, she's fine, Matt; go on.'

'*…at nine sharp. I wandered along and got in among a bunch of tourists. Once inside, changed into an electrician's overalls. Located the presidential suite. Waited for the room service to go and knock on the door. Mr Apte opened the door. A woman got out.*' Matty looked up from the scrolls.

'Go on, git.'

'*…I went up to Mr Apte, said the air-conditioning needed to be looked at. Waited for the room service to leave. Went in the bathroom. Played around with a few switches. Then called for Mr Apte: "Mr Aapte? Sir, is this what is creating the problem?" He came in. The wire was around his neck in a flash. It was a matter of a minute. He was gone. I checked the time. Ten thirty. I then checked his pulse. Nothing. I waited for five minutes. Nothing. I went out the way I had come in. So you see…*'

'Phew maai.' Matty took a breather.

'Well, Matty, I gaugh-aa tell ya, this thins gaugh-me 'air standin' up, alright. Who *is* this bugger?'

'Don't mention his name iyaa.'

'Aamin, what cheek. As if the tossa doan care if he's found-ouu.'

Matty looked at the ceiling. 'Maybe he...'

'Wough.'

'Maybe he *wanted* to be found out.'

'Nouuu. The cold-blooded Indian tossa.'

'A crime of passion, this. You awe-rye, girls? You two don't look awe-rye t' me—do they, Jonnyboy?'

'Thee-hee. Carry on, mayt.'

'Awe-rye then.

'*…So you see how easy it was. As easy as the way Mr Apte accumulated his billions. Now to the third and final, and perhaps the most important question: why? WHY? Because in the annals of corrupt Indians, the name* *of Mr Apte was written in gold. But it was not displayed; no, Mr Apte made sure of that...'*

Sarah had had enough. 'Stop it, Matt.'

Johnny clearly had not. 'Carry on, git.'

'*...His name never came up—never seriously. It was whispered in cabinet meetings, murmured at evening parties, hinted at in underworld gatherings, gossiped at business lunches, muttered at police briefings, insinuated in the Vidhan Sabha, hushed in the Lok Sabha. At all of the above, it was also admired...'* Matty paused and looked straight at Johnny. 'Iyaa—wozz this effin' loukk subaa 'en, aye.'

'I said carry on.'

'*...Mr Apte: combined wealth—nine thousand seven hundred crores. Unpaid taxes—twelve hundred crores. Fictitious companies—forty-two. MPs in the pocket—eleven. Houses in Mumbai—seventeen. Swiss bank accounts—three. Tie-ups with MNCs—nine. Mr Apte—instigator of riots; diverter of rivers; hacker of forests; reclaimer of oceans; devourer of ground water; builder of dams; cauteriser of crops; squasher of the landless; selector of chief ministers; harbinger of wealth. Now dead. Every little helps.'*

'...Theyaa, thazzit.'

Chrissie put her forefingers to either side of her considerable skull. 'O, m-y, G-o-d—me mind's gone numb. Who *is* this bloke? What's a crore? What's a cauteriser?'

'Dee-vee jus ear that or wough. Sweet mother of cheese n' rice.'

'Aamin, this is betta than Conan the bleedin'destroyer, this.'

Matty couldn't agree more. 'Naugh-aff mait. Aamin, ITV loan woov shell out a fortune for sommink like this, inni?'

Johnny threw in the spanner. 'Bugh wough iffits some Asian git sittin' at Brighton beach scribblin 'way like mad an' throwin' the effin trash into the wough-ers?'

'You reckon?'

'Come to think 'bout-ee, there's probably tens of such bleedin' bough-uls floatin' round the couust. Leave it, git...'

'But bugger it, Johnny–'

'Leave it, I said. Lessum old tossa like you find it off effin Italian coust—awe in Zanzi-bleedin'-bar.'

'But, Johnyboy, think. Whough iffits for real? Think, git. This thing's gonna be all ouvaa the telly like a bleedin' rash, mait.'

'You reckon? Noough.'

'Coarse I do. Look. Less juss ring that Trever bloke up at ITV…'

Johnny tittered. 'Yiah. Like you'd 'avis number an' all.'

'No, I doan mean *him,* you wankaa. I mean ITV propaah, inni.

'Yiaa, awe-I. 'Morrow then—first thin'.'

Matty folded the scrolls and tucked them in his back pocket. 'Good. Well, nuff bull for the bleedin' die. Now, woz-at pub we was talkin' bout?'

'Come on then, git. Get a move on, tis gonna close or else.'

The men made a rush for the watering hole. 'Seeya laytaa, girls. We off, we two.'

But the girls had already switched on the telly and returned to George.

'There was a cold day one summer evening…' he sang as he took a shower, the bathroom door slightly ajar.

What aadmi this, standing nanga and singing *Darwaza Khol De…*? Chi. Shaani. Indian, not Chinese. Chi, chi. Yellu hair and billew eyes. This angrez cannot ispeak Inglish. Vy, Vy? Kyonki they live in east Lundun. Not same as Sthoaul. Parantu, sade nal witch. Different, different. Papa told to me. I am talling you naa, not every firangi ispeak Inglish. Black ones worst. Only drugs, no brain. Nothing upstairs. All between legs only. Downstairs, downstairs. Samjhe na?

Bugia, bugiardo, ha mentito. Mi sdario, mentite, mentiamo, mentono, tutti noi bugia—questo e una lezione di grammatico. So sweeeet—what does it mean? It sounds so cute. Like pasta, no? I also like Parmigiani. La Montre? Shit, no I mean hello ji; I mean cheese. Parmigiani is also a high-end watch. How do you mix it with pasta?

Prejudice. How endearing it is. Helpful. Imagine how much we would have to think were it not for prejudices. Makes life easy and it is also human. How human it is. How important it is. How normal it is. To misunderstand and condemn. Bhangi. Condemn and deny. Brahmin. Deny and die. Foreigner. How often do we speak dil se?

What would you rather have—Hindi spoken in Punjabi or Sanskrit? English from Oxford or from the East End where everyone has TB? One is an imitation. The accent, not tuberculosis, which is real, including the imitation. Imitations are more popular—they are affordable. Imitations are shiny and loud. They attract attention, usage, popularity, acceptance. Look at the French—so busy correcting everyone's grammar they have forgotten where they started and lost ground to *les Anglais*. Imagine how much would be lost if a Bengali or an Italian spoke softly or if a Jat said 'please'? What prejudice?

Do dogs have a howling pattern? Birds have a kalarava. What do they discuss? What they have seen or not seen or heard. How do they wake up in the morning, you ullu?

Why is the silence of corruption so loud? *Porca miseria*. The syntax, the grammar, the reach of long hands as deftly as across a piano? How do you say corrupt from head to toe in Turkish? *Dans les pierres* and *sous le vent*?

If the walls of India's offices could speak what would they say? Srutibhedam. Sa, re, da, ni, sa.

Because in the annals of corrupt Indians, the name of Mr Apte was written in gold. He was a *stronza di sorella*, *mangia cane di merda*, *maiale corrotto* and he was a *vergogna nazionale*. Oh, so cute. Where can we find this book, please? Has it been translated? In Khan Market, Shop No 13 behind the Big Chill.

Prejudice is so corrupt. Look at us. The world thinks we are crooked; we think they are racist. Everybody in Karnataka is lazy and had it not been for the Tamilians, the state would have drowned in the Cauvery by now. Had the Italians not built Switzerland, the country would be sitting on a mountain with a few cows and goats. Can never trust an Andhrawadu—food is very hot, like in Sicily. All thieves. Gujaratis are kanjoos, Maharashtrians with their light eyes cannot be trusted and Malayalis learn to swim in coconut oil. And the Germans are like the Sikhs—no culture, no culture. Only beer and girls and fast cars. That's why there are no speed limits in Germany. How cute that the French can't speak English, but it sounds so cute, na? Especially when it is in foreign. White foreign.

Monsieur Apte. *Instigateur des émeutes, derivations des rivières, pirate des forêts, récupérateur des océans, dévoreur d'eau souterraine, constructeur de barrages, cauterizeur des cultures agricôles, squasher de paysannes sans terre, sélecteur de ministres en chef, signe avant-coureur de la richesse. Maintenant morts.* He was an *honte nationale, soeur baiseuse, chien qui mange sa merde, cochon corrompu. Chaque petite geste compte—theyya, theyya thai.* Oh, so diplomatic. French. *Panghat pe aake saiyaan, marode baiyaan*—Hindi in English.

What is the language of lawlessness? Outlaws? In-laws? Lao, lao? Mr Apte: combined wealth—nine thousand seven hundred crores. Would spend some of that in Davos and in the French Riviera buying toys. Ferrari, he said when his Lambo was late. That kind of money is in another league—even God would be embarrassed. Shiny corruption, the type of loot that knows no language, no idiom, no discrimination on the basis of caste and passport. That type of money generates fear, which in turn, generates more money. Fear the laws of anything that speaks all languages, all tongues, without accents. Imagine if a horse barked or a cow hissed? Scary, no?

But this much has to be noticed: the language of greed is democratic. It vandalises all, mutilates everything—from people to countryside to the air to the seas. It also rats on others who try to speak the same language. Do animals rat on each other? Maybe it would be more apt to say, do animals human on each other?

Unpaid taxes—twelve hundred crore; fictitious companies—forty-two at last count. This language of extortion and corruption is what would make shame shudder, greed cower and looters cringe. Even the dreaded mafia has some rules, some honour. An *omerta*, a promise between two pairs of eyes when nothing is said and everything is understood. Honour among thieves is more than three words. It is a long journey across generations. MPs in the pocket—eleven; houses in Mumbai—seventeen. Feel the breeze, the sea breeze. What is the language of the waves that bring messages from distant lands?

What is the language of the guilty? *Sono innocenti? Naan thirida illai? Aiyoo,* Venkataramanaa Govinda—only God knows the truth.

I am honest. Suddenly words appear, in all languages. Letters pour out of pockets. The bounty and mercy of the one who knows all, sees all, speaks all, is solicited. Why bring God into the almirah? What language does God speak? Can you detect an accent or is it very upper class? Swahili?

Swiss bank accounts—three. Nothing heard, nothing felt, nothing seen. Language-less, shapeless, odourless and meaningless. More or less. Greed that can only be felt, not seen. When seen, it is spun, tied and dead. Tie-ups with MNCs—nine. Fiction, addiction. Addicted to money.

Non puo fidarsi di questi Indiani. Dire de si a tutto e poi no, a poco a poco. Essi inoltre non promuovono o proteggono l'un l'altro. Molto facile divide et impera. Hanno pocco sensi di communità. Chiedere loro che cosa costruice loro carattere nazionale e serrano guardare indietro a voi. Ma sono colletivamento bravo a trovare difetti negli altri. Niente è mail copla di loro.

Mr Apte: instigator of riots; diverter of rivers; hacker of forests; reclaimer of oceans; devourer of ground water; builder of dams; cauteriser of crops; squasher of the landless; selector of chief ministers; harbinger of wealth. Now dead. Every little helps. '...Theyaa, thazzit.'

His name never came up—never, seriously. It was whispered in cabinet meetings, murmured at evening parties, hinted at underworld gatherings, gossiped at business lunches, muttered at police briefings, insinuated in the Vidhan Sabha, hushed in the Lok Sabha. At all of the above, it was also admired...

Il suo nome non è mai venuto in su—mai seriamente. Si sussurrava nelle riunioni di gabinetto, mormorè a feste serali, hai fatto capire ai raduni malavita, pettegolozzi a pranzi di lavoro, mormoro al briefing di polizia, insinua nella Vidhan Sabha, *ovattata nel* Lok Sabha. *A tutto quanto sopra, si è anche ammirato*...Oh so cute. I heard Vidhan Sabha and Lok Sabha. These white foreigners, I tell you. They know so much na.

Such a long journey. To futility.

10

1985 – The House of Mirth

The students of St Stephen's college appeared at high noon, having had their fill of unaccounted bowls of rajma, over-generous dollops of aaloo-gobi and not less than ten chapattis to each man standing. Sunlight dazed them into shielding their post-orgasmic eyes even as they munched fistfuls of saunf and misri.

The dining hall overseer, Mr Wilson, was, as usual, left inspecting his student tallies, coupons and sign-ups. *How in Baby Jesus's name can the mess expect to stay afloat under such circumstances?* he lamented silently, then rushed off to the kitchen to scold the head cook, Mr Charles.

Meanwhile, outside, the students stumbled and collapsed on the Allnutt lawns, worried they might succumb to the Curse of Wilson: acute pain in the upper intestine. They had heard from reliable sources—these were gyps bribed occasionally with quarter bottles of Old Monk—of how Wilson habitually compelled Charles to serve half-cooked chapattis that, Wilson knew, when consumed in large numbers, would aggregate in the recipient's stomach to form a giant gooey flour ball with an insatiable appetite for water. 'Will teach the bastards to eat less,' was his reasoning.

The Curse of Wilson struck with regular force at the end of the month, and it was not uncommon to see students being rushed off in rickshaws to the Hindu Rao OPD.

And so, this afternoon, after having licked their cutlery and crockery clean, reasonably certain they had escaped the curse, Akhil and Ajay emerged from the dining hall like wounded warriors and made their way to Rohtaz's dhaba.

'Rots boss, two nimbu paani and one Panama,' mumbled Ajay.

Rohtaz, the eagle-eyed, Wilson-like proprietor, went down on his haunches and swung open the lid of a battered Coca-Cola ice chest. He caught the floating steel bowl and with it gave a few swirls to the stagnant nimbu pani. Once the insect carcasses and other debris had settled, he poured out two portions of his legendary beverage.

Both Akhil and Ajay knocked back their share in one go—their Adam apples shunting back and forth—and thumped the dhaba counter with the empty glasses.

'Put it in my account, Rots,' said Ajay casually, as he and Akhil, while dividing their Panama puffs, drifted slowly beyond the Allnutt side gate and towards the busy University Road.

'It's my turn now, saaley, you have had your three drags,' insisted Akhil.

'Bastard, here. Have to shoot, anyway. Anchoring the Muk-mem,' said Ajay.

'All set?'

'Kind of. I am counting on you to jump in if guys from Hindu make my life miserable.'

'Which they will, you be sure of that.'

'*Sambhal lena, ban-cho*.'

An auto screeched to a halt beside them, catching their attention. The sudden—intentional—application of the brakes propelled the autowallah off his seat, and his seat off the engine that it was an enclosure for. A young woman struggled out from the passenger section. 'How much, bhaiya?' she asked the autowallah as Akhil and Ajay looked on, half-interested.

'Forty rupees,' said the man while repositioning the framed photo of Bajrangbali that had gotten jammed between the handlebar and the windshield.

'How come it's forty?'

'Because I say so.'

'Listen, bhaiya, I am not giving you *one* rupee more than twenty.'

'So you have your own meter somewhere, haan. Where is it? Here? *Here*?'

The woman tried to wrench her bag away from the exploring hands of the autowallah. 'Stop. My bag!'

'Oye saaley, just what do you think you are doing?'

The autowallah turned his head around. 'And who the ban-cho are you two? Her judwaan?'

Akhil threw away the poor man's cheroot and charged. 'Why, you bastard. Ban-cho just you wait...'

Ajay, meanwhile, entered into a conversation, picking up the pieces exactly where he had left them a year ago. 'Oh, hi. Aparajita, isn't it? English honours, no?'

The woman looked at Ajay distractedly. 'What? Yes. Look, this man here...'

Ajay waved his hand. 'Don't worry, Akhil will sort him out.'

'Haan, now what is it, saaley, how dare you?'

'Sorry, didn't know she was your mother.'

'You ban...'

'Arey leave it, ban-cho. Let go of my collar.'

Ajay, thinking nothing of the atypical setting for chatting up a woman, continued. 'So it *is* Aparajita. What are you doing at...'

'What? No, I'd gone home to change. For the Muk-mem debate.'

'You are participating?'

'Listen, can we, maybe later—this man here...'

'Arey, Aks will take care of him. I am Ajay. Ajay Biswas. You remember the name, I hope.'

'Oh...ya, I seem to remember—didn't we meet on the very first day?'

'We did, indeed.'

Meanwhile, at the business end of things: 'Let go of my collar, you bastard.'

'Ban-cho, would you like to do your searching now?'

Aparajita showed genuine concern at the turn of events. 'Look, I don't know, but can you please sort this...'

'Arey, Aks, what's going on, man? You need me?'

'I want my forty. I only asked her politely.'

'Bastard, we saw how polite you were.'

'Look, just give me my fare and I'll be off.'

'So, are you taking part...'

'What...Ya, I am representing our college.'

'You are? Nice.'

Akhil shoved some money in the autowallah's shirt pocket. 'Here—take this fifteen and shoot.'

'...Don't know where you bastards came from...'

'But how come I didn't know? I mean, I am anchoring the show. I didn't see any Aparajit...'

Akhil demanded, dusting his hands. 'What did you say?'

'Oh. A. Balasubramanian, isn't it? I had forgotten your surname.'

'I said, nothing. I am going.'

'Yes, and see that there? That's Maurice Nagar thana. If I ever see you again, forget the fare, you'll be getting whipped with belts. Now get lost.'

'So, are you speaking for or against the motion?'

'Sorry...? Against...'

'So let's go, then. The thing starts in ten minutes...Arey Aks, you still haven't sorted the matter or what, man?'

Aparajita turned to Akhil. 'Is it over? The guy was...'

'Gave him fifteen—there he goes.'

'Thanks a ton. Hi, I am Aparajita.'

'I am Akhil—second year chem.'

'Oh. So *you* are Akhil. Aks, right? I have heard all about you.'

'You have? About me?'

'You have? About him?'

'Well, everyone...you were the first one ever to get Kha-khao's intro on your very first day, weren't you?'

'By everyone, you mean...'

Ajay broke in. 'She means the dhaba crowd.'

'That's *mean* of you, Ajay. And by the way, *you* are known as the wardrobe man.'

Ajay broke away.

'Well, anyway, thanks a ton guys. Akhil, Ajay.'

'Call me AB.'

'And you can call me Aps…'

Ajay consulted his watch. 'We should get going, too. Aks, I'll see you there. I have to get the intro stuff from my room. See you, Aps.'

'Bye, AB. Aks, you coming?'

'Oh, okay.'

Aparajita and Akhil commenced their short walk to the auditorium. This was the first time Akhil had had female company during a walk, and understandably, he was just sticking to the walking.

Aparajita sensed the coyness. She took the lead. 'So, I take it, Aks, you are a rez?'

'Yes. T-10, Muk East.'

'Which block is that?'

'The one next to the chapel.'

'You rez guys have all the fun.'

'Do we?'

'And I have always wanted to see what your Wednesday-special dinner is like.'

'It's nothing great. Just about edible.'

'I'll take it.'

'The paneer is the soya type.'

'I'll swallow it.'

'The chapatti is like rubber.'

'I'll chew it.'

'The lassi is all sour.'

'I'll drink it.'

'And the saunf is always soggy.'

'I'll munch it.'

The words dimwit, jackass, dense, ignoramus, numskull, probably have their etymology traceable to such tête-à-têtes between a young man and a young woman. And the realisation, when it comes, makes you want to offer your skull to a giant French press.

Akhil stopped in his tracks. 'Oh. But you are most welcome as my guest. Sorry I…this coming Wednesday?'

'I'd love that.'

'Great—I'll put your name down.'

'Thanks. Akhil. I need to brush up on a few things. I'll see you inside.'

Akhil gave a thumbs up. 'All the best. The shield is yours.'

Api smiled and hurried off, breaking into a jog.

'Bye…' mumbled Akhil, thinking already of Wednesday night.

Meanwhile, inside the main hall where the prestigious debate was shortly to take place, there was pandemonium. It was difficult to point out the cheap seats. Everyone was whistling and booing. A stronger-than-usual contingent from Hindu College had already begun to debate about what kind of profanity-filled soliloquys would have the most face-contorting, nose-twitching effect on these bunch of Stephanian bastards. While they were making up their minds, Ajay, up on the dais, was trying to sweet talk them into sparing the most nauseous ones for another day.

'…Please, please be seated. Yes, and you, the most wonderful people back there from Hindu College, thank–thank you. Ladies and…Please take your seats…'

'Hindu Hindu Hin-doooo!'

'S-S-C…sitting on a tree…eff-you-cee-kay-i-en-ji.'

'Yes, thank you—please take...'

'Hindu Hindu Hin-doooo. Jitegaa bhai jitegaa—Hindu jitegaa.'

'Thank–thank you.'

'S-S-C…sitting on a tree…eff-you-cee-kay-i-en-ji.'

'Hindu Hindu Hin-doooo!'

'Yes, finally…thank you. Ladies and gentlemen, I am Ajay Biswas, and it is my great pleasure to welcome you to this, the thirty-eighth Mukerji Memorial Debate competition, or Muk-mem, as we call it lovingly.

'As you know, seventeen colleges took part in the initial rounds, and like last year, it has come down to two. Yes—Hindu and Stephen's.

We are honoured to have as our adjudicator today Mr V.D. Menon, the additional solicitor general of the government of India… If I may, sir, could I request you, and principal saab, and vice principal saab, to please come to the stage. Thank you…And Mr Menon is himself a Stephanian, and...'

The picket line at the back went into action immediately.

'Cheaters...cheaters...cheaters...Hindu Hindu Hin-doooo!'

'Yes thank–thank you...and a Rhodes scholar, no less. He was also the winner of Muk-mem in 1967...I now request principal sir to say a few words, and also explain the rules of the competition...Sir, please...'

'Shhh!...Shhh!...'

The prinicpal must have been feeling under the weather, for this time, he kicked off the proceedings by thanking only one person. 'Thank you, Ajay. Ladies and gentlemen. Welcome to Stephen's—and you, too, sirs, in the back there. Welcome. You look just the same since I saw you last—at the interviews.'

The barb from principal saab brought the Stephanian part of the house down. And gave fuel to the Hindu fire.

'Cheaters...cheaters...cheaters...Hindu Hindu Hin-doooo!'

'S-S-C...sitting on a tree...eff-you-cee-kay-i-en-ji.'

The principal took it sportingly. 'It is also a pleasure to welcome V.D. Menon. The country expects, and V.D. delivers. About V.D., I can go on and on, but...yes, now for the rules. Ten minutes to each contestant—no interjections allowed. The motion before the house is: "This House Believes Imperialism and the Raj Did This Country Some Good." And please, stick to the time limit. V.D.'s time is money for the nation. Over to you, Ajay.'

'...Er, thank you, principal saab. So, ladies and gentlemen, may I now call upon Mr Sameer Goel from Hindu College.'

'Hindu Hindu Hin-doooo! Hindu Hindu Hin-doooo!'

'Jitegaa bhai jitegaa—Hindu jitegaa.'

'...Yes, yes, please welcome Mr Goel, a second year maths honours student. Mr Goel will be speaking *for* the motion. Mr Goel—ten minutes.'

The Hinduite began as most Hinduites do, with politeness and courtesy. 'Thank you, Mr Biswas...Mr Menon, Mr Principal sir, Mr Vice Principal sir, esteemed faculty of St Stephen's, and friends. In the next ten minutes...'

Mr V.D. Menon was quick off the blocks. 'Nine...that would be nine, old chap.'

'Yes, thank you, Mr Menon. In the next eight minutes and forty-five seconds, I'll try and put forth my views as to why I think the Raj did this country some good...old chap.'

'Hindu Hindu Hin-doooo! Hindu Hindu Hin-doooo!'

'S-S-C...sitting on a tree...eff-you-cee-kay-eye-en-ji.'

With the debate now under way, the Stephen's principal turned his attention to some urgent matters. *'Good to see you again, V.D.'*

'Thank you, principal saab. It's great to be back. Lots of shouting and screaming, haan.'

'Feels like we are in a mushairaa, doesn't it?'

'Arey, but I quite like it, sir.'

'You think so? At least this year Hindu has agreed to be quiet during the speeches.'

'So no limericks from their end, then.'

'Thank God, no.'

As the clock ticked, Sameer began to argue heatedly, another Hinduite quality. '...Why? Because it's been thirty-eight long years since Independence and what have we to show for it. Poverty? Corruption? An Emergency? A collapsed justice system? Yes, we can say proudly that we are free. But free to do what? Free to plunder the nation's wealth? No, you say. Look at what we *have* achieved. Look at our colleges, our industry, our research institutions...And I hear you ask me: what was it that was better before we kicked the goras out? I'll tell you what was better. For a start, our whole country was governed by just 15,000 Englishmen. And how many administrators do we have now? One hundred and sixteen thousand. Yes, you heard me. One one six zero zero zero. We have ten times more sahibs now—and is the country *really* run *that* much better than when it was under the firangis?

'Ask your grandparents who have seen the Raj. Go ask them: Who gave us a common currency? Who brought the railways to India? Who maintained law and order? Who built the armed forces? Who established all our educational institutions? Who began the process of justice? Of courts? Who preserved our heritage? Who formed the Archaeological Survey of India? Who let C.V. Raman do his experiments in peace? Who gave him the title "Sir"? *Who*? The same people who we call imperialist bastards. And what did they solicit in return, you ask? What was their agenda? Well, alright, they took a little of our freedom away. Yes, they did....'

Mr Menon was taking his duty as the adjudicator most seriously. *'So, how's the situation with the renovation fund, sir?'*

'Oh yes, V.D. In fact, that's the thing I wanted to talk to you about. I got talking to Anirudh— you must know Anirudh?'

'Foreign seccy, na.'

'Yes. So, he tells me there should be no problem in getting tax-free remittances from these NRIs…'

'Well, that's great, sir. I mean…'

'Precisely. V.D. Just follow up on that, will you?'

'Sure, sir.'

Sameer smacked the podium with his fist. 'But balance it with what we got in return—and I know exactly what you are thinking. You are thinking: on balance—was it good?'

'This chap is good sir, isn't he. Shall I, maybe just give him a little hearing?'

'By all means—you are the judge, bhai—and one day, dare I say, the Chief Justice.'

'O-ho-ho, sir. That'll be the day.'

'Well, we wait for it, V.D.'

'Well, thank you, sir…'

Sameer stalled the trembling podium with his palm. '…Was bartering some freedom for all those things of some benefit, after all? Well, sirs and madams, I say *yes* it was. What use is a little freedom anyway? And talking of freedom of speech, which poor man, which Harijan, ever got heard? Which one? And freedom to vote—look where *that* has got us.

'I say this trade-off between freedom and progress was a good thing. Yes, the people of Hong Kong can't decide on their mayor or minister; they can't lead a morcha like our jholawala brothers and sisters; they are forced to buy mostly British goods; and yes, a few unlucky ones got shot in a protest ten years ago. But *each one* of them has some bread on his plate at night. *Each one* has a job. *Each one* is able to send his kids to school.

'Ladies and gentlemen, *ponder*, and *realise*, that those days, the days when there were only 15,000 babus, and discipline, and plenty to eat, and not much freedom to say what you wanted to say—those days were good days. Those days were grand. Thank you, ladies and gentlemen.'

The polite and courteous Hinduites all rose up in unison. '*Wah. Fantastic saaley. Hindooooo, Hindu! Hindooooooo, Hindu!...S-S-C... sitting on a tree...eff-you-cee-kay-i-en-ji.*'

Ajay reclaimed the microphone. 'Yes...thank...thank you, Mr Goel. That was crisp. Er, anyway, our next speaker is Miss Aparajita Balasubramanian from St Stephen's College. Aparajita is a second-year student of English and she will be speaking *against* the motion... Aparajita? The floor is yours.'

A hush descended, the kind that ensues each time a woman is being scrutinised minutely by a room full of single men with a testosterone rather than a dandruff problem.

Time stood still as Aparajita took small and careful strides towards the stage. The audience gaped in wonder. The majestic poise, the goose pimples of thrill visible on her upper arms, the reclining bun speared with a pencil, the perfectly curving hourglass through which poetry travels, from apparition to creation, word by word.

She was not carrying any notes.

And when she placed her elbows on the podium and parted her lips, it was as though a veena had been stirred by galloping fingers. 'Yes, thank you, Ajay...Mr Menon, principal sir, vice principal sir, my teachers, friends from Stephen's, and friends from Hindu...'

The Hinduites clapped and whistled. '*Oye-hoay-hoay-hoay! Maar guyee baazee...thank you, thank you. Shh!! Shhh—arey quiet now saalon...Shhh!*'

'Let me first thank Sameer Goel for putting up a very good defence, a remarkable one. There could be some merit in going back and finding out whether his grandfather was employed in the viceroy's bawarchikhana. And I don't mean any disrespect for the Goel heritage when I say this, but were that to be true, I'll certainly make him *eat* his words today. Not his dear grandfather, no, but Sameer himself. Yes, Sameer—the salesman, the living, breathing, gold-embroidered half-unicorn half-lion crest for that great institution, the Raj.

'Sameer urges us to go and ask our grandparents, our grandfathers, about how good life was in those days. I guess he wants us to ask Lala Chattarmal who was punished with sixty lashes on his bottom for daring to defy the provincial orders that Indians be allowed to only crawl on the streets before Jallianwala. Yes, *crawl*—crawl in the narrow lanes, yes slither, and writhe, on their stomachs.

'...Or shall we ask Chimanbhai who was thrashed and locked up for three months for taking sea water home to make his own salt after Dandi?

'Those were good days, Sameer says, those days before nineteen forty-seven, those dreamy, autumn days when another grandfather, Sardar Gurbakhsh Singh piggy-backed his pregnant wife for seventy miles, all the way from Lahore to Gurdaspur, only to see her deliver his dead son. And shhh! It must be held as a tightly guarded secret that the fate of Sardar Gurbakhsh and forty-three million others was decided quietly over a cup of tea and scones by a few affable gentlemen with sky-blue chalks in their hands and a rough scrawl of the western-frontier map before them. And it must be kept secret that with one eye on the opening overs at Roshanara Club, those benign gentlemen hastily scratched and screeched and squiggled and zigzagged miles upon bloody miles of boundaries and borders. A block of land divided over tea. But what land! A jewel in the crown—a Kohinoor...'

Principal saab was confident the shield was going nowhere. This girl was something. He resumed his chit-chat with Mr Menon. *'Arey V.D., what news of Srinjoy?'*

'Srinj? Not good, sir, I'm afraid. The company made him redundant.'

'Union Carbide, no?'

'Yes, sir. He has filed a writ in the Supreme Court—1,500 petitioners, demanding three hundred million in compensation.'

'Dear God. Dollars?'

'Tushar Raghuvanshi— you know him—is on the case...One clause says Anderson himself must come to Delhi and hand over the money.'

'Good luck with that, I say. What a tragedy.'

'Terrible, sir. A great guy he was, too, Srinj; now without a proper home and car... Has been staying at Taj Man Singh with wife and kids for the past month, poor sod.'

'Bad...'

'I mean, to see him suffer like this, sir...terrible.'

'Still, from such tragedies only do great men rise up...'

'He said his servants, cooks, drivers, all died from the gas that night. Even his dear Panzer.'

'Panzer?'

'His golden retriever. I think that really did him in. He couldn't bear the sight of his Panzer all frothing from the mouth…'

'Bas bas, V.D., I know, I understand. Still, do tell him when you meet him that I had asked after him.'

'Will do, sir…'

The rest of the audience, however, was firmly in Aparajita's grasp.

She tightened the grip. '…After all, didn't those Englishmen worry themselves sick about how and why five million emaciated Bengalis died in forty-three, just vapourised—*whoosh*—in the fifth-worst famine to have hit humanity? They lost their sleep, they couldn't for the life of them understand why, when a narrow gauge track had been thumped on the barren wasteland, when there were hundreds and thousands of sacks of wheat that could be transported, why then did so many die?

'But let's keep that a secret, too. Shhh! No one but Sameer and his Englishmen must know that those trains *did* work, those wagons *did* carry, those tracks *did* rumble under the weight of a million starving eyes, but all the trains took to Bombay—some poor fellow must have switched the lever at the last minute, all his fault. Those trains were meant for the starving and the dying, so how could they have reached the docks, and then how could they have hopped on to giant ships, and then how could they have sailed away to the not-yet-starving-but-might-starve-soon-the-war-is-not-over-yet-you-know? Yes, contingencies have to be made for the white-skinned blood brothers of the dying brownies. Oh, but surely the dying brownies would understand. They always *have*.

'Shh! And let us also ask grandfather Roy Emberton aka Mubisba Nkoango, the slave, now emancipated—thanks Abe, bless your heart—but now in need of some semblance of human rights. Goddamn Yankees. Now look—we have to find a place for these niggers to be dumped. They can't stay on our land, oh no no no, siree, can't have this American dream baloney—that's for us, the Imperialists. Tell you what—let's create a brand new country for Roy. Not near here, but what's the best place...Africa, did you say? Great. So let's make a country for them—we'll call it Liberia. Let them have all their rights there. Oh, they'll be happy. They always are.'

To have reclaimed the attention of principal saab was an achievement in itself. *'I say, V.D., this girl's good.'*

'Wow. She's packing a punch alright...'

'Indeed.'

'Looks like the shield's not going anywhere this year too, haan sir.'

'Well it's up to you, V.D., up to you.'

'She's ripping that fellow apart, isn't she. Bit by bit.'

'Haha, that she is, that she is. I wonder...Balasubra...Bala...no, sorry, can't place her dad.'

Aparajita gripped the podium ledge so tight the mic rattled. 'These little after-pages of our relentlessly progressing world, don't let them spill over on to the history books of cute little English boys and cherubic little American girls who are so happy about what their forefathers did, of how they built so many railways, so many hospitals, so many new countries. Don't let them know of the scummy little Gurbakhsh and his pregnant wife, or the sooty little Roy boy. Or the millions and millions around the world who paid for this champagne called imperialism.

'Or of that grandfather whose job it was to poke a cotton swab in and out of his sahib's point two-two for a whole day—and how, while the sahib perched himself up on the machaan with a thermos of chai and patties of egg, this grandfather was left to tie a goat to the tree and scamper away just in time to save his neck from Sher Khan. Somewhere in the by-lanes of Chandni Chowk, you'll find dusty old back issues of *Town and Country*. And look. There you see the grandfather, standing in the ninth row, third from left, looking with trepidation at the smirking Lord McPherson, first row, sixth from left, a gun in hand and a dead Sher Khan under his foot.'

Mr Menon extended his hand surreptitiously. *'Well, she can't lose now, sir; the shield is yours. Congratulations.'*

'Indeed, indeed.'

Aparajita wasn't done yet. No one knew if she had exceeded the time limit. No one complained.

'But never mind, Sameer. The same lords also doled out a whole lot of scholarships to the needy. Sameer loves them. To him, they are philanthropists, not imperialists. People like Cecil Rhodes. Yes, what of him, Sameer? Oh, but he says, didn't Mr Rhodes hope that his plan of bringing students from throughout the English-speaking world to study at Oxford would aid in the promotion of international understanding and peace? Such a noble cause.

'Before I indulge in what will inevitably be termed as character assassination, let me clarify that I hold no grudge against the many young men and women who furthered their education through scholarships named after these mighty individuals. Their singular aim was to get to the temples of learning, to be in the midst of the best minds, to extend the frontiers of the sciences and the arts, and not worry about what route they took to get there. But for Rhodes scholars Florey or Hubble, we would never have held a vial of penicillin in our hands, or known that the universe is forever expanding. These noble ends more than justified the means and the world is a better place because of many such men and women.

'Ladies and Gentlemen: Rhodes, not the Rhodes scholar, is to blame.'

It was as though Mr Menon had been struck by lightning. *'Oh my. Did she, did she just?...Blast.'*

'Well, I heard it too, didn't I.'

'Good heavens, sir. She's gone a touch too far, I think...'

'Indeed, indeed.'

'This is what dear Cecil said of his Anglo-Saxon race and I quote: "I contend that we are the first race in the world and that the more of the world we inhabit the better it is for the human race."'

Sweat was pouring off Aparajita's face; her eyes shone like blazing coals.

'...And this is what he wrote in his will: "A fund for promotion and development, the true aim and object whereof shall be for the extension of British rule throughout the world, and of colonisation by British subjects of all lands where the means of livelihood are attainable by energy, labour and enterprise, and especially the occupation by British settlers of the entire continent of Africa, and, finally, the foundation of so great a power as to render wars impossible, and promote the best interests of humanity."'

'Best interests. Peace. Humanity.'

'Oh, come on. You didn't plan all this, did you, sir—knowing very well that I was coming...?'

'No no, V.D., what are you saying, man. How can we—we love Rhodes.'

'...The great men who built empires, those imperious men—they set in stone the plans, the intricate designs, the embroidery, for the like-minded to hide their misdemeanours against the vanquished. Hereroes, Aboriginals, Jews, Indians, Asians, are all there—but in the back pages, and you flip the history books before you turn off that night lamp and they are gone.

'These great men believed that the best way to rework their grotesque reality was to remove a small sum from their loot and start a goodwill fund. And so they decided, one fine day, to chuck a few pennies in the piss-pot—their money, blood money, snatched from the land that did not rightfully belong to them...'

Mr Menon clucked his tongue. *'Good Lord and heavens above.'*

'Well, I am with you on this, V.D. She's stretched it alright.'

'I didn't come all the way to listen to this...'

'Well, you do what you have to do, V.D., old chap.'

'Quite, sir. We can always win the shield back next year, can't we?'

'Indeed, indeed...'

'...self-gloating in their aspirations to be remembered as visionaries who allowed countless to obtain excellent education. And how right they were. People still see them as visionaries. So maybe there's a case for an Adolf Hitler Scholarship. You seem aghast. But didn't dear Adolf do a lot for the German people? Did he not pull the nation out of recession? Provide jobs and holidays to millions? Build thousands of roads and hundreds of bridges? Did he not preserve and extend the territories and protectorates of the German Reich? Yes, he did. You only have to go and ask your brothers and sisters in Tanzania, in Ruanda, in Burundi, in Namibia, in Cameroon, in Ghana, in Togo.

And never mind the small matter of soaps made of human fat and lampshades made of human skin.

'Or would you like to study on a King Leopold Scholarship? In which case you would have to take a trek down to the mountains of Congo and ask your brothers there. They are all happy there, the million Roys, the Gurbakhshes, the Chimanbhais. They will be delighted to see you and tell you nice little stories of imperialism over a cup of tea and scones. And they will tell you that you can fight colonialism but you can't fight a colonised mind. It is easy to free a piece of land. But to free a mind—well, that's another story, for another day. Thank you, ladies and gentlemen.'

There followed stunned silence. It was clear that the audience wanted Aparajita to go on. As she walked away, the hall erupted in a standing ovation. Aparajita marched down the steps and took her seat at the end of the first row, wiping away the sweat with her pallu.

Ajay tiptoed over to the podium. '...Yes, thanks a lot, Aparajita. That was, well, that was wonderful...Now. Ladies and gentlemen, please be patient—Mr Menon would, I am sure, like to take a few minutes to decide who...'

Mr Menon coughed and cleared his throat. 'Er, Ajay?'

'Yes, Mr Menon...Oh, you...No no, great, that's great...Er, ladies and gentlemen, great news. Mr Menon is all set with the results already. I now request him to kindly announce the winner of this year's contest...Mr Menon, sir.'

Mr Menon got up slowly from his chair, allowing the audience to see one more time the Savile Row artistry, the John Lobb cobblery, and plain and simple snobbery. He drew out his Oxbridge cufflinks, straightened his MCC tie, and grabbed the mic. 'Yes, thank you. Principal saab, vice principal saab, my teachers, friends.

'First of all, I would like to thank principal saab for inviting me to come and judge this year's debate which, without a shadow of doubt, has been the *best* I have heard in years—on this stage, in the Supreme Court, in the House of Commons, in the US senate, or for that matter, in our parliament. I recall the time when, during one excellent debate in the American senate, President Reagan—who knew me personally, I might add and so did Nancy, by the way—I remember him nudging me with his elbow as if to say: Do they have such good debates over in India, V.D.? Well, I wish Ron were present here today; he'd have got his answer. The speeches were articulated with such near-perfection, that one couldn't—at least *I* couldn't—waver my attention even for a second. So, well done to both of you. But, sadly, there always has to be one winner, even though it was a real close call this year.

'I am delighted to announce the winner of the Thirty-eighth Mukerji Memorial Debate Competition...Mr Sameer Goel of Hindu College.'

There would have been less astonishment had India won a medal at the Olympics. Still, blood runs thick, and so the back seats erupted. *'Yay!...yay... Hindu Hindu Hin-doooo! Hindu Hindu Hin-doooo.'*

'Hindu Hindu Hin-doooo!'

'Hindu Hindu Hin-doooo!'

Mr Menon fashioned a smile and continued. 'So, well done to our cousins across the road...And well done to Miss Aparajita, too. You fought valiantly—and there's always the next time.'

Ajay came forward. '...Yes, thank you, Mr Menon. Now if you could kindly hand over the shield to Sameer...and the cheque, of course...'

It was left for Ajay to conclude the evening. 'So there it is, friends. We come to the close of today's function, and it leaves me to thank our guest, Mr Menon...Thank you, sir; and principal saab...thank you, sir; and everyone else...thank you. Thank you.'

'Hindu Hindu Hin-doooo! Hindu Hindu Hin-doooo!'

'Hindu Hindu Hin-doooo! Hindu Hindu Hin-doooo!'

'Hindu Hindu Hin-doooo! Hindu Hindu Hin-doooo! Hindu Hindu Hin-! Hindu Hindu Hin-doooo!'

As the winner was hoisted on to a hundred shoulders and taken back to the college across the road, stunned Stephanians emerged from the hall shaking their heads.

Ajay rushed down from the stage and waved at Aparajita, who had been joined by Akhil near one of the exits. '*Shit, man*, that was unbelievable—what a bastard, that V.D. Listen, sorry, Aps—you were the best by a long way, man.'

'Thanks, AB—*chalta hai yaar*...Did you like it, Akhil?'

'I have never in my life heard anyone speak so well about anything—*ever*. The shield *was* yours, I don't know why...'

Aparajita ducked through her jhola strap. 'Leave it, guys. How about a nimbu pani, haan?'

Ajay okayed the plan. 'Sure. Listen, how are you planning to go back home? I take it an auto is out of the question.'

'I was thinking, if it's not too much trouble, maybe one of you could drop me...'

'Yes, why not.'

'Yes, why not.'

Aparajita gave a puzzled look. Inside, she knew better. 'Who... then?'

'I can, no problem.'

Akhil slung his arm around Ajay's shoulder. 'Yes alright, I have got to prepare some inorganic notes anyway.'

'But AB, don't you have to close up the hall? I was thinking Akhil can...'

'Oh. Well, in that case, you go ahead, Aks.'

'Alright...'

'I think we should make a move, then...Listen AB, thanks for everything. Anyway, I'll see you at the Wed-special.'

Akhil blushed. 'I have invited her as a guest.'

Ajay put his eyes back in the sockets. 'Well, I'll see you on Wednesday, then.' '*Ban-cho nay pataa li lagta hai,*' he whispered softly.

Aparijata adjusted her jhola strap. 'Sorry, what AB?'

'No, nothing, nothing.'

Akhil turned to Ajay. 'See you later, AB—listen, sign the night reg for me, will you?'

'Alright, alright...you lucky bastard.'

Akhil smiled. It was the smile of the happiest man in the world.

The Khmer-Rouge Chakra. The Tonton Macoute Baton. The Henry Kissinger Chair. The Rhodes Scholarship. The Adolf and Benito Oratory Series. The Billa and Ranga Trophy. The Stalin Kavi Sammelan. The Nirbhaya Chainsaw.

Spot the odd one out. Which one? Rhodes? Why? Because he was rich and white? No, no, not for that, silly. We are not racists. The others were murderers, responsible for cold-blooded slaughter, rape and genocide. Cold-blooded and in the middle of cities. Town hall and all that. You really cannot compare apples and oranges. Certainly not, certainly not—especially in India where we are all white. Or white-like. Even the coconuts are white inside. That's probably why the white racist Cecil John Rhodes made sure his racist scholarship included a few blacks from the colonies.

Grey matter is a white matter. All else is dark matter. No, not dark chocolate. Dark matter. Brahmandam? No, damn it. Black matter. Oh, nuclear fusion. Yes. Fusion. This is not a spelling mistake.

Why are there no dark-skinned news readers on mainstream Indian television? Why is it that scholarships and fellowships to study in the UK in the arts and social sciences rarely spill out of the Lutyens' Bungalow Zone? And on the rare occasion that they do, why are they tied to some father's chair or mother's trophy? Is there a bloodline for scholarships like blood diamonds from South Africa? Add to the sloth the new business of think tanks. After all is done and accounted for and the children are settled in good white schools, time to think and recreate new self-help steps. By this time a generation has kicked in—sorry, paid back—and it is time to repeat the outrage over the chainsaw.

All human beings are racist and class conscious. Let that be said loud and clear. Let it also be said, equally loud and clear, that across civilised democracies, education has systematically sought to level the playing field, to include the excluded—the coloured and the poor. Why are dark people called coloured? What is white if not an amalgamation of seven colours? Thunk, thunk, as think now has a bad name.

White is not uniformly the colour of joy and fecundity. In India, it is the colour of death. Ashen. Vibhuti white. Virgin ash. Ha, how obvious life is when you close your eyes.

Why is it a black Friday and not pink? Why do baby boys wear blue and girls pink? Where did it all start and who is perpetrating it? Oh ho, the new colour of rebellion is pink. Pink bows, pink ties, pink chair, pink commercials. Now that colour has been subsumed and submerged, time to find a new pink. Yellow?

Civilised democracies are full of examples of how universal education has blurred if not totally wiped out the class divide on the basis of birth. Grammar has won over accent, democracy over diction. In India, a handful of people who have apportioned power to themselves through language and birth have fossilised into the worst of all worlds. Where birth had stumbled, money has helped. Beyond a certain volume everything is colourless or colourful.

We are a series of small clubs that are mutually exclusive and deeply suspicious of each other. We hail values no one understands. We bow before gods with sparkling eyes and diamond studs. We establish a pecking order for principles that are universal but give it our own twist. We are scared that someone might find out and call our bluff so we ensure that nothing, but nothing slips out. Not even saliva, or spit. We swallow our own sins, our own fences, our own lies and deceit without realising that one day, we will be victims of the violence we refuse to see, the damage we condone and the destruction we preside over.

See, look, try and understand. When they were being raped and mutilated, we pretended that it was not happening. We called them fascists and Naxals because we understand neither. But these are the words of the educated, the urbane, the sophisticated. What reason couldn't explain, language did. What truth showed, lies fixed. Now that we are being raped and plundered, looted and killed in our own clubs, we pour outrage.

So we get into the rural-rural, rural-urban, urban-urban language for survival. Because none of us has really had to fight for survival, the next meal, or the first job—we are children of privilege. Are we? Or are we children of industrially organized deprivation?

And then natural selection happens. Life happens. New questions throw up others, blowing gaping holes in our language, life and living. Difficult to follow? Try living it, try understanding where your next meal will come from—something that over 350 million Indians fret over every day. Ten years is a lifetime for the very rich and the very poor—same to same. Just that one was born on the right side of the road while the other took a turn. Unwillingly. Error, error. Curse or karma? Where is the error when all is good and pure?

We are truly a house of mirth. Mirth or myth? Mammals, for certain, but beyond that?

11

2003—On the Road

The wellness of a nation is judged by the manner in which its people go about their morning ablutions.

The mandarins who came up with this hypothesis were, in hindsight, prudent enough to have expunged a clause, one that called for appraisal even when the observed were on a train, thus sparing the Pataliputra Express presently lumbering its way through the vast planes of the cow belt. And so, at the break of dawn, with a damp gamchha wrapped around his considerable waist and his janehu wound about his left ear, SP Akhileshwar Kumar Chaubey pried open the toilet door, fearful of what—or who if the bolt on the inside was missing—he might discover on the other side.

SP Chaubey sighed in relief—the cubbyhole was empty. Just as he walked in, the train picked up speed without warning, shaking and rattling uncontrollably.

'Ban-cho, just when you...' cursed Chaubey. He had to let go of everything for a moment and push the opposing walls of the lavatory with his open palms to steady himself. Steady, he thrust his toothbrush in his mouth and went down on his haunches, lodging his two feet on the thoughtfully provided tyrannosaurus-like footprints.

For the next few minutes Chaubey had little else to do but hang his head down and stare at the gravel whizzing past under the round opening that allowed passengers to pockmark the great Indian countryside with their deposits. Ruminating on life in general, and the state of the toilet in particular, Chaubey felt foolish at having commenced on the first of the ablutions without giving a thought as to how in Sita Maiyya's name he would be able to conclude it. Panic struck as he looked around for the omnipresent tin can. His eyes regained their sparkle as he found it, its neck tied to the spout with the help of a muscular chain.

'Saaley kuttey, how am I...' said Chaubey even as he pressed the faucet nozzle to fill the battered can up. Travesty—the chain was much too short. To make matters worse, someone was banging at the door. Chaubey ignored the pleadings, and, with the sort of gymnastic adroitness he usually reserved for his trips to the red-light districts, managed to come clean at the end of it all. As a concluding gesture, he kicked at the can in disgust—it swung around in the air like a jumpy pup on a leash and came to rest faithfully under the spout.

The next assignment—brushing one's teeth—was comparatively a walk in the park, except for the tricky part where Chaubey had to thump the push-button faucet for a few drops of water to rinse his mouth. He replaced his toothbrush on the rack afterwards very carefully, clearly one of those people who treat the toothbrush as a member of their family.

Act three—bath. Chaubey unzipped his Reboak shaving kit and brought out a booklet of soap paper with a duotone Mumtaz all foamed up on the cover. He mulled over the slimy paperback by twiddling his thumb across the sheaf a few times as though it were a bundle of hundred rupee notes, ripping out half and saving the rest for the return journey.

Wholly in concert with the movements of the train, down to the sideways wobble of his salt-and-pepper pot belly, Chaubey turned the shower knob clockwise, then counter-clockwise, then clockwise again—only more frantically, like he was tuning a radio. And his joy knew no bounds when the outrageously corroded showerhead ejected razor-sharp jets of water from precisely five punctures—like sun rays—out of the hundred that poxed its surface.

Chaubey got under the spray, all the time shifting from under one jet to next, and began to lather his palms by rubbing the soap paper, sometimes with such frenzy there was a risk the whole collection might hiss up. As five streams became four, then three, and after a short while, two, Chaubey started to rush his movements pantomimically, fearful of the logical conclusion of the regression series. The two remaining jets, sure enough, turned to a trickle and then vanished, sucked up the showerhead—but not before Chaubey had completed his act. He intentionally left the shower knob as it was, active, roused by the satanic vision in his mind's eye of the in-coming occupant, roosting meditatively, only to be poked in the face by a sudden squirt of the erratic shower. Chaubey choked delightedly at the thought and slapped his belly, producing ripples of unwanted flesh that ran back and forth. Humming and whistling, he collected his toothbrush and unwound the sacred thread from his ear, constructing a pinch and running it all along the length of the thread so as to parch it.

Lockets, charms and knick-knacks dangling, Chaubey unlocked the toilet door and stepped out, scrubbing his head with a second gamchha, building a misty halo around it.

Chaubey now reached his bay and hunched over to look out the barred windows. He realised they were very close to the station, given the sudden jump in slum volume and the caginess with which their train was moving. From the table-rack he picked up his baint and tiptoed to the middle berth where DSP Sharma was lying dormant and open-mouthed.

Chaubey thwacked Sharma's pillow with the baint, once, and then again, forcefully.

'Aag. Ban-cho aag!' hollered Sharma at the top of his voice, looking for immediate paths of escape.

'Where. *Where*?' screamed Chaubey and then doubled up in splits, taking the rest of the bay with him.

As the prank dawned on him, Sharma managed, 'Sirji—you na,' and included himself reluctantly in the general laughter, silently lauding himself for having preserved his subordination and not vented his true feelings which were, roughly, *Ban-cho, if I was your senior, I would have made you sit on your baint for this.* He waited till Chaubey's laughter had subsided to cut down his own grin.

'Arey bhai, Sharmaji, come on, get up, we have reached Mughalsarai,' said Chaubey.

'Ji, sir,' agreed Sharma and crawled out. He was already in uniform and ready to go. Chaubey, meanwhile, rested his back against the bunk stepladder and dusted his khaki pants, after having rescued them proudly from in-between the lower-most bench and its toppled backrest. Next, Chaubey snatched his shirt from the hook; before putting it on, he exhaled against the nameplate and swiped it clean.

'Here, your shoes, sir,' said Sharma, massaging his eyes and slapping his cheeks a couple of times.

Chaubey nodded his approval. 'All ready,' he said after a while, cajoling his baint as the train stopped, lunged forward and then stopped again, finishing with a backward tug.

'You go right ahead, sir, I'll follow with the briefcase,' said Sharma.

'On time, no Sharma?' said Chaubey, ignoring Sharma's previous remark. 'Chalo chalo, bhai,' he said to no one in particular and was showered with greetings from all sides: 'Achha, Chaubey saab, very nice meeting you,' 'Okay, SP saab, have a nice day,' 'Bye bye, Chaubeyji, please, remember my name.'

Chaubey and Sharma reached the exit. Chaubey looked left, then right, and proceeded to rest his foot gently on the platform. Sharma followed soon after. Chaubey nudged the hem of his cap with his baint and asked, again from no one in particular, 'Now, where do we find that Bansilal, hain?'

'His stall is right here, on platform one, sir—he said so in his letter,' answered Sharma, trying his level best to fend off polite enquiries from the gathered coolies.

'Or shall we have some chai-shai first?' wondered Chaubey out loud.

'As you say, sir. Or we can have Bansilal bring us some chai…'

'Good idea. What time is our train back?'

'Nine-thirty tonight, sir.'

'Good. Plenty of time,' said Chaubey as he walked the length of the platform with Sharma in his wake, followed by a posse of coolies.

'*Arey, hato. Bhuttt,*' warned Sharma, trying to discourage the red menace.

'There. There, Sharma, can you see?' cried Chaubey excitedly, as though he had spotted the great Indian bustard after days of struggle with binoculars.

'Ji sir, I see it, too—arey, dhuttt,' said Sharma, pretending to hit one coolie with the briefcase.

Chaubey and Sharma now stood in front of the stall: A.H. Wheeler & Sons (Prop: Bansilal). Throats were cleared loudly. Two discharges landed on the perforated drain cover in quick succession. Realising that the officers were not going to leave soon, the coolies dissipated, cursing the two under their breath.

DSP Sharma was first. 'Who is Bansilal, then, hain?' he asked curtly, bringing his briefcase in an upward arc, then allowing it to drop down clumsily on the magazine arrangements, neatly tearing the glossy cover of *Cine Blitz* in two.

A portly figure emerged from the shadows, proving once and for all that age does not wither away the attentiveness of magazine stall owners. 'I am Bansilal. And you are? Oh. Namaste, saab, namaste.'

Meanwhile, the old lady of yore had lost none of her shrieking abilities. '*...Kindly pay attention! Coming, from, Jammu, going, to, Howrah, Junction...*'

DSP Sharma measured the shape in front of him. 'You are Bansilal? The one who wrote that letter?'

'Oh. Meri kismet. Ji, saab, I...'

'*...the, two, three, three, two, Himgiri, Express, via, Tawi, Kathua, Chakki, Bank, Jalandhar...*'

DSP Sharma spat again, in the general direction of the drain cover. 'I am DSP Sharma and this is SP Chaubey sir. We are from Crime Branch, Mumbai.'

Bansilal was all grace. 'Please. Arey Chotu, what are you looking at, hain? Run and get some chai samosa for our guests. Go.'

'*...Patna, Saheb, Bakhtiyarpur, Junction, Mokameh, Junction, Kiul, Junction, Jamui...*'

'We have come for a little chit-chat.'

'Arey, DSP saab, please. Arey, Chotu. Get two moodas, quick.'

'For how long have you been the proprietor, Bansilal?'

'...Jhajha, Asansol, Junction, is, arriving, at, Mughal, Sarai, at, platform, number, eleven, Thank you...'

Bansilal looked ponderingly at the dipping clothesline on which magazines were hung out to dry. 'Almost thirty-five—no let me see, thirt...'

'Yes yes. Do you have any idea why we are here?'

'I think so, saab. Is it regarding the Apte case? Here, saab, please have a seat. Haan Chotu, now get the chai. Or would you like a cold drink?'

SP Chaubey opened his mouth for the first time. He yawned. He opened his mouth one more time. 'Chai's good. So. Bansilal. When you wrote that letter to our crime branch, was it before, or after, you knew about the reward for information?'

'Before, saab.'

'Come again?'

'I said, after, saab.'

DSP Sharma stepped in. 'Chaubey sir, please let me handle this. These people understand a special kind of language...Haan, so Bansilal, do you realise you have made SP saab come all the way from Mumbai just to talk to you? One full working day lost on this phatichar train.'

'V-very sorry about that, saab. I-I did not know they...'

'You think it's nothing much, to write a letter—the police will just throw it away, kyon? Formalities. Do you understand what formality means?'

Bansilal smothered his face with a gamchha that had last been washed in 1964. 'J-ji, saab.'

'...Kindly pay attention! Coming, from, New, Delhi, going, to, Bhubaneswar...'

'You think you can write anything and we won't follow it up. And-and...Here, is this your handwriting?'

'...the, two, four, two, two, Bubhaneswar, Rajdhani, via, Khurja, Junction, Aligarh, Junction...'

'J-ji, DSP saab, I...'

'...Kanpur, Central, Mughal, Sarai, Junction, Gaya, Junction, Koderma, Adra...'

DSP Sharma smacked the heavily stamped and notated page with his hand. 'What do you mean by writing just this one sentence: "I know who the katil of Apte is. Meet me at Mughalsarai station, platform number one. Your well-wisher, Bansilal, proprietor A. H. Wheeler & Sons". Haan?'

'J-ji.'

'You think you can mislead us? You think we'll take all this lightly, hain? We are not your ban-cho Mughalsarai kotwals.'

SP Chaubey ducked sideways and whispered into DSP Sharma's ear. 'Where are you going with all this, you fool? Get to the ban-cho point.'

'Y-yes, sir. Haan, so Bansilal. We have come to investigate. Start with your story. And listen, one lie, *one lie*, and you know. You know, na.'

'...Kharagpur, Junction, Balasore, Bhadrakh, and, Cuttack, is, arriving, at, Mughal, Sarai, Junction...'

SP Chaubey corrected his cap with a shudder. 'Leave it, Sharma. Er, listen, Bansilal. Don't worry about anything. No one is going to touch you. We'll see to it that you get the reward...get the reward... get the reward...'

The mock echo of the last sentence terrified Bansilal. He was not to know then that 'the mock echo' would go on to become a standard operating procedure for the Mumbai police during interrogations, and that SP Chaubey would get a seva medal for inventing it.

Bansilal mopped his forehead. 'S-saab, I swear on Durga Maiyya I don't want the reward.'

SP Chaubey clucked his tongue. 'O-ho, who isn't giving you the reward, bhai? Don't worry, Bansilal. Just relax. Now start—from the very beginning...Aah, good, very good samosa, bhai. Haan Bansilal, start.'

'...at, platform, number, ten, Thank you...'

Bansilal cleared his throat, and was about to remove the unnecessary when he thought better and gulped it down. 'Sir, one day, I think it was only last week...'

'What day?'

'Tuesday, I think, SP saab. Yes. It was definitely Tuesday—I had just come in from the Hanuman mandir.'

'Proceed.'

'I switched the TV on. And what do I see? Ram-Ram, FashionTV—this saala Chotu must have been watching it all night…'

'Proceed.'

'Mata Rani only knows how many lady customers he must have lost through this, the harami. But the drawer was full of notes so I guess a lot of gents would have come to the stall.'

SP Chaubey looked around for the dented cone and was heartbroken not to have found it dangling anywhere in the vicinity. He didn't know what to do with the clenched fist.

'Proceed!'

'Y-yes, so, anyway, I quickly changed the channel to Aaj Tak—and what do I see? A screen full of headings like, *Boatul main khoon*, *Chaar saal baad*, *Maut ka Djinn*. The reporter was saying, very excitedly, that a bottle had been found in England. This bottle had a message in it that described in detail how a man named Ramrao Apte was murdered four years ago back here in India, in Mumbai.

'That got me hooked, SP saab. But what really shocked me was what the reporter added next—that the message had been written by the murderer himself.'

Bansilal was a born storyteller, SP Chaubey had to admit.

'Hmm, then?'

'Saab, three people were sitting and talking in the studio. One was saying: "Lekin, Kakkar saab, *you* are the weather man. *You* tell me how one bottle—one simple bottle—how can it happen that the bottle travels all the way from Mumbai to, what was the place, Dhingra saab, haan, Cornwall. This is simply unbelievable, Dr Kakkar."

'…and then Dr Kakkar said: "But this is very possible. Things like this have happened before. Once from Canada to Portugal in 19…"…then the anchor cut Kakkar off and asked the third man—he was a private detective from Delhi. The anchor asked: "Dhingra saab, what do *you* have to say about all this?" And Dhingra said: "This is *exactly* like what happened in *And Then There Were None,* the Agatha Christie novel. There, too, just as in this case, the message was in a bottle and the message told of murders carried out by the killer. I tell you, Chaurasiya saab, I get goose pimples by just thinking about the similarity"...and then Kakkar—have you noticed, SP saab, how even after one week, I remember all their names? Because it is fresh as a laal, laal tamatar in my mind.'

'...*Kindly pay attention! Coming, from, New, Delhi, going, to, Sealdaah, the...*'

SP Chaubey was on the edge of his stool.

'Proceed.'

'...*two, three, one, four, Sealdah, Rajdhani, via, Kanpur, Central, Mughal...*'

'Ji. Kakkar was saying that because of some unusual—what did he call it—haan, trade winds. Kakkar said because of trade winds, the bottle went through Suez and the Straight of Gibran and then to reach England it took the help of Westerlies. He was even drawing the route out with a pen...'

'...*Sarai, Junction, Gaya, Junction, Dhanbad, Junction, Asansol, Junction, and...*'

DSP Sharma was feeling left out. 'Yes yes, we don't ban-cho need to know how the bottle reached where it did. And there's nothing called Gibran. Idiot. Anyway, just carry on.'

'Ji...Then, saab, it took me a minute to think. Murder, Agatha Christie, India—and then like a flash, I got it. What if it was Kalki?'

SP Chaubey came closer still. 'Who?'

'Saab, listen, na. I thought, what if it was my Kalki. There was every chance. He could have done it and thrown the bottle in the sea. And how could he have imagined that it would go all the way to England, hain? Anyway, SP saab, I immediately wrote that letter and sent it to the police address mentioned in Aaj Tak. That was on Tuesday, and now I see you so soon. *Meri kismet.*'

'...*Durgapur, is, running, ten, hours, late, from, its, scheduled, time...*'

SP Chaubey was thinking: *If this ban-cho is so good at narrating stories, imagine what his grandmother might be like*. He came out of Bansilal's spell and thumped the magazine rack with his fist.

'Now is that all there is? Do you even know how much chaos you created at our end? All because of your one-line letter. So don't hide anything from us.'

'...of, arrival, and, will, arrive, at, Mughal, Sarai, Junction, at, nineteen, forty...'

'Ji, God promise, SP saab, I have told you everything.'

'...hours, on, platform, number, one, Thank you...'

SP Chaubey twirled and scrolled up a glossy magazine just for the heck of it.

'Now, tell me about this—what was the name?'

'Kalki, saab.'

'Just Kalki?'

'Kalki musahur.'

'Musa– what?'

'Ji, Kalki musahur.'

'One minute...Sharma, note it down. Haan Bansilal, spell it.'

'*Ji,* K-A-L-K-I M-U-S-A-H-U-R.'

'What sort of ban-cho surname is this, hain?'

'Ji, it's not a proper surname. I only gave it to him. He was a musahur.'

'A what?'

'A musahur.'

'What is a musahur?'

'Lowest possible caste. They eat rats, SP saab.'

SP Chaubey gave out the same cry Mahatma Gandhi had given half a century ago. No, not Quit India.

'Hey Ram.'

'Ji, bilkul.'

'And this, this Kalki, he was working for you?'

'Ji, SP saab, he worked at my stall for six years. Then one day he vanished, just like that.'

'When was this?'

'Ji, let me see. Haan, he came in '76, and vanished in...'82.'

'82?'

'*Ji.*'

'1982?'

'*Ji.*'

SP Chaubey was good at maths. 'Twenty-one years ago?'

'Er...ji, SP saab.'

'What the...Ban-cho, this chhokra vanished in '82. And you, Bansilal. *This* was your lead? Some...how old was he when he vanished?'

Bansilal was beginning to fear the surfacing of 'the mock echo' again. 'J-ji, not more than fifteen.'

'So you brought us here not because the killer vanished last week or last month, but *twenty* years ago.'

'N-no...'

SP Chaubey lunged at Bansilal's throat. 'You bas...'

DSP Sharma held him back, just. 'Chaubay sir, *please*. Let me... You ban-cho, Bansilal, you'll pay for this.'

'N-no no, DSP saab, please forgive me if I have made a mistake.'

'You call this a mistake? And you think you'll get a reward. *For this?* Twent...'

Bansilal joined his hands and beat the air like a reciprocating piston pump jack. 'I had good intentions, SP saab, G-God promise.'

SP Chaubey was soothed a little by the oil drilling. He sat back down on the stool. 'And this musahur fellow. What's so special about him that you wanted to tell us? That he can eat rats?'

'N-no, SP saab, Kalki had read each and every Agatha Christie novel. Nine times, ten times. He used to mumble the lines from the novels in his sleep.'

'All?'

'Each and every one, SP saab. I know because I stock all of them.'

SP Chaubey recalled having read a book once but couldn't bring to mind the title. '*Ban-cho.* Was he mad or something?'

'N-no, saab, he was good at his work. He used to sell chai at the platforms and attend to my stall at night. At night, he'd just sit and read all these books.'

'What happened to him? Why did he disappear?'

'I don't know, saab. One night, I waited and waited but he never showed up for his night duty. And then I learnt from other boys and coolies that he had jumped on a train...'

Pen poised just above the notepad, DSP Sharma looked up. 'Which train?'

'I-I don't know, DSP saab; no one knew.'

'Did he go to some school?'

'Ji saab, to our Rail Karamchari Vidyapeeth. It's a school for the children of railway employees. I had arranged for…'

'His father was a railway employee here?'

'No, saab. He had no mother or father with him when he came to Mughalsarai. People say he'd run away from his village in Bihar.'

'Which village?'

'I don't know, saab.'

'Wah. So there's no way to trace him.'

The interrogation had reached a point where there was a risk the interrogated might end up learning more than the interrogators. Certainly, Bansilal now sounded more and more confident that the worst was over. He was beginning to pre-empt the questions even. *Rather strange*, thought SP Chaubey.

Rather strange, too, that they hadn't heard the old lady in a while. She couldn't have dozed off or they'd have heard the snoring. SP Chaubey was starting to miss her. He punctuated his next sentence in her honour.

'So, Sharma, are, we, done, here?'

'Yes, sir, looks like it.'

'And for all our troubles…that ban-cho train journey, the awful toilet, the terrible heat—and now we can't go back before tonight—for all this. What has dear Bansilal given us? That he thinks a musahur, an urchin, with no mother no father, no ata-pata...Bansiji thinks he'll get the reward because he has told us of this, of this, Agatha Christie-reading *tea boy*.'

Bansilal waited with dread for the next rant.

'Let me tell you something, Bansilal. Ramrao Apte was killed by his secretary. The secretary strangled him, the secretary was caught, the secretary confessed, the secretary is peesing chakki at Arthur Road…You want more? Three police officers got distinguished service medals for solving this murder in double-quick time—and one of them is me.'

SP Chaubey paused for effect. 'And now *you* come along and tell me—no no sir, it wasn't the secretary, it was ban-cho some chhotu who ate rats and sold chai and read Agatha…kyon?'

'Err…'

'Kyon bhai, Bansilal? Arey, say something.'

Bansilal would have leapt at SP Chaubey's feet had the magazine counter not been in the way. 'Saab, p-please forgive me for my blunder. I can only...'

'And one last thing. Who else have you told about this Kalki and your Agatha and all this connection? Who else?'

'No one, saab. Not even my wife.'

'...Kindly, pay, attention! Coming, from, Kalka, going, to, Howrah, two, three, one, two, Kalka, via...'

The lady had evidently returned from the toilet. SP Chaubey was also relieved. He smiled. To Bansilal it seemed a cause for anything but relief.

'God promise?'

'J-ji, G-Gaw-Gaw-'

SP Chaubey couldn't wait till tomorrow. 'And we don't need to tell you—or do we?'

'N-no, saab, on my dead body, will I ever open my mouth about this.'

'Good, Bansilal. Good...And what shall we do about your reward, bhai?'

'...Chandigarh, Ambala, Cant, Junction, Kurukshetra, Junction, Karnal...'

'Saab, please don't embarrass me. I don't know what I was thinking to get into all this. *Please*, I am begging you from my...'

'Haan-haan, Bansilal, we forgive you. We really do. Kyon, Sharma saab?'

'Ha-haah, ji, sir.'

SP Chaubey was almost done. 'Hmm...Now, there is *one* thing you can help us with, Bansi babu.'

'SP saab, you just say.'

'Our train back is not till tonight...So, what can we do in this Mughalsarai of yours?'

SP Chaubey's loaded question brought about a momentary silence, where everyone was reading everyone else's mind. And Bansilal had read SP Chaubey's mind perfectly. 'S-saab, now what can a little fellow like me tell y-you, SP saab...'

'...Mirzapur, Mughal, Sarai, Junction, Bhabua, Road, Sasaram, Dehri, and ...'

'Oh. You have understood?'

'J-ji, SP saab.'

SP Chaubey rubbed his hands. 'Wah. Bhai Sharma, our Bansilal is a clever man, hain?'

'He is, sir, he is.'

'He doesn't *look* like a clever man but still. Kyon, Bansi baboo.'

'*...Barddhaman, Junction, has, arrived, at, Mughal, Sarai, at, platform, number, two, thank you...*'

Bansilal swung open the countertop and gestured with his trembling hands. 'Th-this way, SP saab. And DSP saab, please, you can leave the briefcase here if you like.'

SP Chaubey blew away some imaginary dust from his nameplate. 'Arey, Sharma, you can pick some magazines from here. I don't know how long you might have to wait. Kyon, Bansilal, there must be a lobby or a waiting room where you are taking us?'

'There is, SP saab. There always is.'

Three suitcases, one holdall, two tiffin carriers—one with dry food and the other with sambar sadam, aloo and puri and beans curry without coconut—small bag with books, big plastic bag with newspapers and magazines, small pouch for ticket and money, coin purse, another small bag for flashlight, soap and mug, side pouch with slippers and Odomos, one plastic packet with paper napkins and Dettol and another plastic bag with spoons and forks, one flask with hot water and a water bottle. All laden on one coolie who has to carry it to platform number seventeen on the other side of the station while assuring us that we will not miss the train which is not due for the next forty-five minutes. Last heard, that is.

Life is a railway platform.

Now there's zika to compete with malaria, chikungunya and dengoo. Like that only. Odomos, however, remains trustworthy. No Indian has ever checked the sell-by date on the tube flap.

Unpredictable. These damn trains. Never on time. That was the one good thing about the nasbandhi during the Emergency. At least we could cut off the supplies. Old trains, dying trains, dirty trains, slow trains, goods trains, lost trains, different trains, diverse trains, ugly trains—we managed to get rid of all of them. Vermin. No one even noticed. In the dark and remote corners of India, all these trains were dumped and burnt. No one knows, no one will ever know. That was the best part of not having social media. Yes, there was an occasional letter to the editor which no one read. It was almost always in the language of the unwashed masses—Hindi.

Life is a railway platform.

Damn, today, what with Wi-Fi, things are changing. Trains are beginning to arrive on time and there are fewer and fewer vermin. Progress brings problems.

Some trains are all first class. Vatanukool. They smell first class. From the sight to the look to the feel to the people who travel in first class. Here, there's no question of ticketless. Even dogs and parrots have to buy tickets. The cutlery is silver, bone china, white gloves, period lighting, carpets, even in the bathrooms; windows are sealed, and no spitting is allowed. There's a library, a pool table, and a very special five-star restaurant. You have to reserve at least six months in advance. The coupe is never available. Oh, and all windows are tinted and they have silk curtains that glide back and forth on slim rails. People travelling on this train wear nice shoes and socks even if they don't match. Nobody can enter this train. Not even the tea boy. They have their own butler and bearer. There's also a bonsai garden in the card room. It has very short trees—the only artificial thing on this train. Everything else is 'ficial'.

Life is a railway platform.

The turtles wait to be loaded onto the next train. They are grouped in a corner, turned turtle, belly up, unable to move. That is their destiny. Their flapping feet claw the air as if beseeching the gods. Next to them in large baskets are fish—big fish, small fish, red fish, white fish. Some dead, most gasping for their last breath of life. And behind them in large wicker baskets are hens, fifty-seven to a basket, clawing, gulping, staring, dead. Like thousands of Indians awaiting justice in prisons for crimes they never committed, sins they don't know and joys that shall never be theirs. Some inmates are as little as seven. Their crime? They were witness to a crime. Even to get someone to tell them what their absence of crime was takes a lifetime. Thank God scum dies early. There is God, there is hope. There is gold. There *is* hope.

Life is a railway platform.

Despite the shit and the dung, the pigeon droppings and lepers, beggars and tuberculosis coughs, the Mughalsarai junction is a sarai with all its possibilities and impossibilities. A crossroads, a threshold, an avenue, a beginning and an end. It is morning. Everyone is busy. Early-morning sounds of shutters opening and closing, the smell of fresh fruit and the fear of slipping on a banana peel. Morning routines in search of water, rats scurrying from behind bundles of post and on to the tracks on their way to the next platform. Many dogs, stretching, flexing, scratching in preparation for another day when they will have to grab food on the platforms before the beggars get to it.

Life is a railway platform.

There they run after the ticketless compartments. The hunchback and the dwarf, the man with one leg, and that other one whose hands were chopped off so he could beg better. Faceless, aimless, penniless, careless, carefree—they merge into the train like a row of ants, all in a hurry, all following some destiny, some route, nowhere and everywhere. A hospital ward on wheels, wheels on tracks, tracks on a ball, fast, faster. Life is but a queue. Buy a ticket, beggar. We are all in the same boat.

Where are we going? Goods train, express train, fast train, superfast train, non-stop, passenger and mail train. Where do they go after they leave the platform? What happens to all the things that people carry on their heads and hands and shoulders? Do they take them all the way? Do they fall off on the way? How do you know? What do you know? Did you come back to tell a tale?

The more we carry, the more difficult the travel will be. There's a reason extra luggage is charged extra. The less we have, the less there will be to leave. If we come naked, why are we afraid to go naked?

Get real. Our life has never been on track. We have always been on the road to infinity—and we shall never meet. Like ants on a Mobius strip. Samjhey na? Always on the road.

12

2004—A Handful of Dust

Fiddling and fussing with his German silver, Akhil spied through the French windows of the restaurant, hoping the taxi that had just pulled up by the million-watt portico was Aparajita's. It wasn't. Disappointed, he returned to arranging the forks and the knives in curious geometric patterns.

The dinner crowd was beginning to thicken—mostly foreigners with a sprinkling of young and brash Indians asking the manager for tables overlooking the floodlit swimming pool.

Akhil had been to the magnificent Taj Mahal hotel once before. It never failed to unsettle him. Eye-opening opulence protecting itself from blinding poverty. Just outside the hotel entrance, overlooking the waterfront, a row of imported cars. Following close behind, a row of beggars. Which part of human failure was difficult to understand?

Akhil broke away from his thoughts. He saw a cluster of beggars recklessly chasing a Mercedes on their rectangular skateboards, lurching forward with every thrust of their melted hands, unmindful of the twin-barrelled exhaust blow-drying their leprous faces. He jerked his eyes away from that particular slice of life and moved on to the one where ragged kids were unfurling postcard necklaces before a Japanese tourist.

A waiter passed by, clearing his throat, indicating the passing of unpaid-for time.

Akhil slid back into his chair and glanced around the eatery, almost full now—a few black heads bobbing up and down in a sea of pink and blond. Staring down at his origami-ed napkin, Akhil felt achingly alone and unwanted. Soon, though, his morbid thoughts were interrupted by the approaching rustle of silk.

'So sorry, Aks, got caught up in the traffic—worse than Delhi, I tell you,' said Api as she dragged a chair out.

'Not a problem,' said Akhil. 'I came in a few minutes ago myself.'

'This really is ridiculous. You should have a cell phone. Why don't you?'

Akhil smiled. 'Never felt the need.'

'What do you mean "never felt the need"? It's a necessity now, silly.'

'Not for me. Besides, the charges are crazy. Fourteen bucks a minute.'

'Arey, get one if only for the missed-call facility, na. Gosh, you really are an antique piece.'

'Hah, alright, I will soon. But then, who'd call me?'

Api ignored the loaded remark and placed a packet on the table.

'Here, something for you,' she said gathering her sari and sitting down.

'What is it?'

'Sorry, didn't have much time. Picked it from one of the emporiums.'

'Oh, you shouldn't have!' cried Akhil mockingly as he removed the wrapping. 'Nice,' he added, looking at the dagger with an intricate horse-head grip. 'I don't know what to say. Could be of some use, I suppose.'

'The dagger isn't the gift.'

Akhil looked up and smiled. 'I'd figured as much. I last used a dagger in…wow. And what do we have here? Is this…'

Api smiled. 'Nothing much has changed—at least in that part of Delhi, it hasn't.'

'Nothing much…' said Akhil, flattening the wrapping paper out a few times with his palm.

It was a map—but not just an ordinary map.

The hum of being in love makes lovers do silly things. Like drawing a detailed map of places they visited, the restaurants where they held hands, the auto rides they took in the pouring rain, the films they watched in damp theatres with bedbug-infested armrests, the bus rides, the long walks, the Majnu ka Tilas, the Lodhi Gardens, the Ridge, the train stations, the bus stands. The city, its landmarks, its roads, monuments, are redrawn, re-charted, rewritten, with new names, new thrills, new memories. And soon, all that remains of that love is a map.

'Nothing much…' said Api.

Their gaze lingered. Akhil reached for his shirt pocket.

'What *has* changed is this country...' he said, scribbling on the map, and went on, '...what has changed, Api, are its people, its streets. They need to be renamed.'

Api tilted her head to try and make sense of Akhil's doodling. 'Sorry, is that…what are you doing?'

'When everything has changed, why spare the roads? They should be named after our present heroes, not the past ones. The scamsters, the politicians, the rioters, the corrupt—shouldn't we remember their names every time we take a road or visit a monument? Or have they disappeared from our collective consciousness already? Or, as I recall how you put it once—the after pages of our history books—and then you turn off the night lamp…'

'Elephants can remember,' smiled Api. But her smile was more out of irritation.

'Lovely novel, that.'

'Yes, alright, philosopher saab. Now can I get something to drink round here?'

Akhil put the map away. 'Of course. And where the hell is your husband?'

'Don't ask,' said Api. 'At the last minute he told me to carry on. Said he'll come straight here.'

'How a fellow like AB can be so serious about work is what keeps me awake at night,' grinned Akhil.

'He has gone mad lately—wants to get to the top in super-quick time…'

'Dangerous,' cut in Akhil.

'I asked him what he'd do once he was at the top and he said sleep.'

'Well, he certainly has changed since college,' said Akhil, 'Never did a stroke of work back then—but then again, who did?'

'Hah,' agreed Api.

Silence followed.

'Not this time,' thought Akhil and hurried on resolutely. 'I never asked you about…'

'A lot of things,' broke in Api.

'Hah, yes,' said Akhil smiling. 'I never—you never spoke about your plans for a…'

Api knew what was coming. 'What, a family?' she said, as if dismissing the suggestion. 'With him? Ha ha. No, but seriously, we haven't found the time.'

'What, fifteen years isn't enough time?' said Akhil, and then quickly added, 'Sorry—none of my business.'

Api was peeved by this last comment but tried her best to hide it. 'Well, how can you have kids with a man who comes for his shaadi in a lal-batti,' she joked, hoping to play the topic off.

It worked.

'Complete with all sirens blaring?' asked Akhil.

'Ya—and then bang, bang,' said Api, laughing.

'What? He had constables firing in the air? Seriously, Aps…'

'No, silly, those were the car doors. Then he climbed out—bare-chested except for the white thread. And a white dhoti, of course.'

'And I suppose with him all those baskets of mithais and dry fruits…'

'Not to mention ninety decked-up relatives, seven lal-battis, three buses…'

The bowed head of a waiter came between them. 'Er, would you like to order now, sir?'

'Maybe after a few minutes,' said Akhil looking up. 'We are expecting someone. Some water perhaps…'

'Mineral or regular, sir?'

'What's the difference? In the price, I mean.'

'Regular is complimentary and mineral is ninety rupees a bottle, sir.'

'Regular, then.'

The waiter nodded and withdrew.

Akhil resumed the conversation. 'Haan, where were we? Lal-battis, Ambassadors…'

'What a tamasha. And at my end, my uncle and his henchmen—sweat-dripping, pot-bellied, white-threaded—playing nadaswaram. Can make you deaf at the best of times.'

'And what were you doing all this while? Rubbing off all that haldi and chandan, I guess.'

'Yes, something like that. Anyway, Ajay finally took off his sunglasses…'

'The bastard came wearing sunglasses? A white thread, a dhoti and sunglasses.'

'I really thought I was being married off to Rajinikanth.'

'"Married off" being the operative phrase.'

Their eyes met in the ensuing pause. Akhil turned his head to the side and continued. 'Sorry…now where *is* this Rajinikanth of yours, damn it.'

'Ah. Speak of the devil…'

'Say devils. He's brought company.'

Api glanced at the three men standing at the restaurant entrance. 'I hope he is not asking them to join us…'

Ajay, too, had spotted Akhil and Api. He smiled and waved at them. Then he swung round to address his fleet.

'Arey suno, Kharbanda. Can you and Sharma stay put here? Feel free to order a coffee or some soup. They give you free breadsticks along with it—unlimited.'

SP Kharbanda was touched. 'Why, thank you, sir—it's just too hot and humid outside.'

'Yes yes—and I appreciate you two staying back. We might have to rush over to the HQ in an hour's time—wind up the paperwork, you know?'

'Of course, sir. Please don't worry on our account. These look like comfortable seats…'

Ajay feigned a look of regret and said, 'I would have loved to invite you over at the table, but…'

'Arey sir, you are embarrassing us. Moreover, soup and bread would any day be better than what lies in wait for us at home. No, Sharma?'

'Very true, sir. My wife has gone to her maika and the bai—she only knows baingan ka…'

'Achha achaa, ban-cho, DIG saab is not interested in what your bai can…'

'Sorry, sir.'

Ajay cleared his throat in irritation. 'Well, anyway. Kharbanda, Sharma, you'll be fine here?'

'Absolutely, sir, you go right ahead; we'll wait here.'

Ajay started to walk away. 'As you wish. Take care then…'

SP Kharbanda leaned on his toes and called after him. 'Er, enjoy yourself, sir.'

The two officers flung their baints and caps on the nearby sofa and wiped part of the prodigious sweat from their faces and necks. They folded their handkerchiefs neatly and stuffed them down their pant pockets. Not quite knowing what to do next, they stood contemplating whether the horse in the painting on the wall opposite was a goat. Certain that it was a goat—horses don't balance their forelegs on tree trunks and munch foliage.

SP Kharbanda turned to DSP Sharma and said, 'Ban-cho, did you see that, Sharma?'

'I saw that alright, sir. It is unquestionably a goat.'

'No, you idiot. I was talking about *him*,' said SP Kharbanda pointing at Ajay, still meandering his way through crowded tables.

'Oh. Yes, sir. I know what you mean.'

'He'll be tearing his meat away like babbar-bancho-sher. And for us, soup and breadsticks.'

'I know, sir. And soup is an appetiser, is it not. I mean, this is like kicking a man in his stomach just when he is dying of hunger.'

SP Kharbanda rubbed his thumb on his forefinger. 'And all on government expense. See, Sharma? *That's* how it works. In ten years, we have to reach *that* place, *that* table.'

'Yes, sir, I get you.'

'Or it will always be soup and bread-batti for us lot.'

'Very true, sir.'

'How many years do you have left in service, Sharma?'

'Seven, sir, and a few months here and there.'

'Well, in that case, at least *I* have to reach that table in ten years' time.'

'Eh? Er…yes, sir.'

SP Kharbanda sighed. 'Anyway, Sharma saab, no use crying now. This is all written in our kundli. Ban-cho, had I shown some courage at the time and told Bauji I'd like to join the Indian Revenue Service…'

'Lakhs, sir, lakhs. *Crores*. You'd be driving a Mercedes by now, sir.'

SP Kharbanda turned to DSP Sharma with a deadpan expression. 'Or, ban-cho, someone would be driving it for me.'

'Er, that's what I meant, sir.'

'You said it, Sharma, you said it. Anyway, cut to the present and stop making all these khayali pulaos. I bet even khayali pulaos cost a packet here.'

'True, sir.'

'Well then, what are you waiting for? Call that bundhgala and ask him to get some soup and that ban-cho bread.'

'Yes, sir, at once,' said DSP Sharma and waved at a waiter. '…Oye Jawaharlal. Haan, yes you.'

Meanwhile, Ajay had managed finally to reach his table. He produced a lazy salute and pulled the chair out. 'Hi guys.'

Akhil let go. 'AB, saaley, what's this, man? Api was about to leave me and walk out.'

As soon as he had said it, Akhil cursed himself for the choice of words.

Api joined in. 'Yes, dammit. We have been waiting for at least thirty minutes, yaar. What kept you, anyway?'

'Arey bhai, don't ask. The bloody case, what else.'

'So it's just you, is it—the *one* person in charge?'

'Now don't start here, begum—not in front of Akhil. We don't want him thinking it's always me, the reason we get late every time, kyon?'

Api puckered her lips. 'So now it's *my* fault, is it? Yes, that's it, isn't it? We *come* to Mumbai, we *stay* in Mumbai, we *eat* in Mumbai, we *go* from Mumbai.'

Ajay removed his watch and placed it next to the fork carefully, like it was part of the cutlery. He massaged his bleached wrist. 'Oh come on, Aps—be a sport, yaar. Aks, you say something, man.'

'Keep me out of it. You are the one who married her.'

'Achha relax, guys. I'll make up for it. Let's all go to Elephanta tomorrow afternoon. How about it?'

'And back to Delhi…?'

'Tomorrow night, if all goes well. And now, I am *starving.* All I have had since morning is a kachauri…Waiter?'

The waiter sprinted forward. 'Yes, sir?'

Ajay gestured with his hands. 'Yes, get the menu—and some water.'

'Sir, mineral or regular?'

'What's the difference?'

'Sir, one is complimentary, the other is ninety…'

'Get three bottles. And what beer?'

'Kingfisher, sir.'

Ajay looked at Akhil. 'Beer, Aks? I know Aps only drinks my blood.'

'My husband is acting funny today. Just a nimbu pani for me.'

'Aks?'

'Ya, why not. A beer.'

'Good…Listen, two Kingfishers, one nimbu pani. And can I have the menu now?'

'Of course, sir…here.'

'Good. Good.'

Akhil glanced around distractedly and spotted the two officers. 'By the way, AB, I hope those two there are being well looked after? For food, I mean.'

'Let the bastards rot in hell. Did you know, since Monday, *I* have been doing all the investigating, probing, thinking—short of typing the reports, bloody everything.'

Api smirked. 'Finally, AB justifies his salary.'

'Yes, and I suppose one day you will, too, my darling, when the morcha you are leading ends up at a lecture hall rather than Jantar Mantar.'

'Arey stop it, you two—bickering like kids. Reminds me of that autowallah—on Muk-mem day, remember?'

Ajay roared. 'Who can forget? Were it not for me…'

'Oh, sure. Cometh the hour, cometh the wardrobe man.'

'Achha achha, boss, let's order first…Aps? Aks?'

'We'll leave it to you—you are good at ordering.'

'See, Aks? And it's like this all the time...Waiter?'

'…Yes, sir, ready when you are.'

'Ya, we'll have one butter chicken lahori—boneless.'

'Sir.'

'One bhindi nayantara, one kadai paneer…'

'Sir.'

'One dal tadka, raita, some papad …'

'Sir.'

'…And, two—no, make that three—butter naans to begin with.'

'Yes, sir. Your drinks will be with you in a minute.'

'Good. Achaa listen—can you bring some mixture along with the beers?'

'Sure, sir, mixture. Thank you, sir.'

Ajay tried balancing an upended knife. 'Good…haan, so bhai, what's new? What's up? How are things at your end, Aks? Sorry about that night, man. Just couldn't make it, you know?'

'Yes, Aps told me the next day. You came back to the guest house around eleven.'

'Arey what to do, man. I have become a prisoner of this bloody system. But leave all that. Tell me, what's up with you?'

'Nothing much. This and that—you know how it is with research…'

Api let out a secret. 'Our Akhil has become a philosopher.'

'Now is *that* true? Ha ha ha, found science too tough, is it? These brainstorming events you guys keep organising came to naught, is it? Ha ha…philosophising about what?'

'Arey, don't listen to her.'

Api disclosed something more damaging. 'And he's married, too.'

'*What*. Who? Where? When? Bastard. Saaley. What? How?'

'Abey leave it, na. She's talking about my Padmini.'

'Padmini?'

The waiter approached with his hands full. 'Your beers, sir.'

'What? Haan, yes, and there—and nimbu pani for her.'

'Yes, sir.'

'Good...haan, so back to this Padmini bhabhi...'

'Car. It's my great white Fiat, thullay.'

'A car. Oh, Padmini! I get it.'

'*Tube light.*'

'No, but seriously, Aks, forty is no age to be single.'

'Forty hoga tera baap. I am thirty-eight.'

'One and the same. Look at me—married when I was in my prime.'

'Yes, I know about that. Prime pot belly, prime dhoti, prime sunglasses.'

'So you told him, then, did you? Dammit, Aps.'

Api giggled. 'Wasn't my fault. He wanted the truth.'

'But seriously, what's bugging him, Aps?'

'Oh, nothing much. He can't stand the system, hates the way things are, is bugged by the traffic, livid with the water and the power situation, troubled by the literacy rate, objects to the scientific set-up, scornful of our netas, disturbed over corruption, enraged with crony capitalism...Nothing much, really.'

Ajay drummed a quick beat with the fork. 'I *told* you. I *knew* it. India is a great country—but only for pucca Indians.'

Akhil smirked. 'And what am I, bastard—*Jaapani*?'

'No no, you don't get it. Aps, didn't I tell you then, too?'

Api smiled. 'Yes, can't say you didn't.'

'What the hell are you two...'

'You see, Aks, my boy, it is very simple. You are not a pucca Indian anymore. I am sorry to have to tell you that.'

Akhil nodded his head slowly. 'Oh, is *that* right?'

'Yes. And it is so elementary my dear Watsonwa that I am not surprised your miniature brain couldn't catch it. You see, in order to be happy in our country, you have to be *in* our country—*always*. You understand? It is...'

'*Really?*

'Let me finish. In order to not go mad in chaos, you need to always *be* in chaos. You get me now? Man, you experience a few years of order and then come back and think you'll slip back in—into the chaos. Well, it never happens. Here, let me give you an example. Do you adhere to lane driving?'

'Yes, of course.'

'Good. And do you feel outraged when a piddly little bastard weaves his Maruti round your, your Padmini—weaves and cuts it around like he is driving a bike, brushing aside all rules and courtesies of good, friendly driving? Do you get mad?'

'Very.'

'You see? You get mad because you have experienced order and considerate and mannered driving abroad. And you are a fool if you think you'll get all smiles and goodwill if you drive like them, those guys in England or wherever. Well, I tell you, man, *you* are *annoying* your fellow drivers here by sticking to your lane.'

'*You* are annoying me right now.'

'You are adhering to, clinging on to some order, when all around you there is chaos. We Indians wouldn't want to extend our right hand and flick that indicator on—too much effort. It's not worth it. And when everyone on the road won't flick the indicator, it is understood that no matter what, that indicator wouldn't be flicked on. It's telepathy—you understand. *You*, my friend, by flashing the indicator, *you* are the odd one out. *You* are the disturbance. And *that's* when trouble starts.'

Api found herself agreeing. 'I can see his point, Aks.'

Akhil broke in. 'I can see he is talking bullshit.'

'But think, man. If 99% of your fellow drivers here don't follow lane driving, then what the bloody hell are you doing holding on to your order haan? *Try* it. Do as I say. Try weaving all around the place. For one, you'll see the other folks as your brothers—they'll *understand* you. They'll be happy. There is camaraderie among the violators, you know.'

'Well, I can't believe a DIG is advising me to break rules.'

'And that's another one for you to think about. I never break any rules—my driver does.'

Akhil clapped his hands. 'Oh. *Fantastic*, milord. Saaley.'

'And *that's* the secret of survival; correction, anyone can survive—the idea is to survive and be happy. Just allow yourself to be taken in by chaos. And look the other way when rules are being broken.'

'Someone please record this.'

'And a third bit of advice. You hate cows on the roads, you…'

'No, I love cows on the roads. I really do. They remind me that it is *us* who have taken their space.'

'*Mad*. Anyway, if you hate the roads, hate potholes and all that shit, you get a good car with a great suspension. No point cursing the system, getting all riled up with anger and hatred for the municipality, for the bloody contractor who made the road. I mean, that ass isn't worth you spending your few seconds thinking about him. Just get a great car and glide over the potholes, *skim* over them. Life's a dream in the back seat. So throw away your damn khatara and get a car that can handle our roads. Then hire a driver who will violate all the traffic rules. You just close your eyes in the back and think of things you ought to be thinking about.'

Akhil nodded his head mockingly. 'And of course, when you stop at a traffic light, look away from those decapitated, nose-less, ear-less, lip-less…'

'No need to be sarcastic. Get your car windows tinted—a dark tint—and ask your driver to pump up the volume.'

'Wah. DIG saab, wah. Congratulations, Ms Aparajita for being—what was it—*wedded off* to such a man.'

Ajay disregarded the comment and carried on. 'Arey, you laugh at me now, and that's alright. But let me tell you. You can cast and mould and shape millions in this country like you—a million brooders. There's plenty to stew over and curse in India, man. But you got to think: what is my karam? Do *I* have a job? How do I do it to the best of my ability? Bugger the bastard who can't or doesn't know how to. Why the hell should I spend my precious time thinking about that man's ineptitude and incompetence, haan?'

'Absolutely, DIG saab.'

'But think, man. Are you getting paid to do research or has the government employed you to look at those beggars at traffic lights?

And anyway, what have you ever done for them other than throw them your loose change, haan? Believe me, Aks, you'll sleep much better at night. You'll be able to concentrate on what you are paid for. Leave the problems of beggars, traffic, water, electricity to the bastards who are paid to look after those things.'

'And what a marvellous job they have done.'

'Yes, they haven't done much, maybe nothing—I am the first to acknowledge it. But then, bastard, if *you* do their job, who will do yours? No water? Get a water tanker to come to your house every day for hundred bucks. No power? Get an inverter for God's sake. You see? Solve *your* problems and that is how you will have time to think about the things that you are paid to do. Aks, Aks, Aks. Believe me—you *can't* change the system. It is better that the system changes you. It is for your own good.'

'Yes, I can see you made the same points in your UPSC interview all those years ago.'

'No, you are right. I didn't. I told them the system needed changing. And you know what? I told them exactly what they wanted to hear. But in my own small way, I try and do my job…'

'And by gosh, you do. Aps was all wrong—*you* are the bloody philosopher.'

'But this isn't philosophy my friend. This is common sense. Any fool can feel gutted looking at the misery, the filth, the beggars. It takes genuine effort to overlook it all and focus on your job.'

'Now don't you get me started, man.'

'No no, I *want* to get you started. In fact, I *know* why you returned to India, after all.'

Akhil tilted his head and leaned forward. 'Oh, you do?'

'Yes, and I'll tell you. You see, I was in Munich last year—this delegation for fact-finding something, something. Twenty of us.'

Akhil chuckled. 'Let me guess—it must have been in the summer.'

'Yes, June—but why does it…well, anyway. Munich. I was gobsmacked by the cleanliness, the brightly painted buildings, the spotless pavements, gliding buses, people moving about quietly. The whole damn thing shook me to my core. It unsettled me. Quite like the way you get unsettled when some ass weaves around on the roads here. Yes, I couldn't quite place it then but it dawned on me later. I *am* from a different country.'

'A different planet more like.'

'No use pretending I am not. I *belong* to chaos. I *feed* on it. Chaos runs in my veins. And there I was, dropped bang in the middle of order, complete order—everything perfect. I felt misplaced, a refugee, a pariah. I was in shock for the first two days, then shock turned into something much worse—I was petrified.'

'Of what? The guilt of having wasted taxpayers' money on a jamboree?'

'Petrified of my movements. All of them. I couldn't walk properly. I couldn't talk naturally. I was petrified I would make a mistake, that I might involuntarily indulge in a bit of chaos, give in to my natural instinct. And there, you see. That's when I realised I cannot belong anywhere else *but* India. You won't believe it but I spent the last couple of days locked up in my hotel room with a kambal over my head. And so, my friend, you ask: Dear AB, why did you behave the way you did?'

Akhil grinned. 'Dear AB, why did you behave the way you did?'

'The whole thing comes down to this: that I may not spit on the roads here, I may not unzip and pee by the wall, I may not take or give bribes, I may not practise lane driving, I may not do *any* of these voluntarily. But—and here it is, are you listening—but if I did, if I *did* do any of these things, then, my friend, in my India, I can get away with it—scot-free.'

Akhil thumped the table. '*Wah! DIG saab, wah. Satya vachan.*'

Ajay continued. 'And what a reassurance *that* is. Of not violating the laws but being reassured in the knowledge that were you to break them, *nothing* would happen. You see that? I tell you, man, there's nothing like it. Not a feeling in the world comes close to it. Remember, I didn't say this feeling prompts me to break the law; it just *comforts* me. You understand?'

'Perfectly.'

'And that, my friend, is the exact reason why I think *you* came back, too.'

'What rot.'

'Go on, admit it. I have given it a hell of a thought.'

'And sadly, I have given you a hell of a lot of talking time.'

The waiter approached with the food trolley.

Ajay looked up. 'Time out, guys.'

Akhil punched his palm in pretend dejection. 'Dammit. Just when I was about to learn more.'

'You *will*, you will…Yes, the chicken there, yes. Aks?'

'Yes, sir, may I serve you?' the waiter asked.

Akhil raised his hand. 'No, it's alright, thanks. I'll take care of it.'

'No no, Aks, let him. It is his job.'

'Well, DIG saab, I'd like to do his job for now if that's fine by you.'

Ajay threw his shoulders back. 'You see. That's the problem with you non-pucca Indians. I mean, the guy is happy doing his job. It *was* his job.'

'And what's wrong if I came along and *wanted* to do his job?'

'But why? Why deprive him of his pride?'

'His *pride?*'

'Yes, his pride,' said Ajay and turning to the waiter, asked, 'What is your caste, waiter?'

Before the waiter could register the question, Api, who was enjoying the table talk immensely, now asked for some calm. 'Relax, people. Just pass the kadai paneer, please, AB.'

'No no, this is interesting, Aps. His *pride*, AB? You think that by offering to serve myself I have hurt his pride?'

Ajay pointed brusquely at the waiter. 'Sure you have. He gets paid to do that. Those two buggers sitting there—munching all those breadsticks—they get paid to wait for their boss.'

Akhil took a sip of his beer. 'Oh, I see.'

'The guy in the sweltering humidity outside, polishing the lal-batti of our Ambassador. He gets paid to do that. We are all paid to do our job. And we should stick to doing our job—*just* our jobs.'

'Ah. The division of labour. Tell me, do you guys follow the police manual or *Manusmriti*? Advocating the caste system, are you?'

'No, not quite; I was just…'

Akhil was beginning to get a little irritated. 'Just what? There are people who get up every morning and walk the sewer lines. Some tie a cloth around their mouth and drop down a manhole—what's the word—desilting. It is their *pride*, is it?'

'Yes.'

Akhil had had enough. 'You bastard...'

Api came in quickly. 'Hey, Aks, cool it. AB, stop all this. Please. People are staring at us.'

There followed an uncomfortable lull in the conversation, and for the first time, the harmonies of *Take Five* being played live in the background reached their ears.

Ajay touched his mouth with the napkin. 'Hey, Aks, sorry *yaar*, I didn't mean to...'

Akhil was mollified but solemn. 'Just one last thing—to set the record straight. Why I came back...'

Akhil and Api inched forward sincerely.

'In all my days and years at Cambridge, I never once felt it was my country, that it was where I belonged. I met many lovely people, made many good friends. But you know, no matter how much I tried, I couldn't escape the draw—that invisible draw, of my own country...

'Of course, there were other reasons for coming back, too: to work on Indian diseases—malaria, tuberculosis, dengue, leishmaniasis; to try and do something for *my* people, *my* diseases. But the *one* single reason was always *that* one, the one which, I suppose, you can say is a universal reason—that feeling of wanting to be with your own, to not stand out. And in an alien land, when you are all alone and it gets dark outside at three in the afternoon and you know there's only baked beans on toast for dinner, it is *this* feeling that draws on you.

'...*That* is why I came back.'

Ajay placed his hand on Akhil's arm.

'Now—some butter naan, please.'

Api ran her finger round the glass rim, firming up to speak. 'But where is all this worrying leading to, Akhil?'

Ajay concurred. 'Yes, she's right, you know. You can't go on like this, with an attitude that things are so wrong out here at every step, that everything is on its last leg—the buildings, the people, culture, system. You'll go mad.'

'I *have* gone mad.'

'Instead of ignoring irrelevant things, you'll start thinking about *only* them,' Api added.

'Yes, you know, you are right there, Aps.'

Api replaced the napkin, then patted it absentmindedly. 'Isn't that being unfair to your students, to your research? For you to look out of your car window every time you stop at a traffic light, and then for hours on end you can't stop thinking about how that one-legged kid was hopping from car to car, from one rolled up window to another, hopping like mad before the light turned green? And then you can't think about anything else for most of your day. You can't go on like this.'

Akhil became animated. 'Yes, yes, I *can't,* Api. I *know* that, but what can I do? All my country's failings touch me. They go *through* me. I *feel* them.'

'And in doing so you may have ignored your *own* failings, don't you think? The time that you spent thinking about that beggar, or million others like him, that time you might have spent, I don't know, solving a scientific problem, curing diseases. No? Are you being fair to the people you are answerable to? Are you being fair to *yourself, your* scientific ideals? Are you? And then, next morning, you take the local train and see thousands of people squatting by the trackside—and there goes your whole day again.'

Akhil gazed at his reflection in the spoon. 'No, not for *that* particular reason—but I can see your larger point.'

'Not for that? Why? You like it when people shit all around you? Sir Vidia would be delighted.'

'Who? No, what I mean is, in a way, I accept it. I am not perturbed by it. But anyway, that's beside the…'

'No, no, not at all. Now I *do* want to know.'

'You'll laugh.'

'It's been ages.'

'Eh?'

'Go on.'

Akhil dragged his chair forward. 'Look. Your DNA is 99% identical to a chimpanzee's. We…'

Ajay couldn't resist the opportunity. 'I have always suspected that of Api.'

'AB, shush. Sorry Aks, go on.'

'We might have gone on to eat with a fork and a knife, written books, invented computers, but what has made us do all of that is that tiny little 1%. In our heart of hearts, we are still 99% animal. Then why do we turn away when we see someone squatting and performing a natural, animal act? The thousands of pairs of asses have got it right. They do their thing right in front of a moving train, as though it wasn't there. They see *us* as fellow animals but we insist on seeing *them* as something else.'

Api sipped some nimbupani. 'Deep.'

'And Hitler didn't squat on a railway line. No, he just turned out in the best suits and ate the best meals, with forks on the left and forks on the right of his plate, while the body fat of six million kept the fire in his living-room burning. So don't tell me what is civilised and what is not.

'What perturbs me most isn't the uncontrollable poverty of our people, their nakedness, their obtrusive shitting—I can handle that to some degree. What gets me is the falling apart of the most unshakable scientific axiom: survival of the fittest. I know, of course, that I am contracting the evolutionary timeline, and moreover, it isn't social Darwinism, which is nothing but a mangled misreading of the Darwinian evolution itself, that I have in mind. But hear me out for the sake of argument.'

'Go on.'

'Here, the fittest are not the fittest in the true sense of the word. They have somehow bypassed the course of evolution. Found a loophole. The most unfit here have escaped nature's fury, its test.

'A neta siphons the money meant to provide toilets for those now sitting in unending lines. He slices his share from what was meant for housing, water, electricity, schools, hospitals. He gets fat, his people die. He gets fatter, the doctors advise rest. He gets fatter still, the doctors do a gastric surgery. He gets a heart attack, the doctors do a bypass. He continues to drink, his kidneys fail. His people gift him a kidney. He lives. He lives a long life. He is weak, but he survives. Look at the irony. The very person who believes in social Darwinism, who is apathetic to the misery of millions, to their suffering—rather, *he* is the one who inflicts the suffering—and he is the one who survives.'

'But, Akhil, this is hopeless. You can't possibly do anything single-handedly. What can you do except watch?'

'What do we end up holding in our hands at the end of the day? Dust and shit. Nothing to take home. That man squatting, and me standing watching—we have become one and the same, one and the same. You, him, me, everyone—we shut our eyes. A small difference in lid pressure allows us to differentiate between what is worthless and what is worthy. For if we had just closed them gently and not shut them hard, in the soft darkness we'd have put ourselves in the shoes of those shitting millions. We'd have understood how impossibly difficult their lives are, and we'd have thought: what if that man, that woman there, was my son, my sister, my mother? But no, we shut our eyes, instead. *Tight.*'

Akhil crumpled the tablecloth so hard the veins on the back of his hand stood out. 'So damn tight that wrinkles gather on our eyelids. We get the darkness but not the thoughts—they fail to appear. But we *intended* that. And then we look away. We refuse to believe that empathy and compassion are as much evolutionary endowments as is the Darwinian principle of adaptation. In fact, empathy is a trait that has allowed us to survive great ordeals that have come our way during the course of human evolution. But we refuse to acknowledge this. Because we have turned Darwinism into Social Darwinism. Because we believe too much in the selfish gene and too little in the unselfish gene.'

Api and Ajay were silent, their forks suspended in midair.

Akhil threw himself back. 'You're probably thinking what I mad bastard I am.'

'No no…But this is scary.'

'She's right, Aks. Bloody hell, man—you need to take a break.'

'Arey, it's alright, man.'

Ajay squeezed Akhil's hand. 'But you can't keep on like this—you'll be a nervous wreck.'

'AB's right, Aks. Why don't you quit science and maybe join Oxfam or CRY? Handle your dilemmas. Physically *feel* the pain.'

'I haven't been sitting idle. I am doing my bit. Every little helps, you know. Every little helps.'

'That's a nice way of saying it: every little helps. But what *is* this "little". Both of us would like to know. Maybe we could chip in any way we could.'

'Thanks but no thanks. It is *my* problem, *my* disease.'

The subsequent pause in the conversation lasted a long while. The three were taking their time to reflect on what had been discussed.

Ajay jerked into speech. 'Boy, I tell you, all this talk has sapped my dal and chicken away. This is no way for friends to meet after fifteen years. No way.'

Api couldn't agree more. 'We'll find something nice to talk about on the boat to Elephanta tomorrow—something nice, like finding a wife for our Aks.'

'Oh no, not again.'

Ajay tugged at Akhil's sleeve. 'Akhil, my man. I don't know if Aps has told you but I have this cousin in Washington.'

'Stop it.'

'World Bank and all, yaar.'

'Arey just stop this rubbish.'

'No seriously, Aks. AB is right. Only problem is she's a Bong.'

Ajay glared at Api. 'Why, dammit? What's wrong with being a Bong. *I* am a Bong.'

Api was waiting for it. 'That explains it.'

The table resounded with much-needed laughter. Akhil patted Ajay's hand. 'No, look, I am not ready yaar.'

'You are bloody forty.'

'Thirty-eight, you bastard. Thirty-eight.'

'One and the same. So it is decided then—Elephanta tomorrow. Say we meet up at Gateway around one. And then we'll talk of Akhil and Ipsita.'

'Ipsita?'

'Yes, Ipsita. You know what Ipsita means, don't you? The *desired.*'

'It is *you* guys who are mad—both of you.'

'Ipsita, Ipsita, Ipsita, Ipsita.'

'Stop it, stop it, stop it, stop it. And pay the bill—it's late. Who is paying for all this anyway? Oh wait, don't tell me…'

Ajay chuckled. 'Perks. These are called perks. And I deserve them.'

Akhil reached for his drink. 'Dare I ask why?'

'For solving the case in two days.'

'Is that right? And who killed Saane?'

'It's all hush-hush now. CBI wants to announce it first, but I'll tell you. A bastard by the name of Kitla. At the behest of the opposition. Expect president's rule in a week's time. And all because of your dear friend AB.'

'*That* big a story, haan? So how did you—where did you find the body?'

'Arey, these SP, DSPs don't know how to handle all this, man. Saane was shot in the head.'

Akhil raised his eyebrows. 'Was he, now? God. And all your evidence. Pucca?'

'Of course. We caught the guy who did this. Actually, the bastard got popped off in an encounter. Still, we managed to get his sleeper and one thing led to another.'

'Wow. And where did all this happen? Saane's house?'

'No no, a golf course. The bastard was stabbed and thrown…'

Abruptly, Api caught Ajay's arm. 'A bit like *Murder on the Links*, no?'

'What did you say, Aps?'

'I said, it sounds like *Murder on the Links*—the Christie novel.'

'What Christie novel?'

'Arey DIG saab, the whole Saane affair that you described. I said it sounds every bit like *Murder on the Links*. Now, shall we? Or those two chums of yours will start turning to stone.'

Ajay was lost in thought. 'Yes, I see…*Murder on the Links*… You know, I had been wondering about the strangeness of this case. Why do it in the open? Why leave clues? Seemed to me as if the whole thing was a dare…Sorry, where was I? Yes, sorry…no, nothing.'

'So I'll see you guys tomorrow at one, then.'

Ajay paid the bill and grabbed a fistful of saunf from the platter. 'Yes, of course. Listen, can we drop you somewhere?'

'Leave me and my Padmini alone. You go take your lal-battis.'

Ajay and Api got up from their seats. Ajay was helped by the waiter who had stolen a quick glance at the generous tip. His taxes were coming back to him.

From a distance, SP Kharbanda and DSP Sharma saw the table break up. As a reflex, they threw away the breadsticks they were munching and shot up from the sofa.

Back at the table, Ajay gave a high-five to Akhil. 'Hah, chal then, Aks, this was great, man.'

'Ya ya, now get lost you two.'

'Will call you tomorrow. You have a–?'

Api answered Ajay's unfinished question. 'No, he doesn't. Our professor saab here says who in their right mind would want to call him?'

'Jackass. Well, I'll call your lab number, then. Surely you have a student doubling up as a secretary.'

Akhil grinned. 'That's the first passable joke you have cracked all evening.'

Ajay grimaced while Api laughed and twiddled her fingers. 'Bye, Aks, see you tomorrow.'

'Take care, Aps.'

As they left the table, the waiter, while clearing the dishes, noticed the map lying on a chair next to the one where Akhil was seated. He scrutinised it with a keen eye, then pocketed it.

Meanwhile, Akhil approached the officers on his way out. He nodded his head in greeting, smiled, and moved on, which was convenient for the two men, as the real object of their affection was now next in line.

SP Kharbanda touched his cap and cleared his throat. 'Er, hello again, sir, madam.'

'Yes, hello, Kharbanda, and er…?'

DSP Sharma just about hid his disappointment. 'Sharma, sir.'

'Ah, yes. You had a good dinner, I hope, Kharbanda saab?'

SP Kharbanda was speechless for a moment. 'Er, yes sir, very good. All hunger, gone, sir…gone.'

'Well, that's good. Listen, it's a bit late now to go to the HQ. If you could just drop us at the guest house…'

'Of course, sir. This way, sir, please.'

Api placed her hand on Ajay's shoulder. 'AB, you carry on. I'll join you in a minute…Kharbanda saab, any idea where the ladies' room is?'

'Er…no, madam, sorry. But let me find out. Arey, Sharma. You heard.'

DSP Sharma was about to run the errand when Api intervened. 'Arey no no. No problem. I'll ask that woman at the reception. You guys go ahead. AB, I'll see you outside.'

'Alright then. Kharbanda? Which way, bhai?'

You need to pick these little gems up from these bastards, Kharbanda, keep picking them up. Now look at this harami: he knows the way, of course he does—the ban-cho just walked in an hour ago—but still he asks me: 'Which way, bhai?' Beautiful. This is power Kharbanda, real power, and it is displayed thus, subtly.

Kharbanda returned from his yeast-induced hallucination and responded. 'Ji, sir, please, this way.'

'Hmm. Arey, listen, Kharbanda, I need something from you. I have had a thought—might be nothing, but still…'

'Of course, sir.'

'Er…Sharma, can you please…'

DSP Sharma was sick to the stomach. 'Oh, ji, sir. I'll wait for you by the car.'

Ajay waited till he had seen the back of DSP Sharma. 'Haan, Kharbanda, listen. This is strictly between you and me.'

'Of course, sir. As I said—over my dead body.'

'Yes yes, listen, it is this: I want you to give me a list of all high-profile unsolved murders in Mumbai in the past ten years. You understand?'

SP Kharbanda scratched the back of his hand. 'Er, unsolved, sir? But there have never been *any* unsolved murders…'

Ajay could barely hide his anger. 'I am not your sadak-chhaap—I know how you solve unsolved murders.'

'Er…'

'Don't bloody "er" me, Kharbanda, this is too important. You want to be a DIG or not? Or better, join the ranks of the CBI? Up to you.'

The dangling carrots tolled like temple bells for SP Kharbanda. 'Of course, sir—over my dead body. Er, I meant…'

'Shut up. And listen. I said unsolved because I have a hunch the murderer hasn't been caught yet, and I feel that somehow—and it is my gut feeling—this Saane business is connected to one, or maybe even more of those unsolved murders. Because there are—there *have* to be unsolved murders. That list, by tomorrow.'

'Yes, sir, I do get you now. But sir, please, not by tomorrow. I'll get my ass on it twenty-five hours a day, but this thing cannot be done by tomorrow. You have seen the HQ, sir; there are files that are shut and tied off today and the ban-chos don't know where they are tomorrow. And this business—all those files and names of years ago. Please at least give me three-four days.'

Ajay put his foot down, and not just to crush the three-four maxim. 'No, Kharbanda, dammit. I said tomorrow, and I want them, by tomorrow. At the most, you can have till tomorrow afternoon. This is big, *too big*. Even a day's delay means you can say goodbye to all your dreams. So, now that you have *understood* me, may I ask if you have a number—off the top of your head?'

SP Kharbanda glanced around. 'Er, sir, please. This is just between you and me. Officially, there are *no* unsolved murders—my job is gone if this gets out. I hope you understand, sir.'

'Stop making *me* understand. Just answer the bloody question.'

'Sir, don't mind, in the last ten years, at least 170.'

Ajay opened his mouth and then found he couldn't close it. '170. *170.* Man, you guys, you are gods. No one can touch you…*170*?'

SP Kharbanda didn't know whether he was being praised or ridiculed.

'But that's too many for me, Kharbanda. I want a small list, only high profile. Like—yes, exactly like—Saane's. Now *you* know and

I know that this Saane thing is unsolved. But the public will know only of Dev and Kitla, right? So now, how many, like Saane? And I dare you to say three-four. I dare you.'

'Sir, off the top of my head, not more than ten.'

Ajay rubbed his hands. 'Great. We can handle that. Great. Now listen carefully, Kharbanda. I am giving you a free pass to becoming a DIG—by next year, I promise. Now you listen…'

'I am straining my ears, sir. I can even hear the goor-goor in your stomach.'

'Good. Collect as much information about those ten—leave everything else. Ask Sharma to do the Saane paperwork—it's "solved" anyway. This is *big*, Kharbanda—*too* big. If my hunch is right…Now listen—most important–'

'Yes, sir.'

'You need to get all of Agatha Christie's novels—and I mean *all*, and…'

SP Kharbanda sounded worried. 'All, sir? There must be hundreds—er, my daughter's read a few…'

'I don't care if there are thousands. Add them to the HQ library afterwards for all I care.'

'Er, yes, sir.'

'Maybe you guys would benefit a little from the wisdom of Hercule Poirot.'

'Err…'

'Anyway, where was I? Haan, get all of her novels and take down whatever is written on the back flap—you need not read the whole damn novel.'

'Oh, thank you, sir, that's a big relief.'

'I thought as much. Anyway, take it down and make a neat table of two columns. You know what is to be filled in those columns?'

'I think so, sir. In the left column the name of the novel and in the right column, er, whatever is written on the back flap.'

'Good. You surprise me at times.'

Phitay-moo, ban-cho. Now was this praise or ridicule? wondered SP Kharbanda.

'Er…thank you, sir.'

'And let's meet by twelve noon tomorrow—your office at the HQ.'

'Yes, sir, everything will be ready.'

'And listen. Cancel our plane tickets. I cannot go back for at least a week, ten days.'

'Sure, sir.'

'I have to find a way to tell Aparajita this.'

SP Kharbanda nodded his head cheerfully. 'No problem, sir. I am sure madam will understand.'

'Arey, you don't understand women, Kharbanda. I'll go to the gallows for this.'

'Hah, yes, sir.'

'And, Kharbanda, *you* will do the digging—not a whisper to anyone. You got that?'

'Clearly, sir—only *me* and *you*.'

'Fantastic, Kharbanda, fantastic.'

I'd ban-cho bet my striped kachha this was praise, thought SP Kharbanda, clearing the way for Ajay.

Have you ever seen a horse with Pampers? Or a goat with Huggies? Same principle—they don't seem too keen to lug their droppings along with them. Humans, the so-called superior species, are the only species in the animal kingdom that carry their dung on their backs for hours. All the others ease themselves, here, there, everywhere. Like, 80 per cent of India. Which divide is more difficult to accept and understand? Open defecation is an issue because of the absence of facilities to perform them in appropriate places. Otherwise, we leave our droppings everywhere, hoping no one will find them. Like a lot else. Getting found out is worse than doing it—than doing anything. And we do everything khul ke. Deification, defecation—same-same.

Even animals don't behave like this. They don't write on walls. Engrave their names on national monuments. Muthu loves Sharda, or Bitto loves Gunnu, with a heart cleaved in two with an arrow. Such recognisable signs of longing.

There is no street named after a chimpanzee. In the animal kingdom, of which human beings are supposedly the bosses, animals share. Do we? After the tiger has chased the antelope and devoured the royal share, other animals partake of the meal. Right down to the last insect, the kill is shared till there is no trace of it left. The scene of the slaughter is clean, with no space for any diseases to take root. If animals are greedy, they don't show it. Animals don't kill for pleasure or torture each other and later watch it on closed circuit television. They kill when threatened from the outside. Their scores are settled with claws, not guns and cannons. And they don't take selfies with the other monkeys.

In the evolutionary process, we have been animals and monkeys for too long. The human has many more eons to go. Ask anyone who has seen war of the populations decimated, of moving from spot to spot in search of security. The old, the infirm, the baby, they are left behind—human beings don't move in herds. See how quickly we break rules to get ahead, not as a collective but as an individual? Annihilation crosses our mind the moment we are confronted with differences, with other odours and food, rituals and prayers. Massacres are something we are used to. Torture, extortion, defecation, defamation are all activities that attract us.

Hoarding—do animals hoard? They store food for long winter months. We are civilised—that's why we rush to capture, to deprive, to degrade and then to discuss in endless seminars about who is the better killer and who is depleting the world's resources faster than others. We even discuss which form of torture is acceptable and which is not; entire tomes are devoted to what the world's elders deem right. Then comes a new type of war—cyber war, chemical war, another Kurukshetra, another dharmakshetra that changes all the rules. All hell breaks loose as the aggressor is a known entity—one of us who has real ambitions as opposed to something ordinary. We are thrown. We are thrown at the slightest push.

Simple things like, standing patiently in a queue is beyond us. So we criticise others who are orderly, quiet and respectful. That's foreign to us. But the moment we cross the immigration counter in a foreign airport, we become foreign to ourselves. We are polite, courteous;

the bathrooms are cleaner. We even go to the extent of saying please and thank you. A crow in India is no different from a crow in Italy. Pigeons shit all over the place, wherever they are.

And we talk.

Oh, that little girl putting herself through impossible hoops at the traffic light should be sent to the Olympics. She could beat Nadia Comaneci any day, hands down. And the children of our fisherfolk, we should pack them off, too—so many Mark Spitzes and Michael Phelpses in the country. Rope trick, hat trick, snake trick, water trick, air trick, trick trick, we can do it all. It just needs the right attitude. But who has the time? So many problems, so many people. So many people and so few Olympic medals. So many uncles and aunties in selection committees and so many foreign lands to visit.

And we talk.

We talk of humility all the time because we are not humble as a people. Service is not servility. We struggle with that difference. Humility to find talent and nurture it, wherever it exists, and whichever strata of society it comes from, escapes us. If it was truly survival of the fittest, the beggars outside luxurious hotels would have long joined the elite for a meal. We have managed to bend, break, upturn and distort every law of nature to ensure that a few in a country of a billion survive as the fittest while the rest can wallow in hunger, disease and death.

And we talk.

The only time *they* meet us is at the crossroads. Streets named after one family and their friends. Avenues, museums, airports, sports stadia, savings deposits—all fit into three names. Even Switzerland, a country of a few million, has more names than an India of a billion, where history has been written by the vacant and the vanquished, where lies are plagiarised, where freedom is denied, where food is allowed to rot, and from where we call for peace, justice and harmony in Albania. We do this when we cannot walk across the street and share a meal or a song or a game with others.

And we talk.

We prefer the comfort of our gated communities, our answer to the karmic divide. No water, get a tanker; no electricity, get a generator. Food, medicines, healthcare—bring everything in and lock the gates.

Let those who serve us stay outside and break all the rules as long as we can continue to live in our illegal constructions and irrelevant conversations that last for entire generations. On this side, even animals know they cannot pee against the wall. It is from here that we judge the rest of the world for being cold and uncaring—a world where old people are sent to old-age homes instead of living in the warmth of an extended family. Indians never leave their parents and relatives alone. How many times have you heard it said that it is better to be old in India because everybody takes care of each other? Do we? That body lying on the street, those beggars outside religious places are also parents, brothers, sisters, aunts and uncles. Their mangled figures are also bodies, as innocent as ours. Their dreams are also real, as real as ours. But their anger can never be the same as ours. That's where we have fixed the survival step. Naturally. That's what makes our nation a nation of fixers.

And we talk.

We have nervous conversations about a nervous people in a nervous nation. What are we but a handful of dust? We don't have to be, but we are and that's what kills.

13

1987—A Room with a View

Friday, 16 October 1987
Room N3A. Pembroke College, Cambridge

Miss Aparajita Balasubramanian
c/o Mr Krishnan Balasubramanian IAS
S-23 Lord Cornwallis Road, New Delhi

My dearest Api,
I miss you so much I cannot put it in words. I think of nothing else but you. I feel like I am on a sanyas, so far away from you, and thoughts of leaving it all and coming straight back home come to me time and time again. And so I cannot describe to you my mad joy when the porter informed me there was a parcel from India waiting for me. It had arrived in the last week of September (when I was in Delhi, with you). And when I recognised your handwriting, I almost cried. You must have mailed it as early as August. I cannot possibly love you more, you know.

And it had everything that I needed or was hoping I wouldn't have to shell out precious pounds for. I may have to wait a little longer to be in a position to use some of the things. Like the Eveready batteries. I am thinking of buying a radio; the silence here is killing me. Or the

100 gram Nescafé pouches—a kettle is a must now. Coffee is forty pence, tea, thirty, and if you convert all these Ps into rupees, well, you can imagine.

But that sweater! I have not been seen without it ever since I pulled it out of the holdall. It is beautiful. And so are the A.S.-inscribed hankerchiefs. Thanks also for putting in a pack of Reynolds ballpoints and Bittoo exercise notebooks, although at first I was worried at the prospect of being spotted carrying around dear Bittoo. Thankfully, Bittoo is now concealed in brown paper—also so thoughtful of you to have shoved in. The shoes seem a size small but I am wearing them nonetheless. And the zippable quilt: fantastic—most handy. The room has no fan and it gets stuffy at night. Once I tried sleeping with the window open—nearly froze to death. I now sleep all zipped up. There is that annoying feeling of not being able to stretch your legs but this is way better than waking up to find icicles on my eyelashes.

I love you.

And I love you even more for trying (unsuccessfully) to hide the identity of the sender—no letter, no note. Silly of you to think I wouldn't recognise your handwriting, howsoever impossible to read it normally is. Next time, try writing with your wrong hand.

I miss you so much, my Aparajita. You must be angry, I know—nearly two weeks since I landed and this being my first letter. But this is deliberate. As you can see, I am using up one of the Bittoos. It is my intention to write to you every fortnight, so that I can describe all my experiences when I have had a chance to pack them densely—jump up and down them, just as how AB shut my VIP for me the day I was to leave for England. And I am determined that I use up at least half of each Bittoo every fortnight. Happy now?

Yes, to begin. Did you get my postcard from Heathrow? I know—the last thing you expected was a postcard from London with a photo of the Taj Mahal. Blame it on AB. Just before I disappeared into the immigration section at Delhi, he thrust a bunch of postcards in my hand. I can't imagine where he got all those British postage stamps from (his dad's connections, perhaps?), but each postcard was adorned with the bust of a young-looking queen. That's typical of AB—that he can think of getting British stamps for me but not

British postcards. As a result, you got the Taj Mahal while he, the Lal Qila. Dr Rajendran must now be staring at a decked-up lady in a Kathakali pose in front of Madurai temple—that one I posted from right outside Trinity. And principal sir must be wondering, 'How the devil did this fellow land up on a sunny beach in Goa after all that talk of Cambridge?' There are still a few left: Fatehpur Sikri, Golconda Fort, Howrah Bridge. But for you, my loveliest, a Bittoo.

The very first moments. There are eighteen of us, ten of whom are here for their PhDs. They seem a world away from those who have come for a BA tripos (eight in number. including me). I couldn't possibly identify myself with the BA bunch. I mean, one girl had brought along a tanpura—said she can't have 'supper' before she does her daily riyaaz. She invited everyone on the plane, even one Kenyan couple, to come to Cambridge and be an audience. Then there's this girl who kept saying 'O good heavens,' 'deary me,' 'upsy-daisy,' 'now isn't that lovely' at the end or the beginning of every sentence—and this was before we had even landed in London. Oh, and one guy, can you believe it, he was lugging around an acoustic guitar and a cricket bat. Most of the PhD types are from mid-sized to small towns and six of them got married as late as a month before their journey. When will it be our turn? When?

Anyway, we landed, and were promptly told to assemble at the medical approval cabin. My turn came twenty minutes later and I went in. The doctor's assistant was a blonde woman, who said, ''Ave ya lough coom-in todaai, 'en?' I could gather only 'ya' from that. She added, 'Yar x-raaai 'n r'poa 'en, luv.' I behaved as though she had said 'Stachoo' to me—even my lips stayed parted. The lady could have been speaking Malayalam for all it mattered. I mean, before her, my familiarity with the English accent was limited to James Bond and Lawrence of Arabia. And here she was—'Todaai,' 'X-raai,' 'Dijya'. The doctor kept moving his head up and down, right and left, like he was a boxer flexing his neck muscles before entering the ring. After a while, he said, thankfully in a Lawrence of Arabia accent, 'Have you got the lung X-ray and the reports?' 'Yes sir, of course—the reports...Here,' I answered. 'Hmm...and the X-ray. Can I see it?' 'But it must be there, sir,' I said, sounding a little worried. 'Well, I don't see it. Can you see it, Amanda?' asked the doctor. 'Nouuuu,' muttered Amanda. 'Oh, dear,' said the doctor. 'Tsk tsk,' said Amanda. 'Sunk,' I thought. They will now pin me down and shove me inside the luggage X-ray machine (I couldn't see a proper X-ray anywhere). This was a disaster. My lips remained parted. The doctor must have felt pity for me, because at long last, he said, raising his voice, 'Never mind, never mind. Both lung fields are clear. Both domes of diaphragm, CP angles, and both hila appear normal. Heart is within normal limits of size and shape. Bony thorax appears normal. Good. Next.'

He had read my report out loud. I could see the tanpura girl sniggering at the back. I said my thank yous and bolted.

After another hour-long agonising wait, we formed a huddle at the immigration counter. And here we found this old Sardarji, an airport employee who kept barking at us: 'Aiththon, Aiththon', while to the whites: 'From there, sir', 'No, madam, that way, you see?' He waved me on so dramatically that I broke into a haphazard run, coming to rest at the end of a long and impatient line of fellow third worlders. My turn came. At the kiosk, the officer gave me such a stare, Api, that I was certain his third eye would burst out any moment and turn me to a nice little heap of ash. He said, more like growled: 'And what can possibly make us think that you wouldn't go back finally to your country, given the fact there's nothing that you haven't already learnt in your Indian bachelor degree—or have you?' It took me a minute to understand his phrasing. You remember that Beatles song that AB and you have had hajaar fights over? 'There's nothing you can do that can't be done'? Well, something like that it was. Luckily, some nice Indian woman on the plane had forewarned me of such an interrogation. I was prepared. 'Sir,' I said, 'I am thankful for this wonderful opportunity that your country has given me and it is my solemn wish, indeed duty, to learn and then go back to my country and apply that knowledge to the welfare of my fellow countrymen.' I sensed immediately that he knew that I knew that such a question will be asked, and I was sure he knew that my answer was a prepared one. He looked left and right and then burst into a hearty laugh. Then he smiled—and I smiled back. He flicked open my passport and brought down the stamp like he was hacking a kathal with a machete, and said: 'Thank you, sir…Next.'

In the arrival area, we were greeted by the previous year's batch of Indian scholars. Each one of us was assigned a 'parent'—someone who would take care of us in the first few days—show us around the town, get a bank account opened, take us to the supermarket, that sort of thing. My parent (father) was a guy called Bhishma Patel, from second year PhD chemistry and originally from a village in Orissa. Nice guy. He can lift a bicycle with his teeth. Once all our baggage was collected (including the tanpura, the guitar and the cricket bat) we were shepherded to a bus stop outside. It was drizzling and overcast and the wind was fierce, howling, like in the movies. The bus was so silent as if it were gliding on butter. It took us about thirty minutes to leave the city, during which time I never once heard a car or a bus honk. Very, very unsettling.

But the remainder of the journey was worse. From the window I couldn't believe what I was seeing. Such cleanliness, such neatness, crystal-clear air, roads as though they'd been laid only yesterday, just for us, and hour upon hour of the same. I thought this is all wrong, a place can't be this clean. It was terrible. I couldn't bear to look but I did. Like a child, I kept opening and closing my eyes. Couldn't stomach it, had to see it. Fields upon fields of precisely levelled crops and perfectly round hay wheels; houses that were not like the houses we have but exactly how we'd draw a house. I had never felt so sad ever in my life. Not a single car or a lorry switched their lanes all of a sudden. Not one. No weaving, no 'cutting', no honking. What kind of people were they, those drivers, inside those cars and buses? Where would they be letting off all that pent-up anger? Or was it that they never got angry, never did anything wrong, never broke rules? Surely there were divorces, shoot-outs, mental asylums, psychiatrists, prisons, in England? It was perfect and that was my problem. But my feelings were not being echoed around the bus, I could see. Cries of 'Did you see that?' 'Look. Look there, yaar', 'We can never dream of becoming like this, man'. And I thought, 'Thank God for that.' I wanted to run back; most of them seemed delighted to have run away.

We reached Cambridge, a full five minutes earlier than what our driver had promised at the start. One by one, the parents and their sons and daughters were dropped off at various colleges. Bhishma and

I got down at Pembroke (his college, too). It was still drizzling. We entered through a carved wooden gateway that Bhishma said was built in 1347. At the porter's lodge he introduced me to Mr Powell, who then showed me my pigeonhole. Three inches wide, ten inches high, and about ten deep. My contact with the rest of the world. Pleasantries with the porters done, and your holdall safely tucked under my arm, Bhishma then escorted me to where my room was. Along the way, those lawns! Then came the dining hall. I had a quick peek and noticed its wooden tables and benches just like we have in Stephen's, down to the raised floor for the faculty. Then, more faultless lawns, followed by an archway and what looked like a botanical garden, complete with a small artificial pond. How could they concentrate on studies at this place? This was all a bad idea, I kept thinking. I'll fail.

My room turned out to be on the third floor, right on top. A wooden staircase led up to it. Along the way, on the walls, were drawn hands, forefinger pointing to the direction—upwards and still more. I noticed the room had my name printed neatly on the door. Akhil Sukumar. I loved this small gesture, done I am sure as a matter of routine.

We went in. Boy, it was small. Twelve by ten feet at best, and on one side the roof was slanted so that one had to bend down, or sideways, to reach the corner at that end. Thoughtfully, that was where the single bed was arranged. But it doesn't work all the time. Just yesterday I woke up and banged my head properly. One cupboard, a table, a chair and—you'll love this—a note from the senior tutor explaining that '...The walls are not to be disfigured by sticking posters onto them. Poster clips and plastic slit rods are provided for displaying one's preferences. Thank you.' One's preferences. Bhishma took leave and promised to drop by at night to take me out for dinner. Soon, I was alone. And I thought of you at that moment. Then I went to the only window of my room.

The view: It is a normal-sized window—opens outside. No jaali as no mosquitoes here (sorry, no use for the kachuachap that you had packed in). And what a view. It really is magnificent. On my toes, standing up, I can just about see the top of King's College Chapel. Back on my heels, the Old Cavendish building comes into view.

Sitting down, I can see the soot-blackened walls of the Pembroke Street buildings. I think whoever built this room was mindful of how tiny it is, and so decided to make amends by placing the window right where it presently is. A few inches up, or to the right, and you can't see King's at all or the Cavendish. It is placed exactly where looking through it one forgets the constrained space of this room. And this is where I am at present—sitting, window open, writing to you, my sweetest Api.

And if I close the window, I feel I am in a vacuum desiccator. The silence in the room becomes deafening. For the first time in my life I am able to hear the sound of silence—a weak beeping din inside your ears, continues till you want it; open the window and it's gone. All very unsettling, Api, and there's not even the whirr of the ceiling fan. There's nothing except this constant beeping in your head. Something would have to be done or I'll go mad. As if being lonely thousands of miles away wasn't enough; like with those Godrej shaving cream and razors back home—buy one loneliness, get one complete silence absolutely free.

And the smell. Well, this is turning out to be a detailed description of my Chinese tortures, but now of the smell. There is none. No smell whatsoever. Open window, closed window—doesn't matter. It is therapeutic just to recall some of the smells we are so used to. Now let me see: the smell of aaloo-puri, of rust, of coconut-oiled heads, of the suitcase cover-cloth, of shit, of urine, of overboiled chai, of the damp store room, of the aata-glue in the post-office, of sweat, of mixed fruit juice, of water (of the water cooler). And here? Nothing. Nothing smells. I keep the window open most of the time but nothing wafts in. My nose is dying—send me some agarbattis.

Cats. Let me tell you about cats. Every college keeps one. I came across our Pembroke cat, called Jess, one afternoon by the college library. Believe me, Api, when I tell you—at least three times the size of our Indian cats. There it was—jet black, steel-blue eyes, and a collar with a bell attached to it. When I stared at her she responded with half-opened eyes and a measuring up sort of look. She didn't cower or look away like our cats would have. This put me off. I showed my full set of teeth and made a forward motion. Something like this would have made our cat leap back and skittle away with a few protesting meows. Jess did nothing of the kind—she simply looked away, as though she was bored. This was humiliating. Not to be outdone by a silly cat, I then gestured an assault, with my fingers spread open and curled. And you know that I am safe because I am writing this letter and you are reading it, but I tell you, Api, had I not pulled sideways at the very last moment, Jess would have gorged out my Adam's apple in a second. The monster jumped at me, and through the air with such immense speed that the whole instant was—still is—like a great black blur. I have since learnt my lesson: I see Jess prowling or sniffing the path and I turn away and go by another route. Damn. Even the cats here are different. They don't leave the college premises. They meander across the lawns, something that only fellows of the college are allowed to do. They walk away from the food when they feel they are done, sometimes leaving it half-eaten. They basically just sit and survey. That, Api, is the story of the English cat. I am sure it's all white under that black fur.

But everyone else, beside that wretched Jess, is afraid of me. Here are a few samples. Miss Treblecock: 'Mr Sukumar, I am terribly afraid I have not been able to make a cheque yet for the…'. Or Mrs Thornton, the senior tutor's secretary: 'Akhil, I'm afraid the meeting we had planned for you hasn't…'. Even my tutor, Professor Fleming: 'Akhil, I'm afraid that next week's supervision…'.

Now about the appearances. Everyone on the streets here is so well dressed, the women especially. Neat and careful and clean and spotless—not like the goras we see in Connaught Place or Sarojini Nagar. None of those tattered chappals here, those garish multicoloured vests and grimy bermudas, the filthy ghagraas, that unkempt naga sadhu hairstyles—none of that. This came as a shock to me. Perhaps their appearance back in India was deliberate, intentional—an effort to gel in, a holiday tamasha, a 'look'. Discarded all at the airport lounge or on the flight back. All scrubbed off and the real person emerges.

Lesson number one, etiquette. Early-morning breakfast. Mr Sukumar, in queue for his portion of scrambled eggs and baked beans and toast. He says: 'Yes, I want two portions of scrambled eggs.

And give me one portion of baked beans. Also, give me two slices of toasted bread and one coffee. How much?' And pat comes the reply from across the counter: 'Never mind how much. Just, can you put a 'please' and a 'thanks' at the end of every sentence that you just said, please?' And so Mr Sukumar refines his order and has to do all of that 'please', 'thank you' business.

Next: Lesson number two, the civil code. 1900 hours, Market Square, opposite the Guild Hall. Fruit and vegetable stalls. No shouting or hawking. Mr Sukumar eyes a nice ripe mango. Goes all misty-eyed and says: 'How much is that mango?' Quickly remembers lesson number one and tries again: 'Can I have this mango, please?' and again, 'How much, miss, for this mango, please?' The answer that comes out from across is Lesson number two. 'Oii. Waiit fough ya turn, you buggaah—caanchew see (the nose twitches upwards and to the right at this point; the glare is fixed and the eyes contort) I am serving somebodiee? Wheyaa-u fawm 'en?' 'Oh, I am sorry' is all the hurriedly retreating Mr Sukumar can muster.

They are asking me to change, Api, all of them. They are selling me a quiet and peaceful and orderly marketplace when the only marketplace I have ever seen is noisy and riotous, with rotten vegetables strewn everywhere, with vendors shouting their throats out, with people haggling, with ladies snapping off bhindi tips, with motionless cows and howling dogs, with blank men and worried women and wailing kids, with potholes breeding larvae and mother mosquitoes buzzing lovingly above them. But at the end of the day, everyone is satisfied. That's the marketplace I know. What makes them think theirs is the only kind of marketplace there should be?

Just the other day, I remarked on this to my tutor. He took it the wrong way, like most of them do. He said: 'Oh, poor you. Well, it's a mess, India is—but it's getting there, getting there.' They have notions about us. They think we are poor—not just monetarily but poor in every sense. Monetary poverty to them translates into poverty of the body and its soul—mental depravation. Lack of money retards. How can I tell them that no one has sucked up all this filth, this grime, this smell—sucked it up in a syringe millilitre by millilitre and punctured my skull and pushed all of it in? My mind is not my poverty. I am not poor because of the poverty of my mind. And so I want to tell them that I can thrive in my hell. Not survive or simply exist, but thrive. This chaotic hell that surrounds me is just a piece of my clothing. I cannot escape from wearing it but I let it not affect me. But I remained silent.

I don't know why I am telling you all this. I started out writing a letter and have ended up scribbling nonsense, and now it looks like an entry in my diary. This is what loneliness does to you, I suppose. Loneliness and isolation. And here I am, duly sandwiched. The thoughts get all jumbled up. One cannot pry them apart like Dusshasan's limbs, one cannot demarcate their destinations—a letter or a diary. I think I'll stop now. I am exhausted.

How I wish you were here with me. How I wish we were together. I could have shared all these things with you in person. But then my sanyas wouldn't have been a proper sanyas. This—our penultimate act in Ramlila.

I miss you and long to be with you for ever and ever, my sweet darling.

Akhil

PS: A maddeningly prolonged stare at one of the ten problems (drawn below) that I need to solve for tomorrow's tutorial has made me see the veiled implication of this reaction:

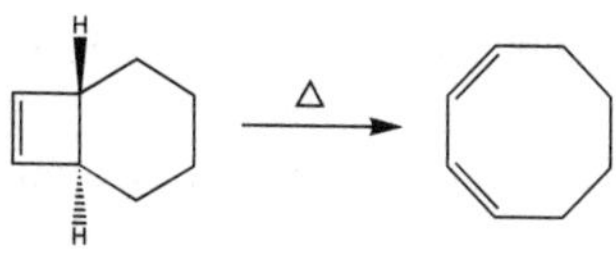

Two unequal bodies, in this case a square and a hexagon, when joined at the hip and heated, become one.

How 'adi' is 'vasi'? Do naphthalene balls tell stories? Does paper have odour? Do trees have eyes? What do they see and whom do they tell what they see? Trees will live longer than you. So will the paper you stored, the letters you saved, the photographs you have hung on the walls of your mind. The stories you never heard, couldn't tell, didn't know, collectively forgave, independently cursed, long as life, short as destiny. You will live beyond you if you don't know who you are.

Invisible laughter, visible grief. Or the other way around—everyone knows so no one does?

And then there were none.

Can't leave the house. So much responsibility, so many things. Things. Locks and keys of empty souls, almirahs full of valuables brimming with grief. Family papers, court cases, property fights, venom and hate, greed and arrangements. Blocks that don't fit into a circle, like a chair with three legs or none. Can't leave the house or the house doesn't leave you? When do you leave your body—any ideas? Before you are dead, during or after? When do you kill others so you can pack your suitcases?

And then there were none.

Storage space is never sufficient. Clutter gives confidence, empty spaces question. Fill, fill, landfill. What is more unsettling—the end of a sentence or the beginning of one, and what if both didn't exist or one couldn't without the other? Innards hanging out.

Empty spaces question. Empty spaces between things that is—more important than the ones between us. Between you and me, between me and myself, between us and our loved ones. Remembered by what you inherit, not what you make of yourself. Complicated, dissected, distributed and agreed. What matters is the arrangement. And in a certain order known to man but unknown to the universe.

And then there were none.

So who begins the story? Your story, my story, our story, their story. The winners or the losers? Who records history—family history, a country's history? History. How long is respectable, how short is the bastard? How real is the arrangement, how false is the deviation? Where is the limit? Is that a cliff or a trough, a road or a destiny?

Who knows. Who doesn't.

Who knows! Who doesn't!

Who knows? Who doesn't?

Is the knower also the seeker or is the seeker and the sought the same? The search is ceaseless. Waves and wounds, waves and wounds, but why is the ocean calm? The kshirasagara is still. This is frustrating. Where is the shipwreck of my soul?

And then there were none.

Who am I? What am I? I am blind and I can see that I am blind. A blindness so bright it blinds. Behind our eyes we bear a loneliness that is our own. We move indifferent and apart, even from the sadness in our hearts. Refuge, subterfuge.

Subterfugees. Living in a subterfugee camp.

The minute we are born, we are in a queue, a number. Take a ticket and stand in line. How long my time is—no one knows. So I require, I acquire, I desire. In preparation and desperation for a liberation I neither understand nor know. Or want. Want-less line, wicked destiny.

And then there were none.

How far back is reasonable memory? How far back do you go? What is the point? Of course, there is. History is important. The history of the important. The history of important things, the history of dates, the dates of important acquisitions, captured for the important, by the important. That's what matters. Keep what is important and destroy the rest.

And then there were none.

How many times have you walked into a house, your house, wondering what is precious and what is not? That chair, those pictures and those hundreds of letters, one from every city in the world. Of people long dead, of relationships long over—of nothingness that fills our minds and hearts. There is a name for it, as there is one for everything that cannot be quantified. Sixteen kilos of kindness and seven of hate, 8,000 photographs of arrivals and departures in airports and cradles, graveyards and stations. Life looking for a place, steels trunks staring at you, steel almirahs laughing at you. They know your secrets, the ones you keep locked in the inner compartments. Is it a kutti Godrej or a jabba Godrej? The turning of the lock brings memories—good and bad—of smells, of distance. What is the distance smell can measure and retain? Marathon or steeplechase?

For how long does a severed head retain the last image of a fast-approaching guillotine?

2007 was a good year—the rains were good, the grapes were not sour, the bottles had special labels. Random is a number.

And then there were none.

Walk into your house and collect everything, the physical possessions and the mental. Collect them and stuff them in a house-sized cardboard box. Clasp its flap and drag your memories down the steps—thud, thud, thud, thud—drag them to the lawn at the back of the house where the sun is shining and the cat snoozes under a parasol. Make a fire to stuff the ashes down your throat. Swallow the poison. It is yours. Bonfire, bon appétit. Burn everything—the papers, the letters, the diaries, the photographs. This fire has no smoke, but this room has a view for those who dare to see that what burns in your heart doesn't have to burn you. Punctuations never end life, only sentences. The souls don't turn to ash.

Walk or else there will be none.

There will never be a record of the 'adi' for a 'vasi' because there were none. The recorder of time and turner of destinies does not own a watch. He too is naked. Or is it a she?

Walk away. Now and naked.

14

2004—Darkness Visible

The evening sun put on such a show of flaming shades across the sky that one could be forgiven for thinking it was Hawaii, not Mumbai. But the heat and the dust stopped that drift abruptly.

Aparajita now regretted having ventured out to the suburbs on a post-lunch whim. Four miserable hours later, she stood outside the giant steel and concrete ogre that was the National Social Sciences Institute, waltzing forwards and backwards but not able to find that precise moment of self-belief and fortitude someone new to a city seeks to cross a busy street. She gave up and hailed an auto. Two crawled over. Aparajita settled on the autowallah combing his hennaed beard.

'Kandivali Station, Baba.'

'Baithiyay,' said the old man.

His compatriot, a young man in khakhi overalls with a grimy tea towel slung on his shoulder, looked on patiently from inside his auto. Seeing Aparajita climb into Baba's auto, the young man yanked his floor starter in a single, almost militant move. The auto roared to life, sputtering all the while he waited for Baba to give way.

But the old man's auto refused to shunt. The young man could hear the thudding sound that every yank of the starting lever made as it fell back on the floor. He climbed out from his auto and came over.

'Kya hua, Baba?' he asked. 'Has she been misbehaving lately?'

Aparajita smirked at the use of the female gender. She eased back on the taut Rexine, noticing, despite herself, a feeling of fondness accumulate inside her for the two men.

'Arey beta, it is Haj time now for the two of us,' joked Baba, patting the handlebar affectionately.

The young man laughed and offered Baba some Rajnigandha, which he accepted matter-of-factly, extending his palm for a few taps of the sachet, then flinging the rubble down his mouth.

Now what, thought Api, curious.

The young man said to baba, 'Chalo, I'll leave you till the station.'

Baba said, 'You will?'

What did he mean by 'I'll leave you', wondered Api. *'Surely he meant, 'I'll take the passenger?'*

The young man now returned to his auto. Api heard the thud of the starting lever and the eruption of noise at her back.

Then, with Baba in his driver's seat—keeping the handlebar even with his left arm even as he dislodged a Rajnigandha remnant from his teeth with the polished nail of his little finger—and Api displaying open-mouthed bewilderment, their auto lurched forward. There it went, gaining momentum, carrying Baba and Api merrily along. It would maintain a reasonable pace and then leisurely, on its own, die, upon which the man following behind would reconnect their auto with his left foot.

The two autos, like a couple, stumbled forward in staggered formation.

It was the ox pushing the cart, and to Api, it was wonderful. The young man, she realised, wasn't going to let Baba to lose his earnings; he wouldn't steal Baba's passenger away.

With every gentle push to her auto from the man's left foot, Api could feel the lump in her throat increase. Soon, she was contrasting her life with that of the autowallahs; the reasons why she had come to Mumbai, her terrible loneliness. Api felt she had nothing, possessed no one. And these autowallahs—happiness and brotherhood. And what of their benefactor's time and petrol? She could have cried, but she was afraid Baba would hear her and turn around and start a conversation.

Baba asked, seeing the station come into view, 'Where shall I drop you, beti?' unmindful that the man trailing behind in his auto was the one doing the taxiing.

'Bas here, Baba,' mumbled Api. She wanted to get down and find a spot where she could cry unseen.

'Achha,' said Baba and whistled, loud enough for the man doing the kicking to hear it. With one last punt he let go of Baba's auto. His job done, the man revved the accelerator and disappeared down the road without once looking back.

Baba applied the brakes and the auto came to a stop right in front of the station entrance.

There was no way Api could say a word, so she thrust a hundred-rupee note into Baba's palm and ran for the platform, refusing to hear the cries behind her: 'Arey beti, this is too much. Arey beti, wait.'

The evening crowd watched as Api skipped the stairway two steps at a time. A line of jostling and elbowing people formed either side of her. Some thought it was a movie take—the heroine jumping off the auto and rushing in to catch the train slipping away with her beloved.

Api asked a man who was staring at her, 'Bhaiya, which platform for the CST local?'

'Here it comes,' said the man, pointing in the direction of the approaching train.

Api ran to the counter and bought a ticket. Because she was going in the opposite direction—towards the city centre—the crowd was manageable. She climbed into the ladies' compartment and searched her way in slowly, looking out of the barred windows, taking in the cool evening breeze. She spotted an agreeable space and sat down.

Across her, two women were talking.

'Arey, just hand me that methi, Kamla,' said one.

'Here,' replied the other while tossing the greens in the air. 'Not much of a bundle for six rupees, is it?'

'Arey, this is loot maar, I tell you; we'll be eating grass next.'

'You don't listen, didi, do you? Why do you keep buying vegetables from Iqbal? I am sure he has a magnet stuck under his pan. Look—this is never one kilo.'

'Yes, you are right—maybe 800, 750 even…Oh, namaste ji. Hello.'

Api smiled at the women. 'Hello.'

'I hope we are not boring you with our chit-chat.'

'No no, not at all.'

'I am Shakti ben and this here is Kamla. And you?'

'Aparajita. Aparajita Biswas.'

'Bungali?'

'My husband is.'

'And you?'

'Madrasi.'

Shakti ben drew her breath in. 'No. Really?'

'Yes, why?'

'You are not *that* dark. And you have fish-shaped eyes. You look more like a Bungali to me. I find you are very attractive.'

Api laughed. 'Well, thank you Shatki ben. That's very kind of you. You should tell this to my husband.'

'Shouldn't do that—they get very possessive otherwise; start behaving as if their wife is Aishwarya Rai, no less.'

'So you think it's better to be ugly in front of your husband?'

'If you can help it.'

'Hah, thank you. I'll keep that in mind.'

Shakti ben commenced the plucking of methi leaves. 'You are not from Mumbai, right?'

'Yes. How did you guess?'

'You are sweating like anything.'

Aparajita reached for her pallu and glanced upwards. 'I wish the fans were working. How long till CST?'

'Plenty—at least twelve stops in-between. You'll reach CST by eight-thirty. Is somebody coming to pick you up?'

'What? No, I'll take a taxi.'

The interrogation continued. 'Here on vacation?'

'I thought I was, but all I have seen this past week is Gateway. And today's Elephanta trip also got cancelled.'

'Alone?'

'No, with my husband. These vegetables…?'

Shakti ben cleared her sinuses and raised her head. 'Arey, this is our daily routine. Where's the time these days, you tell me, haan. We'll reach home by nine, with kids darting all over, screaming dinner, dinner. This is the only way to save some time, Aparajita ben.'

'That's clever.'

'You can see our preparations for tonight's dinner: Methi matar and aloo gobi...What does your husband do?'

'He's a police officer.'

'My family has a few policemen but not *one* posted in Mumbai. My rotten luck. Life would have been so much easier.'

'I suppose.'

Shakti ben wiped her nose on her blouse sleeve. 'And what about you? Do you work?'

'I am a lecturer at Delhi University.'

'I thought so. You look like a lecturer. Where is the sari from?'

'Fabindia. It's Rajasthani print.'

'You should come to our Gujarat. Our prints are the best.'

'If I may ask, Shakti ben, what do you do?'

'Arey don't be so shy, Aparajita ben. Ask, ask anything.'

'Yes, well...'

'Both Kamla and I work in a jewellery shop in Borivali. Seven to seven, every day except Sunday. But I hate Sundays—that's when I have to listen to all this jhik-jhik of my husband and kids. Monday to Saturday I am my own rani. The only jhik-jhik I have to listen to is of my darling Kamla. Kyon ri, Kamla?'

Kamla nodded.

'Twelve hours, and Saturdays, too—that's a tough life, Shakti ben.'

'Arey, I am lucky I have this job. So many women I know are stuck in their matchboxes, poor things. This way, I am away from all that. And today was my weekly trip to the beauty parlour, too...See?'

Shakti ben brought her face forward and craned her neck. 'Nice, no. And see, see the brows? Ten rupees only.'

'Haan, good job. A practiced hand.'

Shakti ben gesticulated with the bundle of methi in her hand. 'And my husband? He doesn't even notice these things.'

'Shakti ben, everyone's looking at us. A bit softer please…'

'Arey, Aparajita ben, these are all my friends. I know each and every one of them.'

Aparajita glanced around the bay. 'Surely not…'

'With my eyes closed, then what. They are my life, Aparajita ben—the happiest time of my day is spent here, in their company, in this ladies' compartment, slicing vegetables and chopping onions. Even if I was sacked from my job, I'll keep taking this train every day without fail. Kyon, Kamla. No, Durga?

'That beauty sitting on your left? That's Durga ben. Her husband is a dabbawallah, and over the years, he has come to know of some amazing recipes—and now because of Durga, I know of them, too.'

Aparajita turned to her left. 'Hello, Durga ben. Aparajita.'

'Namaste, Aparajita ben.'

Shakti ben pointed across the bay with a cauliflower. 'And that one by the window? That's Madhu. Marathi. She makes the best srikhand in the whole world.'

'Fantastic.'

'This coach is my *true* home. *This* is the real Mumbai. People—it's the people who make the city.'

Aparajita tucked a lock behind her ear and smiled. 'How true.'

Shakti ben reorganised her bulk and settled it in the lotus position. 'So, tell me…how long have you been married? You have any children?'

Aparajita was taken aback with this new and bizarre line of questioning. Out of politeness but with an unsure voice, she answered: 'Er, since '93—eleven years. No, no children.'

'Eleven years. And when were you engaged?'

'Engaged. Oh, let me think…1990.'

'Three years you waited? That's too long.'

'That's what Ajay—my husband—thought.'

'But you didn't think likewise. And why no children? You'll need them when you are sixty. And how old are you? Arey, don't be shy. I am forty-nine myself.'

'Thirty-seven.'

'Now it's too late to have children. But why don't you have any?'

Aparajita was beginning to have second thoughts about this newly found friendship. She recalled her train journey across Europe a few years ago where, for five days and five nights, across nineteen countries, with countless different cuisines to comment upon, with the ever-changing weather to despair at, new languages, different dialects, not one person exchanged a word with her. Not one person, not one word. And now this.

'Er, Shakti ben, if you—if you don't mind...'

'Arey Aparajita ben, why are you feeling shy, haan? Tell me—will I get down with you at CST? Am I going to follow you all the way to Delhi?'

'No no...'

'Then? Listen, too often we think we don't want to talk to anyone, that we are alright as it is. But you know, that's where this ladies' compartment comes in. I was just like you on the first day that I started using this train. And let me tell you, there was this wonderful woman called Tulsi ben—passed away last year—and it was just like this. Me shy, like you, and Tulsi ben, sitting opposite, just like I am now. And she told me the words that I am telling you now.

'...Life is too short. Only strangers become our true friends. They want *nothing* in return. They know the other person is going to get off in a minute and will be gone forever. They just lend their ears. They are, strangers are, the *most* unselfish people you can find.'

Aparajita could feel a tug at her heart. This was a new experience for her, opening up to someone she had met a minute ago. And she had to agree that Shakti ben's words said had a ring of truth to them. *The world is full of kind and warm people,* she thought, *and it has taken me fifteen years and a train and an auto ride to find two of them.* She nodded thoughtfully.

'...And she said, "Shakti ben, use this time as your Amritanjan. Tell us your problems, your worries. *Use* me. Use *us*, Shakti ben."'

Aparajita placed her elbows on her thighs and cupped her cheeks. 'How wonderful.'

Shakti ben wiped her brow. 'Yes, and I tell you, Aparajita ben, I cried—there and then. The tears wouldn't stop. I told her everything, absolutely *everything*. There was so much to tell. And she, and Bimla ben, and Kanta ben—they took it all; like Bhagwan Shiv, they drank all that poison. And suddenly I felt so free, so alive; all my sadness went out of this very window you see here.'

'That's so wonderful.'

'And I haven't looked back since. You can say I am the sarpanch of this compartment; maybe because of my age, or maybe because, before she left us for heaven, Tulsi ben made it known. And this is the *best* responsibility I have had in my entire life. Durga ben here knows more about me than my husband ever will.'

'Arey Shakti, I also know more about your husband than *you* ever will.'

Shakti ben flung a pea at Durga. 'Durga, you mui...So you see, Aparajita ben. In your world you pay thousands just so you can go and talk to—what do you call them—yes, mind doctors. You pay thousands. In here, it is *free*. And let me tell you, we might not be doctors, but when patients get together to share their problems, who needs a doctor?'

Aparajita could have cried. 'You people are amazing, Shakti ben.'

Shakti ben smiled. 'So, now…'

'*Anything*. Just ask anything.'

'Why no children?'

'I can't have any.'

'Who said so—the doctor?'

'Yes.'

'*You* don't believe a word of him. I know a swamiji—not your nakli sadhu type. I'll take you to him. I'll take care of all costs, don't worry. You just tell me when we can go.'

'Really, that's too kind of you, Shakti ben. But we have been to a hundred hospitals, done a thousand tests. We may go for adoption sometime soon, maybe; yes, maybe.'

'As you wish, Aparajita ben. Still, give my offer a thought. Dauktary hasn't got the cure for everything—and you know where to find me.'

'That I do. Thanks, Shakti ben. I think I could cry now.'

Shakti ben reached over and patted Aparajita on her thigh. 'Arey arey, get a hold on yourself, Aparajita ben.'

'Yes…thank you for this, Shakti ben. You do not know how much you…'

Shakti ben massaged the thigh lovingly. 'Bas, bas, Aparajita, bas, bas.'

Aparajita hadn't realised the train had hardly moved in the past half-hour. Now she noticed they had stopped altogether. The train rocked and pitched, making her extend her hands and grab the window bars.

Slowly, tiredly, they began to move again.

Shakti ben pushed the baby cauliflowers away and cleared some space for the next assignment. 'Pass me the matar, Kamla…Unusually slow today, isn't it.'

'Oh, I know why, didi. It's because of that rail minister. I read in the newspaper while you were getting your eyebrows done. Flagging off a new train, he is today. All lines to the south will be like this.'

'These ministers. Who cares if thousands are home late in this heat. Our Aparajita will miss her dinner now…'

'Arey no no, Shakti ben.'

'Was it love marriage?'

The query jolted even the softened-up Aparajita. 'Hmm? Sorry, what, Shakti ben?'

'Was yours a love marriage?'

'Oh, haha. Yes, I suppose you can say that.'

Shakti ben clucked her tongue. 'Oh, I know. Your husband was a rebound, your second choice.'

Aparajita was too shocked to answer. Shocked because of the outrageous candidness—shocked because it was true.

'I can see it, Aparajita ben, I can feel it. Behind that calm face, there's just the opposite in that mind of yours. You loved someone else, didn't you? You loved that man to death, didn't you? And that man ditched you, like they all do in the end.'

Aparajita shook her head vehemently, tears welling up in her eyes. 'No no, it wasn't like that—at all—no it wasn't…'

'But you loved him to death.'

'Yes.'

'Then *you* ditched him?'

'No.'

'Then? He fell into a ditch?'

'T-thaa.'

Shaki ben was unrelenting. 'The family, wasn't it? Your family? His family?'

'My fam…'

'Your family? Why. Was he no good? Did he not have a job?'

'No, it wasn't like that. He was fantastic. And yes, he loved me to death and I loved him beyond death and everything was right—his job, his future…'

Shakti ben was on the edge of her seat. 'What were you before you became a Biswas? I mean, baaman, bania, what?'

'It wasn't me; it was my father.'

'Oh.'

'And my mother.'

'Bhagwaan…'

Aparajita sobbed into a bunched-up pallu end. 'I couldn't do a thing. I lost the battle.'

'No you didn't. *You* ran away is what you mean. I have seen it happen so many times.'

'It wasn't as simple as that, Shakti ben. My father swallowed half a bottle of sleeping pills—right in front of my eyes…'

'*Hey Bhagwan. Kalyug…kalyug.*'

'And then, right there, he passed on the bottle to my mother, who without as much as batting an eyelid, swallowed the rest.'

'*Kalyug…kalyug.*'

'Both my parents landed up in the ICU.'

'*Hey* Ram.'

'My mother went into a coma…they couldn't save my father.'

'*Ram…hey Ram.*'

'That last moment with my father—he held my hand but he couldn't speak. He had the ventilator on with all that oxygen mask…'

'Ram…'

'But he said what he wanted to through his eyes. He said what he wanted to, I was sure.'

'I am very sorry, Aparajita ben…'

'My whole world, everything, destroyed in a matter of days…'

'Very, very sorry.'

'Suddenly I was the sole breadwinner. An invalid mother, wheelchair bound, who also talked to me only through her eyes. And the talk wasn't kind. Eyes, do you know, can speak a lot?'

'…I understand, Aparajita ben.'

'Anyway…that was the last time I met Akhil—until now...'

'Akhil?'

'Yes.'

'Oh. And all this was in…'

'1990.'

'And where was your husband in all this?'

'No, he didn't picture in all this. Me, Akhil, him—we were the best of friends.'

Shakti ben had stopped shedding the pea pods a long time ago. 'So, how did you and your husband…'

Aparajita smothered her runny nose with her upper arm. 'He was the only other man in my mother's eyes. She wrote down his name on a piece of paper after I had pretended not to understand her when her eyes kept pointing to Ajay.'

'Oh…'

'Nothing could be done or delayed further. My fate was sealed.'

'But you did delay it—the marriage, I mean. A full three years beyond your engagement.'

'That was the period in which I got all those tests done.'

'Oh…Tell me, Aparajita ben—did you love your husband then? Do you love him now?'

Sepia flashbacks rushed through Aparajita's mind in response to that question, browned and blotched and tattered stills from her life: school school college college college Ajay Akhil Ajay Akhil Akhil Akhil Amma Appa Amma hands hands held held Ajay Akhil Akhil kiss loving arms longing arms kiss kiss Akhil roof moon moon tree moon shade rains rains Akhil Appa Appa Ajay loving longing longing Akhil crying crying fan fan rope fan Akhil crying longing Akhil Ajay Akhil…Akhil.

The roulette ground to a halt.

'No.'

'And do you still love this, this other…Akhil?'

'*Yes.*'

'Then, why...why?'

Aparajita hid her face in her hands and cried.

'I think I know, Aparajita ben. You delayed your marriage so you could get all those tests done. And after you knew, you thought, you have got nothing to offer Akhil. And you still think that? Even after all these years, you still think that? Do you? Is that what marriage means to you? Children? And that, too, blood children, Aparajita ben?'

'It is a lot more complicated than that, Shakti ben, a lot more...'

'Tell me. Let me drink all your poison.'

Aparajita closed her eyes and opened them again, to allow the tears to dribble away. 'I know my Akhil. I know he loves me still, but after all that happened to me, my family, after what they said and did, I sat back and realised—what you meant just now. Of course, marriage isn't just children, of course not. But if you can see from my eyes, my marriage to Akhil would have been a selfish act on my part. The companionship of marriage, the comfort and satisfaction that one expects from it...One thinks, "*That's* the one for me", and the man thinks exactly the same thing and we choose each other from a sea of people. We *choose* a partner because we expect something in return—the companionship and the safety of it. I realised I wanted Akhil *for me*...'

'But Aparajita ben, that's one way of looking at it. Didn't he want you, too? Of course, he did.'

'Yes, of course. That urge to be together, to get married, to stay together—that urge is based on self-interest.'

'But it's the same between any man and woman; just the truth, that's all.'

'Yes, but I wanted to *give* him something. I felt my whole life was meant to give him that one thing.'

'What. A child?'

'Yes, but not just a child...'

'So what if you cannot bear one—there's nothing more noble and fulfilling as adoption.'

'Yes, you are right, Shakti ben. But it wasn't just the question of giving him a child.'

'Then?'

Aparajita pinched her hand in anguish. 'Oh, how can I tell you... You won't understand.'

'Try me; tell it to your sister.'

'I...'

'Bolo...'

'I wanted to dilute his blood. Oh, it's too warped, the thinking. You'll hate me; you are hating me already.'

Shakti ben came over to sit next to Aparajita. She pulled Aparajita's head with both her hands and placed it on her shoulder. 'No I am not, Aparajita ben. I don't understand at all, what you just said, but I respect you for having fought all this way, for having tried all options...But make me understand.'

'It's too difficult, Shakti ben. I don't even know *how* I told you what I just did. I haven't told it to anyone before, not even Akhil.'

Shakti ben got up and returned to her seat. '...So what is it, what did you mean when you said dilute...'

'For you to understand this, I would have to tell you thousands of years of our history, the history that, in one sense, can't be termed as such, because it is still the present. It is not history, Shakti ben, but to the present, it is the curse of history...

'Who can erase it? Who can make us ignore it? *No one.* People have tried—great mahatmas have tried. But the mahatma left and this curse stayed.

'Education, learning, knowledge—they have got nothing to do with it. It inflicts us all; rich and poor, illiterate and learned, landowner and landless, man and woman, child and the newborn.

'We are born with it—that taveez that's tied to the limb of a newborn, it *is* that, that *is* this curse. And it was my failure to change the way my people thought about this curse; it was under this curse—as a child of this curse—that I thought, what my best offering to my Akhil was not just the offer of my hand for him to hold and walk in times good and bad; not the offer of my body for him to fulfil his physical desires; the best I could give to him, I thought was my silent protest, my retort: the offer to dilute his cursed blood...'

'Cursed blood? What do you...'

'Not to wipe out his sorrows for him, not to win his battles for him, but an offering to remove the weight of this curse from his children instead. To halve it, with the hope that with time, it would get halved again, and again, and again, *and again*, until one day, the cursed blood of Akhil would no longer flow in any living vein; it would be diluted, gone, erased...

'And when I found out that I couldn't even offer that little to him, I gave in to my mother's eyes, and became Ajay's wife.'

'But who—what is, this Akhil of yours? What is his curse, as you say?'

'Oh, Shakti ben, that's all for another journey.'

'Still…'

'He is a Chamaar.'

'A what?'

'A Chamaar.'

Shakti ben let out a scream. 'Bhagwaan. Hey Bhagwaan…hey Ram…Harey Ram! Oh, Aparajita ben—hey Sita Maiyaa. Of all the people—Aparajita, Aparajita ben. Of *all* the men to choose from in this world. Of all the…'

'I can see even you aren't unaffected by this curse. It's impossible for you, too…'

'Oh, Aparajita ben, but it has to be. It *must* be so—impossible. It *is* the way of the world. Ben, ben, ben…And what has become of him, this Chamaar.'

Aparajita clutched the edge of the bench and squeezed hard. '*Akhil.* His name is Akhil.'

'Yes, well, what has…'

'Well, it's a long story, too long, Shakti ben…Almost 8.30. Look, it's pitch dark outside…'

Shakti ben turned her head and looked out. 'Yes, it is.'

Something caught Aparajita's eye, something strange. 'Except for the light coming from the coaches of that train. Isn't it odd, what you see? Two trains running side by side, maintaining similar speed…'

Shakti ben had also noticed this curious occurrence. '*Haan*, it is certainly strange.' She wanted to return to the discussion but Aparajita was transfixed.

'...look...total darkness, but you can see those people by the light of their compartments. A parallel world, a different set, a...a...Oh my God. Oh God! Did you...Did you see that?!'

Shakti ben jumped out of her seat. 'Oh God, yes! Hey Bhagwaan! Harey Ram! Kalyug!'

The whole bay had seen it. Small girls came rushing in and gripped the window bars and tried to push their heads through for a better look.

'Shakti ben, Kamla—*do* something. That man is stabbing him. Oh God! Can you see it?'

Shakti ben was trying to get through to the window for a better view. She pulled a child away and extended her arms through the bars, waving them hysterically. 'Arey, do something—pull the chain! Let's all shout and alert the passengers of the other coaches. They might not...they couldn't possibly have seen what we have just seen...Shout! *Shout*! Someone pull the chain! Look away, Aparajita ben, look away!'

Aparajita stifled her scream with her fist. 'Oh God, no. He has done it. That man's dead, I think. Someone please do something. Call the police. What have we just seen. He is dead. That man is dead. I saw it with my own eyes. He used a knife—or a dagger, was it? Look! He's thrown it out the window!'

Shakti ben grabbed Aparajita by her arms. 'Aparajita ben. Get a hold of yourself. Look away...'

Aparajita noticed the dagger now lying on the tracks, the light from the train compartments making its steel glint. The bejewelled jade-coloured grip sparkled, and the horse-head...Aparajita froze. 'Oh God, no...No! It can't be. It just can't...'

'What? What can't be?'

'What time is it? Where are we? I must get down.'

'Aparajita ben, you can't! We are moving...'

'But I must. How far is IIT from here? Someone please pull the chain. Here, I'll do it.'

Shakti ben shook Aparajita by her shoulders. 'IIT? But we are past it. And look. Someone *has* pulled the chain in that train. It's alright. The police will be there in a minute. Calm down, ben, you need to calm down. No, don't pull...'

Aparajita broke away and pulled at the chain with all her strength. 'But I must. Oh God. What have I seen! I must, I must…Give way, move. *Move.*'

'But you can't just jump out like that, Aparajita ben. Wait.'

Too late. Aparajita jumped from the slow-moving train. She stumbled as she landed on the rubble, but managed to steady herself and run across the tracks to the other side in full view of the stunned passengers who watched her until she receded to a dot on the open stretch.

Shakti ben remained plastered to the window bars, mesmerised. '*Bhagwaan.* She jumped.'

Kamla was on the adjoining window. 'What a woman, didi.'

'But if you ask me, Kamla, a little screw loose.'

Kamla detached herself from the bars and grinned. 'You mean, *mad.*'

'A complete nutcase.'

'Still, a hell of a timepass, wasn't it?'

Shakti ben smacked Kamla on the head with the back of her hand. 'You mui. Now pass me that cauliflower.'

Myself Jam.

Venkataramanujam. And your good name? My berth is lower. I have tied my new Samsonite suitcase to the leg of the seat with a Swiss lock. It will rattle a little. Sorry for the inconvenience when you sit down. Your wife can take the upper berth. The step ladder is here. Little dirty. Cleanliness in India has gone to the dogs—Swachh Bharat or no Swachh Bharat. What can the train do when people are dirty? Yourself? Ah, Patwardhan, I see from your VIP tag. Chitpavan? Brahmins, no?

Good, good. The journey will be peaceful. I saw on the list that the fourth passenger is a Bengali brahmin. Very good, very good. Bengalis are good people, like us south Indians. And like you Maharashtrians. Quiet, cultured, God-fearing, and classical music inclined. How else do you explain why so many singers come from our regions? Only

Devi can explain. The fourth Bengali passenger, he can keep his harmonium on top there, between the berths, next to the fan, behind the tiffin box.

Ah, the train finally moves. One can say goodbye to the station filth. Yes, yes, just throw the plastic cup under your seat. Cleaner will come to pick it up. You only have to look away and lift your legs when he sweeps it out.

Just coming back from America, California, after visiting my son. First baby. Boy. Boy. His. My wife is staying back—to bathe the baby every day in olive oil and help with cutting vegetables and washing clothes. Custom. We have a three-month visa but I had office work. Little leave only. What to do?

My son went on an H1 visa and is now permanent citizen of America. Mows the lawn every weekend. Also barbecues. He eats a little meat and is social drinker only. Nothing at home—no, never, not even onions. Outside also only due to friends. What to do. Good fellow; when he knew we were coming, he filled the fridge with vendekkai, katrikkai, shundakkai, pavakkai—all available in Mountain View, little cheaper than Palo Alto, but a little costlier than San Jose which is full of loud Mexicans. But in Mountain View, so many Indians I saw, it looked like Pondy Bazar in Mambalam. Only Ratna Stores was missing. Otherwise noise, smell, people—almost the same.

Brilliant boy. First class first throughout. Only self-taught. Was playing chess from age two. IIT, IIM and then Stanford. Started tuition in India when he was eleven. Other colony boys when they were three. But he took tuition only when eleven and that too only for calculus. Maybe because of pollution. Sinus. But now big house in Redwood City and has white Americans for neighbours. No blacks on their street. You take 101 from San Francisco airport, get off Middlefield exit, go till you cannot go anymore, then turn left and from there it is a straight road to his house. I used to walk every day to the mall. In fact, spent all my time in the malls. Even got idli and vadai there.

And there's also a Hanuman temple nearby. Swimming pool also, but my daughter-in-law does not wear a bikini. One piece. Like a sari—one piece. From a good home, in Tirunelveli. Very, very homely. Watches only Tamil and Hindi films all day, about gods and goddesses. Does not stir out of the house. My son also good husband. Handicap 24 because he cannot leave home. Otherwise, he would have handicap 4. Life is about give and take. Some adjust here and there.

Oh, my wife also has a handicap. She is hard of hearing. But she has packed food for the whole journey and some pickles, too. You can also have. We have extra spoons. Nothing like Indian women, I tell you. What is there in foreign—you tell me what is there in white skin? We are also returning from Seattle. Our son is also very brilliant—IIT, IIM, Harvard. But he married a foreigner and that too, black. Too black. What can one do, world is so globalised nowadays. Her parents are from Burundi. I didn't even know such a thing existed. Much darker than Obama. Much, much more visibly dark. Real black you should see, but how can you. Like in Africa. Cannot see her at night, so black it looks like blue. They have one issue. A girl. As dark as Obama. Grey you can say. Diluted, by the grace of God. Her name is Abigail Varalakshmi. She will be attending bharatanatyam classes soon. Also judo but we are not happy as she will grow muscles like that Williams who plays tennis. Sari blouse will not fit. If she marries a white man when she reaches the marriageable age, we are hoping children will be almost white. Dilution.

That is our only hope. Dilution. Only hope, I tell you.

Where are you going? We are also going to Bangalore. We will be getting off at the Cantonment. We have one unmarried daughter. Very clever. Plays the veena. Only one problem. She wears thick glasses. So many refusals. But she is happy and very adjusting type. Doesn't use any make-up. Not even snow. She taught our daughter-in-law Cindy how to make all the dishes that my son likes. They often have guests, so we also taught her some foreign dishes—cabbage bake, potato bake, all without onions. You know these foreigners, they only eat bread. No culture. No music. Only hippies playing guitars.

She is studying BCom in GAS—Government Arts and Science College. Will pursue PhD after marriage. In America. We are looking in America. Good girl. No bad habits. Goes straight to college and comes straight home. Her name is Soundarya. She can also play the tabla—but not much as that gives muscles. There's one more thing.

Her menses were late and my wife was very worried. She is also a manglik. Do you know any good astrologer in Bangalore? We are Iyengars.

Shameless we are not. Insincere we are. Kind we are not. Curious we are. Stylish we are not. Clumsy we are. Modesty escaped us, leaving behind arrogance. We all went to IIT, we all went to IIM, we all speak English, we are all brahmins, we will all go to heaven where we will find that our creator may have had another view of all what we hate and love.

We are probably the only people on earth who rush inside a train that is not scheduled to leave for the next two hours. To catch a seat in a fully reserved train where we too have an assigned seat. It's just to 'catch' that little extra—konjum something. Or me, myself and my own. How is it possible for complete strangers to discuss minutely private details about each other and then get off the train and walk away without so much as a goodbye? How is it possible to share a meal one instant and swear at each other the next? How is it possible that with so much brilliance brimming over, India has not placed too many innovations in the global market? Any? Indians do very well when they go abroad. Didn't you hear that on your train journey? Didn't your train journey educate you enough?

Train journeys are where we let all our complexes hang out, where we smell a high-caste fart and taste a low-caste pickle, where nothing is taboo, where we mingle and detach, mingle and detach, where our darkness is visible.

By the way, there was something very fishy about that Bengali woman on the upper-side berth. She was travelling alone. No bangle, no sindoor, wearing a Punjabi salwar and talking on her phone all the time. Eessh. Everything is even more visible when it is dark.

15

1990—The Death of the Heart

The young man held the ketchup bottle away from his body, its plugged nozzle pointing at the omelette. He slapped the base repeatedly with his palm but to no effect. In anger, he repositioned the upturned bottle and started to knife the space above the omelette over and over again. A river of glossy red pulp gushed out all at once, bloodying the plate. The young man put down the emptied bottle and spread the ketchup evenly on the omelette with a few caressing strokes of his butter knife. Satisfied, he shrouded the murdered egg with a slice of white bread and commenced the sawing, pinning it with a fork first. Scarcely able to wait any longer, he put down his knife and picked the quarter portions up with his fingers and inserted them, one after another, into his wide-open mouth. With closed eyes and buffalo-like jaw grindings, the young man embarked on his evening tea at St Stephen's cafeteria.

As Akhil, seated with Api on the adjoining table, watched the young man devour his omelette, he was reminded of that culture-colliding anecdote involving one of his college friends, Vishwas Bhatia.

'Saali, French bitch,' had fumed Bhatia all those years ago.

'*Who*?' had pushed the attentive circle of friends hoping to hear something nauseating. 'Arey my French girlfriend, yaar.'

'What about her, ban-cho?'

'Bloody she broke up with me, man.'

'No, seriously?' had commiserated the circle cheerfully.

'Yes. And you know why?'

'*Bata jaldi, saaley.*'

'She couldn't stand my soaking the omelette with ketchup. Ban-cho, *I* never got angry when *she* ate all those beef momos. Saali hypocrite.'

'What a bitch. Anyway, to hell with her and that *Alan Frenchie.*'

'Alliance Français, bhosdi ke.'

'Whatever. Forget her, bastard. Hop on to Bagga's Lumraytta and start going to Max Mueller Bhavan for German lessons.'

'What are you talking about, ban-cho?' Bhatia had enquired, half-interested already.

'Serious, man,' had counselled his friends. 'Bagga's hajaar positive he'll be pillion riding a German pataka within a month. Look, here he comes—*Guten morgen*, Bagga.'

Akhil broke away from this joyous recollection and paid attention to the worried look on Api's face.

'Hey, what's up?' he asked.

'No, nothing,' said Api, not looking up from her scrambled eggs.

It didn't overly worry Akhil to see Api in this state. D-day nerves, he thought, that's all. In fact, nothing had overly worried Akhil ever since the start of his week-long trip to India. Everything had been planned beforehand in Cambridge—even this meeting with Api today at the college café.

Akhil was staying on the campus with Dr Rajendran, his old chemistry teacher. It was high summer and the college was closed. But the café was open, to serve those small number of unfortunate honours students who'd stayed over to repeat their subsis.

The café was almost empty, and when the young man paid up and retreated down the steps licking his fingers, Akhil and Api were the only customers left.

Akhil was not of this world today, meeting Api as he was after three interminably long years. He was into the second year of his PhD at Cambridge, having fared exceptionally well in the Natural Sciences Tripos. Only when he was well settled into his PhD had he decided to test the waters as far as marriage with Api was concerned.

He had written her long, convincing letters, telling her he could now say he had done well in life, was on his way to becoming someone she would be happy with. He told her how, after his PhD, he wanted to come back to India and start a lab, how life was one smooth, upward curve from now on. He told her all this, and of course, Api was happy and delighted and agreed to Akhil's proposal. They decided after a few months that the time had come for Api to tell her parents about him. Api did so eventually and a date was set when Akhil would come and meet Api's parents. Today was that day.

'You haven't said a thing for the past twenty minutes, yaar,' said Akhil.

'Hmm? Sorry, what, Aks…' mumbled Api, forcing back a smile. She looked drained and feverish.

'*I* should be the one all worried and trembling. I am the one meeting your parents, remember. They *are* expecting me, aren't they?'

'Yes, of course.'

'And you have told them everything?'

'Hmm? Haan, yes…'

'Hey, wake up, sleeping beauty. When do you think we should move?'

'In a few minutes; we are expected at six.'

Akhil swivelled round and waved. 'Arey, Bhaiyan?'

The cheerful and pencil-moustachioed Bhaiyan came toddling over. 'Haan Akhil, bolo.'

'How much, boss?'

'That's two scrambled eggs—twelve rupees…six toasts—ten…one pot tea—that's twenty-five total.'

'Here, that's two hundred—for you and Harimohan and Jagdish.'

'Thanks, Akhil. Where's AB?'

'In Calcutta preparing for his UPSC. I am flying there on Thursday before I finally fly back. Had to come to Delhi, as you know. Well, we better be going now…'

'See you around, Akhil. Come back and file a report on how things go.'

'Will do. Come, Aps.'

The two made their way out and walked slowly towards the Allnutt South exit gates. Api remembered something. 'Aks, what was all that about filing a report? They know?'

'Of course.'

'Great. So now everyone knows.'

Akhil smiled. 'Arey relax, yaar. It's not that I am going around distributing marriage cards, is it?'

'But before it has even happened!'

'Why. You think something might go wrong?'

'Shut up, na.'

'You aren't in two minds now, are you?'

'Oh, shut up, Akhil! This isn't funny.'

'What? Hey, is something the matter? You okay? You aren't hiding anything from me now, are you?'

'Of course not. Just...just, let me be, for a few minutes.'

'Okay, *okay*,' said Akhil and hailed an auto.

The autowallah heard the call and pulled over.

Akhil nodded at the driver. 'Cornwallis Road.'

'What?'

'Cornwa...Sujan Singh Park.'

'What?'

'Suj...Arey yaar, near Khan Market. You know? Never mind, I'll give direc–'

'No, I know. That'll be fifty.'

Akhil patted the meter.

'Isn't working.'

'Achha yaar, take fifty…Api, get in.'

'But, Aks, fifty? That's double the…'

'Arey leave it, na. It's a special day. Haan, chalo boss. And listen, take the Outer Ring Road—not through Filmistan, okay?'

'Add five more, then.'

'Arey, you take ten more, yaar. Can we move now?'

The man swung the handlebar and took a sudden U-turn, disregarding the oncoming traffic. Cars and taxis swerved and screeched, and those on motorbikes and two-wheelers banked severely and weaved around the auto, shouting the usual rich pickings from the ma-behen word list. The autowallah waved these off as harmless sledging and propelled his machine to speeds not meant for three undersized wheels.

Akhil hadn't noticed a thing. He tickled Api on her back. 'Hey…'

Api shrugged it off.

'Hey, Api.'

Api pushed the adventurous hand away.

'Hey, Aps, I love you.'

'Yes yes.'

'What yes yes? Hey, Api, I love…'

'Oh, be quiet.'

Meanwhile, the autowallah, who had seen the goings-on at the back through his wing mirror—and approved of them. He decided to give the lovers the kind of thrill and adventure he thought lovers craved. He revved the handle to its maximum limit and made his apparatus behave as though it was on two wheels, not three.

Within five minutes, they had reached the ISBT traffic light, which the autowallah ignored ruthlessly. It took them another five to pass all the final resting places of the great Indian men and women, with some heaths reserved already for the future crop. Seeing Rajghat come into view, the autowallah bowed his head and closed his eyes momentarily.

For Akhil, they might as well have been travelling in a bullock cart. 'Hey, Api, my love…'

Api showed her irritation. 'What?'

'I am thinking, if all goes well, you could come with me to England for a few weeks now itself, haan. Don't worry, I have saved enough. What say you? A little pre-honeymoon. Hey, Api…'

'Oh, shut up, Akhil, please.'

'What shut-up wut-up, yaar? Don't know what's gotten into your bheja. Arey where else will they get such a handsome and dashing son-in-law, hain?'

'Oh, please, Shh.'

'Dashing, charming—arey BA tripos, that too a Geoffrey.'

'Geoffrey?'

'Yes, Geoffrey. Geoffrey Hurst—First.'

'You are *mad*.'

'Not a Desmond.'

'What?'

'Desmond Tutu—a two-two.'

'Oh, shut up.'

'What more could any loving parent ask for? No?'

'Quiet.'

With his good eye on the wing mirror and the glass one on the road, the autowallah rocketed past India Gate. Their speed seemed to stretch and warp the ten or so ice-cream handcarts to about a hundred.

Akhil came to life. 'Boss, take a right from here and then a U for Himayun Road.'

A qualified U-turn specialist, the autowallah raised no objections.

'Now take a right at the petrol pump...Now second left—haan. Haan, bas bas bas. Stop right here.'

The auto screeched to a stop, leaving behind three skid marks on the road, like the familiar lines on Iyer foreheads.

Akhil rummaged through his wallet. 'Fifty-five?'

'You said sixty.'

'*Arey, yaar*, here—take seventy. Happy?'

If the autowallah was happy he didn't show it.

Akhil struggled out from the auto. 'Come, Api—you go in first.'

'Oh God oh God oh God oh God...'

'What? *What?* Hey, just relax.'

'You go first, Akhil.'

'Hey...'

'Don't argue. Just *go*.'

'Alright, alright.'

Akhil stood at the main door, ran a cursory hand over his hair, and pressed the bell. The door opened, revealing a man with three lines on his forehead, wearing a half-sleeve shirt and a zari-work veshti.

'Hello sir, good evening.'

'Oh, welcome, Sukumaran, welcome. I am Appu's father. Come, come. I hope you had no trouble with the traffic. Come in, come in...'

'Thank you, sir. Come, Aparajita...Sukumaran? Hey, Aps, what's this Sukumaran—or has he just muddled it up.'

Api pushed Akhil in. 'No, he hasn't. You are Sukumaran, *not* Sukumar. Remember that, *please*—for my sake.'

'What. But why…'

'Please make yourself comfortable, Sukumaran,' said Api's father, trying to gather his veshti and walk at the same time. 'I am sorry the wretched desert cooler broke down this afternoon. This heat must be a terrible change from Cambridge, no? Come, sit. No, sit there. That's at least by the window. I'll call Rukmini. Appu, please see where your mother is.'

'Yes, Appa.'

Appa sat down on the sofa with a thump and waited for the 'fissing' sound to subside. 'And tell her to bring all the goodies. I tell you, Sukumaran, er…'

'Akhil, sir. Akhil Suku…'

'Yes, I tell you, Sukumaran, Appu's mother makes the bes-*t* vadas. You like vadas?'

Akhil grinned. 'My record is thirteen—without the chutney and the sambar, of course.'

'Hah. That's very good, very good. We must arrange for a vada competition one of these days—old man's still got some fire in his belly, you know.'

'We must, sir.'

'I can understand your eagerness, hah, after years of baked beans and fish and chips.'

Akhil couldn't agree more. He nodded. 'Yes, sir.'

'Appu has told us all about you. Had we any inkling, we would have arranged for this meeting much earlier.'

'Well, thank you, sir.'

'And how is work, Sukumaran?'

'Guess it's alright, sir. I am into my second year of PhD. Things haven't really started rolling yet but I hope they pick up soon.'

'That they will, that they will. The important thing is to enjoy yourself. Maybe Appu hasn't mentioned, but there was a time in my life when I could have gone to England to study.'

'She did mention it once, in passing.'

Appa threw his arms up in the air. 'But my father put his foot down, said where is the need? Stay put and join IAS. Hunh, join IAS—like it is some military service. I had to break my back to pass. It was like smashing a hundred coconuts daily with your forehead.'

'It is really tough, isn't it, sir. I mean the exam…'

'I missed the foreign service by two spots, *two tiny spots*. We could have been eating vadas in London. Ah, but it's alright, can't complain. There have been plenty of opportunities for tours. I was in Paris last summer.'

'Haven't been there yet, sir.'

'But nothing like home, Sukumaran. Ah, here come the vadas.'

Appa caught hold of Api's arm. 'Come Appu, sit.'

'Appa, you talk whatever you have to, I'll be upstairs…'

'Arey, come, come. What is there to talk? We have seen the boy and we couldn't be happier. Come, sit.'

Api took a seat well away from Akhil.

'So, Sukumaran, you have plans to come back? Finally, I mean.'

'Yes, sir. Maybe after a post-doctoral stint. That way, it'd be easier to find an academic job here.'

'Arey, boys like you will have no problem, no problem at all. The jobs are for the taking—so well qualified and everything.'

Akhil reached for a vada. 'Let's see, sir.'

'Here, some filter coffee?'

'Thank you, sir.'

'You know, that reminds me. Don't mind, Sukumaran, but you Iyengars…'

Akhil thought he had misheard. 'Er…what, sir?'

'When Appu told me of your Sukumaran surname, I got thinking—the fellow must be an Iyengar only.'

'But…'

'I laughed. What strange luck for an Iyer to marry off his daughter to an Iyengar. Strange and eccentric ways Lord Ayappa works, I tell you.'

Akhil couldn't comprehend the beseeching, pleading, desperate stares of Api. 'Er, sir, maybe, there is some mis…'

'Yes yes, where was I? Oh, the filter coffee—yes Sukumaran, don't mind, but you Iyengar fellows have a habit of serving your coffee in cups that have a false bottom. It's true. You people are famous for it. Once, at a friend's place—he's an Iyengar—I took a few gulps of the coffee and I thought, *what* fantastic coffee. And then when I went for my third gulp—there, that was all the coffee there was.'

Akhil was beginning to get worried. 'Er...'

'But splendid fellows, you Iyengars. I have no complaints. I mean, after all, it's only us Iyers and you fellows that are second in position to those Nambudris, no?'

'Sir, let me...'

'So what, I say. Still top-notch one hundred percent brahmins. And what can one say about those Nambudris—their damn noses up in the sky. And I don't believe in all this first position-second position business, all this caste-waast—it is taking this country down. Iyers and Iyengars at the same level, tied second, is what I say. No? Arey, I am boring you will all this nonsense. But I thought it was important to reassure you at the very beginning that we think very highly of Iyengars, most highly.'

'Sir, if I may...Api, will you please...'

'Appu—I mean, we—we are of Srivatsa gothram. And her star is Rohini. Is that alright?'

'Sir, what?'

'Srivatsa. Our first ancestor. You can say our Adam. And let me see—your *gothram* might be...you have any clue? You fellows are Vaishnavites so it must be...Oh, the name's on the tip of my tongue. What is it, what is it? Sadamarshana? Koudiniya? Arey you youngsters wouldn't even have had a proper horoscope made. Anyway, when setting the date of marriage, we will enquire from our Panditji.'

'Sir, can I pl...'

'Appu told me about your having lost your parents in a car accident. I am very sorry. But I would like to tell you, Sukumaran, that in us, you have found your new parents.'

Akhil's thoughts were a muddled mess, what with Appa's ramblings and Api's stares.

Appa, meanwhile, had no such worries. He rambled on. 'When do you think we can set the date for marriage? If possible, we'd like to get it done and over with by this year-end. I know you are in the middle of your PhD, but my grandmother is ninety-eight and there's nothing she would like better than to see her great-granddaughter married off before the she takes on her journey to the heavens. Anyway, we are not conservative. We leave it to you. I have told you our preference, that's all. And don't worry about having to take Appu to Cambridge after marriage—no problem at all. Let her complete her studies here and then we'll see what happens.

'Sir, about the Iye...'

'And of course, Appu being our only child, did you ever wonder—I don't suppose you gave it a thought—but didn't you think it was odd why a pucca Iyer girl was called Aparajita?'

'No, sir, I didn't.'

'See, it's a Bengali name. It means, *the one who cannot be vanquished*, and it's a long story, but maybe now is the time to tell you. You see, we had Appu only after twelve years of our marriage. Something wrong with her mother, they said. We had lost all hope. Even Lord Ayappa had turned his back on us. We are only human. Who is to know how the lines of our hands may twist and turn and go some other way? Rukmini proposed the idea of us adopting a baby but I must tell you, Sukumaran, I was apprehensive. I mean blood is blood after all and the outer world is a nasty place. Who is to say the baby you adopt, even though guaranteed by the agency of being a brahmin, turns out not to be so. Ooh—the very thought!'

Where is this going, thought Akhil.

'...so then, there was this Bengali friend of mine—great fellow, and an IAS of course. He took us to this village near Darjeeling—his guru's ashram. We walked barefoot all the way from Calcutta, your auntie and I. The guruji had one look at both of us and told us there and then what our problem was. It was incredible—his aura, his presence. He told us to stay in his ashram for a fortnight and arrange for a few havans, carry out pujas. I remember he would ask just Rukmini to accompany him for long walks in the forests, to tell her, I suppose, not to lose any hope, that the Supreme Being was always there to hear and act. And sure enough, nine months later, we were blessed with our Appu. We decided to pay our respects to the Bengali guruji and gave Appu a Bengali name.'

Akhil didn't know what to make of the story. He remained silent.

'Aiyo, Sukumaran, I am the one here talking on and on; you say something, bhai. And let me just add that we would prefer to have the ceremony in Kerala style. You can take a brahmin out of Pallakad but you can't take Pallakad out of the brahmin. Haha.'

Akhil cleared his throat. 'Sir, I think there's been a terrible misunderstanding. I mean…Aparajita? Would you like to clarify the…'

'I am sorry, Sukumaran, but I didn't get that. What misunderstanding?'

'Aparajita…?'

'Leave Aparajita—you tell me.'

'Sir, I am Sukumar, not Sukumar*an*.'

'I don't understand.'

'I am not an Iyengar, or even a brahmin. I don't know what and why Aparajita told you…'

'What do you mean you are not an Iyengar. What are you then… Appu? What's going on?'

Akhil cleared his throat. 'I am a Chamaar.'

'A what?'

'A Chamaar.'

'What Chamaar?'

'In your scheme of things, the lowest of the low. Or as you might think, someone masquerading as a human.'

'What exactly do you mean? You better tell me clearly, boy.'

'I am a shudra, and within shudras, I am a Chamaar. A Chamaar!'

The exclamatory end to the last word whisked away all sound from the room. There was deathly silence. Appa opened his mouth many times—slivers of spit stretched and contracted between his quivering lips—but he couldn't say a word. Then, as though hit by a tidal wave, he sprang up and started beating his skull with both hands. 'Oh my God! Aiyyo Ayappa! Lord Ayappa! Rukmini? Did you hear that! How dare you deceive us, boy. How dare you deceive my daughter!'

Akhil was taken aback. 'Your daughter? She knows…'

'No. No, Appu, no! Tell me this isn't true. Tell your Appa this is a lie. You bastard monkey. I'll kill you with my bare hands. Get up. *Get up!*'

Akhil tried to calm things down. 'Sir, I know you are agitated, and this has come as a shock to you, but I was under the impression that you were aware of…'

Appa was yelling uncontrollably. 'Aware? I was *aware*, you said? How *dare* you even think that I can call you to my house and discuss marrying my only daughter knowing fully well that you are a, a– oh, Ayappa! What have we done! Why are you punishing us like this?'

Akhil retreated to the sofa but did not sit down.

'Don't keep standing there you thief, rascal, you monkey. Get out!'

'Sir…'

'Rukmini? Call the police.'

'Sir, please, at least listen to me. My caste is something I have no control over. *Who* decides all this? *You* could have been a shudra.'

'Why, you filthy bastard, how dare you even say such a thing!'

Akhil pleaded with his hands. 'I *love* your daughter. I'll give her all the happiness in this world—and she knows it. Ask her, sir. She loves me more than I love her, just ask…'

'*You* leave *her* out of this, you stinking…Appu! Go upstairs. Now!'

Aparajita, too terrorstruck to be coherent, simply mumbled. 'Appa, please try and understand…'

'No no no no, *no*! Go upstairs—*now*. If you want to see your parents alive then do as I say…'

Akhil clenched his fists behind his back. 'Sir, please. I am prepared to do anything you ask of me—*anything*. I am prepared to convert. Yes, I'll become a Muslim if you say so.'

'How dare you! That's only slightly less worse, you dirty little…'

'You want me to undergo a blood transfusion? To drain off my "cursed" blood? I'll do it.'

'And you think I am a buffoon? I know my biology. You may come out of the clinic with good blood but after a few months your bone marrow will resume supplying you your own Chamaar blood. You don't fool me, boy. There's no such thing as a two-month brahmin. Now get out. And just you dare see my precious Appu again. I will gouge your eyes out and feed them to…'

'Alright sir, I'll go. I would, however, like to hear what Aparajita thinks of all this.'

Appa bared his teeth. 'You *wish*. Get out. Out of my sight, out of my house, out of my mind, out of my daughter's mind—*Out!*'

Akhil tried one last time. 'I have no interest in prolonging your misery, but as I said, if I can hear from Aparajita…'

'You don't believe me, do you? You want her to suffer, is that it? Alright then, you'll see her suffer. You'll see her watch both her parents die right here in front of her. You'd like that, wouldn't you…Rukmini! Get that bottle of calmpose from the medicine cabinet.'

'No, sir, please…'

Appa wagged a finger ferociously. 'I'll show you what true sacrifice is.'

'Please…'

'*No*. Now you wait.'

'There's nothing left to wait...'

Akhil started walking towards the main door.

'No, don't go. See this—you must see this.'

Appa heard the door click shut. He turned around and shouted on the top of his voice. 'Rukmini! That Chamaar may have gone but you bring Appu down here, *right now*. And for the last time, where is my bottle of calmpose?'

Akhil stood on the steps of the main entrance. Try as he might, he could not take a step; his legs were rooted, frozen. He could hear Appa's shouts and screams but could not understand them as they were now entirely in Tamil. He thought at that instant of Aparajita, but to his horror, he found he could not put her picture to it. He kept repeating her name, in the hope that, sooner or later, the name would recall the face. But no. There was no face—only the letters of her name formed and zoomed in and out. The shock had kept back the face, the tears, everything. The shock had taken complete control of the body and the mind.

Slowly, Akhil detached his left foot from the step, then the right. Strength returned as blood rushed through his limbs.

It had gone dark and the street lamps were flickering to life. He came out on to the road and kept on walking.

Many years later, he would recall that he had walked all the way back to college, tracing the exact route he had taken earlier that day.

Chamaar.

The shoe fits but the soul doesn't.

Jhini jhini bini chadariya;

Kahe ke tana, kahe ke bharni

Kaun tar se bini chadariya.

Kabir. What strings are your body, mind and soul made of?

My soul, your soul, our soul.

Dhikku ver-illai Deanna sharannai, sang Papanasam Sivan in front of the Kapalishwarar kovil. Nowhere to go. *Pap* is which language and what direction? The Chamaar who escaped the pap smear is rickety and diseased, cancerous and oozing with pus, but human and nowhere to go.

Chamaar. Gucci.

We are weaves of the same cloth, hues of the same dissonance, notes of the same song. We are the same chadariya. Are we not?

Chamaar. Gucci. Chamaar. Ferragamo. Chamaar. Clarks. Toucher and tanner of leather, maker and wearer of belts. So at what point does sin enter into it? During marriage negotiations, or when the *kaapi* tumbler has a false bottom? Tearing, tanning or torn between ordinariness and the song of the creators? Did someone get shortchanged because some God decided a few of us could?

It could have been worse. Karim Abdul Jabbar. Muslim Bhangi. Jamadar. She could have brought in a rat with rabies.

Chamaar. Shoemaker, tanner, Gucci, catwalk, Milan. No Milan here. Just mayhem because our sheets and weaves are only as long as our bodies, our human bodies. Akhil thought he was human till he wasn't. Two-penny opera—loose change. Jugaad.

How on earth could a Tamil brahmin girl, a pure and creamy *thair sadam* with a strong lineage of saints and sages and intellectuals roaming around the world and in jungles of concrete and trees, not be called Urvashi, Rambha, Menaka or Tilottoma? Menakai, Rambhai, Tillotamai, you stupid Punjabi.

In this land of so much sun, so much sin. So much sun that disinfects only the shit mounds on the roadsides and the railway tracks but does nothing to the sin. Sin. What is sin? Where is sin? You will never know how strong you are till you are broken. Breaking is not a sin. Not learning from it could be. How many people think when things go topsy-turvy, there may be a bigger reason, a grander learning around the corner? Where did Api fit into all this? She harmed herself. No, she harmed three souls. Is the intellect ahead of the body or missing a few births here and there? How can an intellectual giant be an emotional pygmy?

So much sin is attached to everything—this when our gods tell us there are no permanent sinners. All because of television, the internet and foreigners from Nigeria. Polluting India. *Ram Teri Ganga Maili.* What? Are you mad? *Ganga Tera Pani Amrit.* Rishi moolam, nadi moolam. And quiet flows the don. Not the river. Like Aparajita, which means the one who cannot be conquered. What is sin? Who are the sinners? Api doesn't know.

Chamaar—licker of thread and feet, maker of chappals and sometimes shoes and daring to dream. That is the worst part. Daring to dream. Daring to dream of a good education, of being an integral part of society, of marrying a brahmin. No blood transfusion can correct that karmic message. None.

Foreign Chamaars are okay, Tod, foreign Chamaars are fine. Try and understand, Salvatore, their hide is white.

Anno Domino, BC, DVC, OBC, AC/DC, Pink Floyd. Rascal. Changed his name to fool an innocent Indian girl. To touch a girl in this land of seven rivers, mountains and notes is to insult her mother, her mother's mother and all mothers' mothers. He came home and cast a shadow of filth.

Love marriage in the land of swayamwar. Love marriage. What has love got to do with marriage? Heart? There are so many cardiac surgeons amongst us. Why go there with them? And even the heart has upper chambers and lower chambers and the two can never meet. In fact, the heart is divided into four parts, just like the caste system. Nothing can bypass anything. That is the rule, the law. And this is the problem with quotas. The polluted blood can access the upper chambers of India when in reality, without quota, they would be ciphers. Vermin. Contained and destined to keep to the lower chambers. And once they cross the road and come to our side, they entice our daughters in bars, restaurants and lungis.

Love. How dare anyone talk of love before marriage. Love should be banned. *Banned.* You go to college to study. You go to college to study physics, mathematics, chemistry, biology, history, English—*our* subjects. But then these lower-caste people, and *that* community people, they come along and also end up studying physics, mathematics, chemistry, biology, history, English—our subjects. Our subjects end up studying our subjects. You know why? Because they can then lecture us on history. Our history, as if they belong with us. They study English to correct our English but it takes a brahmin to tell them why the great George Bernard Shaw questioned the rain in Spain. Whatever you say, their accents, punctuation, grammar will give them away even if they are fair-skinned shudras and bhangis. Style don't come easy, boy! Boy! Nigger! Wog! Chamaar!

Look at India's telephone directories under the alphabet C. Chakravarti, Charukesi, Chattopadhyay, Chidanand, Chaitanya is what you will find. If they are so intelligent, why don't we find Chamaar in the telephone directory? Basics.

But what does a shudra know about all these important matters? It's not us who keep them down and trodden; it is them, for howsoever much you try and help them, they will go back to their roots. Intellectuals like us need roots because they set us free. These lower-caste people need roots for routes—into our homes, into the hearts of our innocent womenfolk, into our libraries. Them. Them! Chamaar DNA. Chamaar bone marrow. Chamaar love. Do you now understand? Do you?

Yes, it's best they marry a foreigner from Scandinavia. Ingmar Chamaar, Nils Bhangi, Olof Jamadar Henriksson. It even sounds better in foreign. And maybe in seven generations when bloods have mixed and re-mixed, they will produce pink babies with black hair. Then they can apply to the elite Indian universities. For now, it is better to apply to white countries for funds. These foreigners, they cannot tell the difference between sex and love. The only difference between Denmark and the bhangi colonies in India is space. More space, more litter.

All in the upbringing, all upbringing. In their homes they have mosquitoes, nothing to eat and sewage water to bathe in. That's what they deserve for having dared to dream. In our homes, we have books. We don't need to eat, sleep or bathe, for a true seeker of knowledge is not bound by desires and trousers. For us, all else is detail. All else is detail. Our floors are clean as our minds, our windows are open as our hearts, our speech is flawless as our music and the only smell in the house is that of knowledge mingled with sugar, coconut and ghee.

We in India are not like foreign parents who don't know what their children are doing. Father going with someone, mother going with the gardener, postman and personal trainer. How can you blame the children? Rubbish in, rubbish out. Sex all the time. Even in the kitchen. That's why they don't know how to cook. Why does anyone with a brain need a table in the kitchen? Kitchen is for cooking only, where women cook and men eat and after all the men have eaten, women eat what is left.

Dirty brain. The watchful eye of Indian parents has ensured that nothing dirty like 'that' is ever done before marriage. We will go on the internet hunting among complete strangers to marry off our daughters, but heaven help the child if she falls in love with a stranger who has no gotra or rashi. If a girl goes 'astray' and wants to marry out of caste, it is the solemn duty and responsibility of parents, friends and family to bring the cows home to graze. The grass is always greener this side, and our beasts are better.

This is the land where women are worshipped and this is the land where all the lands come to seek salvation. If that doesn't work, there's always Tik-20 or kerosene. Nothing like a good oil bath in kerosene. First soak the hair; you don't have to go all the way—just a little distance to be maintained from the object of fire. Light the match and hold it for show. You will see everybody and everything will fall in line. Ignite, good night.

We need to ensure that the heart does not beat everywhere and anywhere and especially not in front of the public. Extend your loving arm and wrench it out from between your child's broken ribs, stomp on the throbbing lump, pummel it, squeeze it in your bloodied fist so tight it begins to ooze out through your fingers like curd rice during lunch. Suck, yes, suck, suck all love from it and then toss it away to die by the roadside bin.

It's just a body part, silly. Appendix.

16

2004—Under the Net

'*OUT OF ORDER. INCONVENANCE REGRATED—BY ORDER, MUMBAI POLICE*' said the child-like scrawl on a torn fragment of a whiskey carton left dangling on the grille of the antiquated lift.

'Bloody bastards, shit,' scowled DIG Ajay Biswas as he stood opposite, pondering his options. He turned his attention to the dusty, perforated plastic board by the lift and let his gaze wander from top to bottom, trying to decipher the names and words that were made up of white plastic letters, some missing, most limp. In due course, his eyes spotted 'MHINDR PATAP KHABAND' with its designation 'SUPRITENDENT OF LICE' linked with ten white plastic dots. The designation was further led on by such dots to 'SEVENTH FLOUR, ROOM NO. 714.'

Ajay grunted. 'Bastard Kharbanda,' he said out loud and took to the stairway, avoiding pulling himself by the railing of the wrought iron and Burma teak balustrade, having seen the grime and the paan-juice deposits it was layered with. The seven floors became the seven peaks of a mountain range. After he had conquered the second, Ajay wished he was carrying an oxygen cylinder. His pace slowed. Older policemen with unreal pot bellies went past him lithely, some taking two steps at a time. After the third peak, Ajay began to gasp for breath. He did not think twice now about latching his palm onto the handrail to gain that slight advantage while hauling his body up. He turned midway to the fifth floor and paused, looking at the fifteen or so steps that would take him to the fifth peak. His thoughts were jamming up, his feet unsteady. It looked impossible.

Ajay wiped his forehead and the back of his neck with his handkerchief and put his foot on the next step. He had forgotten why he was climbing the stairs. The expedition had taken over his senses completely. Survival, to garner that extra bit of strength, was what was on his mind now. *What for? What for did I come here to the HQ?* he repeated the question with every new step. Eventually, he stood on the fifth plateau, facing the steps for the sixth and beyond, knees moving involuntarily from side to side, but not quite touching each other, like cymbals.

Water! He looked around, and even with his doped senses he could make out that this was the floor where they hoarded broken furniture. Sofas shrouded in old cobwebs spilled out rusted springs and nibbled foam. Green Rexine-sheathed tables with three legs stood in mourning alongside crippled woven cane chairs. Eastman portraits of great leaders and slain prime ministers lay strewn, coffinned in mock wooden frames and shards of glass.

Hopeless, beaten, defeated, Ajay pulled at the banister with trembling hands and began his ascent. He recalled the famous last scene of a Ray movie—*Seemabaddha*—where the manager Shyamal returns home from work, all energised and cheerful, anticipating a good evening in, and then comes home to a dead lift; and how the camera follows the man throughout his painful climb up the stairs, right up until his sweat-dripping nose touches the door of his apartment.

'Ki holo. Tumi oto geeley geley keno?'

'Aar bolona. Lift ta cholchhey na, shiri diye utthtey holo.'

'Paakhar tolaay bosho.'

'Shit!'

By saying the last word out loud, Ajay realised he had reached the summit—all this while talking to himself, indulging in unconnected thoughts, like a factory worker by the conveyor belt. And now, back to being DIG Ajay Biswas, the journey—the expedition—rapidly turned irrelevant. All he could think was: *Ban-cho, don't look shattered and worn out in front of Kharbanda. Act cool.*

And so, even though his watery eyes had spotted the door with a handpainted sign that said SP KHARBANDA, he hesitated, looked around, and then walked to the door with a handpainted sign that said MAN. Once inside, with his senses shaken up by the methane clouds from the flush-resistant deposits left behind by man, he rushed to the sink, turned on the plastic tap and splashed some water on his face. Next, he dipped his comb in running water and raked his hair with monkey-like frenzy. He unbelted, unbuttoned and unzipped his trousers, he straightened his shirt all around and then raised the trousers back on. He pinched the shirt loose from his waist, a little from the left, a little from the right, then polished his shoes on the back of his trouser legs. Finally, he sucked in the foul air and drew out, through sustained gargling, a lump of phlegm that he spat at the sink with angry force.

Once outside the toilet, Ajay walked with large and urgent steps towards SP KHARBANDA, did not knock, barged in and without wasting his breath any further, said hurriedly: 'Good afternoon, good afternoon, Kharbanda, first things first. Some chai and samosas, anything to make me forget that bloody guest house lunch.'

It worked. Taken by surprise, Kharbanda and Sharma found no time to ponder over the reason behind the slight but noticeable tremor in their superior's voice.

'Oh, hello, Ajay sir, hello, a very good afternoon,' said SP Kharbanda, and then, 'Arey Sharma, some chai-shai. And tell that Kishore harami to save all that sugar for his daughter's dowry. And listen—get the samosas fried again if they are soft…Please, Ajay sir, come.'

Ajay rubbed it in. 'And, Kharbanda, you didn't tell me the lift wasn't working. It's a good thing I spend an hour every day at the gym back in Delhi. Climbing all those hajaar stairs.'

'*Oh,* very sorry, sir. Here, please take my chair…'

'Arey keep sitting, Kharbanda.'

SP Kharbanda got hold of the backrest with both hands and swung the chair in Ajay's direction as an offering. 'No no, sir, please, I insist. It is what they call nowadays, sir, ergonomica…'

'Yes yes, Kharbanda, now don't you start on some story of yours. We have truckloads to do today.'

'Of course, sir. Myself and Sharma have been up all night, sir, including this morning.'

Ajay sank into the lush leatherite. 'Aaahh…this chair sure feels good. Sorry, did you say "Myself and *Sharma*"?'

SP Kharbanda bit his lip. 'Er…'

'I heard you say Sharma, didn't I?'

'Sir, please give me a minute to explain…'

Ajay rushed forward and was soon hit on the rear by the backrest that was following close behind. 'Kharbanda!'

'Sir, please, just one minute…'

'Didn't you hear me say last night, just you and me? Just *you* and *me*.'

'Yes, sir, I did—and I promise on Ganpati Bappa that it is just you, me and Sharma…'

'Ban-cho, Kharbanda.'

'Sir, last night, after dropping you and madam, I came straight back to HQ. You can imagine my worry as to where to start with the search…'

'I don't bloody care. You defied my orders. This force works on orders.'

'…Then, sir, I must have, in my anxiety, mumbled about the unsolved-solved files. But it was audible enough for our Sharma.'

'This is totally unacceptable. This is a direct violation of my orders.'

'And sir, in hindsight, it was godsend—that my mumbling was audible to Sharma…'

'You have gone ekdum mad, Kharbanda. And you thought by making all this public you are going to take me down with you? You don't know me, Kharbanda, not half—not even one-tenth.'

By now, even Ajay had realised SP Kharbanda's mouth and ears were connected to entirely independent neural networks. SP Kharbanda continued. '…And then he said: "Arey, SP saab, why do you worry? Please take me as yours and DIG saab's disciple and I'll bring you all those files before you can say…" Well, I won't like to tell you what he said after he said "before you can say", sir, but believe me…'

SP Kharbanda's perseverance with his screenplay-like account brought unexpected results. Ajay seemed to have calmed down.

'Believe me, sir, the bastard's been up whole night. All the files are now at this very table, sir—right in front of you. See it with your very own eyes, sir. They are all there—all seventeen.'

'I thought you said ten last night.'

'Three-four here and there, what does it matter, sir.'

Ajay swivelled, slowly, menacingly, like Bond's adversaries. 'Well?'

'Yes, sir, so poor Sharma…'

'So he has become *poor* Sharma now.'

'Poor Sharma has been climbing ladders and balancing himself on one leg to get us all these files. Not only that, sir, he has gone round the city thrice this morning, visited every bookshop, all pavement stalls, too…'

'For what?'

'For all those Agatha Christie books, sir. Our set is almost complete except a few that we have been told are now out of print.'

Ajay slapped the armrest. 'Jesus. So he knows about this Agatha Christie hunch of mine, too. Dammit, Kharbanda.'

'Arey sir, Sharma is like my younger brother. I have looked after him like a mango sapling all these years. He will gladly shield me with his very own chest in an encounter.'

'Spare me your bullshit, Kharbanda.'

'Me and him are like Ram-Lakshman jodi. Our little secret is quite safe between the three of us, sir, believe me. Please sir, please. I beg you. There was no choice. The work was too much, just too much. Since yesterday night, Sharma and I have been at it without any rest. How could I have managed it all on my own, sir? Please don't be angry now, sir, be happy—it would mean a lot to me.'

'Hmm…and this Sharma you say is 100 per cent reliable?'

'His reliability is unquestionable, sir. I trust him more than my wife.'

'*That* does put my mind at rest.'

'Thank you. And believe me, sir, three heads are better than two. You only said so.'

'When the bloody hell did I say so?'

SP Kharbanda was insistent. 'You did, sir. God promise. And, sir, there is one more thing.'

'*Now* what?'

'Sharma said he would bring a surprise for you at this meeting.'

'What? A ban-cho kathal?'

'He didn't tell me, sir, but he said he will present it to only you and he said it is big.'

'So it *is* a kathal.'

SP Kharbanda risked a laugh. 'Sir, you na.'

'...Anyway, Kharbanda, I still would have preferred you calling me last night and asking my permission for including Sharma in this.'

'I am sorry, sir, but it was too late and...'

'Yes yes. Now all this Sharma has done. What have *you* been up to? And don't tell me you have been busy supervising him.'

SP Kharbanda pulled up his sleeves and got ready for a demonstration. 'Sir, you won't believe me but all the joints of my fingers are now refusing to crackle. See? I bend them to breaking point and no sound. Watch this.'

'What the bloody hell are you...'

'Who do you think has been making all those tables, sir? First I had to make a table for those seventeen good-for-nothings. Then, since early morning, I have been making this Agatha table. Bastard Sharma just keeps getting the novels—already it is running to twenty-seven pages, sir. We still have some novels missing but...'

Ajay was genuinely impressed. 'Bhai wah. I am genuinely impressed, Kharbanda.'

SP Kharbanda decided to milk it. 'And, sir, you na—scolding your disciples.'

'Arey arey, sorry, Kharbanda, I didn't...I was only...Achha bhai, I am sorry. Now cheer up, man.'

'Arey sir, *please*, no mention. And now with Sharma also in the team, we will hit bullseye in no time.'

Ajay rolled over to where SP Kharbanda was standing. 'Well, there is this one last thing. This Sharma—he isn't expecting any reward, any promotion for all this, is he?'

'Arey sir, have a large heart. What will the poor fellow want anyway, haan? We will throw something at him later.'

'Alright, Kharbanda, you have your say here, too. But keep me out of it. I can't be seen distributing laddoos to every Tom, Dick and Harry. You take care of Sharma.'

'Of course, sir.'

Ajay looked around the room. 'Good. Well, where is Sharma, then? We'd better start on this as soon as possible. Where is he?'

'He'll be here in a minute, sir, with chai and samosas.'

'What's taking him so long? Call him…that reminds me. You might get a call from Aparajita. She demanded that I give her your number after that Elephanta thing had to be cancelled. If she calls, just tell her sir is in a meeting with some crime branch harami or something.'

'Er, so you managed to cancel Elephanta, sir? And you have told madam about the ten-day extension?'

'Arey one thing at a time, Kharbanda. She nearly mauled me when I told her I cannot make it this afternoon. The other news I'll have to be more tactful while breaking it to her.'

'Where is madam now—guest house?'

'She said she might go over to this, some social institute in Kandivali.'

SP Kharbanda knew his city, something rare for a policeman. 'Yes sir—National Social Sciences Institute.'

'Yes, whatever. Now where the hell is Sharma?'

'Yes, sir…Arey Sharma? *Sharma.*'

DSP Sharma could be heard a good minute before he actually took shape. 'Ji, ji, yes, sir, coming, coming…Sorry, sir. The re-frying of samosas took time.'

DSP Sharma unloaded the feast on to the exquisitely gilded baroque teak table shrouded unfortunately with the gaudiest Sunmica one could find east of Thane. The Martian-producible run of letters, numbers, dashes and slashes that vandalised the ledge would have set Gödel rethinking his Incompleteness Theorem.

'Here, sir, please have some. They are nice and hot. And some tea. Sugar is separate, sir.'

Ajay reached for a samosa. 'Arey Sharma, come closer to the table, bhai. Why are you hiding behind that curtain, hain? Come, come. Kharbanda has been singing love duets in your glory. Man, these samosas are good. Kharbanda, I take two sugars.'

SP Kharbanda jolted into action. 'Er, yes sir, of course.'

Ajay mumbled when he could. 'So, Sharma. You are in the loop now, aren't you?'

'Er, yes, sir.'

'And you do know what being in the loop means?'

'Of course, sir, he does.'

'Let *him* speak, Kharbanda.'

'Of course, sir, I do. On my dead body, sir, if that's what you mean.'

'That is *exactly* what I mean.'

'Of course, sir.'

Ajay received the tea with both hands. 'Because, you see, Sharma, once all this is over, we are going to be, well, how shall I put it…'

SP Kharbanda interjected. 'Allow me, sir. All of us are going to kick Khandala in the and take a cruise to Switzerland.'

'Yes, Kharbanda, spot on. Something along those lines, anyway. There's no cruise to Switzerland.'

'There isn't? That bastard Trilochan.'

Ajay took a sip and immediately felt ill. 'Well, you get the point. And especially you, Sharma. Once you are promoted—and of course, you would skip a rung or two along the way, we'll make sure of that.'

'Well, a heartfelt thank you, sir.'

'Yes yes, save all your thank yous for later. But what I mean to say is this: not *one* bloody word of all this—to *any* person living or dead. You understand? Kharbanda? Sharma?'

'Of course, sir.'

'Good. Now, can we clear up this samosa and all these cup-shup?'

DSP Sharma rushed forward. 'Yes, sir.'

'Good. So, let us begin.'

SP Kharbanda put his reading glasses on, last used when he was studying for his SSLC. 'Sir, both tables are ready. Here is the unsolved table, if we can…'

'And one more thing: all these table-shaybles are to be burnt once we are done.'

'Of course, sir.'

'Good. Haan, Kharbanda…'

'Yes, sir, this table here is the unsolved table. You can see all seventeen entries.'

Ajay tried dislodging a dhania seed with his tongue. 'Hmm…go on, go on.'

'And this one here is the Agatha table. As I had told you, sir, some information is missing here.'

'Which novels couldn't you get, Sharma?'

'Sir, six.'

'Names.'

'Sir, *By the Pricking of My Thumbs, Nemesis, Sleeping Murder, The Clocks, A Caribbean Mystery* and *Dead Man's Folly*. Sorry sir, but I looked all over the…'

'Yes, well, let's carry on. So six entries cannot be made. Actually make that five, hahah. I have read *Sleeping Murder*. Miss Marple's last case, I think.'

'You have, sir? Great.'

'Well, this, and another one, I can't quite remember the title. And then...none...something like that. Arey, it was all over the news sometime last year, wasn't it? You know, with that message and bottle and Cornwall, bhai. And then nothing came of it.'

SP Kharbanda knew the answer to that one. '*And Then There Were None*. I know all titles now, sir. Please ask me any.'

'Later, Kharbanda, later. Have you read any, but? And you, Sharma?'

'Er, no, sir. Where is the time? But sir, about this one, I want to give you a gift, sir…'

Ajay waved his hand. 'Later, later. We are digressing again. Okay, so how many entries have you got in the Agatha table?'

'Fifty-seven, sir.'

'That's fantastic, Kharbanda. Extraordinary.'

'Thank you, sir. And that's not all, sir. With your anticipated permission, I have also made a third column.'

'You have?'

'Yes, sir.'

Ajay glided forward. 'Show.'

SP Kharbanda leaned on the table and pushed his glasses down from the bridge of his nose, impersonating distinguished professors and honourable judges when they want to look like distinguished professors and honourable judges.

'Here, sir, you see. I thought going over each and every description every time—for every unsolved fellow, I mean—would be just too much trouble. So I have arranged the novel names and descriptions under headings—poison, shooting, stabbing, pushing over hill, hitting on head, coming under car, drowning...You see, sir?'

'Yes, I do. Great work, Kharbanda. You have started to surprise me more often than I thought you could.'

'Thank you, sir. Actually, it was Sharma's idea, I have to admit.'

'Really. Well, Sharma, good going.'

'Thank you, sir. Sir—about that gift, sir...'

'Later, bhai. Good. So now we have both tables in front of us. Well, what are we waiting for, hain? Kharbanda, you take the Agatha table; Sharma, you the unsolved. I will plan out the whole strategy.'

'Ji, sir.'

'Achha, before we start on these unsolved fellows, I have this keeda—I just want to make sure about this Saane guy. Kharbanda, have you made a "golf" heading?'

'I have, sir.'

'Well, what does it say?'

'Two novels, sir, under "golf": *Why Didn't They Ask Evans?* and *The Murder on the Links.*'

Ajay snapped his fingers. 'That's it, that's the one. Just read me the description of *The Murder on the Links.*'

'Sure, sir. "*The Murder on the Links:* The most bamboozlingly possible plot; a neat succession of clues. —*New York Herald*".'

'Uff, Kharbanda, spare me the bloody blurbs, man. Just the description, dammit.'

'Y-yes sir, sorry. "For God's sake, come! Unfortunately, by the time Hercule Poirot received Monsieur Renauld's urgent plea..."

For the sake of literary propriety, Ajay felt obliged to interrupt. 'And please—slowly, clearly. And he is "Paw-ay-row", not "Poii-rott".'

'Yes, sir. "...urgent plea, the millionaire was already dead, stabbed—lying in a freshly dug grave on the golf course. The police think they've found the killer. Poirot has his doubts. A second murder proves him right".'

'Hmm...And the other one. What was it? Read that one.'

SP Kharbanda shuffled the loose pages like a bookie. 'Yes, sir. *Why Didn't They Ask Evans?* "During a round of golf, while retrieving the ball, two men find instead a dying man, fallen from a cliff, whose last words are peculiar: Why didn't they ask Evans? Bobby and Francis would love to know. Unfortunately, asking the wrong people has put the amateur sleuths' lives in mortal danger."'

'Ban-cho. You see now?'

'What, sir?'

Ajay slapped the table this time. 'It *is* the man I thought it was.'

SP Kharbanda was at sixes and sevens. 'Sir, I don't understand...'

'Arey, Kharbanda, the bastard who cleaned up Saane, bhai. He has combined the two novels. Saane was stabbed on a golf course—that's *The Murder on the Links*. Saane was found all broken-shoken 30 feet below—that's *Why Didn't They Ask Evans?* You still don't get it?'

'Oh. Yes sir, I do. I do now.'

'We are on the right track, Kharbanda. We have hit a gold mine, what?'

'We have indeed, sir.'

Ajay punched the air. 'We have done it, Kharbanda. You see? You see now the power of deduction, the power of investigation—a *proper* investigation?'

There was not a dry eye in the house. 'You are a genius, sir, a total genius.'

Ajay was pleased but remained calm. 'Arey leave it, Kharbanda, just leave it. Don't you bullshit me now.'

SP Kharbanda had already thought of a eulogy that could be fitted neatly to a paragraph. 'On my dead body, sir. I mean it. All these Mumbai crime branch hotshot ban-chos—and I include myself in their bastard group,' sir. I mean, here comes a young, dashing, really intelligent officer from Delhi—and within a matter of a day, he has single-handedly solved not one, not two, not three, but what looks like ten murders. Sir, I am certain they would have to create a new post for you. Even the topmost ones don't do justice to your brain power.'

'Arey Kharbanda, leave it, bhai. You na. But thanks. Man, I can't wait to *solve* these other *unsolved* bastards. Bring them on.'

'Absolutely, sir. The first one...'

Ajay twirled a tuft. 'Wait a minute, Kharbanda. I think we should go about it differently. Why don't you put the unsolved folks under the same headings as you did for Agatha? Easier that way, no.'

'Great idea, sir...Sharma?'

'Yes, sir, here is the list.'

Ajay cut in. 'No, Sharma, you keep hold of the list. Just tell me how many people fall under the following headings. Ready?'

'Yes, sir.'

Ajay fell back on the chair, and because of the German ball bearings-driven tilt- tension-controller system, kept falling back until in panic he paddled the air with his arms. He reclaimed his dignity and cleared his throat. 'Good. Train.'

'Yes, sir, just a minute, sir. Train...train...trai...'

'If you must, do the counting in your bloody head.'

'Yes, sorry, sir. Tr...one. Only one, sir.'

'Good. Gun. Shot, I mean.'

'Yes, sir. Shot...shot...that's two...there's three...five, six...six. Sir, six.'

'Six? That's a lot, isn't it. Almost one-third. Okay, good. Next: poison.'

'Yes, sir.'

While DSP Sharma was spotting the number of times the word 'poison' appeared in the table, Ajay winked at SP Kharbanda. 'Kharbanda, this is good, na.'

'Brilliant, sir, brilliant. We are learning from you all the time.'

DSP Sharma cried out suddenly. 'One, sir. One.'

'Good. Train, shot, poison—anything else? Yes, how about serial?'

'Sir, serial?'

'Yes yes, serial. Bhai, one after another but all connected. Kharbanda, you tell him.'

SP Kharbanda clicked a dental consonant. 'Arey Sharma, like that Shah Rukh Khan in *Baazigar*.'

'Oh, I get it. Sir, nothing that stands out as such. Except these three brothers...'

'Okay, put them under serial; we'll find out shortly. How many headings thus far, Sharma?'

'Sir—train, plane, gun, poison, serial.'

'Good. How many unsolved left?'

'Sir, six.'

Ajay shut his eyes and pinched the bridge of his nose. 'Hmm...we have covered outdoors. How about indoors? Anything that stands out among this six? Where were they killed, for example? Home, hotel, something like that.'

'Yes, sir, one minute. Two killed at a political rally...'

'Yes...'

'Sir, one in a hotel—our own Taj Mahal hotel, sir. Found strangled with electric cable. About this one everyone knows, sir. Ramrao Apte.'

Ajay opened his eyes. 'Who?'

'Apte. That message and bottle thing, sir—last year. It was connected to *And Then There Were None*.'

'Of course. Apte.'

'Ji, sir. This was the gift I was telling you about.'

'Look, don't distract me, Sharma, I am in the zone right now.'

DSP Sharma placed a file on the table. With his fingers he goaded it towards Ajay. 'The gift, sir. Here, this file.'

'What is it?'

'This is the whole Apte file, sir.'

Ajay pushed the file away. 'Why are you giving it to me? And you call such things gifts? And anyway, if I remember correctly wasn't the bastard's secretary convicted for the murder?'

'He was, sir, he was. But the reality is different, I think, sir.'

'What do you mean?'

DSP Sharma pushed the file forward again. 'It is not official; it is not to be mentioned *ever*, sir. It is my humble gift to you, sir. It will help you.'

Ajay was beginning to enjoy file tennis. He pushed the file back in DSP Sharma's court. 'Look, Sharma, I…'

'I was one of the officers sent to investigate that message and bottle theory, sir—after it came out in the media.'

Ajay sat up. 'You went to Cornwall?'

'No, sir, to Mughalsarai.'

Ajay tried to suppress a laugh. '*Mughalsarai*?'

'Yes, sir. Let me tell you the complete story, sir. I was sent under SP Chaubey.'

Ajay looked at the ceiling fan for one moment. 'No, don't know him.'

'He was transferred to Jharkhand last December, sir.'

Ajay was fast losing his patience. 'Please, Sharma, look…'

But DSP Sharma had won the toss and elected to bat. 'Myself and Chaubey went and met a fellow called Bansilal. Bansilal had written a letter to the crime branch saying that he knew who the killer was. This Bansilal gave us a name, sir, of a boy who worked at his book stall at the station. Bansilal said that this boy had read every Agatha novel there ever was written. *Each and every*. Bansilal was sure that the killer had to be this boy.'

'But then the secretary? I…I don't quite get it. Why was all this never made public?'

'We couldn't, sir. Chaubey sir himself had caught the secretary and was awarded a medal for it, sir.'

Ajay reached for a paperweight and gave it a mighty swirl. 'Wah. The thing just goes on and on, haan.'

'I…I couldn't go against Chaubey sir's orders, sir. He made sure we kept this Mughalsarai thing under wraps.'

'Ya ya ya. I, *I*, always. *I* couldn't this, *I* couldn't that. Kyon, Kharbanda. You are very quiet. Sure you didn't have anything to do with all this?'

SP Kharbanda shook his head vigorously. 'W-what are you saying, sir? No no, of course not. I barely knew Chaubey.'

Ajay turned to Sharma. 'Anyway. What can I say…thank you for this...this gift, Sharma. I am honoured.'

'My duty, sir. Form one honest officer to another.'

'Speechless.'

DSP Sharma gestured with his eyes. 'Open it, sir. There's that message from the bottle in there. Read it, sir. It is thrilling. You feel as if you are sitting right next to the killer as he is writing it.'

Ajay put a stop to the monkey business. 'Sharma, not now. Later. Look, we have derailed completely here...just go back to what...Yes, any other, besides the political rally and the hotel?'

DSP Sharma was deflated but dare not show it. 'J-ji, sir...One is at home—but this is more like a domestic than anything else, sir.'

'Dammit, no one asked you for your opinion—just yet anyway.'

'Sorry, sir. Yes, sir. And finally, sir—this is interesting—bastard killed in a library.'

'Library.'

'Yes, sir.'

'Well, put it down under "library", then. I think that's enough for the moment. Let's start with what we have got and we'll move to those rally and home and hotel ones later.'

'Yes, sir.'

'Good. Kharbanda?'

SP Kharbanda tilted his head. 'Sir?'

'Arey, I mean ready?'

'Yes, sir.'

'Sharma?'

'Yes, sir, waiting for the gun.'

'Good. Let's begin with this library fellow. Sharma—give me the lowdown on this guy. Then, Kharbanda, I'll ask you what you have in the Agatha table, alright? Go, Sharma.'

'Yes, sir. The name is Yashwantrao Palnitkar. Two-time mayor of Mumbai.'

'Yes yes, I think I know the guy. Was murdered in the Bombay Gymkhana.'

'Yes, sir. November tenth, '99. Body found in the library of Gymkhana club, sir. Death by strangulation—the verdict of the coroner.'

Ajay drummed the table with a pencil. 'Saala, bastard. One would be hard-pressed to find a more corrupt dog, no Kharbanda?'

'Yes, sir. Sold off 30 acres of mill land at one go. Thousands lost their jobs overnight. You saw that food court, sir, when we were on our way to the morgue? A cloth mill had stood there for seventy years...'

'Yes, well...'

DSP Sharma covered his cough with his fist, or tried to. 'Er, sir.'

'Yes, Sharma?'

'Sir, it says the case was solved within a fortnight.'

Ajay looked at SP Kharbanda naughty-eyed. 'Kyon bhai, Kharbanda?'

DSP Sharma continued excitedly. 'Sir, it goes on. It seems the murderer was an ex-police officer, someone called Khare. Khare confessed to the killing—said 5 of those 30 acres belonged to him. Unfortunately, it says here, sir, Khare was shot dead while trying to escape from the Arthur Road Prison, sir.'

'Arey Kharbanda, you are exceptionally quiet.'

SP Kharbanda scratched his upper arm nervously. 'Er...no, sir, I was only...'

'Bas, bas. Now, what have you got in Agatha?'

'Yes, sir. There are four under the library heading, sir: *The Murder of Roger Ackroyd*, *The Body in the Library*, *The Murder at the Vicarage* and *Lord Edgware Dies*. I have also included murders that happened in a study.'

Ajay asked, in all seriousness, 'Now, why have you done that?'

'Study is like a library only, no?'

'Accha achha, go on. Obviously *The Body in the Library*.'

'Yes, sir. *The Body in the Library:* "Colonel and Mrs Bantry are shocked to find the dead body of a young platinum blonde on the floor of their library, strangled to her death. Nobody in the village of St Mary..."'

'Arey Sharma, just ring the bell and ask for some chai.'

'Sure, sir.'

'Haan, Sharma, sorry. carry on.'

'Yes, sir. "...the village of St Mary Mead seems to know who she is, but everyone has a theory about the crime. But Miss Jane Marple, St Mary Mead's resident sleuth, always seems to be one step ahead of them"...the end, sir.'

'Yes, this seems to be the one. Library, strangled. Except I don't think Palnitkar was a platinum blonde.'

SP Kharbanda couldn't resist. 'He was a platinum ban-cho, alright, sir.'

'Hah, that he was. Well, put Palnitkar's file aside Sharma—case number one solved. I mean "truly solved".'

'Yes, sir.'

Ajay did a 360-degree turn and ended up 720 adrift. 'Go on. Shall we take the train next?'

'Sir?'

'Arey, train, Sharma. Train.'

'Yes, sir. Train. Man named Rajwardhan Singh Khedwal. MP from Bijnaur, sir. Found dead, stabbed on 10 June 2001 in his first-class AC coach…'

'Bastards always travel first-class AC, don't they? And those who vote for them? Unreserved compartments for them lot…carry on, Sharma.'

'Yes, sir. This Rajwardhan—body was found by the TTE. The coupé was bolted from the inside and the police had to get in by breaking the window. File says he was a huge Thakur vote bank. Also, a friend of Bhaiyaa Raja.'

'You mean *the* Bhaiyaa Raja?'

'Yes, sir. Er…case solved within a week. File says he fell out with Bhaiyaa Raja. Criminal case against Bhaiyaa Raja himself is pending in Allahabad High Court, sir.'

Ajay threw his head back. 'You see, Kharbanda? Skeletons tumbling out with breakneck speed. But why was Mumbai police involved—their jurisdiction doesn't run on till bloody Bijnaur, does it?'

'Er, no, sir. The train was Mumbai-bound. Body was discovered at Mumbai Central.'

'Ah. Anyway, over to you, Kharbanda.'

'Yes, sir. Four cases under the "train" heading: *4.50 from Paddington*, *Murder on the Orient Express*, *The Mystery of the Blue Train* and *The Girl in the Train and Other Stories*, sir.'

'Alright, start.'

SP Kharbanda put his glasses back on. 'Yes sir, *4:50 from Paddington*: "Elspeth McGi-l…McGilli…sorry sir, what is this McGillicu-ddy…'

'Uf bhai, it's not important. Change it to Rampyari if it makes you comfortable, goddamn…'

'Er, yes, sir. "Rampyari is generally not given to hallucinations. Until she boards the Paddington train for St Mary Mead and becomes a witness to a murder. She claims she saw a man killing someone in a train running parallel to hers—a crime no else apart from Rampyari believes ever really happened. Except for her friend Miss Jane Marple…"'

'Hmm…no, not this. Go on, next.'

'Yes, sir. *Murder on the Orient Express.*'

'Oh yes, I have heard of this one, but unfortunately haven't read it.'

SP Kharbanda spoke the words before he had a chance to open his mouth. 'Where is the time, sir.'

'Shut up.'

'S-sorry, sir. Yes, *Murder on the Orient Express*: "While en route from Syria to Paris, the Orient Express is stopped dead in its tracks by a snowdrift. Passengers awake to discover that a wealthy American has been brutally stabbed…"'

'Aha. We are getting somewhere now.'

'Yes, sir, "…brutally stabbed to death in his private compartment. Incredibly, that compartment is locked from the inside…"'

Ajay smacked the Sunmica. 'Bingo.'

'Yes, sir, "…With no escape into the wintry landscape the killer must still be on board! Fortunately, Hercule Poirot is also on board."'

'So how the ban-cho did the killer get out after cleaning up Rajwardhan, with the windows intact and the coupe bolted from the inside? Well, what did the Mumbai police have to say about this... Sharma?'

DSP Sharma dug deep. 'Let me see, sir…Er, sorry sir, no mention of this puzzle.'

'I knew it—bastards. Arey, these are the small keedas that make an officer out of a donkey. And *you* guys? I shudder to think if this saala Poirot was working for Mumbai police. All his grey cells would have turned ash white on day one. Anyway, hop on to the next one, Sharma…'

'Which one, sir?'

'I don't know…try plane.'

'Yes, sir. Oh, this man everyone knows. Manochar Kangda.'

'The beedi king?'

'Yes, sir. Died on the plane—Indian Airlines flight IC134, Bhopal to Mumbai, 2 December 2000. The autopsy report says multiple organ failure, massive overdose of an anti-cancer drug. Killer turned out to be his personal physician, a man called Ramnath Powar, who was with him on the flight.'

'Good. Kharbanda?'

'Yes sir. Two cases: *Death in the Clouds* and *Passenger To Frankfurt*.'

'Go on.'

'Sir. *Death in the Clouds:* "A French woman dies mid-air on a plane crossing the English Channel. A poison dart indicates murder. That she was notably ugly provides a clue, albeit a cryptic one. Fortunately for justice, the famed Belgian detective Hercule Poirot happens to be aboard. In fact, evidence points to him as the perpetrator."'

Ajay tapped his chin. 'Something not quite gelling…'

Kharbanda, though, was confidence personified. 'Why, sir, I would think it is watertight. This Manochar—you haven't seen his photographs, have you, sir? The ugliest gandu in town…'

'Oh, stop being an ass, Kharbanda. Our guy doesn't choose his victims based on their looks. I mean he has left out our present CM, hasn't he?'

Kharbanda tittered, then said, poker-faced, 'Maybe he isn't done yet, sir.'

'No. Something else. Just read a few under poison.'

'Er, sir, there are too many.'

'How many?'

'*The Crooked House, Appointment with Death, A Pocket Full of Rye, The Mysterious Affair at Styles, Three Act Tragedy, Sparkiling Cyanide, The House of Lurking Death, The Pale Horse, Five Little Pigs, Sad Cypress, The Mirror Cracked from Side to Side* and *Curtain*, sir.'

'Damn. Well, read a few...'

'Yes, sir. *Crooked House:* "In a sprawling, half-timbered mansion in the affluent suburb of Swinly Dean, Aristide Leonides lies dead from barbiturate poisoning. An accident? Not likely. In fact, suspicion has already fallen on his luscious widow, a cunning beauty fifty years his junior..."'

Ajay was fast losing patience. 'Bas bas. And Kharbanda, it is crooked and not crooked, like cooked with an "r". And lush-us not lusk-eye-us. Dammit, man.'

'Sorry, sir. Print is too small.'

'Yes, of course.'

Kharbanda looked away and as he did, caught a glimpse of Sharma and found him sniggering.

Ajay played around with a quill-shaped golden pen, part of a government-issue gang of four. 'In any case, this deals with barbiturate. Next.'

'Sir. *Appointment with Death:* "'You do see, don't you, that she's got to be killed?' Ominous words for Hercule Poirot to overhear on his first night of vacation in the Holy Land. They come true, among the towering red cliffs and the ancient ruins of Petra when a tourist is murdered in full view of her fellow sightseers. A tiny puncture mark on her wrist is the only sign of the fatal poison that killed her—digitoxin. And not surprising. The 'horror of a woman' was loathed..."'

'No, not this one either. Digitoxin, it says. Let's try another one.'

'Yes, sir. *A Pocket Full of Rye:* "The innocuous cup of morning tea left Mr Rex Fortescue dead. Early investigations revealed the culprit to be a deadly poison called taxine—an alkaloid found in the seeds of yew tree berries. Everyone agreed that the shocking thing about his murder was that the contemptible tycoon wasn't knocked off sooner. But when two less-deserving souls fall victim to the killer, Miss Jane Marple is engaged to solve the mystery. The only link appears to be buried in a not-so-innocent verse. So what's the rhyme and reason behind the playful hint? The answer draws the shrewd sleuth into the heart of a family secret—and an increasingly menacing game that's anything but child's play."'

'I think this could be the one. Arey Sharma, you said Manochar died of a massive overdose of some anti-cancer drug. Does it say which one?'

Sharma came back to life. 'Yes, sir. Taxol.'

'Hang on a second. Was Manochar suffering from cancer?'

'Sir, the autopsy report states no tumours of any kind were seen in various organs...'

'Then why the hell was taxol administered?'

Sharma looked at Kharbanda and then back at Ajay. 'Beats me, sir.'

'Think, you idiots. Think.'

Sharma looked at Kharbanda once again, and this time decided not to revert his gaze to Ajay.

Ajay slapped the desk. 'Unless...Oh God. Wow. You evil Mumbai police bastards. No wonder there are two autopsy reports.'

The last time Sharma was this confused was at a Friday evening get-together organised by his department, when the right-hand side of the menu had appeared irreconcilable with his dear allowance.

'But, sir, I don't see what...'

Ajay slapped the desk once more. 'I get it now. How convenient for a beedi king to die through an overdose of a cancer drug. And quietly, the bastard who wrote the autopsy, quietly he turned taxine into taxol. *Genius*. If only you guys had spent this much effort in solving a goddamn crime...'

Sharma snubbed the castigation, principally because he couldn't understand it. 'Er, sir, I think we have cracked this one, too.'

Ajay sighed. 'Yes, so that's three done and dusted. Bloody slow progress, what. It's approaching seven already...okay, Sharma, where were we. Ya, hop on to the serial...'

'Yes, sir. The gruesome and shocking murder of the Hirwani...'

'Oh to hell with the adjectives, Sharma. Just the case, the damn case.'

'I am sorry, sir, but that's how the report starts...'

'Never mind how the Shakespeare who wrote your report began his story. They are all stories, aren't they, all your stories. *Start*.'

'Y-yes, sir. The murder of the Hirwani brothers. Three brothers, sir—20 April 2002...'

Ajay scratched behind his ear. 'That's the other thing. All these murders are quite recent in time. Anyway, go on.'

'One was hit on the head with a hammer, one was strangled and the third brother's skull was banged against a wall. All three found murdered in their office, here in Bandra.'

'What office?'

'Oh, didn't you know, sir? Hirwani Builders. Second-largest construction firm in the whole of western India. Were building the 100-metre dam on the Krishna, sir. Twenty-thousand villages were...'

'Yes yes, carry on.'

'Sir, all found dead. The murderer nabbed after a month.'

Ajay gave out a mock cry. 'Oh, yes.'

'A man called Lakhanbhai—another builder. Case is pending in Mumbai High Court, sir.'

'Good. You, Kharbanda?'

'Yes, sir. Two cases: *The A.B.C. Murders* and *And Then There Were None*.'

'Go on.'

'Sir. *The A.B.C. Murders:* "Alice Ascher is bludgeoned to death in her shop. Next to die is Betty Bernard in Bexhill—strangled with her own belt. Then, Sir Carmichael Clarke's skull is crushed in Churston. An urgent hunt is launched for the fiend, nicknamed as the A.B.C. murderer. Racing against the clock, Poirot tries to be one step ahead of this ruthless killer."'

Ajay almost got up from his favourite chair. 'Don't tell me. The names of the Hirwani brothers. A, B and bastard C, aren't they?'

'Sir?'

Ajay brandished his arm like he was fencing. 'Arey, their initials.'

SP Kharbanda felt a chill run down his spine. 'Ganpati Bappa. I am getting goose bumps all over my body, sir.'

Ajay was shouting. 'I don't care about your goose bumps, man—the names.'

'Amarmani. Brijmohan. Chimanbhai.'

Ajay punched the heavens. '*Yes!*'

This time SP Kharbanda was wholly sincere. 'Sir, you are a top-to-bottom genius.'

'*You* bloody keep quiet, Kharbanda. All this was happening right under your bulbous nose and you couldn't smell a thing. And because of you some bastard named Lakhanbhai is languishing in his langot somewhere in an eight-by-eight at Arthur Road.'

'I know, sir. That's three, no, six down already. This is so much more than we expected. We have to think carefully now, sir. Maybe, maybe use one disclosure for one promotion. Stretch it, I mean.'

Ajay broke a pencil in two. 'Shut up. *Shut up*.'

'Sorry, sir, I was just–'

'Kharbanda, how can you even think like that, haan? Anyway, now's not the time. So much has to be done to finish this whole thing. We have to first catch the real bastard who did all this. I bet you hadn't even taken *that* into account.'

SP Kharbanda realised he had erred. He decided the best way out was to err some more. 'Er...'

'What er?

The knock on the door saved SP Kharbanda. Ajay asked irritably. 'Yes? Who is it?'

'Sir, chai.'

'Finally. Two sugars as usual. So how many till now, Kharbanda?'

'Six and counting, sir.'

Ajay tapped the new pencil on his forehead. 'Arey. What about that Apte fellow? Why are we assuming you morons caught the right guy—the secretary, I mean.'

'True, sir. In fact if my hunch is correct...'

'You and your hunches, Kharbanda.'

'Err...'

'Where is that file you gave me, Sharma?'

'On your table, sir. Sir, sir, first please read the message, sir.'

Ajay opened the file. '*Quiet*. Talking like a five-year-old. Hmm... this? This is the message?'

'Ji. We had great trouble getting it from those Scotland Yard banchos. Finally, Interpol...'

'Yes yes. Here—read it, Kharbanda. And slowly.'

The entire Kharbanda family tree had not done as much reading as SP Kharbanda alone had in the past hour. He now stepped forward and took the ragged sheet from Ajay's hand and began reading.

Mumbai...Thursday, eleventh March, nineteen ninety-nine. This may take a while to reach you. In any case, you will be the first to learn of when, how and why, I murdered the 'Pride of Bombay' Mr Ramrao Apte.

Let me begin with the answer to the first question: when? This morning. Ten-thirty. Presidential suite. Hotel Taj Mahal. So, the complete answer to the first question: I killed Ramrao Apte on Thursday, eleventh March, nineteen ninety-nine, at ten-thirty precisely—I confirmed.

To the second question: how? I arrived at the Taj at nine sharp. I wandered along and got in among a bunch of tourists. Once inside, changed into an electrician's overalls. Located the presidential suite. Waited for the room service to go and knock on the door. Mr Apte opened the door. A woman got out. I went up to Mr Apte, said the air-conditioning needed to be looked at. Waited for the room service to leave. Went in the bathroom. Played around with a few switches. Then called for Mr Apte: "Mr Aapte? Sir, is this what is creating the problem?" He came in. The wire was around his neck in a flash. It was a matter of a minute. He was gone. I checked the time. Ten thirty. I then checked his pulse. Nothing. I waited for five minutes. Nothing. I went out the way I had come in.

So you see how easy it was. As easy as the way Mr Apte accumulated his billions. Now to the third and final, and perhaps the most important question: why? WHY? Because in the annals of corrupt Indians, the name of Mr Apte was written in gold. But it was not displayed; no, Mr Apte made sure of that...His name never came up—never seriously. It was whispered in cabinet meetings, murmured at evening parties, hinted at in underworld gatherings, gossiped at business lunches, muttered at police briefings, insinuated in the Vidhan Sabha, hushed in the Lok Sabha. At all of the above, it was also admired.

Mr Apte: combined wealth—nine thousand seven hundred crores. Unpaid taxes—twelve hundred crores. Fictitious companies—forty-two. MPs in the pocket—eleven. Houses in Mumbai—seventeen. Swiss bank accounts—three. Tie-ups with MNCs—nine. Mr Apte—instigator of riots; diverter of rivers; hacker of forests; reclaimer of oceans; devourer of ground water; builder of dams; cauteriser of crops; squasher of the landless; selector of chief ministers; harbinger of wealth. Now dead.

Every little helps."...The end, sir.'

Ajay felt a drop of cold sweat drag its way down from the back of his neck. 'Bloody hell, I tell you.'

'Nice, no.'

'Shut up. Let me think, let me...Kharbanda, jot down whatever I say.'

SP Kharbanda snapped his imitation Mont Blanc, a Chinese fake—the shape was identical but the golden words 'Mount Blank' on the cap gave it away—from his shirt pocket and clicked the nib out. 'Ready, sir.'

Ajay let his head fall back and closed his eyes, like he usually did at the barber's. 'This guy's English is quite good for a start.'

'Ji, sir.'

'Despite your pronunciation.'

SP Kharbanda was about to write that.

'Anyway, so can't be that—who did you say, Sharma? That stall boy.'

'Ji, sir. Bansilal said his name was Kalki musahur.'

'What sort of a ban-cho surname is that?'

'He was low caste, sir, a rat eater. Bansilal said he had run away from his village.'

'Well, this is no village English.'

DSP Sharma was confident. 'Not at all, sir.'

'Also, looks more like a killing than a murder. You get me?'

'Er, no, sir.'

'This guy killed Apte not for his money or for business reasons. I think, I think...I...goddamn. Shit. Just see the rest of Apte's friends here...'

SP Kharbanda was having difficulty keeping up. 'Sir?'

Ajay sat up with a jolt. 'Ban-cho. They are all rich bastards, aren't they? But they are corrupt bastards as well. All of them seem to have cut corners. Someone sold mill land, someone else agricultural land, someone was building a dam. You see?'

SP Kharbanda was trying really hard. 'Kind of, sir.'

'They are all connected, Kharbanda. This guy is meting out his own justice to them.'

'Ganpati Bappa.'

'Yes. And I'll tell you one thing. Our man can't be a stall boy. What was the name? Kalki musahur. Unless he is not what he was all those years ago.'

'Ji, sir.'

'This guy is educated, refined, confident—can get close to these bastards. He doesn't want their money. Doesn't want their power or fame, either. Our man is a serial killer with a conscience.'

Some of the words were very new. 'J-ji, sir…conscience.'

Ajay snatched the letter from SP Kharbanda's hands. 'Look. What does he mean by this, this last line, *look*. "Every little helps." What is this every little. Obviously, he is polishing off these men. But who does it help? Who. Those mill workers? Those farmers? Every little… helps…ban-cho, why do I get the feeling I have heard this same line somewhere? Somewhere recently, too…every little…'

Ajay sprang up from his chair as though someone had shot him from underneath it. 'No. *No*! Oh my God!'

SP Kharbanda was breathless in anticipation. 'What, sir. Please tell us.'

'But no. How can it be? *Oh my God!*'

'How can what be, sir?'

'Shut up a sec, Kharbanda. You know someone by the name of Akhil Sukumar?'

SP Kharbanda was taken aback. 'W-what are you saying, sir? Your professor friend?'

'Yes, my professor friend.'

'C-can I ask you, sir, what exactly is in your mind? Maybe three heads are better than one—you only said so.'

'Shut up. You remember our dinner yesterday, Kharbanda?'

'Ji, sir. Very hard to forget.'

'During our conversation, Akhil said the line, "Every little helps".'

'But, sir…'

'No one. *No one* uses this phrase here. I have never heard it before in my life—and I have been out and about. No, it is too quaint, too English. And Aks—I mean Akhil, he said this when we asked him what had he been doing to set his house in order. I mean, he was distraught by this ban-cho country. Who isn't, but his pain was special.'

SP Kharbanda was unsure. 'If you say, sir, but…'

Ajay closed his eyes and slid on the chair. Ten minutes went by. Not a word escaped Ajay's lips. To Kharbanda and Sharma, it appeared as though their boss had gone into deep meditation. In fact, it was anything but. The shock had to be absorbed, that too in public. Appearances had to be maintained. Choices had to be made, between friendships and stardom. And ten minutes was all it took for the mind to rationalise the discovery. *It was all a long time ago, the friendship—all in the past. And besides, how many times did we met these past fifteen years? What if I hadn't thought of writing him an email; what if I hadn't met him at all last week? He has changed and so have I. So have all of us. Sad, but life goes on. What was that about time and tide…?*

Ajay opened his eyes and looked straight at Kharbanda.

'My God, Akhil, what have you done. *Why*?'

'Don't you worry, sir. We'll bring in the professor and make him talk. And we know how to make people talk…'

Ajay threw the paperweight in SP Kharbanda's direction. From now on, it was going to be a delicate balance between exhibiting one's love for duty and friendship; and Ajay, a man of, by and for the system, had mastered the art.

'You bastard, Kharbanda, you'll do no such thing. I will skin you alive and…'

'S-sorry, sir, just a thought, just a thought.'

'Keep that thought to yourself, then. Akhil is my friend. He was my best friend, dammit. Yes, what he has done—and we aren't even sure if he is behind all this—but if he is, then it is up to me to beat him at it, not bloody *beat* him, you understand? All what we have at present is circumstantial. We need more, something concrete.'

'Yes, sir, of course, I am sorry.'

'Now listen, all is not lost. Look for clues. Look, *look*. We'll get to him, somehow…no? You don't trust me?'

'No no, sir, what are you saying. We have reached this far only because of you…'

'And I don't think interrogating Akhil would bring out much. In fact, it would take us further away.'

'If you say so, sir.'

Ajay growled. '*Yes*, I say so sir, Kharbanda. If Akhil is responsible for all this, the very fact that he hasn't hesitated one bit in being so close to me these past few days...well, you get me?'

'Yes, sir.'

'So all we can do is wait. Maybe I'll think of something. Set a little mouse trap for my clever friend. Leave it to me.'

'Yes, sir.'

'And listen—for the thousandth time, and more than ever—*not* a bloody word to *anyone*.'

'Of course, sir. Sir, if I may. There is one important thing we haven't discussed.'

'Yes, tell me.'

'Sir, the best-case scenario—we catch this killer, whoever he might be.'

Ajay was getting impatient. 'Yes...'

'Sir, that would be a *calamity*.'

'What the devil do you mean *calamity*. I thought this was precisely why you two had your eyes bulging out for, isn't it?'

'No no, sir, you don't understand. The cases.'

'What cases?'

'Have you thought about the cases, sir? Let me explain. All these cases are, well, *solved*. People...people now very high up, they have got medals for solving these very cases. Now *you* come along and you *unsolve* them and then *solve* them again. Well, what about those medals and promotions? All those people—what happens to them. You see? No, sir, best to leave it like this, on second thoughts. In my humble opinion, sir.'

Ajay waved a finger at SP Kharbanda. 'Well, keep your humble opinion and your second-rate thoughts to yourself, Kharbanda. What would you prefer—becoming a DIG and a super-duper-star, or content with licking the boots of your incompetent third-rate officers? Haan?'

'Err...'

'Bastards. All of you. Well, I don't care what happens to the medal of a donkey. We have, *we* have done what *they* were supposed to do in the first place. *We* deserve all those medals that they have pinned to their stinking wardi.'

'Sir, I get your point. Just that a lot of mud would fly…'

'Then let it. Remember the best-case scenario—you would have jumped right above those very officers, well at least most of them. And I would have pole-vaulted to the bloody top, from where I can always keep an eye out for you two.'

SP Kharbanda's heart skipped a beat in relief. 'That is *exactly* what we wanted to hear, sir. Any trouble, you please keep an eye out for us.'

'Of course I will. Now will you two stop stirring and ladling your khayali-pulaos? We have work to do.'

SP Kharbanda felt as though he had returned to work after a holiday at the spa. 'Yes, sir.'

'And one last thing…Yes? Now who is it? Come in.'

The door flung open and a man rushed in, desperately short of breath. 'Sir. Sir!'

'Yes, who the hell are you?'

'Sir, myself Gokhale. Inspector Gokhale, sir.'

'Yes, whoever—don't come barging in like this. We are busy, can't you see?'

'Sorry sir, but there has been a terrible…'

'What?'

'Sir, we heard on the walkie-talkie. Mr Vilasrao, our railway minister. He has been stabbed to death, sir. Stabbed to *death!*'

Ajay's cup dropped to the floor. '*Jesus*. When? Where?'

'Just ten minutes ago, sir. In a train, no less.'

'How did you get to know? Who told you?'

'Around a hundred people, sir. They all witnessed it.'

'What do you mean, man. It was in the open?'

Inspector Gokhale caught his breath. 'Almost, sir. Mr Vilasrao was killed in a train, and his murder was being watched by these hundreds in the adjoining train, running parallel…'

Ajay was already running towards the door. 'Shit. *4.50 from Paddington*.'

SP Kharbanda was trying to catch up. 'Ganpati Bappa. We have got him, sir!'

Ajay had by now reached the stairway. He hesitated, but then going down is so much easier than coming up. He yelled at the top of his voice: 'Kharbanda! Sharma!'

'Sir!'

'Get the tables, the files—let's go, man. Lady luck is on our side.'

Fingerprints remain, to date, an important piece of identification in any criminal investigation. Or for that matter, even to get a passport. It is that vital. That's why we leave them all over. Because we are a nation of clean chits. There is a national clean chit on which all crimes, however heinous, are written. Some of us tick all boxes. But the chit has to be clean. Band-box clean. Wah. Clean cheaters.

Forensic originates from the Latin word *forensis*. It means on stage, in a public setting, before the forum. It is a form of legal evidence as well as a category of public presentation. We don't need it because everything is in the public domain. The truth will come out. Eventually. After the burgled and the burglar are both dead and the inspector has retired and the law would have followed its own curse. No crook in India is afraid of facing the law because there isn't one. When it comes down to it, we visit places of worship to atone in full public view. Entertainment, entertainment and entertainment.

A billion people and we have one DNA fingerprinting machine. Sometimes out of order. A billion people and we have no proper institution in the country that studies forensic science. And if one were to start it, fingerprints would be manufactured. In India, cutting off the thumb of a dead person to ensure ration and pension by proxy is not uncommon. If we can manufacture a thumb, we can manufacture evidence. We are all a biometric pass. Thumb, index finger, middle finger, ring finger, little finger and a little coriander and green chillies for the small change.

Lie detector. Damn fool. Why on earth do we need a machine like that in the land of Satyamev Jayate? At the rate with which we tell the truth, it would shudder, cringe, contort, hiss, steam and break down. So much truth, so little electricity. So much truth, so many power cuts.

It is time to admit that our forefathers and foremothers made a blunder. The tiger isn't our national animal, pink panther is. Why rummage through the crime scene wearing space-age suits when you can solve cases just by reading jacket blurbs? All these infra-red, ultraviolet, DNA, she-NA—bad Western influence, that's all they are. Hunh, we are an 8,000-year-old civilisation, older than crime itself. Remember that—older than crime and the origin of crime. We watched it take birth on the banks of our holy rivers, we saw it take its first baby steps and then snatch a lady's purse and run like mad. *'Pakdo! Pakdo usko!'* 'Don't worry, madam. He's not going anywhere. We know where he lives.'

Deduction, my friend—Ramanujam, Raman, Khorana, Chandrashekhar, Bose, Inspector Clouseau—use your brain. Make up stories, then read them to the judge.

No seriously, why is it that our sleuths are always air-dashing here and there in search of lies when truth is sitting right next to them? Why must they run when truth stands still—sthir. Why are we always *zeroing in* on the criminals, chasing thieves, connecting with counterparts all over the world when the culprits are hiding under the bed? Why are we always *swinging* into action—Darwin needs evidence? Monkey.

What we cannot do at home, we cannot do elsewhere. We cannot find the evidence because we have decided to lose it, never find it and occasionally refer to it to remain credible. Like readymade idlis, there are readymade sentences generally pointing in the direction of truth. We have completed the interrogation, a few witnesses have to be examined, new evidence has been unearthed, in light of the new evidence that is unearthed there is a new angle, our investigators have been sent to Mars. No one is coming back because no one has gone anywhere.

We like to blame others for what we have hidden. So black money is always 'stashed' in Switzerland. It is physically impossible to stuff a crore or any other currency in a bank unless it's a barn. It is common knowledge that criminal money always travels faster than an investigation. You can sell drugs in Medellin, buy a few paintings in Hong Kong and wire the money to the Isle of Man without moving from your desk. Leave it to the mouse. Yes, yes, mouse, stupido. That thing which moves your right hand round and round, up and down, this way and that.

Swiss bankers wonder what a lakh crore means. They understand million, billions and trillions, but a lakh crore? They should train in India to know how money is 'stashed' in education, infrastructure, land, sea and spectrum. In passing they may also learn that money does grow on trees. Not that they are green behind their ears but a rich vocabulary never harmed anyone. Especially Indian money vocabulary that can outsmart the smartest sleuths the world has ever seen, much less worked with.

So our sleuths—calling them detectives would sound too close to Char so bees—travel to New York when the fingerprints are in Switzerland. They then travel to Sweden because the fingerprints have moved to Turkey. So they go to Hong Kong because they cannot speak Spanish. Not speaking a language is important. So much can be lost and found in translations.

So why even bother to learn English? Why bother with disciplines like forensic science, criminal law, cross-border treaties and Fevicol? What, Fevicol? No, no, Interpol. Interpol. This is not a travel agency.

Why worry about understanding the difference between the accused and the convicted when we have nothing to hide? We have absolutely no reason to worry about being under the net. Ask the next mosquito. They have never had it so good and now even have competition in the form of other vectors, like new dons in the neighbourhood. See, life imitates art which imitates art all under the same net.

Relax, no one will ever get caught in India. We are not fish. Neither are we firangipani. We are 'zimble' human beings who do not want to get caught with our hands in the till. Now if that is not a fair request, what is, thambi?

17

2004—The Sound and the Fury

The Sukumar lab at night resembled Crawford Market during early evening. Packed and chirpy. On the thumbtacked cloth board by the entrance, a full-page newspaper cutting of the wagon wheel of Laxman's 281 at Eden Gardens, pinned cruelly over with photocopied pamphlets that jostled for visibility: An Idiot's Guide to Electroporation, Murphy's Laws for Scientific Publishing, 10 X Buffer Compositions, Tissue Culture Protocol. Next to them was a greeting card that had Samantha Fox bubble-asserting 'Night time is right time'.

The Sukumar lab, like most research labs, was a microcosm of India's ethnic diversity. The Himachali Gitaram hummed Rafi as he pushed sodium wires in a three-neck containing diethyl ether, the thin silvery wires sinking listlessly into the ether like jalebis in hot ghee. The UPite Krishen was taking optical density measurements of cell cultures at the spectrophotometer, drumming the instrument lid with his knuckles. The Madrasi Swetha was measuring out five microlitres of radioactive phosphorus, concurrently patting her thighs, now with the inside of her palm, now with the outside, mesmerised by MS. The Bengali Anamika was carolling along parts of Runa Laila as she wrote up the day's work in her notebook. The Haryanavi Alka was writing a letter to her husband of two months and keeping an eye on the dripping nickel affinity column. The Punjabi Siddharth was rim-rolling a carbon dioxide cylinder by the Laminar-hood—it wobbled dangerously before coming to rest—while he tapped his feet to Mika. And finally, the man without roots, Akhil Sukumar, was inside his office at the far end of the lab, as he always was post dinner until midnight or even later.

It was science at work and everyone seemed as blissful with their lives as they possibly could, or at least until Aparajita Biswas came charging in and knocked hard at the door that said Prof A. Sukumar.

'Yes? Come in…' said a voice from inside.

Api cracked open the door and stood half in, half out.

'Api!' said Akhil, his jaws dropping.

'Akhil,' replied Api, surprisingly gently, then closed the door behind her.

'Hi. What are you doing here?'

'Was passing this way and thought why not check up on you. Tried the house first…'

'What a surprise. Where's AB? Haven't heard from him since he rang the lab in the morning to say Elephanta was cancelled. Gita gave me the message. How did you find my lab? Sit, sit, sit. What would you like—some coffee? How have you come?'

'Oh, I took the local—from Kandivali. I thought I should come and congratulate you on a job well done.'

Akhil showed surprise. 'Wha…what. Sorry, I didn't…'

'But tell me. How did you get back so quick?'

Akhil gave a nervous smile. 'Dear Api, I don't know what you are talking about.'

'Really. Oh, come now, Akhil, no need to be so modest.'

Akhil shook his head. 'Api, I repeat, I have absolutely *no* idea what you are on about. Anyway, if you must know, I have been in the lab since 6 pm.'

'Oh you have, have you? And I suppose you haven't even had time for dinner, poor you.'

'What's got into you, Aps? What's going on—will someone please fill me in?'

Api exploded. 'Shut up, Akhil. Just don't say a word.'

'Are you alright, Api? Please tell me, I am beginning to get a little worried now.'

'It was all for my benefit, wasn't it? Just to show *me*.'

'What? *What,* Api?'

Api looked straight into Akhil's eyes. 'So you *have* showed me. So I *have* seen it. Now what? Now what happens, Akhil? *You* have to tell me. I cannot understand you; maybe I have never understood you.'

'Look, this has gone too far. Either you tell me what's going on or you...'

'Or *what*? I am next? That's it, isn't it? I am next. So go on, then. I am right here before you...*do it*, like you killed that man in the train. With the dagger I gifted you.'

Akhil pretended to get up. 'Alright that's it...'

'So this was your "every little helps", was it? But is this your last "little"? Oh, but wait. It can't be ...'

'Listen, Api, please...'

'It was *all* for my benefit, wasn't it? You wanted to demonstrate how easy it was for you, this "little". You wanted to show me your power. You *knew* I was in the other train, didn't you? Yes, you did.'

Akhil pushed a cardboard carton towards Api. 'Here—read the label on the box. What does it say, haan? *Read* it.'

'...Sukumar. L-32 Chemistry Department, IIT Powai. Ph: 25722545. One Italian crust, onion and capsicum. One garlic bread. 160 rupees.'

'Read on.'

'7.30 pm.'

Akhil fell back on the chair. 'Satisfied?'

'But...but how can it be? I saw *you*, Akhil. I saw you kill that man. I saw you stab him. It was you who...'

'You saw me? You saw my face?'

'But it *had* to be you. There's no getting away from it. You used that dagger I gave you. And then I saw you throwing it from the window. It's still lying there on the tracks, for all I know—my gift.'

'So you are saying I can defy Heisenberg's Uncertainty Principle—that Akhil Sukumar can be at two separate places any given time. Haan?'

'But, but…'

'But what, Api? You thought the guy who killed the railway minister—you thought that was me?'

'I…yes…'

'And now. What do you think now?'

Api looked away. 'I…forgive me, Akhil. I couldn't see how it…what a fool I have made of myself, gosh, what an ass. I am so sorry…'

'You needn't be, Api.'

'Hah, well, there you are right? I cannot even begin to ask for…'

'No, I mean you need not be sorry. Look—it is time for you to know. You weren't entirely off the mark.'

'Wha-what do you mean by that?'

'It wasn't me you saw in that train there. But in a way it was. Yes, you can say I got it done.'

Api gripped the table ledge. 'No. *No.*'

'I got the job done. But it's not what you think. I didn't pay for it or anything like that.'

'You have an accomplice.'

'Yes. Someone who'd do it anyhow, without me telling him to.'

'*Him.* So who is *he*?'

'I am sorry, Api. I can't tell you that. At least not yet.'

'*No.* You mean…how…how many more, Akhil? And how many more to come?'

'*That* I can tell you. One more.'

Api shook her head. 'No! God, no Akhil. My *Akhil.* Tell me this isn't true. *Tell me.*'

'Will you hear me out? Will you at least listen to my story?'

'*Your* story? What *is* your story, Akhil? That you have murdered innocent people in cold blood? Is that your story? How dare you.'

Akhil leaned forward. 'Api—listen to me. If *I* hadn't told you, wouldn't you have gone home thinking I was eating a pizza and not killing that minister? *I* told you, Api. I chose to tell you.'

'Thanks a lot, Akhil.'

'I am tired of it all, Api. I can't go on. *I can't.* I want to tell you the reasons I have done all this.'

Api smacked her palm on the table. '*No*. I don't want to know. I don't want to grant you the pleasure and satisfaction of having explained your crimes away.'

'I am *not* trying to explain them away. I have committed them, dammit. I am not happy that I have committed them, but neither am I sad.'

'You are not sad? You are not sad that you are a murderer? What has become of you, Akhil? What have you turned into? What did you want to do with the blood of innocent people?'

Akhil raised his voice. 'Don't call them innocent, Api!'

'Oh, so what else are they? Do tell me of their sins, then, *Judge* Sukumar.'

'They were anything but innocent.'

'And who proclaimed them guilty? *You*?'

'*Yes*. But along with me, a hundred, a thousand, a million others…'

Api got up then sat down. 'No, no, *no, NO!* Don't you dare. Don't you dare try and water down your crimes by making millions accessory to it. You *alone* killed them, Akhil.'

'Yes, I alone killed them. What makes you think I am shirking my responsibility?'

'*Wah*. You call this your *responsibility*?'

'It became my responsibility.'

'Oh, I see. So you are the policeman, the magistrate, the high court, the Supreme Court all rolled into one, is it? Responsibility. You have got some gall saying this.'

'Perhaps responsibility is the wrong word.'

'A little late for realisation to dawn, isn't it Akhil?'

'Let me finish…'

Api hissed through her teeth. 'No, you let *me* finish. There is a word for this—it's called murder. But you have far exceeded the sphere of that as well. You have become Shiv, the *destroyer*.'

'Just listen to me, Api, ple…'

'You are Akhil no more. You are *Shiv*.'

'Listen, Api…'

Api got up. 'I can't sit here and turn into a confession chamber for you, Akhil. You better find a church for that. And a father who will keep saying "Yes, child" and absolve you of all your crimes.'

'Listen to me.'

Api made for the door. 'I loved you, Akhil. I *love* you. I have seen many sad and terrible days in my life, and you know most of them, Akhil—but this...Goodbye, Aks.'

'Half a million people. Would have perished within a year…'

Api turned around.

'What?'

'Reduced to eating mango kernels. Relieved—food at last—then dying a slow and horrible death because of the poison. Come, sit.'

Api sat down gingerly, on the edge of the chair.

Akhil continued. 'Half of those would have had no option but to arrive in Mumbai and sell their bodies in return for some food. But emaciated, pus-ridden bodies don't go for much—five, maybe ten rupees a go…'

'Wha…'

'The children. Yes, the children, pushed from their swings hung on trees that are now to be uprooted to make way for swanky malls, that would then have shops selling toys, all kinds of them. But those kids would only be allowed to stare through the windows…

'Whole families, villages, hundreds of them, squashed to dust, with only charpais left for those families to balance them upturned on their heads and walk barefoot, Indian file, to somewhere, to some distant wasteland…'

'What are you…'

'And Saane would have accomplished all of that, each and every part, in a matter of three years…'

Api was confused. 'Saane? How does Saane come into this? You mean you…'

'Yes, your "innocent" Saane. The very Saane who leased 20,000 hectares of prime agricultural land to the highest bidder. Ever heard of SEZ? The special economic zone? Well, he leased all that land. And mind you, it was not wasteland, but agricultural land.'

'Saane did that?'

'Yes. And I won't bother to tell you how much he stood to make out of all this, this "innocent" transaction. The final signing ceremony was scheduled for next month.'

'Half a million people?'

'Maybe more, Api, much more. But no, you wouldn't call this genocide, would you? After all, it's all legal, innocent stuff, isn't it... That was Saane and *The Murder on the Links*.'

'But what's Agatha...*No*. You mean that message in the bottle stuff last year? No, Akhil.'

Akhil carried on. 'Twelve thousand families currently making ends meet in matchboxes, recycling the water with which they bathe, recycling it for drinking—can you picture that? Mothers walking to the ends of the city to find a job, some job, *any* job. Their children, kicked and beaten, their husbands forced to pull the thela, barefoot, in the sun, on the tarred road that has turned all sticky with the heat. Have you ever tried to test your feet on the burning road? How long do you think you can last? Ten seconds? Twenty? Imagine those men, pulling the carts for miles. Why? Because those eight mills in which they were employed for twenty years decided to change into Mediterranean-style condominiums. That was Yashwantrao Palnitkar and *The Body in the Library*.'

Api was crying. 'Oh, Akhil, stop. Stop, Akhil!'

'Manochar Kangda—you know him? Directly responsible for providing livelihood to 80,000 children, all between the ages of six and ten. Why? Because of their little fingers—the way they can fold the tendu leaf into a beedi. And what do these children of Manochar get in return? Two rupees a day. But wait. Mr Kangda was all above board. He was a proud signatory to the National Child Labour Eradication Mission. He was "innocent", Api. That was *Death in the Clouds*. You want more?'

'No, Akhil, no...'

'Ramrao Apte. Go find out what he did. Go discover his claim to fame. How many thousands he killed, uprooted, burned, ran over, tortured. That was *And Then There Were None*.'

Tears were falling on Api's lap. 'Oh, Akhil...'

'But it is never "And then there were none", Api, *never*. They keep coming, like the spawning of a thousand asurs—swords drawn and charging—from a single drop of their father's blood. There *is* no end, Api, no end. Raktabeej is amar.'

'Then why, Akhil? *Why?*'

Akhil clenched his fist and brought it down on the table. 'Because every little helps. *It really does*. Ask those millions who are at least breathing today—ask *them*. Maybe my "little" was *my* effort to slow down the conveyor belt on which they were squatting, slow down its rumbling roll towards the survival-of-the-fittest pit. Maybe all in vain, but sti...'

'No...'

Akhil's eyes had turned bloodshot and were glistening. 'In any case, Api, I tried, you know. And I am tired now, I can't go on. I am sorry, Api, that you had to go through all this. Nothing is worse than seeing you cry like this...'

Api reached out and pressed Akhil's hand. 'But, Akhil, what made you so convinced that this was the way? Were you, are you, still convinced of it? How did it come to this, this self-annihilation?'

'Call it what you will, Api—but it is not fatalism. This country runs on fatalism. The one who is consigned to, becomes resigned to his place or position in society. A *rung*—that's what everyone holds close to their chests here. Look at what we are taught since birth. Whatever happened happened for the good and whatever will happen will also happen for the good. *What does it mean*? Isn't it a call to sit back and observe, to not take part in the battles that confront you? A call to accept one's fate—an *a priori* judgement? Whatever happened, happened for the good. Never has a philosophy been advocated that is so simple to understand and yet so utterly devastating when followed.

'Yes, great mahatmas have appeared from time to time, Api, and intoned reclassifications—Harijan. Dalit. *Children of God*. What children of God, Api? *Which God*? Calling a bhangi a Harijan improved nothing. The old cataloguing still remains as firm as ever. The children of God still pick shit while the "other" children of God shit. *The children of God* have become *the children of Manochar*. Maybe they always were.'

Api wiped her eyes with her damp pallu.

'Self-annihilation is not everyone's cup of tea, Api. After all, it runs counter to the basic tenet of the survival of a species—to go against the wishes of one's brain and its primeval wiring. It is difficult—not impossible, but rare—to be a kamikaze. Do animals commit suicide? I don't know. But I have wanted to, for a very long time, too long a time, Api. Somehow, every time I thought of going through with it, something prevented me—someone always provided a ray of hope. It has been missing for a long time now, Api. I am shrouded in darkness. I don't possess a shadow anymore. I could have just gone, you know. It would have been easy—a slit of the wrist, a jump from the building. But this time around, I became the provider of this ray. Maybe, I thought, I can be of some use before I take my leave…'

'Isn't your life worth living? Haan?'

'When exactly does a human life become worth living, Api? What if you knew that you are going to die, say, in a year's time, would you live that one year all happy and smiling at strangers and saying "Lovely weather"? Maybe.'

Api flicked a tear from her eye. 'Maybe…'

'But maybe when you stop valuing your own life, you begin to value that of others. You say, "To hell with it. I have got only a year left anyway." The funny thing is, this thinking works only when you have got a year left. I mean, people don't start doing good deeds when they think they have *only fifty* more years left to live, now do they? Of course they don't, because if you *did* start to think like that, there'd be no war, no hungry and thirsty and dying people, no emaciated, displaced refugees travelling millions of miles.'

Api tilted her head forward and looked deep into Akhil's eyes, with sadness and love.

'So what is your quantum, Api. One year? Five years? Surely not more than five years. But a human life means *so* little, like that of an ant that you crush under your shoe. Only a war makes you realise this. You—miles away from the front—you prepare yourself for the news of your soldiers' deaths. A small war—we can spare a thousand; a world war—alright then, a million, maybe ten. But in peace time, that *same* human life regains its significance. Remember last year, when thirty firefighters were trying to save the life of that one man, that Indo-Pak war veteran, trapped in his burning house? And that same man would have died unnoticed on the front in '71. *We*, the society, *we* judge a life's importance. But what if I don't wait for you to condemn me or glorify me? What if I volunteer?'

Api shook her head. 'No…'

'There are millions who are dying even in peace time, or didn't you notice, being so transfixed with that news of those firemen and that one man trapped in his house? Is your peace time so different from my peace time? While you are desperate for that one man to survive the fire because it makes you feel good, while you are desperate to forget the millions who are trapped all over the world but don't have thirty hoses trained on their burning bodies, while you are kind and desperate, what the hell should *I* do? Tell me.'

'Oh, Akhil.'

'Can I balance *one* life—mine with those million lives? Believe me, Api, when I tell you that I am convinced my life isn't worth living. To carry on day after day like an ox that quietly ploughs through a field all its life. You say I carry on like this till I am seventy? *Why*? What have I got to live for, haan? Who to share everything with? It's time to twist those propellers, Api, time to twist those propellers…'

Api squeezed Akhil's hand. 'But what made you think you weren't already doing your bit, your "little"? Didn't you say you wanted to work on "my diseases"? Who's to say that you wouldn't have come up with a new drug for tuberculosis?'

Akhil gave a wry smile. 'Working on my own? On a yearly budget that's less than the monthly cafeteria allowance of a Pfizer employee? Who are you kidding? And even if, let's say, I did manage to come up with a new drug for tuberculosis after twenty years—what about it? Are you not aware that most diseases are curable already? And what's the purpose of most new drugs anyway—a 10 per cent improvement over the existing drug. Lesser side effects.

'Tuberculosis, Api, is completely curable. I stress, *completely*. And yet, two million die every year because of it—these are *WHO* numbers. The drugs are there already. No, it's something else. People die, not because of the lack of a drug, but because these deaths are of *no* importance in the eyes of the state. The protraction of a disease has got nothing to do with the availability of the drug meant to cure it. The real culprit is the apathy and failure of the state. *It's a game.* The minister says next year we'll get the deaths down to sub-two million levels. Sub-two million. These are *people* they are talking about, people who can't even get forty-year-old anti-TB drugs, and you are waiting for a rainbow to appear after fifteen years courtesy my research efforts?'

'But…'

'Science and Antakshari have a lot in common. Biding my time. That's all I was doing, Api, biding my…'

The poignant splendour of 'Für Elise: Blumen aus einem Buch' broke the conversation.

Api rummaged her purse to find her mobile. 'Oh, sorry I…'

'No, take it, take it.'

Api flicked the phone open ruefully and placed it by her ear. 'H-hello…'

'Hi sweets, this is AB. I have been trying your cell for God knows how long! Where the hell are you, Aps?'

'I am alright—on my way back to the guest house.'

'Shit, Aps, there's been a murder on the suburban. I have just reached the spot. Do you know who…'

Api wiped her nose with the back of her hand. 'Yes, some railway minister.'

'Oh, so you know. Where are you?'

'On my way. Should be back in half an hour…'

'Well, take extra care. Guys here are on full alert. They anticipate mobs on the streets. Where exactly are you?'

'AB, I said I am fine. I'll talk to you when I get back.'

'Listen, I'll be late, Aps. This could be very important. I think this murder is somehow linked to Saane—and the Apte…Go straight to the guest house, okay? Take care, alright?'

'Ya, you too. Bye.'

Api flipped the phone shut and dropped it in her purse.

'That was AB. I think he has an inkling, Akhil. He just said he thought this murder was linked to Saane.'

'Clever dickey, our AB.'

'Why would he say that, especially when he said he's just arrived at the crime scene?'

Akhil smiled. 'Unless he has read *4.50* and connected it with *Links.*'

'He never tells me what he is thinking. It is still a long shot that he's aware of *4.50.*'

'You never know.'

Api sighed And said, 'Now what, Akhil?'

'Nothing. As I said, I was prepared for this and I am prepared for what happens next.'

'Are you? And who will believe anything you say? You think the police will…'

'I don't want anyone to believe me. And yes, it *is* in my plan to make sure that I don't go unpunished.'

'W-what do you mean?'

'I want a favour from you.'

'AB's on to you, Akhil. It is best you come with me to the guest house. Together we can make him understand.'

Akhil shook his head. 'No, Api, no. No one needs to be made to understand.'

'Akhil, will you listen to me for a change? We will—*I will*—explain it all to AB, I really will. AB can give you a patient hearing. But you need to understand, too. If those who you killed committed a crime, then you did, too. There's no getting away form it, Akhil. We wi…'

'Look, Api, I need this thing from you. Now either you do it or I'll have to make do without your help.'

Api lowered her head and looked away.

'I want you to keep all this under wraps for just a couple more days, just till this weekend. Look, no one can help it if it comes out on its own—and it might in all probability now that AB's on to it, but it might be that he may want to hold on for a little longer just to tie all up loose ends, link all the connections. And two days is all I need. So will you please help me in this, please, Api?'

Api felt dizzy. 'Wha-what is on your mind? What is going to happen in a couple of days?'

'I'll give myself up. I must, however, get to one last thing...in Batia.'

'Batia? Where's that? You are not going to tell me, obviously.'

'*I will. I will.* I will tell you about it when I am there. I must be off tonight, to avoid being called for questioning by A B. Just tell him that you haven't seen me since last night if he asks. I'll contact you in two days' time.'

'You are off tonight?'

'Yes, I'll take a train—any train going that way. I have your mobile number.'

Api squeezed Akhil's hand with firmness. 'Can I come?'

'*What?*'

'Maybe I should have chucked it all a long time ago, Akhil, but it's never too late...'

Akhil rubbed Api's hand gently. 'Yes, it *is* too late, Api, *too* late. Now go—there might be trouble on the streets soon.'

'I don't want to leave you, Akhil. I've got a bad feeling. Tell me what's going to happen in Batia, please Akh...'

'Look, Api, I can't. Trust me. Now *hurry*.'

'I want you to know that I understand why you did what you did. I cannot possibly absolve you, but I understand. I...'

'Good girl. Now stop crying. Come—you have a taxi waiting?'

Api nodded.

'Then come, let's go...I'll come back, you know.'

Api moved her head slowly. 'No, you won't, Akhil, I know you won't.'

What was all that about, eh? Sixty years. Seventy years. Eighty. We die a thousand deaths every day anyway, don't we? And turn into trillions of vibhuti particles. Or is it ashes? Alright, you can call it stardust.

It could have been perfect.

Almost perfect, that is. Woman meets man. They are attracted to each other. Love blossoms, they progress. He wants to set up India's best research laboratory, study communicable diseases and she wants India to grow up and take charge. They dream separately. They dream jointly. There's fire, there's passion, there's energy, devotion, dedication, a sense of necessary sacrifice and there's hope. But above all, there is that space and that time where everything is possible. Can't be explained by any other word except udaan—flight. Soaring comes close, but sounds imperfect.

Udaan is that coming together of space and time where the two can leap, without a net, without a belt. Their love is so binding, it sets them free. Their roots are so strong in their knowledge and in their curiosity that it gives them that push for a leap of faith. For life is exactly that—a leap of faith. When you are allowed to leap, that is.

Desperate, decisive, dainty, daunting, daring, dreadful, doleful—all rolled up in an ambition for India. So frighteningly impulsive, like the birth of a star, an unknown trajectory. The only way it can ever be. This was not an atlas; it was a compass called heart and for them the only direction it pointed was upwards.

What happened then, what the hell happened? Life, that's what. Life happened. It just slipped in. Without a warning, quietly, in all its fury. Gates clanked into place, fences were erected, doors closed, windows shut, and so did all the nine entry points of life—nostrils, eyes, ears, nabhi and the two unmentionables. Vital when we live. Instant obsolescence when we leave our body.

Then life also died. It decided that it wanted to die because something was choking it, strangling it. It had been decided that life had to be dead, by hook or crook. Life took itself into its own hands and *preponed* its death. Took its own life. Akaala mrityu does not depend on God. You can also kill yourself. What has suicide got to do with our creator?

Then life happens differently. We fail in our exams, we cannot afford to go to school, we miss the bus, we are forced to eat nothing. We are forced to live a life of poverty. We are forced to live a life of privilege. We are forced to succeed, forced to fall by the wayside. When life takes over in all its fury, we can stop neither wind, nor water, nor fire, nor earth. When life takes over, we are not even a speck in time. But we think about that speck, think about it all the time. We are overwhelmed by the littleness, the pettiness, the absurd and the cunning. The observer and the observed become one, they merge.

Aham Brahmasmi. What? *Tat tvam asi.* What? So no difference between Chamaar and Iyengar, then. So why all this food poisoning?

What did you say? Stream of consciousness? If we are consciousness, then why can't we be the river, the fountain, the ocean of knowledge and a space of peace? Life is a conscious battle; the *Bhagavad Gita* is a book for the warrior, for the seeker. It is about war, a just war, the story of war within in our body which is the dharmakshetra and the kurukshetra. Which one do you choose? To kill is also your dharma but you cannot decide how and where. That is not the unknown. That is the known. Karma is a calculation, a very precise calculation, an inexorable rolling and re-rolling of time and action—timely action.

You have to be blessed to encounter evil, otherwise you will not be able to seek the knowledge that will set you free. You have to be ready for the opportunity that disguises itself—good and bad, wanted and unwanted. Being unprepared will be unforgivable. The study of the strike is as demanding as the strike itself. Arjun, about to let go of the arrow, is that perfection that we strive for in our search for freedom from disease. It must make sense, it has to. All else is ordinary.

Is that reasonable? Who is free—the arrow or Arjuna? The one who has been set free, or the one who has set free? The unreasonable is also part of reason. The unwanted is also part of the wanted, the despised is also the part of the desired. Such is the tragedy and the glory, such is the miracle of what we call life. What is truth without knowledge and what is knowledge without its completing corollary in death? Death of a body, not death of consciousness, completeness.

Satyam, Gnyanam, Anantam, Brahman. Millions of years of coding and decoding, a book on a war, a lecture on a battlefield, a call to kill one's own, a right to kill evil. Dharma. Knowledge is not only power, it is also compassion, laughter, love, mirth. Power that is binding is powerless. We spend entire lifetimes looking for directions when the one direction we should accept, evades us—the direction of simplicity, the path to nowhere. Where are we headed? Into a rat hole? Congratulations, we are bound to find more rats there. Api took Akhil with her too down that road. Who was captured by whom here? How can a free soul be captured? Was it all a lie?

Philosophy is the science of reality. It must not be misconstrued as being scholastic, religious, theological or mysterious. This is a truth without a second. This truth has no other version.

Tat tvam asi—you are it. You are the truth. You are advaita—there is no other. Akhil and Aparajita lived that for a fleeting second. In this janma. For *it* was it.

Aneka Janma Sampraapta Karma Bandha Vidaahiné
Atma Gnyanam Pradaaneya, Tasmai Sri Gurave Namaha

Could it be that Akhil and Api had freed themselves from the cycle of karma accumulated over several lives and were truly free? A freedom that was the envy of those around? Nah. Api was the arranger in this life. She derailed everyone—some consciously, subconsciously. Several lives crashed together.

'Several lives'. Like the multiverse?

Atma gnyana is liberating, after all. When you possess no shadow, there's no looking back.

Life is the born and the unborn, the pleasure and the penance, the sound and the fury. Akhil and Api knew this, but they were trapped. One in a method of life and the other in life itself. External tentacles, internal tentacles. Bolo kitne tentacles?

18

2004—The Unbearable Lightness of Being

The sun-baked coaches of the Darbhanga Express bumped along the scorching rails, leaving their occupants to absorb all the shocks and the jerks. There they sat, packed to the rafters, some by the open doors, some in the toilets, moving from side to side like car wipers, bled of all energy or, perhaps, trying to conserve it for greater, even more brutal challenges that somehow always lay ahead.

To the eyes of an eagle gliding above in the cloudless sky, it would have seemed as though a Moses formed of rusted iron and corroded tin was parting an ocean of yellow dust. Except for the train and a few pipal trees swaying to the cruel blasts of the loo, the eagle would have spotted no other movement. Even the water buffaloes stood unmoving in ankle-deep sludge that was a pond once. The train ignored them, speeding past as though on a mission.

In one of the coaches, amid a murmuring, nibbling, drinking, smoking and sleeping mass of humanity, sat Akhil Sukumar, looking out through the barred windows, waiting apathetically for the next fishplate pounding—the metronomic dhugh-dhugh-dhugh-dhugh.

Two days, three trains and countless kullarhs of chai later, Akhil and his companion were nearing their destination. But theirs was a journey where time had lost all meaning. Watch is a human invention and to consult it is a human choice.

The train came to an abrupt halt. Someone had stood by the rails flagging a ten-rupee note and the driver had obliged. After a while, the train lurched forward and in three or so pulls caught speed again.

The man sitting opposite Akhil said, 'Saali, this heat.' No one paid any attention.

Soon, a little boy in tattered clothes entered the corridor. He was followed by a thin man with small-poxed cheeks and a harmonium around his neck. The little boy was blind; there was caked skin and muscle where the eyes had once been. The duo could be heard from a distance. The thin man was pumping the harmonium in quick short bursts orphaned as and when he raised his arm to cover his ear with the palm. They were rendering a Hindi song that, over the years, the consortium of Indian beggars had appropriated as their clarion call. With his bleating partner in tow, the boy commenced feeling his way through the bays with extended arms, exaggerating his blindness.

'*...Gareebon ki suno...woh tumhaaree sunegaa...*'

'Oye,' barked the man who had complained earlier of the heat as the singers approached his and Akhil's bay.

'*...tum ek paisa dogay, woh dus laakh daygaa...*'

'Oye, saaley.'

'*...gareebon ki...*'

'Oye, easy on the harmonium, ban-cho.'

The thin man stopped pumping his harmonium. He bunched his fingers and took them to his mouth. 'Arey saab, help this blind and deaf and dumb boy. Here, read his sad story...'

The man brushed the pamphlet that the man held out away from his lap. 'Keep that in your pocket. He was only blind till last year, wasn't he? And today he is deaf and dumb, too, haan? Ban-cho, you have seen *Black*, that's why, isn't it? Now bolt up that dubba and scoot.'

'Hunh. Chal Chotu, to the next compartment...'

The man looked around the bay and gave a wry smile. 'Saala. Did you see that, friends? No honesty, is there...Boss, will you pass me your lighter?'

Akhil obliged. 'Here.'

'Thanks...and a cigarette?'

Akhil broke into a chuckle. 'Hah…here—Gold Flake. Will that do?'

'That'll do solid, boss. I am Arif Mohammed. You can call me Arif. And you two? Are travelling together? Here, the lighter.'

Akhil reached for his lighter. 'Thanks, Arif. I am Akhil and he is Chander.'

Arif gave an aadaab. 'Akhil, Chander, very happy to meet you, boss.'

Akhil lit one up himself. 'Going to Batia?'

'No, Akhil mian, further down, to Firdauspur.'

'So, what do you do, Arif?'

Arif made a sorry face. 'Loan business, Akhil bhai. Saala running from this village to the next with all these farmers defaulting. Once I was after a ban-cho who had defaulted on his ox.'

Akhil exhaled at length. 'His *ox*. I didn't know one could get an ox in EMIs.'

'*Of course*. And they cost a lot if you didn't know—sixty thousand is the going price. Anyway, this haraamzada lured me along to an animal fair, made me sign all the papers for an ox he said he liked the look of. And what do I find after three months? Huzoor this, huzoor that, I can't pay the EMI for this month. The crops failed. Ban-cho. Is it my problem that the crops failed? Anyway, I caught him and his ox by their collars and dragged them both to the police station. That was one full year ago. The police hammered a khoonta in the courtyard and tied the ox there. Now they ask the farmer to appear in person every month and force their chai-pani from him and my firm asks me to do the rounds every month to get *their* chai-pani. I am fed up, boss.'

Akhil tried to switch lanes. 'You must know Batia, then.'

'Of course. It's along the route. Not more than five-ten minutes from now, in fact.'

'How long does the train stop at Batia?'

Arif slapped his thigh. 'Stop? Hah. For as long as you want, boss. There is no scheduled stop at Batia—nor at Firdauspur, for that matter. Just pull the chain and get off as fast as you can. You seem new to these parts…'

'Yes, we are going to Batia.'

Arif made a worried face. 'Not loan agents, I hope.'

'We work for a water company. Going to Batia to collect samples.'

'Arey. I can see the kiln. Batia station is five minutes walk away. Now is the time. Pull it.'

Akhil got up, looking flustered. 'Just like that?'

'Of course. Look, I'll do it for you—in exchange for the Gold Flake.'

The three men rushed over to the exit. In his excitement, Arif didn't notice that Akhil and his friend weren't carrying any suitcases. He dislodged the chain handle and pulled at it with all his might. 'Here, now hurry. *Jump*.'

Akhil patted Arif's shoulder affectionately. 'Thank you, Arif mian—and good luck with the ox.'

'Hah, thanks Akhil bhai, Chander bhai,' replied Arif as he flicked the singed filter-tip on to the tracks.

Akhil and Chander hurried to the side and watched the train pass them by. The only piece of luggage between them—a small leather bag that contained some plasticware and a few credentials and letters—was slung across Akhil's shoulder.

Chander fashioned a bandana out of his white handkerchief and tucked the edges behind his ears. 'Batia. After all these years…'

'Twenty-eight, to be precise.'

'You look a bit grim, Kalki. Memories all rushing back, haan?'

Kalki smiled. 'Come, Chander, let's walk to the station. Might find someone there to take us to the village.'

Chander followed behind at a sluggish pace. 'What's the big hurry? Here, hand me the water thermos.'

Kalki unzipped the leather bag and took out the thermos. 'All this while we haven't had a drop and you want it now.'

'...Aaahh. That was needed. What a day. 46 degrees, at least.'

Kalki glanced at the station. 'No one on the platform.'

'What, in this heat? What is it they say? Only a mad dog and an Englishman. But look—under that neem. Isn't that…Kalki, it's Bhola. Our Bhola! The bastard is now a tongawallah.'

Kalki nodded. 'Yes, it *is* Bhola.'

Chander approached the tonga and patted the mule on the rear. 'Arey....Arey tonga. Hey you.'

Bhola emerged from under the canopy rubbing his eyes. 'Who, what…Oh, haan haan, saab. Please come, please come…'

'Will you take us to the village?'

'Where in the village, saab? It's some distance from here—at least thirteen furlongs.'

'Sarpanch's house.'

'Twelve rupees, saab. Come saab. Here, let me dust the seats a little. Sit, sit.'

Kalki squeezed in next to Chander. 'Let's go.'

'Yes, saab. Huck-k-k-kaa-huckkk…k-kaa-huckkk.'

'What is your name?'

'Bhola, saab. Tck-kaa-hukkk...tck-kaa-hukkk…Bhola.'

'You have been in these parts long?'

Bhola gave the mule an almighty whiplash. 'Born in Batia only, saab. Haven't even been to the nearest town. I take great pride in saying that.'

'Yes, some achievement. Tell me: is the Badey Thakur still the sarpanch?'

'Why, yes of course, saab. Do you know him?'

'We corresponded with him six months ago. We are here because of that.'

'Great man, Badey Thakur.'

'Is that so?'

'Yes, saab. Never forgot his neechi jaat people. Batia has a bhangi school, bhangi hospital, bhangi well. What more can we people ask for, saab? Tck-kaa-hukkk…'

'Looks like Badey Thakur has made a little bhangi idyll for you.'

Bhola nodded. 'Has been our sarpanch for close to forty years.'

Kalki asked Bhola what he had been wanting to for some time. 'And, besides the bhangis, any other neechi jaat in Batia?'

'Not anymore, saab, but used to be. Musahurs, they were called. Bad people, saab, rat eaters. Good riddance, if you ask me.'

Chander pulled at Kalki's sleeve. 'Leave it, Kalki…'

'How far are we from...'

'Two furlongs more. To Badey Thakur house you said, na saab?'

'Yes.'

Chander squeezed Kalki's arm all of a sudden. 'Look, Kalki, the pipal. And, and...oh, Kallu, our burnt houses. Still standing...'

Kalki stared blankly at the scene before him. Hollowed-out ruins taken over by wild creepers; baby pipals sprouting from every possible crack in the soot-covered walls; termite-ravaged doors unhinged and reclining, waiting to unhinge further and detach from the threshold.

Kalki saw Amma trying to break open the door from inside. He saw his sisters pulling and pushing at the window bars, crying and shrieking till the flames engulfed even the shrieks...He looked away.

'There, that's your house. Nothing's changed, Kalki.'

Kalki remained silent. His heart was pounding.

'These houses, Kalki, still standing. *Why?*'

Bhola thought he was being spoken to. 'What is that you said, saab?'

'I said, what is this route—all these burnt houses.'

Bhola whipped the mule. 'Oh, this is the Batia Aitihaasik Smarak, saab. These were musahur homes. They were torched, what, almost thirty years ago. Badey Thakur had said, let this be an example to anyone who dared to challenge the Thakurs. Huck-k-k-kaa-huckkk... even got our local MLA to come and inaugurate it. That day, each and every Batiara's chhati swelled with pride.'

Chander crouched forward menacingly and said sofly 'Saala, bastard, I'll kill him, Kalki.'

'Leave it, please, Chander.'

Bhola continued. 'There was a great uprising that night thirty years ago. I was there to see it all with my own eyes, saab. The musahurs did something terrible to our Badey Thakur. Twenty musahur families, maybe twenty-five—I don't remember—they were locked up in their homes and everything was set on fire. Next morning there was not a single musahur left in our...'

Kalki interrupted curtly. 'Leave it, we don't want to hear about it. How far to go now?'

'Not long, saab. There, you can see the haveli already.'

Kalki and Chander saw the Thakur haveli gradually come into view. Closing their eyes was more painful than keeping them open.

Bhola reined in his mule. 'Tck-kaa-hukkk...hurrrrahhh-hukkk. Here we are, saab. This is the Thakur haveli. Foohh, this heat…'

Kalki and Chander got down. 'Here, twelve rupees. You want some water, Bhola?'

'No, no saab, I'll take it later—from my well.'

'As you wish.'

Bhola bowed with folded hands. 'Thank you, saab. Just go right ahead. Badey Thakur is usually in the inner veranda at this time of day. You might have to try coughing gently a few times to break his afternoon nap…Achha, saab.'

Chander touched Kalki on his arm. 'Listen, Kalki, you alright with this?'

'Yes, let's go inside. Let's meet the great man.'

The two approached the haveli. It looked deserted, even abandoned. The awning above the gateway of the extended threshold was tattered and weathered by the incessant sunlight. In the heat, the facade of the two jharokas that flanked the breadth of the haveli seemed to melt and stretch, the war scenes depicted by their embellished frescoes animated. Kalki and Chander walked slowly past the great bargad tree, noticing that its tentacles had reached over one of the side walls and deep into the haveli itself. The wrought-iron birdcages that dangled from its branches were empty, their little doors wide open.

The place bode ill.

Kalki thumped the nose ring of the growling lion on the wooden door. No one answered. He pushed at the door. It opened freely, then seemed to gain momentum, going the full quarter arc that was allowed it.

Kalki and Chander stepped in.

The fountain was dead, its spout corroded and covered by verdigris. A pigeon fluttered in noisily and perched itself on the ornate rim of the chalice-like structure, and just as it did, the main door of the inner courtyard swung open. The men stopped in their tracks. It was the wind. The door slammed shut soon. The two hurried on to the main courtyard.

Badey Thakur was taking his siesta, as Bhola had said.

Kalki stood over him. 'Looks like the great man is dozing.'

'Dreaming of some great things, I'm sure...'

'A-Ahum...Ahum-a-hum! Badey Thakur? Badey Thakur.'

The great man got up, then fell back. He tried again, this time succeeding. 'Huun...? What...who, who are y-you?'

'Good afternoon, *Badey Thakur.*'

'W-what...? You have to speak a little louder, I can't hear properly.'

Kalki raised his voice. 'We said, good afternoon, Badey Thakur.'

'Haaṇ, good afternoon. What can I do for you?'

'We are from the water company, from Mumbai. Remember we had corresponded six months ago? Well, we are here to see you regarding that.'

'Oh, haan haan. So you did get my reply, then.'

'Yes, Badey Thakur, and we are very grateful that you could take some time out...'

'Er, you are...? I am sorry, my memory these days...'

'I am Akhil, and he is Chander.'

Badey Thakur gestured with his hand. 'Well, have a seat, have a seat...Very hot, isn't it?'

'Ji, Badey Thakur.'

Badey Thakur looked under the cot for his hookah. 'And in this heat, no one dares to come out of their houses. You must have hardly seen anyone on your way here.'

'Hah, that is correct, Badey Thakur. Not one person, come to think of it.'

'Yes, kabristaan is what Batia becomes in this heat. So, tell me.'

Kalki opened the leather bag as he spoke. 'Ji, Badey Thakur. It is like this—very simple. The plan is to install a state-of-the-art water purification system at the well, so that the water from the well goes directly into this system and comes out all clean and ready to drink. Here—this is exactly how it will look.'

'Wah.'

'Ji, Badey Thakur. The water can then be drunk straight from the pipe—no further filtering.'

'And none of this kaulra, chechak, kutta-khansi...?'

'Ji, Badey Thakur. These, er, diseases you mentioned...I mean, we could first install the system, say for a well that is the dirtiest. For example, maybe a bhangi well...'

Badey Thakur shook his head. 'No no, install it for the Thakur well first. The system should be seen as a thing of pride for the village. People will come from far and away just to see it. And why worry about the bhangi well. They are immune to all these diseases anyway.'

'Ji, Badey Thakur, as you say.'

'So when will you come and install it?'

'In a month. As soon as we have analysed the water quality of your well. The system has to be fine-tuned, you see. We would need some samples.'

'Of course. My servant will take you to the well. Mahi Ram? *Mahi Ram*!'

Kalki replaced the brochure in the leather bag. 'We would have preferred if you showed us the well. You see, the water samples have to be taken in the presence of the sarpanch. That's the company regulation.'

'Oh. Come then, I'll take you to the well. It is not very far. Here, give me a hand.'

'Ji, Badey Thakur.'

For an old man, Badey Thakur certainly could step on it. Kalki and Chander found themselves breaking into a jog.

'Come along, come along...'

'Ji Badey Thakur. We must thank you for your ready acceptance of our company's plans, Badey Thakur. It's not always like that—in other villages, I mean.'

Badey Thakur took the compliment warmly and turned philosophical. 'Arey, we must see the light and move forward. I don't believe in holding people back. All these rituals, these traditions, these are holding our great country back. I don't know whether you have taken a round of our village, but you will see for yourself how much I have done for these lower castes.'

'Ji, Badey Thakur. We saw a few things on our way here. The bhangi school building looks very impressive and so does their dispensary.'

'You think so? Well, that really pleases me—to see my selfless efforts being appreciated by outsiders. And mind you, in a couple of years you must come back. I'll myself ask you to install a similar system for the bhangi well. I don't believe in depriving these people their due—in due course, if you get me.'

Kalki smiled. 'We get you alright, Badey Thakur. No wonder people here call you a great man.'

'Haha…here we are.'

'Yes.'

There they were. The Thakur well. It seemed like yesterday.

Badey Thakur beamed. 'See for yourself. Full 20 feet across.'

'Indeed, Badey Thakur. Can we—if you don't mind—climb up the parapet?'

Badey Thakur hesitated. 'Er…you are a Thakur? Bania? Baaman?'

'Ji, baaman, Badey Thakur.'

'Well, then, by all means. We have to keep the purity and the sanctity of the place. You understand, I hope.'

Kalki nodded. 'Completely, Badey Thakur. The purity—at all costs.'

'Snatch the rope of that ghoomra and take all the samples you want.'

Kalki put one foot on the parapet. 'Ji. Come, Chander…Oh. That is very deep, Badey Thakur. I'll get vertigo just by looking down.'

'A good 80 feet, Akhilji. Arey, I have seen it when it was only 40 feet deep. Those harami kolawaaley set their factory up 2 miles from here, and ever since then we have had to dig further down every year. They suck out most of the ground water, you see.'

'Indeed, Badey Thakur. Would you mind coming up the parapet—just so that you can certify the…'

Badey Thakur was not one to step back from a challenge. 'Why not? There's still some ghee tel left in these legs, kyon.'

'Ji, Badey Thakur. Come. Here, take my hand.'

'Thank you, Akhilji…A-aah.'

'Deep, isn't it, Badey Thakur.'

Badey Thakur took a step back. 'Hahah…well, you were right about the vertigo. Perhaps you better begin your sample collection while I get down and…'

Kalki put a friendly hand on Badey Thakur's shoulder. 'What's the hurry, Badey Thakur? Won't you like to stay for some entertainment?'

'Entertainment? What are you saying, Akhilji, I don't understand…'

Kalki hissed the word. 'Entertainment, Badey Thakur.'

Silence overpowered even the trees and the birds.

'What entertainment. Again, I do not…'

'Perhaps I should make it clearer. Here, have a look down. What do you see?'

'What do I see? I see a well, that's what I see. And now, I'd like to get down if it…'

Kalki grabbed Badey Thakur by his neck. 'But look again—in there. Can you see Baldev? Your Baldev. No?'

Badey Thakur tried to wrench his neck away but the grip was firm. The blistered hands that for thousands of years had scrubbed and washed and scavenged and polished and massaged and fanned and scraped and served and toiled for him, those hands had finally made a grip, and the grip was firm.

Kalki dragged Badey Thakur by his neck to the edge and forced his head down. 'Still, nothing, Badey Thakur? Look. Look closely. Baldev is calling for you. He is calling your name.'

Badey Thakur stammered. 'B-B-Baldev. My s-son Baldev? I-I don't know what you…'

'No? Chander? Would you please care to show Badey Thakur?'

Chander took a step forward. 'Yes of course, Kalki. It would be my pleasure.'

Badey Thakur froze. 'Kal-Kalki? What Kalki? I thought you said Akhil. Kalki? Oh my God. Hey Ram…'

Kalki smiled. 'That's right, Badey Thakur. Good you remembered God at the right time. It always helps.'

'Wha…what, what are you going to do? Are you mad? Wha…get me down immediately!'

'As you say, Badey Thakur. Your wish is our command—as it has been for centuries.'

Badey Thakur thrashed his arms wildly. 'Get me dow…'

'There you go, you *bastard*!'

There was a moment of silence, a moment that lasted as long as the well was deep, and then the luxurious, almost elastic, detonation of the water, followed soon by that noisy, splashy gulp, and then the silence again.

Chander looked into the void. 'He is gone, Kalki.'

'And not a soul to see him go.'

'Except a mad dog and an Englishman.'

'Hah…'

Chander looked at Kalki. 'You ready, Kallu?'

'Wait. I have a little promise to keep. Won't be a minute. Give me your mobile.'

'We have all the time, all the time in the world.'

Kalki pressed a few buttons on Chander's mobile.

'It's ringing,' he said.

There was a click and then some static. Sweat was pouring down Kalki's face. He opened his mouth but, unsure, smothered it with his palm.

'H-hello. Is that…is that you, Akhil?'

'Hi, Api. Me again.'

'Where the hell are you? The p–, the whole damn force is on the lookout!'

'That's alright.'

'What do you mean "that's alright"? AB went public at a press conference this morning, although I think he hasn't revealed everything; just that all those murders are connected.'

Kalki shuffled on his feet. 'Good for him.'

'Come back to me, please come back to your Api. Hel-hello? Are you there. Hello?'

'Listen, Api, I haven't much time.'

'Wha-what's going on?'

'I called to keep my end of the promise. Tell AB I can be found in Batia. Also tell him that he will find this, other man, I had told you about. Tell him he can find us inside the Thakur well, in Batia.'

'Thakur well? Akhil, please tell me what's going on. Are you alright? Why don't you come back here—to me? Come back to me, Aks!'

Kalki was shaking all over. 'There isn't enough charge left on the phone, Api. I want to tell you how much I have loved you, how much I still love you. Forgive me for giving you so much pain. So much pain. So much pain that you stopped feeling it. So much pain. Forgive me, Api...'

'No, Akhil, don't say all this. Come back to me, just come back to me. Come back, my Akhil...'

'I will, Api, but not this time round. I hope you'll understan...'

'H...hello? Akhil? *Hello*. Damn it, signal. Hello, Akhil? Hel...'

Kalki stared at the phone, then shook it and waved it in the air. 'Api? Hello. Ap, Api?'

Chander laughed. 'The signal, Kallu?'

'Hah, bastard, here too...Well, Chander, come here, saaley. I love you, man, and I am sorry for everything...'

Chander held Kalki so tight he couldn't breathe. 'Don't say a word, saaley...Me first, Kallu.'

Kalki stopped Chander with his open palm. 'No man. It's always the Englishman first.'

'And the dog follows, hah.'

Kalki held Chander by his hair. 'Alright then, Chander, once more, forgive me.'

Chander smiled. 'I forgive you.'

Kalki let himself go.

Chander closed his eyes and waited for the familiar sound.

It came. It went.

Chander, eyes still shut, waited a good minute. Then, calmly, he too jumped in.

What is gravity if not birth? What is density if not death?

To escape, does one soar or plummet?

From now on, we will not use terms like gutter rat—a term that originated because of the plague in London. But we have no plague. Why should we? We bathe every day, unlike foreigners, who do only dry-cleaning. That's why they need so much scent. Perfume.

We hereby declare that all foreign words are cancelled. Foreign hands, too. Legs they can show and we can keep.

Words have a long history, a geography, a culture, a usage, a space, an anointment, a status, a sound, an identity.

Words have a density.

Musahur sounds almost like French. *Monsieur Mousahoor, autograph, s'il vouz plait?* He could have done that. Passed off as a perfume that you sprinkle at will. Donned robes and worn shoes that reeked of new money. It is so easy to be true, yet we spend entire lifetimes chasing neon lights. It is so expensive, yet we turn into paupers chasing untruths.

Akhil was a thinker and he was interested in something else. In enzymes. In bacteria. In chemistry. In cells that multiply to cause a disease that humanity cannot entirely fathom. He had dreamed of placing India at the cutting edge of science and technology. Of fighting water-borne diseases and food-borne killers that flourish in filth, of fighting tuberculosis, malaria, dengue—*my diseases*, he had said. Faith. Yes, faith in the propensity of human beings to dare to dream of a disease-free world. How difficult is that to imagine? Instead, he encountered filth of another kind—filth that has kept India naked and begging and dirty and sick. Filth that walks on two feet trying to skirt around filth.

'I will come back, Api, but not this time around,' he had said. And now he sinks to the bottom of the well like a stone. It all depends on the angle that life provides you. Some stones skip on water, others sink.

Let's be honest. The omens weren't good. Someone had spat at his emerging head, remember? But there's always a next time for everything. Maybe next time, he will be born in the holy land of Bethlehem. Or Benaras. Maybe next time, they will have a globe in the Ramakrishna Mission School. Maybe next time, he will *buy* Agatha Christies to read them. Maybe next time, he will also be able to play the clarinet. And speak French or Italian or Swedish. And not be called a bhangi. Or a Chamaar. Or a musahur. Only monsieur. Maybe next time.

How many janmas to the next platform, please?

To the glory of life after death. For you crushed this one under your foot like an ant.

After all, God doesn't give with both hands. But Monsieur Mousahoor had gambled. He knew health is wealth. That is why he always wore a clean pair of socks. Signature.

He knew all railway platforms except one. Platform number Gangotri. That is a little far. Next life, for sure, with all the good karma he accumulated in this one. Maybe that well in which he currently travels is really a wormhole. Maybe he will emerge on the other side of it, into a life of joy and splendour. Maybe.

To the glory of life after death. For you whipped all the joy out of this one.

This is the problem of coming up too fast in life. In one life, you can only go to school. In the next one you can also be born as a mongoose because you never know which karma is performing. The only way out for him in this life was doob maro, doob maro. But even that sounds better in French: *Il veut péter plus haut que son cul.*

Slow down. One life at a time, my friend. Easy does it. Don't jump platforms.

To the glory of life after death. For you slashed at my throat before the blood of freedom could nourish my brain.

But tell me, please. Please! Why was he born at all? Why did he live? Do bhangis and betis, jamadars and silkworms, have karma? Do they?

To the glory of life after death. For you promised me heaven on earth but pushed me into a manhole instead.

He never lived, so how can he die?

To the glory of life after death. Oh, this unbearable lightness.

Epilogue: 2005–A House for Mr Biswas

What should be the suburb is really the heart of the city.

Lutyens' Bungalow Zone: an area of a few square miles, inaccessible to the native as recently as sixty years ago is now *the* most sought after property in the country. Bribes are paid, transfers are made, friends are stabbed, enemies are pampered, seats are bartered, ministries are swapped, and at the end of it all, the victorious can move into a ninety-year-old bungalow with twenty-four-hour power and water supply, with twenty-foot-high ceilings, with a gravel path approach, with a lawn to die for.

Meanwhile, in the suburbs of Delhi, dwell fourteen million humans of the same colour and features. They work hard, they sleep less, they travel on buses, they disappear down manholes, they die in road accidents, they pay bribes to the power and the water people, they wake up every morning with a tin bucket in hand and rush to the only tap in their crumbling tenements, they survive another day, another week, another month. Then, exhausted, they come on the weekends to the heart of the city with their children and their parents and lie on the cool green grass by India Gate. They remove their socks and dip their two feet in the boat-club pool and wiggle their toes. They look around and see roads that are protected from the sun's fury by hundred-year-old jamun tress, neem trees, imli trees. They see the roads merging at roundabouts as big as the parks where they live.

They see in those roundabouts the seasonal flowers in full bloom, the art deco fountains bursting with energy, they see that no one can enter the roundabout gardens as they are cordoned with spiked chains and iron railings. Then they get a little adventurous and start to stroll about one of the tree-lined avenues. 'Look, that must be the home minister's house', they point to their kids. 'And look there. That is 7 Race Course Road, the prime minister's residence.' But their sightseeing is interrupted rudely by a lathi-wielding constable who looks up and down them and asks them to get lost.

The heart is still inaccessible to the native, and a thousand years from now, when archaeologists stumble upon the mythical city of Delhi, the most well-preserved ruins they shall find would be of Lutyens' Pompeii. The tumblers and the vases of great sultanates and dynasties will once again be on show.

The departing British handed over to the native something magical—his own land. The native received that land with watery eyes and a lump in his throat and now that he had the government sanction and the constitutional right to walk on the soft lawns, smell the flowers, collect the jamuns, drive on the boulevards. Now that he was free, he quickly made it his and only his. And over the years, many of the Lutyens' bungalows have become imposing shrines of refuge, away from the heat and the dust of the matrubhoomi, with the accompanying green acreage giving way to swimming pools paved with Italian marble. And those obtrusive colonnaded porticos, a reminder of the whimsical draughtsmanship of a scornful white man, have been torn down and replaced with mock Mughal-Greek-Tudor architecture, all to the delight and satisfaction of the victorious.

There they sit, but you cannot see them—fenced away as they are by stitched-up cane—but there they are, perched on a rattan in their manicured lawns, with their sprinklers whirring gloriously, providing a welcoming mist to their golden mornings, with their dogs already up and running, retrieving Frisbees and *Indian Expresses* and *Jansattas* and...oh, look: There he comes, the cummerbund-ed servant with the frilly turban, and he brings the first flush on a silver tray, and the silver teapot is teacosied in a velvet wrap, and the wrap is embroidered with silver zari, and the perfectly shaped sugar cubes are arranged in a silver bowl, and at hand is a pair of silver tongs to pick up the cubes, and rich, frothy milk sloshes gently in a silver beaker, and to absorb the ugly cup rings, between the silver cup and the silver saucer, is wedged a ruffled blotting paper, and silver spoons are in abundance.

And the lord? He snaps the pages of the newspaper and doesn't even bother to look up and acknowledge all that silver.

There they sit and from there they rule. And when they die, their next of kin miraculously get the same bungalow to live in for the next fifty years.

And it was in such a bungalow, over such a lawn, amidst such flowers, under such trees, surrounded by such servants, that the recently appointed police commissioner of Delhi, Ajay Biswas IPS, was pacing up and down, shouting, 'Arey Gokul, oye Ramkhilawan. Where the hell are you buggers, dammit?'

The servant heard his sahib's call and threw away his bidi. 'Aaya saab.'

Ajay boomed. 'Damn it, Gokul. Have you filled the vases up? And where's memsaab?'

'S-she's upstairs, saab.'

'Well, call her and…wait. I'll get her, you get the living room ready.'

Ajay hurried over to the foot of the stairway that led to the upper floors.

'Aparajita?' he shouted. 'Arey, where the devil have you disappeared?'

Api emerged from a room tying her hair into a bun. 'Why are you shouting, bhai? Relax.'

'What relax, yaar? It is seven-thirty already, and…'

'You know the Dilliwaalas. Call them at seven and they start trickling in at nine.'

Ajay was insistent. 'Arey, go na please. See if Parwati has fried those prawn papads.'

'Uff. Alright.'

Ajay turned his attention to the goings-on in the living room. He accosted someone dusting a Degas ballerina. 'Arey, Gokul. Has Ramkhilawan put the marquee up on the lawns?'

'Pata nahin, saab.'

'Well, find out. And get some angithis fired up there. Now go. And before you go, where is Pillai?'

The servant scratched his head. 'Must be in the kitchen, saab.'

'You goddamn Indies. "Must be", "pata nahin", "think so". Bloody, when are you people ever sure, hain?'

The servant nodded, having not understood a word. 'Ji, saab.'

Ajay decided it was Pillai's turn for a dressing down. He started for the kitchen.

'Pillai! You were supposed to…'

The piercing ring of the doorbell stopped Ajay in his tracks. He heaved a sigh and ran a hand through his mane before opening the door.

'Oh, hello Paul saab, hello Mrs Paul. Please, come in, come in.'

'Hello, commissioner saab…Splendid bungalow, yaar.'

'Thank you. I hope you didn't have much trouble finding the place.'

'Arey no no, not at all. I recently got my lal-batti installed with that GPS-she-PS, bhai. Now I keep telling the missus: chalo let's get lost just for the heck of it.'

Ajay faked a laugh. 'Do come in. Arey, Mrs Paul, hand me your shawl. No Jeeves here, unfortunately.'

Mrs Paul gathered her shawl and handed it over grudgingly. 'Jeeves, er, was your earlier butler? Christian, was he? We used to have one years ago, called Samuel…'

'Arey missus, you bhi na. Always joking-shoaking. Don't mind her, Ajay saab.'

Ajay guided them to the living room with tender pushes and prods. 'Come, come. Aparajita will be with us in a minute. Keeping an eye on the food front. Meanwhile, what can I get you?'

'Only Johnny boy will do tonight, commissioner saab, kyon?'

'Of course, Paul saab. And for you, Mrs Paul?'

'I will have some red wine, if you have it. If not, then some Jaljeera.'

'Of course, of course. Red wine, and Johnny Black for you, Paul saab—coming up.'

'Thanks, old boy.'

Paul saab gave the place a once-over. 'You had the interiors done before you guys moved in?'

'Just the putai-shutai. Aparajita thought we'd slowly fill the place up with this and that, you know.'

'Bad idea, commissioner, what with transfers and all.'

Ajay handed Paul saab his clinking Johnny. 'We are hoping they would let us stay in Delhi for at least a couple more years.'

'Why not, why not? After all, you are the golden boy of the force, bhai. Superceding everything in front of you and all, haha. And your wife. Is she working?'

'I bloody well hope so, or we might have to end up ordering from Claridges.'

'Arey, no no, I meant as in a job-shob.'

'Oh. Yes—she's a lecturer at DU. And talking of the devil, here she comes...'

Api entered the living room and smiled warmly at the guests. 'Hello...'

'Aparajita, this is Mr Dhiraj Paul, joint commissioner. And this is Mrs Paul. Sorry, didn't catch your name, Mrs Paul.'

'Madhumita.'

'Hello, Madhumitaji; hello, Mr Paul. Pleased to meet you.'

'Likewise, Mrs Biswas, likewise. I was just telling Ajay what a splendid bungalow this is. The old-world splendour almost makes you forget the bitter January cold in here.'

The ensuing lull in conversation only added to the impact of the barb.

'Oh. I didn't mean to...'

'No no, you are right, Paul saab, quite right. I'll get some room heaters brought in here at once...Here, your drink, Mrs Paul. And let me just find ou...'

The shriek of the doorbell made Ajay slosh Mrs Paul's wine as it was being handed over. 'Oh, the wretched bell again. Please excuse me a minute.'

Ajay scurried over to open the door, dragging Api with him.

'Oh, hello, Ghai saab. Please come, please come in.'

'Hello, hello, commissioner saab, how are you? Please meet my Mrs...'

'Hello ji.'

'Hello, Mrs Ghai, welcome. Aparajita, this is Mrs Ghai.'

'Hello, Mrs Ghai.'

'Hello ji.'

Mr and Mrs Ghai were escorted to the living room.

'Ghai saab, meet our joint commissioner, Paul saab. Paul saab, this is Ghai saab—IG, CRPF.'

'Finally, we meet.'

'My pleasure, Paul saab, entirely my pleasure.'

The doorbell was like a hungry child. Ajay replaced his glass on the side table. 'Oops. The bell again. Please sit, sit. I won't be a minute. Api? Come.'

The couple retraced their journey, secretly wishing they had been allotted a two-bedroom flat and not this butler-demanding Alcázar. Ajay swung open the door.

'Kharbanda! Great to see you. As usual, late by thirty minutes. And you must be Mrs Kharbanda. And this, little Preeti.'

DIG Kharbanda shook the hand till Ajay unclasped his hand. 'Hello sir, so great to see you. Very sorry we are late. Hello, Madam...'

'So nice to see you, Mr Kharbanda.'

'Great, great...Listen Kharbanda, please feel at home. I'll just rush to the front and check up on the ammo.'

'Please go ahead, sir. Er, I'll join you in a moment.'

Ajay left for the front, leaving his wife behind. Aparajita smiled awkwardly. DIG Kharbanda remembered something and felt his elbow-patched tweed at various places. '*Oh!* and Mrs Biswas, this letter is for you. We have had it for a week now. I am sorry we should have come and given it to you earlier, but you know how it is. Where is the time?'

Api took the envelope, amused by the ten or so stamp marks, official scrawlings, and that ubiquitous secret code embedded with dashes and slashes. 'Oh, thank you. Yes, it is addressed to me alright, but...'

'The address is of the guest house where you and sir stayed when you were in Mumbai last summer. I think it must have remained there for a few months, until some police guest recognised your name and redirected it to your house in Delhi.'

'Yes, strange...'

'And by the time this letter arrived in Delhi, you people had already shifted to this new house. The letter must have remained at your old house for a month at least.'

Mrs Kharbanda thought it prudent to warn her husband. 'What are you doing ji? Finish up the story fast, no.'

'Oh. Sorry, sorry. Yes, to cut a long story short, we found this letter the day we moved into your old house, which was last week. I could have delivered it to sir, but I thought I'll give it to you in person as we were coming here tonight.'

'Well, thank you very much, Mr Kharbanda.'

DIG Kharbanda tried his hand at wit. 'Not anything urgent, I hope.'

Api looked tired and weak. 'Hah...'

'Are you alright, Mrs Biswas? You look a little tired.'

'Arey no no, Mr Kharbanda, please. Gosh, we have been standing in the doorway and talking. Please come in. The living room is down the corridor. Ajay will have some drinks for you. I'll join you people in a minute.'

DIG Kharbanda entered the upper echelons of the Indian police service with stateliness. 'Thank you, Mrs Biswas. Come along now, Preeti, Mohini...'

Mrs Kharbanda nudged her husband as they shuffled in great excitement over to the living room. 'You na, ji. Always going on and on about everything. Where was the need? You could have just given her the letter...'

'Uff, missus, just go to that ladies jhund. And keep your mouth shut and ears open...Oh, hello, sir.'

Ajay reached for his colleague with open arms. 'Ah, there you are, Kharbanda. Come, come...Paul saab, Ghai saab, this is Mr Kharbanda, DIG, Delhi Offences Wing, and shortly to be shifted to CBI, no less.'

Ghai saab raised his glass. 'Hello, Kharbanda saab. Bhai we have been hearing just too much about your amazing work—yours and Ajay's, I mean.'

'Thank you, sir.'

'No sir-var here, bhai.'

DIG Kharbanda had been practising just the right laugh for such occasions for months. 'Hahah. Thank you, Ghai saab.'

Ajay tapped DIG Kharbanda on his shoulder. 'What will you have, Kharbanda?'

'Anything, sir. But Scotch would be nice.'

Paul saab took a hefty slurp of his favourite drink. 'Where is your missus, Ajay? Don't see her here.'

'In the kitchen maybe, Paul saab. Dinner won't be long, I assure you.'

'No no…'

Got him, the bastard, thought Ajay. 'In fact, let me just go and check up on her and her lieutenants.'

'You do that, you do that…'

Ajay grabbed a fistful of cheesy bites. 'I'll be back in a minute.'

The conversation turned to the mundane with Ajay gone. '… Haan, so Kharbanda saab, how do you find saadi Dilli?'

'Great, Paul saab, great. Coming to Delhi was just the change I wanted.'

'Shall I top you up, Paul saab…?'

'Yes please, Ghai saab. No holds barred tonight, hahah. Haan, Kharbanda, you were saying…'

Ajay reached the engine room and found Pillai at the deep end.

'Pillai, how are things?'

'We are running a little late, saab.'

'I can see that. And where is Aparajita?'

Pillai swiped at the sweat from his forehead with his finger. 'Memsaab has just gone upstairs. Will be back in five minutes, she said, saab.'

'Yes yes. Listen, tell Gokul to put on that white safari suit with brass buttons I got for him yesterday. And make sure he comes in with the starters in five minutes, no more. You got that?'

'Ji, saab.'

'I repeat: Gokul in five minutes, and with some ice, too.'

'Ji.'

'And when memsaab comes down, ask her to come over to the living room.'

'Ji.'

Meanwhile, upstairs in one of the bedrooms, hidden away from all the commotion, Aparajita tore open the envelope with trembling hands. She detatched the folds of the delicate sheaf that looked as though it might crumble to pieces on being handled. One teardrop fell with a plop on the first page. She smudged it away and read on.

Mrs Aparajita Biswas
c/o Ajay Biswas IPS
Atithi Guesthouse
Pedder Road, Mumbai – 400026

Dearest Api,

Would you believe me if I told you there has not been a single day, right from that Muk-mem evening all those years ago, till that afternoon at the railway station last week, when I have not thought about you? I went away from your life Api, but you didn't go away from mine. What else was there then, that was left for me? It's a terrible plague when I realise that I can only spend my happiest moments, as and when they come, with no one else but myself. Of what use is that? To think that one day I'll die alone. In the end, when you come right down to it, human life hangs only on hope. And what of me? Kept to my own, my achievements become a curse, a disease I cannot cure myself of. No, I must destroy myself. Destruction of self is the…

Can you believe it! You just swept in a few minutes ago. Now look what you have done? Here I was, all ready to write a long one, when suddenly I find you standing right in front of me. On second thoughts, you have saved me a lot of time. I can now skip large chunks that I think we have discussed already.

And you are right—it was a confession chamber that I wanted. The desire to...

There was a knock on the door. Api bunched up the letter instinctively.

'Yes?'

It was Pillai.

'Arey, memsaab, you are here? Saab is calling you. The pulao is done.'

'Thank you, Pillai.'

'You are crying, memsaab…Is everything…everything is alright, memsaab?'

'Yes, yes it is, Pillai. Tell Ajay I'll join the guests in a minute.'

'Ji, memsaab,' said Pillai, retreating.

Api uncrumpled the pages carefully:

…The desire to confess is as deep a human trait as any. To confess in the hope that one may be absolved, or to confess for no other reason than just to confess? That is the dilemma we face. I am far beyond absolution, Api. And who else but you do I have as my chamber, you tell me?

There is something that you—and perhaps Ajay—would never have discovered, and so I'll tell you now. My real name is Kalki and not Akhil. I am not a Chamaar but a musahur.

AKHIL SUKUMAR is KALKI MUSAHUR and KALKI MUSAHUR is AKHIL SUKUMAR.

I accept there have been better anagrams but this one's served me alright till now, I guess. In hindsight—of course, in hindsight—there always was an Akhil inside Kalki. What I hadn't figured out was just how much Kalki there was in Akhil. Just how much Kalki there is in all of us.

I was born on a bloody road. The blood was my mother's. My sisters couldn't find a midwife in time. There was no way my mother could get relief from the upper-caste well, and so they tell me that my sisters ran to some puddles to fill their little mouths up and ran back to where my mother was almost dying of pain and then spat out some water on her face and the rest down below on mine. That's how I came into this world.

My family ate rats and picked up shit for a living. I wasn't proud of what they did but I was proud of them. Then some terrible things happened to me and my family, Api, that I can never tell you and never will. But what you do know about your Akhil is true: that he is an orphan from Bhopal and that he loves you more than anyone can ever love you.

Before I became Akhil, I sold tea and tended to a bookstall at the Mughalsarai railway station. It was there that I read all of Agatha Christie. Before my tenth class exams, I ran away from Mughalsarai all the way to Bhopal. I had overheard someone mentioning a Ramakrishna Mission Orphanage and School in Bhopal that took in children like me and prepared them for the tenth and twelfth boards. And anyway, there was nothing that held me back at Mughalsarai.

I stayed at the orphanage and the school for two years before I came to Stephen's.

Prior to my tenth boards, they asked me to fill up my religion and caste. The damn thing's tied to my tail like a rock, Api. To the world, I am, always will be, my caste. I was afraid to mention musahur as it could have given my identity away. I filled in Chamaar.

Now when I look back, I think that was the day when I decided to finally stand up, decided to opt for a lower caste. Because on that day, I had the opportunity to become anything—brahmin, bania, khatri. And everyone would have believed me, of course. That day, Api, I chose my caste, and I chose Chamaar. I chose it because I wanted to show to the world what a lower caste can achieve as a lower caste. And, Api, you can say from that day on, I met my life on my own terms.

But I still couldn't get you, Api, I still couldn't. Do you hold it against me? I could have kept quiet that day, when your father mistook me for an Iyengar—Sukumaran he called me. You loved me so much that I think you wanted me to be quiet. But, Api, will you believe me when I tell you that I loved you even more and that's why I corrected your father? For fifteen years, I have asked myself, would being a Sukumaran instead of Sukumar really have made that much of a difference to me? I love you, Api, but the answer is yes.

I must wind up.

My accomplice is my childhood friend Chander, who also suffered at the hands of the Thakurs of our village. To have him along was not my idea. He found me out some ten years ago by sheer chance. He was working at a pharmaceutical factory in Himachal and I had gone there for a conference. I helped him find a job at IIT as a lab attendant. Only a couple of years later did he tell me of his intention, of what he thought his aim in life was. It wasn't much different from mine.

Strange are the ways of providence. Of all the DIGs in this world, it had to be AB who was handed the Saane case. Anyway, it was all coming to an end. I couldn't have gone on. I wanted it to end, I wanted to be found out; it was just an absurd coincidence that of all the people, it was you who made the connection. You and your dagger.

It is always terrible to kill a fellow human being. For what I did, I must pay. Of course, you might say, who's to decide on the severity of the punishment and that a voluntary punishment would be a token one. You'll have to wait a little longer to find that out. I'll try and call you from Batia one last time. I hope you get this letter before you leave for Delhi.

Once I am dead, my dearest Api, the residual oxygen in my cells will help prolong a dying minority of chemical reactions. My nails will grow for a few more hours, so will my hair. My RNA will be translated into heat-shock proteins. Eventually, there will come a time when my body performs its very last reaction—maybe a few hours after I am gone, maybe a bit longer, hard to tell.

But I know that you'll help me perform that last chemical reaction. My last breath will have your name.

Yours,

Akhil

Api stared at the page for a long time, then got up and walked over to where the dressing console was, in a niche by the bedroom window. She pulled the second drawer out, the one that stored the general medicines, and began ransacking it for the small white plastic bottle of calmpose.

Meanwhile, down in the dungeons, Paul saab was explaining weather patterns to DIG Kharbanda.

'And by the time the rains arrive…Oh, come, come, Ajay. I was just telling Kharbanda that you two are the new poster boys.'

'Kya Paul saab.'

'Arey seriously, bhai. Especially after five of our colleagues stand suspended because of you.'

Ajay scrambled for a nuanced response. 'Yes, we are sorry to hear that. It wasn't our intention, you know, Paul saab.'

'Of course, Ajay, of course. I only feel for Chaubey—the others can go to hell—but Chaubey was just six months away from his shawl and his clock. Still, you guys did what you had to. And solving twelve so-called solved murders at one go—and then catching the real killer as well. Bhai wah!'

'Thank you, Paul saab.'

Ghai saab gave a mystified look. 'Arey, I didn't know it was you guys who got the killer. I thought it was the UP police. That IG Ravinder said he…'

Paul saab poked Ghai saab in the chest. 'Arey, Ghai saab, that Ravinder talks through his ass. You mean, you don't know the whole story? Kya yaar, Ghai, which world do you live in? Refresh our Ghai saab's memory, will you, Kharbanda?'

DIG Kharbanda took a large sip before his put his drink down. 'Er, sure, Paul saab…Ghai saab, you know na, that our man was killing desh bhakts on the lines of Agatha Christie novels?'

'Yes yes, that much I…'

'Well, this fellow turned out to be some laboratory attendant at IIT. We found his house to be full of Agatha novels. Turns out he was going through them one by one.'

Ghai saab shook his head slowly. 'What a bastard.'

'He was a low caste from a village in Bihar called Batia. His family was burnt alive by a Thakur sarpanch thirty years ago. Revenge, Ghai saab, a simple story of revenge it was. And that's not all. The fellow—I think Chander was his name—he went all the way to Batia in the end, killed the same sarpanch, and then went on the run.'

'I had heard something about some professor at IIT also getting…'

'Yes yes, Ghai saab, I was coming to that. This Chander then comes back to IIT and shoots this professor—his name was Professor Akhil—and this was so tragic as our Ajay sir knew Professor Akhil very well.'

Ghai saab turned towards Ajay. 'Is that so? I am so sorry, Ajay saab.'

'Yes, Ghai saab, I couldn't bear it for months. This professor was my best friend back in college. Carry on, Kharbanda.'

DIG Kharbanda lobbed a peanut in his mouth and continued, mispronouncing a few words early in his sentences because of the munching. 'Ajay sir's best friend was shot in the head by Chander. You must have seen it all on Aaj Tak. Those camera close-ups. It was all over the media—a brilliant professor murdered. Last July it was…'

Ghai saab knocked on his forehead. '*Oh.* That was the time I was in Paris on a fact-finding mission. Ajay saab, my very belated condolences.'

'Thank you, Ghai saab. Go on, Kharbanda.'

'We—I mean, only through the extraordinary efforts of Ajay sir—we knew beforehand of the Agatha Christie connection. We made a list of people who had been borrowing her books from all the libraries in Mumbai. And bhains-ki-aankh. We got Chander's name. It was touch and go. He had his passport and air tickets ready but we swooped down on him at his home and after a protracted shoot-out, we killed him.'

'Wah. Five stars to you, Ajay. And also to you, Kharbanda.'

'Thank you, Ghai saab.'

Ghai saab sipped his drink with concern. 'And this professor friend of yours, Ajay. How come the poor fellow got caught up in all this?'

'Ghai saab, what can I say? My friend had helped this chap get a job at IIT. And in the end...I-I am sorry, I get emotional just thinking about it.'

'Yes, of course, Ajay saab, I am sorry to have brought it up.'

'No no, it's alright, Ghai saab.'

'...So, why the hell did this low caste—this Chander—why did he kill the professor?'

'Why do you think, Ghai saab? My friend's full name was Akhil Sukumaran.'

'I still don't...'

'Sukumaran, Ghai saab, Iyengars. Brahmins of the first order—Vaishnavites, you know. And my poor, brilliant friend was killed for no reason other than the fact that he was a brahmin.'

Ghai saab drew his breath in. 'My God. I am so sorry to hear that. This is kalyug, Ajay saab, kalyug. All we can do is wait for the tenth and final avatar Kalki to come and redeem us.'

'Indeed, Ghai saab, indeed. Some more Johnny for you?'

Ghai saab's reply was drowned by the doorbell.

'Damn, the bell again. Will you excuse me a minute, Ghai saab?'

'Please, Ajay, please. Here, give me the bottle.'

Who am I?
Aham Brahmāsmi

I am the seeker and the sought
I am the giver and the got
I am the thinker and the thought

Akhanda mandalākāram
Vyāptam yena charācharam
Cogito ergo sum

I am the fragmented and the whole
I am the logic and the lore
I am the child of man
I know no end
And so I never began

Ya devi sarvābhuteshu
Chetanetyābhidhiiyate

I am the seed of a plant
That grows in the world
That does not exist

I am the real and the imagined

I am the Rat Eater

Acknowledgements

We thank Nitin Valecha and Praveen Tiwari, Bloomsbury India, for their help and encouragement, and Shreya Chakraborti, editorial manager, Bloomsbury India, for her incisive suggestions and editing.

Two passages from this book have appeared earlier in articles published by Ranganathan. The *Hardtalk* transcript used in Chapter 9 is courtesy the BBC.

Anand Ranganathan
Chitra Subramaniam
May 2019